Neil Broadfoot worked as a j⌇ national and local newspapers, including *The Scotsman*, *Scotland on Sunday* and the *Evening News*, covering some of the biggest stories of the day. He now provides media relations advice for a variety of organisations, from emergency services to government and private clients in the City.

Neil is married to Fiona and is a father to two girls, meaning he's completely outnumbered in his own home. He lives in Dunfermline, the setting for his first job as a local reporter.

No Man's Land

Neil Broadfoot

CONSTABLE

CONSTABLE

First published in Great Britain in 2018 by Constable

This paperback edition published in Great Britain in 2019 by Constable

Copyright © Neil Broadfoot, 2018

1 3 5 7 9 10 8 6 4 2

The moral right of the author has been asserted.

A CIP catalogue record for this book
is available from the British Library.

ISBN: 978-1-4721-2758-7

Typeset in Minion Pro by TW Type, Cornwall
Printed and bound in Great Britain by Clays Ltd, Elcograf S.p.A.

Papers used by Constable are from well-managed forests and
other responsible sources.

Constable
An imprint of
Little, Brown Book Group
Carmelite House
50 Victoria Embankment
London EC4Y 0DZ

An Hachette UK Company
www.hachette.co.uk

www.littlebrown.co.uk

For Mum and Dad, who've been there for me all the way from the scalded pink jotters to here

PROLOGUE

Connor Fraser collapsed against the church wall, rain-slicked granite driving icy needles into his back and shoulders. He focused on the sudden chill, tried to use it to clear his thoughts, calm the white noise of pain and confusion and rage.

Blood pumped over the hand he had clamped across the wound to his leg, hot and slick between his fingers. He took a deep breath, ignored the flash of pain in his chest, exhaled a cloud of steam into the night air.

The voice drifted from the shadows, as warm and cloying as the blood pouring from his leg. 'You okay, Connor? Watch your step. Last thing we want is you slipping and breaking your neck. Been enough death here recently.'

Connor looked into the darkness opposite, trying not to think of what had been left there only days ago. Knew now it had been a message for him. A message crafted in blood and pain, designed to make his life a horror story.

His attacker slid from the shadows, moving closer. Connor saw muscles tense, the final attack close. The knife rose slowly, flaring orange as it caught the glow from a streetlight overhead.

Connor braced himself against the church wall, tried to draw strength from the ancient stone. 'Come on, then,' he hissed, dragging his gaze from the ghost in front of him. 'I've not got all night, and this is getting fucking boring.'

Another smile, almost genuine this time. 'Mr Take Charge, huh, Connor? I always liked that about you.' A glance down at the knife. 'Well, if you insist.'

Connor pushed off the wall as hard as he could as his attacker lunged, using inertia to make up for the weakness in his leg. He surged forward, the fury and pain finally erupting from him in a roar that filled his ears, drowning out even the hammering of his heart.

They collided in a tangle of limbs and fell to the cobbles, writhing. Connor's leg was engulfed in agony as he jerked the wrong way, the sudden pain forcing another scream from him. He felt small, hard fingers scrabble across his face and twisted away, eyes searching desperately for the knife. He grabbed for it, felt the crazed strength of his attacker behind the blade, inching it closer, closer, to his face.

He took another breath, tasted blood at the back of his throat, and gripped the arms that were quivering with the effort of driving the knife towards his face. He thought about letting go for an instant, the knife digging into the soft flesh under his chin, the blade slicing sideways and down to tear open his windpipe, blood and gristle splattering onto the cobbles. He could let it end with him. Let his blood be the last.

Couldn't he?

CHAPTER 1

Edinburgh – three days earlier

Run!

The word was a shriek in his mind, an imperative he could not ignore. He charged forward, shrugging off the hands he felt on his shoulders. Ignored the sudden panicked shouts of his name as he crashed through heavy double doors at the back of the High Court and onto the street.

A clatter of feet behind him, a voice shouting: 'Stephen! Stop! Shit! Tango Alpha to team leader, he's gone. Repeat, asset is on foot, heading . . .'

He pushed through the throng in front of him, ignoring the indignant shouts, the burning, dazzling flash of cameras and the clamour of questions.

Run!

Stephen lurched across the street, new shoes slithering across the cobbles, aiming for the gate and the News Steps he knew lay beyond. Took them three at a time, each impact on the age-smoothed stone juddering through his body and driving the breath from him.

He looked up, realized he was running straight for the looming stone wall at the bottom of the stairs, where the path twisted to the left, then on down the hill. He skidded through the turn, colliding

3

with a heap of tattered blankets tucked into the corner of the landing, felt something soft yield against his flailing feet.

'Ah, ya fuck!' a voice grunted, the blankets rearing up like some kind of threadbare monster. A pale, thin face glared at him, eyes wide with shock, outrage and pain.

Stephen kicked himself free, dived for the next flight of stairs, reached the bottom and picked up speed on the slope that led onto Market Street. Waverley station was only minutes away. He could duck in, pick a train, any train, and just go. Leave it all behind and . . .

A figure appeared at the mouth of the alleyway, all shoulders and back, blocking his path. Stephen's roar was part shock, part fury. No station for him. No escape. Not now. He tried to slow down, but momentum conspired with the slope to confuse his co-ordination and balance. His feet tangled beneath him, the world tilting as he toppled forward, concrete rushing up to meet him.

A dark blur of motion in front of him, then hands on his chest, stopping him smashing face first into the ground. His stomach gave a cold, oily flip as he was spun around and upright, then slammed into the wall of the alley, breath driven from him in a bark.

'Easy, Stephen, easy,' the man said, grip tightening on his lapels as he spoke.

'Connor, man! Fuck!' Stephen spat, squirming in the man's grip. 'Where the fuck did you come from?'

Connor Fraser gave him a you-know-better smile. 'Come on, Stephen, really? Obvious which way you'd go. Most of the press packing out the front of the court, only way for you to go was the back door, especially after I showed you the way when I took you up those stairs this morning. It was fifty–fifty you'd make a run for it, but I thought I'd cover the bases, just in case.'

Stephen fought for breath, felt his eyes prickle with heat. Waited a beat, fighting to keep his voice even. 'Ah, come on, man. Just let me go, okay? My dad'll blame Robbie, not you. He's the one I got away from. Just let me go. Tell Dad you couldnae catch me. Please?'

Connor shook his head slowly, eyebrows rising in something like apology as he eased his grip, allowing Stephen to move away from the wall. 'Sorry, I can't. You know that. Besides, where would you go?

And what would you do next? No, better to go home. Be with your family. You've got a dad who only wants to look after you. Let him.'

Stephen glanced over Connor's shoulder towards the station. He felt a brief tug of regret, and sighed. Where would he go? It wasn't like he could just fade into the background – he'd been plastered across the headlines for a week now: *Star's Son Key Witness in Murder Trial*. With the trial ongoing, the press had refrained from picking apart his life, digging into the corners he didn't want them looking into. But now that he'd done his part, given evidence that almost guaranteed a conviction, they would be on him. Scrutinizing his life. Wanting him to comment. His dad's agent had already warned him that the media interest would be intense. Wherever he went, this would follow him. Connor was right: better to face it here.

He took a steadying breath, nodded. Connor studied him for a second longer, then took a step back, letting Stephen move onto the path. But he didn't let him go: one hand was still clamped around his arm. Just in case.

Stephen let himself be led the short distance to the end of the alleyway, felt no surprise when he saw a black BMW parked at the side of the road, idling. The driver's window buzzed down, Iain Robbins nodding to Connor as they approached, eyes darting over Stephen.

Connor guided Stephen to the back of the car and opened the door for him to get in.

'Look, Connor, I . . .'

Connor held up a hand. 'No problem,' he said. 'I know what it's like. You did a brave thing today, Stephen. Not everyone would have the balls to stand up and tell the truth the way you did. But you did it. Now you have to deal with the fallout.'

A flash of panic made Stephen's legs twitch, the thought of running darting through his mind. But then he stopped. Calmed himself. It was done. He couldn't change that now. Best to pick up the pieces.

He ducked into the car, Connor swinging the door shut behind him.

'Come on, then, Iain,' he said. 'Let's not keep Daddy waiting.'

* * *

5

Connor watched the car pull away, heading down Market Street. Waited until it got to the roundabout and turned left, heading for Stockbridge and Stephen's home. He wondered what John Benson would say to his son when he got there, pushed the thought aside as he clicked open his earpiece channel. 'Team leader to Tango Alpha, asset secured. Lid full. Going off comms.'

He didn't wait for an answer, just removed the earpiece and slipped it into his pocket. Then he pulled out his mobile and called Robbie Lindsay's number.

'Connor, man, fuck. Sorry, he got away from me. Fast wee fuck, he—'

'I don't want to hear excuses, Robbie.' Connor glanced up the News Steps Stephen had just sprinted down. Kid was lucky he hadn't broken his neck. 'You were primary on Stephen. There was no way you should have let him get enough distance between you and him to make a break for it, especially so close to an unsecured exit.'

Robbie mumbled an apology, took a breath. 'You going to tell Jameson?'

'Do I have a choice? You let an asset slip out of the pocket in an exposed area. We were only lucky that he followed the path I'd already shown him and had limited options for escape. Imagine what would have happened if he'd managed to get past me and was hit by a car or something.'

Silence fell on the line. Robbie didn't need to imagine. John Benson was one of the biggest names in Edinburgh, a former fan favourite at Hibs who'd moved into TV punditry and presenting when his footballing career had petered out. Stephen had enjoyed living in the shadow of his father's success and played the role of spoilt celebrity brat, the usual blend of parties, paparazzi and sex keeping the media interested.

But it had all gone wrong for Stephen one night three months ago when, sharing a noseful of party favours in the toilets of one of Edinburgh's more exclusive clubs, a hanger-on called Roddy Davis had got into a row with another clubber and, in a rage, produced a knife and slit the man's throat. Stephen had made a full statement to the police, and was called to be the star witness in the trial, which

6

had generated a full-blown media circus. John Benson had called in Sentinel Securities, the same close-security firm that had looked after him when the partying got a little too hard and the crowds a little too rowdy.

'Look, I'll think about it,' Connor said, focusing again on Robbie. 'But for fuck's sake, catch yourself on, okay? This isn't a game.'

Robbie sighed down the line. 'Aye. Okay, Connor, sorry.'

'Right, get on home, then, and get your report to me by Monday.'

'Aye, thanks, man.'

Connor killed the call, headed for the News Steps. He had seen Stephen collide with someone up there and wanted to check that whoever it had been wasn't hurt. He was halfway up the stairs when his phone buzzed in his pocket. He knew who it would be. 'Lachlan, how are you?'

'Connor,' Lachlan Jameson boomed, voice as clipped and precise as the moustache he insisted on wearing. 'What news this fine day?'

Connor rolled his eyes. Did he really think ordinary people still talked like that? 'Not much,' he said. 'Just wrapped up with Stephen Benson at the High Court. He's on his way home now. Iain will stand perimeter with Jodie, keep the press at bay.'

'And what about young Lindsay's performance?' Lachlan asked, a hint of impatience creeping down the phone line.

Connor winced. Shit. The old man must have been watching the case on the TV. 'Let's just say he needs a little work,' he replied. 'Couple more months of training and Robbie should work out nicely.'

'Is that an offer?'

Connor mouthed a silent curse. 'Oh, no,' he said, 'no way. You asked me to run the close protection and security around Stephen and his family while he gave evidence. Job done. Iain and the team can handle the rest. Besides, I've got a long weekend coming up, remember?'

Jameson grumbled his displeasure down the phone. As a former soldier, there was something about 'time off' that he just couldn't understand.

Maybe, Connor thought, if he knew what I've got to do, he'd go a little easier.

'Fine, Connor, fine. Just remember, though, if Robbie's not an asset, he's a liability. If he's not cutting it, we cut him. This is a business, after all.'

Connor bit down on the sigh he felt in his chest. Typical Jameson: officer class, saw the grunts as cannon fodder, disposable. Not if he could help it. 'You want me to come into the office and write up my report now?'

'No, no, it's fine. Just head home, type it up and email it to me by close of play. Besides, you'll want to get back to where the action is anyway.'

'Oh?' Connor said.

'Seems there's been a murder in Stirling, not far from where you stay. Not a bad break for us, keeps the trial further down the news schedule. There isn't a lot of detail at this stage, but sounds fairly grim. Maybe you should come into work after all – might be quieter than home tonight.'

Despite himself, Connor laughed. 'Not bloody likely,' he said. 'And, besides, murder investigations aren't my thing any more. Let some other poor sod deal with it.'

'Better them than us,' Jameson agreed. 'Enjoy your time off, Connor.'

Before Connor could reply, the line went dead. Jameson always wanted the last word.

He flipped open the news app on his phone and found the story. It didn't add much to what Jameson had told him already. Body found up near the castle, police saying the death was being treated as suspicious, with 'definite lines of enquiry being followed'. Translation: it's a murder, and we don't have a fucking clue yet.

The byline of the reporter who had written the story contained her Twitter handle: @donnablake1news. Instinctively, Connor flicked over to his Twitter app, scrolled through her timeline and clicked follow. After all, it never hurt to stay informed.

CHAPTER 2

Stirling

From beyond the police cordon, DCI Malcolm Ford heard the soft purr of tyres on cobbles as a car made its way up St John Street towards Stirling Castle. He locked onto the sound, like a shield against the soft, incessant squealing behind him. It was like a grotesque ear worm, a song he kept hearing in his mind. Insidious, maddening. Irresistible.

Look at me, it whispered. *Just turn and look.* Instead Ford gazed up into the clear August sky, closing his eyes against the sudden memory of what lay behind him, trying to draw heat from the day to banish the bone-deep chill that forced him to clench his teeth to stop them chattering.

Look at me, the squeal sang behind him, louder this time as the wind picked up. *Go on. Just one quick look.*

Ford opened his eyes and, making a half-turn, forced himself to focus instead on the scene in front of him. He was on a small lane that ran between the Holy Rude Church and the old bowling green that lay behind the imposing frontage of Cowane's Hospital, which dated from the seventeenth century and backed onto the town walls. At this time of year, the place should have been bustling with tourists, eagerly snapping pictures as they took in the whitewashed stone and grey slate of the hospital and wandered around the gardens that surrounded the bowling green.

Today the area was sealed off – crime-scene tape draped across the gates that led onto the lane, two officers posted there to keep curious passersby away and a growing number of reporters and camera crews in check. Tourists had been replaced by SOCOs, the carefree wandering giving way to an agonizingly slow fingertip search of the area. Crime-scene photographers, using massive lenses and harsh flashes, were capturing every grim detail. In the centre of the green, a large white tent shimmered in the breeze, hastily erected to protect as much of the immediate scene as possible.

A similar tent was being erected behind Ford to preserve the primary crime scene and contain the sheer horror of what was there. But he knew better. Containment was impossible now. They could shield it from sight, but it was too late. The damage was done. He would see that image for the rest of his life, revisit it in countless dreams, dwell on it in quiet moments driving home or sitting up during the nights when sleep would not come. It was branded into his memory. Part of him. And, somehow, he had to try to make sense of it. And the twisted motivation that led to it being there.

He shuddered again, blinking rapidly as his eyes moistened. He coughed once and dug out his notepad, glaring at the pages, trying to fill his mind with the facts, quell madness with the mundane.

The discovery had been made a little after six that morning by a normally spry and vital pensioner, who was now under heavy sedation at Forth Valley Hospital. Ford hadn't yet listened to the 999 call Donald Stewart had made but, from the edited transcript, he knew it was little more than a stream-of-consciousness rant of horrified disbelief punctuated by snippets of detail.

Stewart had been out for his morning walk with his dog, Minty. As usual, they had made their way up a long, twisting path called the Back Walk, which led from the Albert Halls at the bottom of the town, hugging the old town wall as it snaked around the cliffs on the way to the graveyard and the castle. Making a loop, they would walk back down St John Street and head for home in Abercromby Place, a typical central Stirling street of neat hedges, spotless pavements and Victorian townhouses hewn from granite and sandstone. Stewart was obviously not short of money, Ford thought. A point worth remembering.

But that morning Stewart had never made it home. Walking past the Holy Rude, the dog had slipped his collar, squeezed under the gate and charged into the lane, yapping and barking. Noting the gate was unlocked, Stewart had followed – and stepped into Hell.

The report of what he had found, the thing which called to Ford now with its soft squeal, descended into a litany of swearing and sobs for God's mercy. Ford nodded silent approval. He'd seen too much in his job to believe in God, but if ever he wished there was one, it was today.

He set his jaw, took a deep, hitching breath. Thought of Mary, who would be at the university now, where she worked in the IT department. Mary, who would hold him in bed when he moaned in his sleep, listen to him as he spoke, tolerate his silences when he couldn't find the words. Not that he would have to do much explaining on this case: it would be on every TV station and front page soon enough.

Bracing himself, he turned, letting out a small sigh of relief when he saw the SOCOs had finished erecting the tent. He nodded to one he recognized. Even swathed in his white jumpsuit, hood and mask, the huge outline and pendulous gut of Jim Dexter was unmistakable.

He heard the squealing again as he approached the tent. Soft, maddening. Almost, he thought, excited now. *Yes, Malcolm, that's it. Come and see me. I've been waiting for you.*

He stepped inside, earning a cold glare from another forensics officer standing in the middle of the space. Ford held up a hand, indicating he wouldn't get any closer. He wasn't sure he could, even if he wanted to.

The tent had been erected on a small section of perfectly manicured lawn just to the side of the ornate arch that made up the main entrance to the church. The wind picked up and there was another squeal. Some primal instinct to run caressed the back of Ford's neck as he looked at the source of the sound, the object that had called to him, begging him to look. Just. One. More. Time.

In the centre of the tent a slender steel spike had been driven into the lawn, swaying gently with the wind. Impaled on it was a head, the spike entering just below the left side of the jaw and exiting just above the right temple. It put the head at an obscenely jaunty angle, giving it an almost quizzical look. It was little more than a twisted knot of waxy, ash-grey flesh. Lank dark hair was plastered to the forehead, while fluid from the ruined eye sockets soaked the cheeks and mingled with blood so dark it almost looked like oil. The rest of the body was in the second tent on the bowling green, and Ford dimly wondered if the injuries he had seen on it had been inflicted before the head was removed. Given the expression on what remained of the face, he thought so.

The face was a rictus scream of agony, the mouth forced open impossibly wide. Despite his revulsion, Ford was seized by the sudden, almost irresistible urge to step forward, remove the object that had been crammed into the mouth to release the scream it must have stifled. Instead, he looked away, stomach roiling, acid burning the back of his throat as he stared at the thick pink rat's tail hanging from the mouth and trailing over the lower jaw, like a perverse line of drool.

CHAPTER 3

The landscape seemed to decompress as Connor drove west, the urban sprawl of Edinburgh and its suburbs giving way to the open fields and greenery of Linlithgow and West Lothian as he headed for Bannockburn. The radio was full of breathless reports about the murder, each station finding ever more inventive ways to say the same thing over and over again. He finally settled on Valley FM, more out of habit than preference. It was a typical local radio station – all nineties music and terrible jingles for small firms in the town – but he found the traffic reports useful. And it was on the station's website that he'd read the first take on the story.

Donna Blake sounded older than he had imagined from her Twitter profile. The picture there – open smile, perfect make-up and just the right approachable twinkle in her striking blue eyes – gave an impression of youthful enthusiasm and likeability. A reporter who wanted to hear your story. But the voice drifting from the radio was deeper, more tired than he would have thought.

She went through what Connor had already read, telling listeners that the victim had been found in the grounds of Cowane's Hospital. Investigations were ongoing, and a post-mortem examination was due to be held. The report then cut to what Connor thought must have been a press conference, the harried voice of a DCI Ford struggling to be heard over camera flashes and the background murmurs of a room full of excited reporters.

'A definitive cause of death has yet to be established, and the victim has yet to be identified. Extra officers will be deployed in and around Stirling town centre, and we would appeal to anyone who was in the vicinity of John Street, Cowane's Hospital or the area around the Old Town Cemetery and castle at the top of the town between ten p.m. last night and six a.m. this morning to come forward.'

The report cut back to Donna Blake as she gave some background on the area in which the body had been found. Connor tuned it out, his attention shifting to the two massive horse heads that loomed up over the horizon, the metal sculptures glinting in the late-afternoon sun. At thirty metres tall, the Kelpies were an arresting sight and, to Connor, vaguely menacing. They had been built as part of a project to extend the Forth and Clyde Canal, a monument to Scotland's long use of horses in industry. But there was something about them that seemed designed to intimidate, one staring straight ahead, the other frozen with its head flung back, as though it was rearing to throw off its rider.

He shook his head, bearing down on the accelerator and enjoying the surge of power from the Audi's V8. The car was veering danger-ously close to flashy for his line of work but it was, apart from the flat, his only indulgence. And, besides, his mother would have approved. He was almost sure of it.

He came off the M9 onto a twisting A-road that he enjoyed just a little too much, reluctantly slowing as he came into Bannockburn. As he passed a car dealership and a petrol station, it struck him again how normal the town seemed, the banal markers of modern life giving no hint of its extraordinary place in Scotland's history. In 1314, the armies of Scotland and England had met in fields close by and, over two long, brutal days which cost more than fifteen thou-sand lives, Scotland had prevailed. Connor had studied the battle at school, its sheer scale and savagery capturing his young imagination.

He ignored the satnav, taking the turns that led to his destina-tion from memory. As ever, a creeping dread chilled him as he drove, his thoughts descending into a confused jumble. He indicated and turned off the road, the static of crunching gravel filling his ears as he drove up the long, sweeping driveway that led to the main house.

Pulling into a space under a small grove of neat trees, he killed the engine, then climbed out of the car.

It was a clear August afternoon, the wind calm, the sun warm yet not overbearing. Despite this, Connor felt clammy, overheated, as though he had just finished an intense session at the gym. He loosened his tie and the top button of his shirt as he glanced up at the building in front of him. It was a Victorian-style sandstone mansion, the bottom floor dominated by two huge picture windows that flanked the open front door like sentries. To the left of the main house, connected by a glass corridor, sat a smaller, more recent building, like a modern block of flats, trying its best to blend in with its grander neighbour.

What would he find when he stepped inside? Would she be waiting for him, or would it be only the sickness that increasingly wore her face? Would he be greeted with a smile or suspicion? And how would he tell her what he was going to do this weekend?

Steeling himself, Connor headed for the care home's main entrance, hoping that someone he recognized was at the reception desk. At least then he would be guaranteed one friendly welcome today.

CHAPTER 4

She felt like a teenager again, sneaking something illicit while her parents were distracted, filled with the fear they would come back and catch her in the act. But this time it wasn't a boyfriend or a cigarette or a stolen drink with a friend. No, this time it was her laptop.

Donna hit the power button, wincing as the sound of the Mac chiming into life filled the flat. What the hell was she thinking? Why did she still let them get to her like this? She wasn't a sixteen-year-old who had ruined her life and it wasn't the 1960s. She was thirty-four, had studied for two degrees, forged a career in a male-dominated industry in which women were still expected to handle the puff pieces and soft news. If she'd been married they'd have been delighted by a grandchild, probably be pushing her for a 'little brother or sister' for Andrew.

But there was the problem. She wasn't married, a fact of which her parents – her mother in particular – reminded her every time an opportunity arose. And, unfortunately, as Donna needed them to help with childcare when she was at work, the opportunity arose far too often for comfort.

Leaving the laptop to boot up, she headed for her bedroom, and the crib in which Andrew had finally decided to take a nap. She peered in cautiously, focused on his chest, watching it rise and fall gently, the dummy in his mouth jerking occasionally as he sucked.

Again, she felt the amazement well up in her that this tiny life had come from her.

As she leant closer, watching his small chest rise and fall, she brushed a strand of hair away from her face and absently tucked it behind her ear. She had changed out of her work clothes and slipped on her favourite pair of maternity jeans – she was almost back to her pre-baby figure but the elasticated waist was comfortable – with a hoody and let her hair hang loose. She knew her mum would disapprove of her fashion choices – 'Dress the part, Donna, always dress the part' – and the irony of it made her smile. Just you wait, Mum, she thought.

Her looks weren't intimidating but she had something that caught men's interest, which she resented and didn't understand. She knew she was generally seen as overly serious, and on the odd occasion when she let her guard down, her laugh could shock those who didn't know her well. Her piercing pale blue eyes amplified her serious demeanour, giving her gaze an intensity she knew some weren't comfortable with. It hadn't been an issue in papers or on the radio, but now? She had a habit of letting her thoughts leak out in a cold glance, and she had never been able to meekly agree if she thought her bosses were in the wrong. But that was the career she had chosen, the life she had planned. Until Andrew. She had not been desperate to have children. In truth she hadn't been sure she wanted this one, until the first moment she'd held him. She felt a pang of guilt at the thought, resisted the urge to pick him up, stroke his warm, smooth cheek and sniff the thick mop of hair that was so like his father's.

She remembered her first meeting with Mark Sneddon in the newsroom of the *Chronicle*, the attention he'd paid her, telling her she was 'just what the newsroom needs'. Standing up for her with the editors, arguing for her stories, sharing contacts, encouraging her to take risks, go for the political-reporter job she wanted. It was only later, when someone told her to watch what she was doing because Sneddon had a reputation, that she had the uneasy feeling she was making a mistake. But by then it was too late.

Way too late.

She crept away from the cot and back to the living room. Checking the baby monitor beside the laptop, she opened her email account. After wrapping the report for Valley FM, she had copied the audio file and sent it to an old friend at the local bureau desk for Sky. Donna had met Fiona Clarke when they both worked at the *Western Chronicle* – the *Westie* – in Glasgow. Back then, Fiona had been on features while Donna had remained with news.

It crossed her mind that perhaps she should have followed Fiona's example, not stubbornly insisted on sticking it out on news. But news was the toughest gig and she wasn't going to concede that she couldn't hack it. She might have been better off if she had: after yet another round of redundancies targeting the features desk, Fiona had taken a payout, while tapping her contacts for a sidestep into broadcasting. She'd pocketed the redundancy money and found a better-paid job. Worked her way up to her current role as a senior news producer – and raised a finger up to her former newspaper bosses by regularly getting the stories they couldn't.

With news reporters not eligible for the redundancy payments, Donna had stuck it out, telling herself she was an old-school newspaper hack, refusing to acknowledge the terror of being front and centre that broadcast required. She liked being a newspaper reporter because she could get the story and leave – no need to be in front of the camera, judged or even mocked by millions watching at home. But not now. Now it was different.

She felt a sudden pang of panic – had she been wrong? About Mark, about her job, about every decision she had made? Was that why she was now swallowing her fear and pursuing a slim chance in broadcasting? What if Fiona thought she was being too pushy and said no?

Her heart skipped when she saw the message she was waiting for.

FROM: Fiona Clarke fclarke@skynews.com
RE: Stirling murder. Local reporter covering?

She paused for a second, finger hovering above the trackpad. Muttered a silent curse, angered by her sudden indecision. She hadn't been like this before Mark. Or Andrew. But now . . .

She shook off the thought, stabbed at the trackpad and opened the email.

Hi, Donna, long time no hear! Hope all is well with you. I hear you're a mum – congratulations, and welcome to the non-sleep brigade! Denny is four now, growing so fast and with an opinion on everything.
I listened to the package you sent over. It's good stuff, and it's clear radio suits you. Good to know you're freelancing, I'll keep you in mind for the future. As for covering this story, I'm sorry to say that, with the coverage it's getting, the bosses are shipping in the big guns, so there's not much work going at the moment. That said, keep in touch. If you get a good line on it, especially with you being local, let me know and I'll see what I can do.
Let's get a catch-up soon!
Fx

Donna leant away from the laptop, breath hissing from between clenched teeth. Shit.

She looked around the room, let the quiet soothe her. It was a small, characterless flat, a new-build in an estate just close enough to the town-centre postcode to be described as 'Central Stirling'. But she loved it. It was the first home she had owned and everything in it was hers and Andrew's. No nervous waiting for the key in the lock – would he come home this time? She felt a wave of self-loathing wash over her. Why had she let him come and go, believed him as she'd told herself lie after lie? He just needs time. I'll play it cool. I'm giving him space, the impression I don't really need him. I'm independent and strong: he'll find that irresistible.

In hindsight she realized she had done the opposite. She'd sat at home letting him pick and choose. She had put it all on a plate for him. She shuddered at how naïve she had been. She'd made it so easy for him. Too easy.

She scanned Fiona's email again, forcing herself to read more slowly. How had she ever thought she, of all people, could become a TV reporter? It seemed ridiculous.

But there, at the end, a glimmer of hope: *If you get a good line on it, especially with you being local, let me know and I'll see what I can do.*

Donna shut the laptop slowly, hardly aware that she was biting her bottom lip. Fiona had been right. And wrong. Radio did suit her. For the moment. But she had no intention of staying there, letting her insecurities hold her back again. After Andrew's birth, and the nine glorious months of maternity leave when it was just the two of them, she'd realized it was time to get back out there. This time, she was going to grab every opportunity that came her way. Valley FM was a stepping stone. She didn't want to be the reporter in the background any more, slipping in quietly with a few questions in her notebook: she wanted to be fronting the news. Since the shit-storm surrounding her pregnancy and the trauma of Andrew's difficult birth, her priorities had been clearer, her resolve firmer. She was beyond caring what people thought, wanted only to show them that they were wrong about her.

And if she had to scoop every other reporter covering the Cowane's Hospital murder to prove herself, then fine. She knew just how she was going to do it.

CHAPTER 5

It was only a ten-minute drive from Bannockburn to his flat, along roads he normally enjoyed, but Connor had lost his taste for it.

It had been the worst kind of visit. She was there and she was not, as though she was in a darkened room with a single swinging light bulb, the harsh glare stripping the shadows from her mind for precious moments, then plunging her back into darkness and confusion. She had ranted, she had cried. She had hugged him, asked how he was, then looked at him with nothing but addled pleading in eyes that were growing dull and too used to tears.

It had started three years ago. Small things at first. An inability to finish her beloved *Times* crossword. Forgetting where she had put her reading glasses or the cigarettes she insisted she no longer smoked. But his mother had assured him Ida Fraser's condition was manageable. His grandmother needed a little more help around the house. That was all. Nothing for Connor to worry about. Certainly no reason for him to come back from Belfast to check up on her.

Looking back now, Connor wondered how much of his mother's reluctance for him to come home was based on a desire not to disrupt his life, and how much on her desire for him not to see his gran. Because if he'd seen her, he'd have known. Before it was too late.

Nothing much happened for the next few months. Connor would make his regular calls home, speaking either to his mother or his gran. They told him everything was fine, and he put the stress he heard in their voices down to the new circumstances they were finding themselves in. After all, Ida Fraser had always been a fiercely independent woman, her determination forged in the sixties, when being a single mother abandoned by her husband was still seen as a failing and a social curse. To have to accept help from her daughter-in-law – whom she regarded as not good enough for her darling son Jack – must have put pressure on them both, especially since darling Jack would no doubt pull his normal disappearing act as soon as things got tough.

Over time, it faded from being an issue into a fact of life. His gran was getting on a bit: she was bound to forget things. And by then Connor had his own problems to deal with in Belfast, and the issue was forgotten.

Until that night. And that call.

He remembered it all too clearly. He was down in the Cathedral Quarter of the town, trying to calm the sting in his knuckles and the panicked clamour of his thoughts with Bushmills and Harp. He'd been ignoring the phone most of the night: Karen was calling and he didn't know what to say to her. Didn't have the words.

But then he'd glanced at the screen and seen a different caller. Gran – mobile. Connor had experienced a moment of vertigo, the room tilting nauseatingly as adrenalin flooded his veins and burnt away the blurring effects of alcohol. His gran never used her mobile. Barely knew how to turn the thing on. He had a sudden image of her lying on the floor in her living room, surrounded by the wreckage of the table she had crashed through, reaching for the mobile in her pocket, calling the one person she knew would always answer.

He was out of the pub before he knew it, phone clamped to his ear, the cold of the night only partly to blame for the chill he felt deep in his guts.

'Hello, Gran? You okay? Listen, if there's—'

'Connor, son,' she said, cutting him off. Her voice was level, rough with tears she had long since exhausted. 'I'm sorry to call you this late at night, but we have to talk.'

'What? Gran, what's wrong? Are you—'

'It's your mother, Connor,' Ida replied, her voice a blunt, hard thing of extended consonants and flattened vowels. 'I'm sorry, son. She asked me not to tell you, not to worry you, but it's getting bad now. And you have to know.'

'Know what?' Connor asked, his lungs leaden, the air around him hard to inhale. 'Gran, what's—'

'Call her,' Ida said. 'Get her to tell you, son. But please, just come home.'

He didn't bother calling, instead booked the first flight home. Knew it was bad the moment he walked through the front door.

His mother was in the living room, wrapped in an oversized cardigan that only emphasized how much weight she had lost. She had always been a small, vital woman, her hair flame red, her porcelain skin dappled with freckles, flares of red in her cheeks and across her neck. But the woman in front of Connor that day was dull, anaemic, her hair peppered with grey, her skin waxy and parchment thin. Only her eyes were familiar, the brilliant green of the pupils refusing to give in to the yellowing of the whites.

She didn't speak when he knelt in front of her, just leant forward and wrapped skeletal arms around him in a feverish hug.

Bowel cancer, the doctors said. She had kept it quiet to start with, dismissing it as just an infection, something that would pass. But it hadn't passed. And now, with the cancer having spread its black, snaking tendrils through her, there was nothing to be done.

Claire O'Brien Fraser died three weeks later. And while the loss devastated Connor and his father, it had pitched Ida into the abyss.

The doctors said the stress of Claire's death had exacerbated Ida's dementia, increasing its severity. But Connor knew better. His mother had been his gran's tether to reality. And with her gone, she was adrift in her own mind.

Connor went home, glad to be away from Belfast and the nightmare it had become. After a stint in Edinburgh, he moved to Stirling, using some of the inheritance his mother had left him to place his gran in the care home at Bannockburn. The rest he used as a deposit on the flat and the car. If his father objected, he said nothing to his son. Not that that was a surprise: Jack Fraser had been clear all his life that Connor was a bitter disappointment.

Home for Connor was a garden flat on Park Terrace, close to the affluent King's Park area of the town. The street was wide and lush, with manicured gardens and carefully trimmed trees. The house Connor's flat was in reminded him of the care home, the cream sandstone now seeming to glow like amber in the evening sun.

A narrow driveway led off the road to a parking bay at the back. Connor pulled into it, switched off the engine, grabbed his kitbag from the boot, then descended the small stone staircase to his flat. He unlocked the door, disarmed the burglar alarm and stood in the silence for a moment. Satisfied nothing had been disturbed, he made his way down the hall, past the kitchen on his right and a bedroom on his left, to the living room. It was a large space, the far wall dominated by floor-to-ceiling patio windows that looked out onto a small paved area and granite wall that the previous owners had disguised with a miniature Japanese garden.

He dropped his bag, took a breath. Switched on the TV, more to drown out the silence than from any desire to watch anything. The news channels had moved on to other stories, but still he saw the words 'Stirling' and 'horror murder' more than once on the ticker at the bottom of the screen.

He went back to the kitchen and poked his head into the fridge. Nothing. Shit. He'd meant to stop on the way back, get food for the weekend. And beer. After his visit with his gran, and what he had to do next, he needed it.

He hadn't had the heart to tell her. She was too confused, too fragile. Or maybe that was cowardice. Either way, it had to be done. This weekend, he was going to clear out her home, get it ready to put on the market. He didn't want the money for himself, but he did want it to make sure her care was provided for. But, with her dementia stripping her of her memories, how could he tell her he was about to remove any physical reminders of her life by packing up her home of thirty years?

He stepped back into the living room, stared blankly at the TV as he tried to work the tension out of his shoulders. He had been bracing his neck the entire time he had been with his gran, almost as though he was waiting for her to throw a punch.

He sighed, then headed for his bedroom and the kitbag that was packed and ready. A workout was what he needed. Something to take his mind off his gran, his mother and the past. The report for Lachlan Jameson could wait.

He changed and headed for the door, hefting his bag over his shoulder. The gym was only a half-mile away, and the walk would serve as his warm-up. He set off down the street, already running through the workout he would subject himself to.

He didn't notice the figure across the road, watching him from the shadows. Didn't hear the whisper that drifted into the night.

'Hello again, Connor.'

CHAPTER 6

The splash-back from the toilet bowl peppered cold water across his burning face. It only increased the roiling in his guts and he retched again, vomit made acid by the vodka he had drunk earlier to steady his nerves spattering the bowl. He felt his pulse hammer in his temples, vision pulsing in time with his heart. Drew a shaking hand across his mouth as he took ragged, hitching breaths. Fought for control, screwed his eyes shut, dark sparks dancing across his vision, and focused on his breathing.

Then, in that darkness, the memory. That call. Cold. Remote. Businesslike.

His eyes snapped open and he doubled over once more as his empty stomach spasmed. He felt an incredible pressure build in his head, as though it were about to explode. Dimly, he hoped it would. After a moment, he collapsed, chest heaving, his back against the wall of the office en-suite.

At first, he had thought he would be okay. The call had come just after eleven a.m., directly to an anonymous pre-paid mobile to which only the caller had the number. The message had been, like the voice, cold and efficient, with just a hint of something darker beneath the cultured tones.

'It's done. Check the news. You should be very happy.'

The call ended before he could say anything. Not that he could speak at that moment. He stared at the phone, a suddenly alien thing in his hand that radiated a numbing cold. He nodded and cleared his throat, horrified at the tickle of laughter that bubbled inside him, then stole a glance at his office door and his assistant, who sat just beyond.

He pocketed the phone, smoothed the lines of his suit and walked to the door, his face contorting into a well-rehearsed smile. It wasn't hard. He'd been living behind a mask for the last twenty-five years. 'I've got a conference call on some casework,' he said, in the measured tone he had perfected years ago. 'Can you hold all calls and see I'm not disturbed, please?'

'Of course,' Margaret said, blinking up at him from behind thick glasses. She had been beautiful when they met – young, vibrant, flawless. Now the years had etched thin lines into her waxy skin, twisted her elegant hands into gnarled twigs and slackened a jaw that had once been firm. He used to lust after her. Now he pitied her.

He retreated into his office, made sure the blinds were angled for privacy, then went to the cupboard beneath the wall-mounted TV. He took out the bottle of vodka and one of the crystal tumblers stacked neatly beside it. Poured a large measure, took bottle and glass back to his desk, loosened his tie and gazed dumbly around the room. The enormity of what had happened seemed to scream at him in the silence.

It's done.

He felt the numbness recede, like the tide going out on a forgotten beach, as panic rose. He took another mouthful of vodka and held it in his mouth for a moment, willing it to burn away the rising terror. It didn't.

He swallowed, spotted the TV remote on his desk and watched his hand drift to it as though it wasn't connected to him.

It's done. Check the news.

He didn't want to. To see it splashed across the TV would make this nightmare real. Of course he had had no choice, been forced to act by the greed, short-sightedness and self-serving arrogance of others but still . . .

It's done. Check the news.

He stabbed at the remote. The TV flared into life and he turned the volume down. It defaulted to the internal TV channel: a florid-faced man with bad teeth and worse hair was lecturing a sparse, uninterested audience on a topic only he was interested in. He flicked to the news channel and his breath caught when he saw the caption: 'Breaking news: murder in Stirling.'

A striking woman with perfect make-up, her expression grave, spoke into the camera: '. . . was made at approximately six o'clock this morning. Police have confirmed this was a sustained and brutal attack.'

He fumbled for his glass, felt the veneer of control crack as the camera cut to the police tape strung across the entrance to Cowane's Hospital, the white SOCO tents visible just beyond. The camera pulled back, the reporter taking full frame.

'I understand the post-mortem examination will begin shortly, to ascertain both cause of death and the identity of the victim.'

With that, the dam broke and the terror surged. He lurched for the en-suite, the vomit exploding out of him almost before he'd had the chance to raise the toilet seat. It was as though his body was trying to expel not just the vodka but a lifetime of guilt and lies.

Now he slumped in front of the toilet in the office he had given so much for, the office that had ultimately led to the death of the man on the screen. The man who, as the reporter had just said, would shortly be identified. The man who would not be the last to die in Stirling in the days to come.

CHAPTER 7

The gym was a twenty-four-hour place just off Craigs Roundabout on the main road into and out of the centre of town. It was Thursday-night busy, the working week burning off the Monday-morning resolve of many, leaving the weights free for the truly dedicated.

Connor got changed and entered the main hall, nodding to familiar faces. He wedged in his earbuds and hit play on his phone – Bach's Cello Suites. He'd been in enough gyms to know that high-energy dance or heavy rock was the preferred soundtrack, but neither worked for him. For Connor, the gym was all about the work. About pouring everything into the weights and pushing himself to the limit, where exhaustion and endorphins would conspire with the music to calm his mind. And, besides, he'd seen enough movies to know that torture scenes were always more effective when set to classical music.

After a warm-up on the rowing machine, he worked his way around the weight machines, alternating pulling and pushing exercises as he pummelled his upper body. And all the while he kept glancing towards the free weights, checking if they were unused, waiting until they were quiet and the real work could begin.

Fifteen minutes later, Connor was sitting on a weights bench, head between his knees, concentrating on the 50-kilo dumbbells he had just used for twelve reps of an Arnold press as he tried not to throw up. He could feel his muscles swelling with blood, his skin growing tight as his pulse thundered in his ears. He shut his eyes, concentrated on his breathing. Jumped when a cool hand touched his shoulder.

A petite blonde in the gym's unflattering purple uniform smiled nervously down at him, unease and concern fighting for supremacy in her eyes. He took a deep breath, popped out the earbuds and smiled up at her. 'Jennifer, sorry. Just finished a set . . .' He trailed off, partly because he didn't know what else to say, partly because nausea was still scalding the back of his mouth.

Jennifer MacKenzie's smile became more confident. Great teeth, Connor thought randomly, feeling a sudden burning in his cheeks that was nothing to do with exertion.

'No problem, Connor,' she said, the hint of a Glasgow accent giving her voice a singsong quality. 'Just wanted to check how you were doing. You looked like you were going at it pretty hard there.'

She'd been watching him? Shit. 'Yeah.' He shrugged. 'Been a long week. Needed to unwind a little. Anyway, how you doing?'

The unease tightened her face again, her eyes shying away from his. 'Ah, you know, same old,' she said, aiming for levity and missing. She half turned as if to go, then hesitated.

'You sure you're okay, Jen?' Connor asked. They'd known each other for a few months, since Connor had started coming to the gym. Friendly nods at first, then chats between sets that had stretched into lingering conversations. They'd threatened each other with coffee or a drink on several occasions but never got round to it. He wondered if that was what was bothering her, or something else.

'Yeah, I'm fine, really,' she said, eyes still not finding his. 'Look, I'd better let you get back to it.'

He looked at her: the slumped shoulders, the nervous flicking of a strand of hair behind her ear, the shallow breathing. Nerves. Definitely. 'I'm almost done,' he said, not knowing the decision had been made until he started speaking. 'You got long to go on your shift? I can hang around if you'd like – we can get that drink?'

Her eyes darted back to him, warm gaze fixing on his. 'I'm on till ten,' she said. 'If you're sure . . .'

Connor glanced up at the clock on the wall above the mirrors. Ten to nine. Plenty of time. 'No problem,' he said, leaning forward and wrapping his hands around the dumbbells again. 'See you in Reception.'

'Yeah. Cool. See you then!' She flashed him another smile and was gone, busying herself checking that the free weights had been racked and everything was tidied away.

Connor hefted the weights onto his lap then, with a kick of his knees, muscled them up to his shoulders. He stared at his reflection in the mirror and started to press the weights up. When his muscles began to burn in protest, he thought of Jen's smile – and wondered what else lurked there.

He took his time with the remainder of his workout, easing back on the intensity, wanting to be able to raise a glass without his hand shaking. But as he worked, Jen's smile refused to leave him. That nervous, almost fearful glance, the words that were almost said. Could his reaction have scared her when she'd startled him? If that was the case, why would she agree to go out for a drink with him? And why, for that matter, had he asked her?

He showered and dressed, a thin sheen of sweat coating his back, the afterburn from his workout, then checked himself in the mirror. *The image of your grandfather*, he heard his gran whisper in his ear. *Forget all that Fraser blood. You're an O'Brien, son. Plain and simple.*

Growing up, he had never seen it, his grandfather a towering presence whom Connor feared and adored in equal measure. But now, standing in a Stirling gym, his body pumped up by a workout his grandfather would have mirrored at the gym he had assembled at his own home, he saw it: the same broad shoulders, the back that seemed to flare in a too-wide V for the rest of his frame; the heavy jaw that was just the right side of thuggish, making his prominent cheeks and blade-straight nose seem delicate and at odds with the rest of his face. But while his features were his grandfather's, his eyes were his mother's, the same luminous green, like chips of jade. He shook himself, raked his fingers through his short, copper-flecked brown hair, then took a deep, steadying breath, amused and a little annoyed to find he was nervous.

He walked back into Reception, glancing up at the clock on the wall: nine fifty-five p.m. He was early. He sat on the couch that faced the security-locked rotunda doors that made up the entrance, content to wait. He was just fishing out his phone when Jen appeared, her cheeks bright with colour, her breathing fast and excited. 'Just finishing up. I'll only be five mi—' She stopped, staring through the glass front of the building to the street beyond.

Connor saw the colour drain from her face, her body tensing with the trepidation he had seen in the gym earlier. No, he thought, this was worse. This wasn't unease. It was fear. He tracked her gaze as he stood up. Saw the outline of a car on the street. 'Jen? You okay?' he asked, keeping his voice neutral and his body facing the entrance.

Rule one: never turn your back on the threat.

'Y-yeah,' she stuttered, dragging her gaze from the window. Her eyes were wide, her skin pallid. 'Sorry, Connor. Look, maybe this isn't such a good idea. I'll see you another time and we can—'

'Jen,' he said, his voice soft but firm. 'It's no problem. Five minutes, okay? Meet me here. If nothing else, I can walk you out. Last thing I want is you to be alone on the street. Imagine what that would do for my reputation.'

She forced a smile for him, then darted a glance at the door. 'You sure?'

'Yes,' he said, holding her gaze, answering the question she hadn't answered. 'Go and get changed. I'll see you here. And take your time. No rush.'

Her mouth opened, then closed, a conversation dying on her lips. 'Okay,' she said after a moment. He nodded and walked back to the couch. Phone forgotten, he stared out of the window and the shadow that hunched there.

And waited.

She was back five minutes later, her uniform swapped for jeans, T-shirt and a leather jacket. She'd brushed her hair and applied make-up, which only accentuated how pale she was. She nodded at him, eyes skittering back to the entrance.

He pretended not to notice. 'So, what do you think?' he asked. 'Drink? Something to eat?'

'Hm? Oh, sorry. How about a drink? We could walk into town, head for Baker Street?'

No. 2 Baker Street was a pub near the centre of town. Connor hadn't been there often, but the beer was good and the surroundings comfortable. It was only a ten-minute walk, most of it close to the road. Perfect.

They headed out, Connor making sure he stepped onto the street first. He checked to his right: the car he had spotted was still there, a black Mercedes saloon, reflections from the streetlights rippling across its polished bodywork.

Jennifer stiffened when she saw it, took an involuntary step closer to him.

'You okay?' he said, looking down at her, making sure he kept the car in his peripheral vision.

'Yeah, yeah, fine. Look, I'm sorry, Connor. Let's get to the pub. I can buy you a drink and maybe,' she glanced over his shoulder again, 'maybe I can ask you a favour.'

CHAPTER 8

The house was in almost total darkness by the time Ford got home, the patio light a single beacon in the night. Home was a three-bedroom detached in Bridge of Allan, a small town a ten-minute drive north of Stirling. He and Mary had moved there more than twenty years ago when she'd taken her job at the uni; the campus was close by. With him transferring to what had been Central Scotland Police from Edinburgh CID, it was perfect. And although it was only a stone's throw from work, Bridge of Allan had always felt separate to him.

Until tonight.

He killed the engine, watching as the dashboard clock winked out as he pulled the key from the ignition. Ten thirty-five p.m. A fourteen-hour day. Not unusual. Setting up a major murder investigation was always a laborious, time-consuming process, but with the merger of Scotland's eight forces into Police Scotland, it had become a bureaucratic nightmare. And with a staffing crisis that made investi- gating anything more complicated than a parking ticket a logistical headache, a murder – especially one as public and brutal as this – piled the pressure on everyone, particularly the man in charge. During a catch-up call to Ford after the press conference, the chief constable had made that all too clear.

Ford grunted as he hefted himself out of the car, lower back aching dully. He found his key and opened the door, stepped inside and locked up behind him. Then he kicked off his shoes and headed for the living room.

A single light illuminated the room, thrown by the large reading lamp Mary had set up in the corner behind the couch that dominated the far wall. A small side table had been placed beside his chair, with a bottle of Glenfiddich on a tray, a half-filled glass and a small water jug. A note was propped against the bottle. He didn't need to read it to know what it said.

He picked up the glass and sat heavily in his chair. Heard weight shift upstairs, knew Mary would be in bed, reading. He'd told her years ago not to wait up for him, that there was no need for both of them to be exhausted. But she never listened. Whenever there was a big case she wouldn't sleep until she'd heard him walk into the house. It was their ritual, learnt long ago through bitter experience and arguments that still echoed from the walls. He and Mary had a rule. When he was on a big case, if the hours were long and the circumstances grim, he would sit, have a drink, collect his thoughts, decompress, as he tried to re-enter normality.

It was Mary's idea, born of too many arguments when she had faced him as he walked through the door, stunned and drained by the violence and horror he had seen, unable and unwilling to shape it into words for her. Now she would pour him a drink, leave him the note, and go to bed to read. *Just the one, Mal. If you want to talk, I'm here. Take the time you need.*

He took a sip of the whisky, enjoyed the sensation of it scalding his throat. Closed his eyes, tried not to think of the horrors he had seen that day. The squeal of a steel spike bobbing in the wind. Of dead, ruined eyes glaring at him from the head impaled on that spike. Of the corpse, reduced to little more than flayed meat, lying on the cold steel of the pathologist's table.

And of what they had found next.

Dr Walter Tennant had worked with the police for as long as Ford could remember. He seemed somehow timeless, an eternal, comforting constant amid the chaos Ford confronted in his work. No matter the case, no matter how brutal the death, Tennant had faced it with the same resolute good humour, a warm smile and a bad joke always on his lips. He was a big man, bearded, with a barrel chest, hulking shoulders and hands that Ford thought were more suited to a rugby player than a pathologist, yet he had seen him work on the dead with a quiet grace and, yes, an elegance that astounded him.

But not that afternoon. This was something new. Something that had robbed Tennant of his defiant good humour, his poise and grace. The sight had chilled Ford almost as much as the temperature-controlled mortuary, and underscored for him the sheer savagery, the malevolence of what he was facing.

The body had been washed and stripped, then laid out on one of the steel tables with the high gutters that would catch the blood and viscera that the post-mortem examination released. At Tennant's insistence, the head had been similarly prepared – a complex under-taking as, before anything could be done, the object had to be removed from its mouth.

Tennant worked quietly, the only sound his breathing. Turning the head, examining, probing. Ford's stomach lurched when Tennant leant in close and prodded the jawline with a finger. 'Hm. Dislocated.' He made a further survey, ensuring his assistant – an ashen-faced young woman whose name Ford couldn't remember – took pho-tographs when needed. Then, in one quick, fluid motion, he pulled the animal from the mouth, which gaped like a dark wound. 'I'm no expert,' Tennant said, 'but it looks like a domestic rat to me. Big but unremarkable. We'll look at it later.'

With that done, he picked up the head, then carefully laid it at the top of the table, a sliver of steel glinting between it and the rest of the body as the spotlights revealed the full grotesquery of what lay before them.

'Well, well, well,' Tennant had whispered, a hand rising to scratch his beard. He caught himself: his gloved hand hovered inches from his cheek and he stared at it for a moment, as if it was new and alien to him. He shook his head, a silent admonishment, then dropped his hand, looking at Ford with eyes that were as bright as the spotlights overhead. 'Malcolm,' he said, his voice hardening, 'you don't have to stay for this, you know. I can get it done and send you the report. From the look of . . . ah, this,' he waved a hand at the body, 'it's not going to be pleasant. I can already see the telltale signs of internal bleeding and multiple fractures. You might not like what you're about to witness.'

Ford felt as though he'd swallowed a mouthful of sand. He stood there, pinned, his mind screaming at him to get out, get away from this horror, as far and as quickly as he could. But then, even as he opened his mouth to agree, he heard it. The whispering squeal. The one that he knew would haunt his nightmares.

Look at me, it sang to him. *Look at me.*

'No, Walter, thanks,' Ford said, the words thick and heavy in his throat. 'I need to be here. I need to know.'

Tennant said nothing more, just changed his gloves and went to work. He kept up a running commentary as he worked, noting injuries and violations with the businesslike tone of a surveyor listing maintenance points on a dilapidated house.

And all the while Ford watched, fighting the icy chill that permeated his body, focusing on Tennant's voice as he tried to drown out that singsong squeal.

The full examination took a little more than an hour, Tennant seeming to regain his composure as he worked, as though the familiar routine of disembowelling a corpse somehow comforted him.

When it was done they retreated to his office, a small anteroom that was as cold and clinical as the main examination room. Ford knew Tennant was married with two grandchildren – away from work he couldn't stop talking about them – but there was no trace of that life now. No pictures, no mementoes, no trinkets from his family. They never spoke about it, but Ford understood. Just as his decompression time with a whisky was his ritual, this was Tennant's way to shield his family from the unwanted knowledge of violence and death that his job brought him.

Tennant made coffee with a small kettle in the corner of the room, then barricaded himself behind his desk. The mug looked tiny in his hands, and when he lifted it to his lips, Ford saw a small tremor. 'So,' he said. 'What do you think?'

Tennant gazed into his mug, as though the words he sought were in there. 'Savagery,' he said finally, not looking up. 'Utter savagery.

Whoever the victim was, he was subjected to a prolonged beating with a blunt object – a metal bar or a baseball bat. One kidney ruptured, every rib broken. Severe bruising and damage to the groin. Seven out of his ten fingers broken. And whoever did this paid particular attention to his primary joints – the knees, ankles and elbows all show signs of multiple fractures.'

Ford nodded, the question he didn't want to ask filling the room. 'Was he . . . ah . . . Well, did he . . .'

Tennant looked up, the coldness Ford had seen earlier flashing back into his eyes. When he spoke, his tone was as lifeless as the body that lay on his table. 'If you're asking if he was alive when he was decapitated, then it's impossible to give a definitive answer. But . . .' he took a shaking breath, held it, then exhaled '. . . if you want a guess, from the pupil dilation and petechial haemorrhaging to the ragged nature of the wound, I would say he was. And he was thrashing.'

'Jesus,' Ford whispered. He felt as though he had been plunged into darkness, left to fumble around an unfamiliar room by touch alone. And again he heard it. That singsong squeal. Soft. Discordant. Insistent.
Look at me.

'Indeed,' Tennant replied.

Ford shook himself. When he spoke again, his voice was almost normal, but he hated the whine of desperation he heard. 'Walter, this is a fucking nightmare. Have you got *anything* at all that might help me?'

The pathologist looked down again, studying the naked tabletop in front of him. 'If you mean identifying him, then dental is out of the question. There was a lot of damage done when the rat was forced into his mouth, and by the look of it, he suffered repeated blows to the head. But his fingerprints are intact, mostly, and of course, we can run his blood, see if we get a match.'

Ford whistled between his teeth. All valid procedures. All time-consuming. And after the media circus of the press conference, the chief was baying for a result. A quick one. 'Anything else?'

'There's only one thing,' Tennant said, leaning forward, 'and this is off the record, Malcolm. It's pure conjecture on my part, based on what I found. My theories won't appear in my report.'

Despite himself Ford felt a thrill of excitement. 'At this stage, I'll take it. What?'

Tennant glanced out of his office window back to the main examination room. 'You heard me say when I was examining him that there was a small tattoo on his left pectoral muscle.' He pointed to his own chest at roughly the point he had noted the inking on the corpse.

'Yeah. Is it significant?'

'It may be. As I said, there were serious injuries around his joints – knees, ankles, elbows. The tattoo may explain some of that.'

Ford had listened as the doctor talked, waves of cold cramps washing through him.

Now, sitting in his living room, he looked at the note Mary had left. *Just the one, Mal. If you want to talk, I'm here.* He laid it aside, poured another whisky and sipped slowly. He ignored the squealing in his mind and put together facts he did not want to know.

A body. Brutally beaten. Every major joint in the arms and legs broken. A rat forced into the victim's mouth before he was decapitated, probably while still alive. And on his chest, beneath the bruising, a small tattoo. A tattoo that gave Ford the outline of a picture he didn't want to see. It was a simple design. A hand, palm out, fingers held tightly together, thumb locked parallel.

A hand. But not just any hand.

A red hand.

The Red Hand of Ulster.

CHAPTER 9

Eleven o'clock on a Thursday night, and Baker Street was winding down for the evening. The students had cleared out for the night-clubs, leaving only a smattering of locals and a couple who could only be tourists, given their mahogany-tanned skins, too-white smiles and choice of clothing: chinos and a T-shirt for him, jeans and an 'I love Scotland' sweatshirt for her.

Connor made sure they got a table at the back of the bar, facing the front door. He kept the conversation light at first, inanities about work, who was doing what at the gym, what Jen had planned for the weekend. He watched her nerves dissipate as she spoke, the tension leaving her shoulders, the colour returning to her cheeks. He knew the Mercedes had followed them from the gym, breaking off only when Connor had turned into a side lane that was impossible to drive along. He had listened for the clunk of a car door and the clatter of footsteps to catch up. Heard nothing. And, since they arrived, he'd seen no one enter the bar whom he deemed a threat.

He watched as Jen drained her glass, then nodded to it. She gave him a shy smile, considered, then said, 'Oh, go on. Just one more. I'm working tomorrow.'

He headed for the bar and ordered their drinks – vodka and tonic for her, a whisky with ice for him. He didn't want it, but he liked to chew the ice cubes.

'So,' he said, as he sat down again, 'you going to tell me what the favour is you were going to ask?'

She blinked rapidly, as though waking from a dream. He saw tension jump back into her posture as she sat away from the table, hands spinning the glass as her eyes darted between it and him, unsure what to focus on.

'Ach, that,' she said, releasing her glass to wave a hand dismissively in front of her. 'It was nothing, don't worry about it. It was just . . .' She let the sentence trail off, busied herself with her drink.

Connor watched her for a moment, letting the suddenly awkward silence drag out as he made a decision.

Fuck it. 'Okay,' he said, 'but if it's something to do with whoever is following you in the Merc that was outside the gym, I can help.'

Her head whipped up, eyes filled with electrified panic. For a moment, Connor thought she would leave, but then she took a breath, centred herself. When she spoke, her voice was almost even. 'How did you know about . . .?'

'It's my job,' he said. 'I saw the way you reacted when you saw the car at the gym, and whoever was driving didn't make much of an effort to disguise the fact they were following us. I'm surprised the driver hasn't stepped in here, which means they either figured out where you were heading or have what they needed.'

She looked at him as though for the first time. He'd been intentionally vague when they'd spoken about his work in the past, saying only that he worked in security, letting her jump to the conclusion that he was a doorman of some sort.

'I'm not judging, Jen,' he said, when it was clear she was still processing what he had said. 'Jealous ex, stalker, over-protective dad, I don't know. And I don't really care. As long as you're okay. And I'm saying that if you need it I can help.'

She took a slug of her drink, eyes reddening either from the alcohol or whatever she was feeling. 'Good guess,' she said, the hint of a smile tugging at the corners of her mouth. 'I'm sorry, Connor. See . . .' she blew air '. . . it's my dad. He does, ah, well, a fair bit of business across the Central Belt, and he gets a wee bit protective at times. He's back in Edinburgh, but he likes to have one of his employees keep an eye on me, just in case.'

Connor made a mental note to check out Jennifer MacKenzie's father as he ran what she had told him through his mind. It made sense, and it explained why the driver hadn't followed them into the pub: he'd seen Jen with a large-built man, in a public area, heading for a pub. No doubt reported it, probably called it a night. 'So it's not a problem?' he asked.

'It's a fucking pain in the arse,' she said, her words hard with anger and resentment. 'I know Dad means well, but I'm sick of seeing a car sitting outside the gym whenever I'm working a nightshift. I mean, Paulie – Dad's guy – is nice enough, but it's like a slap in the face, isn't it? Does he think I can't look after myself?'

Connor nodded. Wondered again about her father, what type of man would go to such lengths to protect his daughter – and from what.

He considered his glass, looked around the pub. It was dying. And he still had that report to write. He downed his whisky, caught a chunk of ice between his wisdom teeth and began to worry at it. A vague alarm was sounding in the back of his mind: there were more questions he should ask her. But he was tired, the workout starting to bite at his muscles. 'So if it's not that, what's this favour you wanted to ask me?'

She looked away, suddenly shy, a mischievous smile on her lips. She followed him in downing her drink, then held his gaze, flashing him those amazing teeth as she smiled. 'How do you fancy a tour of my place?' she said.

CHAPTER 10

Matt Evans took a moment to appreciate his surroundings. He was locked in a toilet cubicle, the sharp sting of bleach unable to hide the smell of stale shit that hung in the air. He concentrated on keeping his hands steady as, with his credit card, he chopped at a line of fine white powder on top of the cistern. He separated the mound into four white lines about six centimetres long, then stuffed the foil wrap back into his pocket.

On your marks.

He bent his head to the powder, flushed the toilet, then snorted up the first two lines. There was a brief, bright flash of pain, then his nose went numb as the powder headed for his brain. A moment later the front of his head went gloriously numb. Somewhere, he could hear an engine revving.

He dabbed quickly at his nose, waiting for the cistern to refill. Already, he could feel the coke kicking in, giving his thought synapses the boost they would need for the night ahead. His gums felt dry and bitty, as though he had just rubbed a towel over them, but that wasn't a problem: he had something to deal with that.

Cistern full, he flushed again and snorted up the final two lines of coke.

He paused for a moment, the euphoric rush forcing him to his knees, then stood up and dusted himself down. He left the cubicle and went to the washbasins to check his reflection. Mousy dark hair beating a hasty retreat from his forehead, leaving an exposed patch of skull no amount of clever combing or hair-gel contortions would ever conceal. Blue eyes that were bloodshot and bleary, set back in dark, hollow sockets that mapped out years of long nights. His beard, or the scraggly, irregular growth on his face that betrayed he was too lazy to shave, was flecked here and there with patches of grey.

'Getting old, Matty,' he whispered to himself. He ran a hand through his hair, plastered on his best shit-eating grin and headed for the door. Already the coke was coursing through him, making him excitable and nervous, turning everything up a notch.

Show time.

He bustled into the studio, ignoring the cold stare of disgust Gina shot at him from the production suite as he settled into his chair. He pulled on his earphones, adjusted the mic and tried to get comfortable. His heart was racing now, sending daggers of ice shooting through his veins. He took a deep breath, felt something catch in his nose and dabbed at it hurriedly with a tissue.

'For God's sake, Matt.' Gina's voice boomed through his headphones, clipped and clinical, chilled with contempt. 'You've got two minutes to air. You ready for this?'

He looked up and through the window into the production office. She sat there behind the desk, imperious as a queen. Back ramrod straight, chest thrust forward, long hair cascading over her shoulders and glistening like burnished bronze in the overhead lights. Matt felt a stab of rage. Who the fuck did this stuck-up little bitch think she was? He hit the button that activated the mic, putting him through to her. When he spoke, his voice was a low, soothing purr. It was the voice that had saved his career, the voice that would fill the airwaves 'from Stirling to California' in the hours ahead. Matt liked the line, even if the California in question wasn't the land of palm trees and movie stars but, rather, a small former pit village in the hills near Avonbridge. The voice that would shake the whole country, if he didn't get the answer he wanted soon.

'Sorry, Gina, got a little tied up in the toilet.' He leant back and patted his ample stomach for effect. 'All good now and ready for the night. What's first?'

Gina exhaled noisily, the sound echoing in his ears as the mic amplified it. After a moment, she started to run through the schedule for the show, the first segment, the adverts, any new sponsors. Matt tuned her out, the words meaningless static as he watched her and nodded, all the time wondering what it would be like to grab her by the throat and squeeze, squeeze, squeeze . . .

His four-hour shift, laughingly called the Midnight Hour by the marketing bods at Valley FM, was about to begin. Matt had his own name for it: the Dead Zone.

What he didn't know then was how accurate the nickname was about to become.

CHAPTER 11

Ford was back at his desk at seven the next morning, too many thoughts and too little sleep conspiring to give him a snarling headache. Randolphfield, a brutalist concrete office block with dull grey walls and too-small windows, was quiet at that time of the morning, the incident room yet to fill with officers and the chaotic bustle that a murder inquiry always generated.

Tennant had written up his report and emailed it through late last night and, as promised, the tattoo received nothing but a cursory mention as a potentially identifying mark. Ford stared at the image on the screen, the harsh flare of the pathologist's camera bleaching the greying skin a waxy white colour, giving the bruising around the tattoo a sickening glare that did nothing to calm his stomach.

The moment he reported his suspicions, it would create a chain reaction. With the current uncertainty in Northern Ireland and sporadic terrorist activity across the UK, law-enforcement agencies were on high alert. And news that a man's murder had all the hallmarks of a paramilitary-style punishment beating, and that the victim had had a Loyalist tattoo on his chest, would do nothing to dampen those fears.

The thought of the case being taken out of his hands, passed to the Specialist Crime Division, or possibly even MI5, gnawed at him. He saw that head every time he closed his eyes, heard the singsong squeal in his ears the moment he let down his guard. Who could inflict that level of brutality on another human being? Ford was no stranger to violence, but this was something new. Almost like a malignant leap forward in the evolution of evil. Not surprising, perhaps, in the age of tweeting madmen and bigotry packaged as patriotism, but still Ford had to know. Had to look whoever had done this in the eye.

The blood and DNA samples had been sent for cross-matching to see if they corresponded to someone they had on the database, and the description they had managed to cobble together by looking beyond the victim's horrific injuries was being cross-checked with missing persons, but still the waiting maddened him.

He tried to distract himself by sinking into the mire of paperwork and bureaucracy that was the hallmark of any major investigation. He filed overtime requests – which would no doubt be denied – made sure the press office had everything they needed, wrote a brief for the chief constable, updated the case log, assigned duties for the day . . . It just never seemed to end. He had been told, along with every other police officer in Scotland, that the merger of the eight forces into one would make everyone's jobs easier as the single force created 'synergies and efficiencies'.

All it created for Ford was a major fucking headache.

He leant back, away from the screen, blinked, then stood stiffly and walked across the room. The blow-up had been pinned to one of the whiteboards that lined the far wall, a silent scream with its own gravitational pull that seemed to suck all the attention in the room towards it. He wondered again about the wisdom of pinning the picture up where everyone could see it: the head on the spike, ruined eyes glaring out at them, challenging them to find whoever had done it. Ford knew a couple of the officers thought it was going too far. Even for those accustomed to violence and death, it was unsettling. But he wanted, *needed*, it to be there. A reminder of what they were facing, of the madness that was, even now, out there somewhere.

The thought that had haunted him last night rose in his mind. Was this an isolated killing or the start of something more? The dumping and staging of the body at a tourist hotspot in the heart of town without being seen suggested meticulous planning and execution, which was hard to reconcile with the sheer sadism of the killing.

But would that be it? Would they be satisfied with one kill, or would they want – *need* – more?

He was staring at the picture, lost in the dark labyrinth of his thoughts, when his computer gave a soft chime. He turned and walked back to it, saw he had a new email. His breath caught in his throat as he read the subject line, heart hammering with excitement and trepidation as he opened it. He read the message quickly, then double-clicked on the attachment.

He read greedily. Felt the ramifications squeeze his gut into a bilious ball of tension. He looked away from the screen, back to the picture of the head that glared at him from the other side of the room.

A head he now had a name for.

CHAPTER 12

Donna was sitting on the couch when her parents arrived, Andrew cradled peacefully in one arm, the phone clamped to her ear. She nodded a greeting and saw, from the pinched expression and hard set of her mother's jaw, that there was going to be trouble.

One problem at a time.

'Oh, come on, Danny,' she said, turning her attention back to the call. 'There must be something you can give me, anything – I'm desperate here.'

At the other end of the line, Danny Brooks gave a long, frustrated sigh. They knew each other from Donna's time on the *Chronicle* in Glasgow, had worked as reporters together. After the cuts that had driven Fiona Clarke to Sky, Danny had followed the well-worn path that led from journalism to PR and ended up working for Police Scotland. He saw all the press releases the police sent out. More importantly for Donna, Danny also saw what didn't make it into the press releases, the details that were deemed too sensitive for public consumption.

And, thanks to Danny's fondness for working practices that would have made a Murdoch blush, he owed Donna a favour.

'Look, I gave you everything I could yesterday,' he said, in a self-pitying whine that made Donna want to grind her teeth. 'Most I can tell you is it looks like the victim was tortured.'

'Yeah, but how? Come on, Danny, I need something on this, a line, an angle, to get me ahead. This is important.'

Danny sighed again. She could almost hear the thought stumbling through his head, and bet he was scraping his hand over his shaved scalp. It was why he was so bad at the casinos they'd visited after a late shift: Danny had so many tells he might as well have been broadcasting his intentions via megaphone.

'All right,' he said, voice flat with resignation. 'I'm not sure how much use this is, and then that's it. We're even. Okay, Donna?'

Donna agreed, knowing they were nowhere near even. He'd hacked the private messages of a cabinet secretary at Holyrood, and all to expose his grubby little secret of an affair with his counterpart on the opposite benches. Not that Donna really cared that a senior politician had been caught with his pants down, but if the government ever found out that he had not only been hacked but had used public money to keep the journalist quiet . . .

Nah. It was going to take a hell of a lot more favours to settle that debt.

'Go on, then,' she said, feeling her mother's gaze fall on her again.

'Okay. The victim was definitely tortured. It was fucking obvious from the way the body was found and the state of the poor old bastard who called it in. And he's known to us. Everyone's talking about it. They got an ID on the victim. Whoever it is, he's got previous.'

Donna swallowed the bubble of excitement that was rising in her throat. 'I take it there's no way . . .'

'Not a fucking chance,' Danny said. 'Even if I knew, I couldn't tell you. But that's the thing. I don't know. Whoever he was, they're keeping his name close to their chests. Need-to-know kind of stuff.'

Donna thought back to the press scrum at Cowane's yesterday. To the harassed DCI who had given a faltering, uneven statement to the press. Clearly not a big fan of being front and centre. She sympathized but, like her, he'd have to get used to it.

'Okay, Danny,' she said. 'Thanks. Say hi to Jill, will you?'

'Yeah,' he replied, in a petulant tone that reminded her of how much she disliked him at times. 'And I mean it, Donna, this is it. You want anything else, go through the Stirling press team.'

'Danny, we both know that's not going to happen,' she said, cutting the call before he could reply.

She put the phone down, her dad taking that as a signal to get out of the room. He murmured an excuse about putting the kettle on and scuttled away. She watched him go, then turned back to Andrew, who was still sleeping contentedly.

'So what was that about?' her mum asked, jutting her jaw towards the phone.

Donna returned her level gaze. Her mother had never approved of Donna's career choices or her life in general. Andrew had built something of a bridge between them, but still the disapproval simmered. 'Work,' she said. 'Following up on the murder I worked on yesterday. It's a big story, national. If I play it right I could really get something out of this.'

'Hmm.' Her mum's eyebrows arched.

Donna felt a snarl of anger, forced it down. She didn't want to lose her temper in front of Andrew. And the last thing she needed was her mother storming out in a melodramatic huff. 'Mum, I really appreciate you taking him today,' she said, standing and offering Andrew to his gran, who took him willingly. She looked down, eyes softening, arguments melting away.

Donna watched her mother, heard her dad bustling around in the kitchen. 'Thanks, Mum,' she said softly. 'This means a lot. It's a big story. If I play it right, it could really open doors for me.'

Irene Blake looked up at her, something Donna couldn't name flashing in her eyes. 'That's all for the good,' she said. 'But just remember what comes first. We love taking Andrew, but he needs his mother. Especially since his father is nowhere to be seen. And you chasing stories and trying to restart your career won't help him.'

Donna took a deep breath, tried to compose herself. She was about to speak when her dad came into the room, carrying a tray of tea and biscuits like a peace-offering. He looked between his wife and his daughter, reading the tension in the room, nodded, then set the tray on the coffee-table in front of the couch. He flicked Irene a look, an entire conversation passing between them, then gave Donna a smile. 'You got time for a cuppa before you head off, love?' he asked.

CHAPTER 13

Matt Evans fell back into himself, jerking into consciousness from the oblivion he had been drowning in. His heart was pounding as his lungs clawed for air. He blinked, trying to focus in the gloom, panic and confusion wrestling for supremacy in his mind as he sifted desperately through the jagged shards of his memory.

What had happened last night? And where was he?

He swallowed, took another deep breath, the smell of stale urine mingling with something nauseatingly sweet that burnt his nostrils. He forced himself to think.

Smell. Something about the smell. Something . . .

His breath stopped, the gloom crowding in on him as the memory formed in his mind, panic arcing through him like electric current. He let out a sniffling whimper as his eyes filled with tears. The smell. The smell of leather and polish. He remembered.

He had come off air at the usual time, skipping out of the post-show production meeting, eager to be free of Gina and her scorn, wanting nothing more than to get home, check the tapes one more time. He had started walking, scrolling through his phone, felt a slight irritation that there were no messages waiting for him. No *Want to see you* or *How about I come over?* Not a problem tonight, he needed time alone. He pushed the thought aside, started looking for the number of a taxi company he used. Paused at the junction where the industrial estate ended, laughed when he saw a taxi crawl towards him, its light on.

He covered the distance to the cab slowly, wanting to make the driver wait, establish who was in charge. Reached the car, opened the door and slid inside.

The interior smelt of leather and polish, a typical private-hire taxi. 'Evening, sir, where to?' the driver asked, without turning round.

'Wellgreen Lane,' he said, slumping into the seat, his mind already turning to the bottle of white that, along with a block of cheese, made up the contents of his fridge. It would go nicely with the coke he had left. And tonight he would enjoy it alone. No company or conversation, just him and something to watch. Solitary pleasures.

'No problem,' the driver said, indicating then pulling out. Evans heard the soft click of the doors locking as the car accelerated.

He watched as the streets slid by, clutches of students heading home after nights out, people huddled in front of takeaways or at taxi ranks, the streetlamps staining everything a sepia hue. He closed his eyes, thought of climbing the stairs to his flat, the first kiss of chilled wine on his lips.

'What's the flat number?' the driver asked, his voice as dull and monotonous as the sound of the tyres hissing over tarmac.

'Anywhere here is fine, pal,' he said.

The car pulled in, Evans contorting himself in the seat to get his wallet. He glanced up reflexively, looking for the meter so he could get the cash he needed.

There wasn't one. 'Hey, pal, what's the . . .'

The words died in his throat as the gun slid between the front seats, glinting like a blade as it caught the streetlights.

'Don't worry about it, Matt,' the voice said, in a tone that made Evans's bladder give way, hot urine flooding unnoticed into his lap. 'This one's on the house . . .'

Tears slid down his cheek. The gun. That barrel. He couldn't take his eyes off it. He was babbling, heard his own pitiful mewling as he promised money and anything, anything at all, just as long as you leave me alone and let me go, just please . . .

The flash of the muzzle was blinding in the darkness, the sound strangely muted. There was a moment of pain, and he looked down, saw the dart embedded in his leg even as the world began to swim. Then nothing. Only static, like a radio tuned to a dead channel.

And now he was here. In some darkened, unfamiliar room, lying on a mattress stained with his own piss. Through the drug-induced fog of whatever he had been shot with, he vaguely remembered waking during the night, wailing for his captor to come and free him, straining against the chain that had been clamped to his ankle and attached to a steel support girder close to where the mattress had been thrown.

The tears began slowly at first, then dissolved into hitching sobs that filled the gloom and seemed to taunt him as they echoed around the room. Panic seized his mind, sweeping away rational thought with images of pain and suffering. He thrashed around, the chain clanging almost musically off the girder, the soundtrack to his suffering.

He had known this was a possibility as soon as he had started this. But sitting in a warm flat, the afterglow of orgasm heightened by coke and smoothed by wine, it had seemed an abstract idea, a vague possibility. Something that happened to other people. Not him.

Now, as the door squealed open, a dagger of light stabbing into the gloom from the room beyond, he understood it wasn't a remote risk but an absolute reality. He had found his get-out-of-jail-free card, played it, and lost.

He shrank away as the figure stepped into the room. Even as reason dissolved into terror, he knew what would come next. Questions and pain.

And after that he would die.

Badly.

CHAPTER 14

Connor was on his third set of press-ups when he heard it. He paused, ears straining, scanning for the noise. It was faint, just a background murmur, but distinctive, a crunch-crunch of feet on gravel.

He grabbed his shirt as he made for the door, swung it open noiselessly, then padded up the stairs, pausing at the third step from the top, knowing that going further would put him in the line of sight of whoever was circling his car. He popped his head up briefly, then ducked down. Thought of Jennifer. Her smile. *How do you fancy a tour of my place?*

He stood up and took the last three stairs casually, feigned surprise when he saw the man pacing around his Audi, casting admiring glances and approving nods as he did so.

'Morning,' Connor said.

The stranger froze mid-stride. He was a squat, wide man, the immaculate suit he wore doing nothing to hide his slab-like arms and a gut that looked like fat but would, Connor knew, be like hitting armour plate. Connor had never met him before, but he knew exactly who, and what, he was. He'd met men like him many times. He knew the drill.

'Nice car,' the man said, small, hard eyes darting over Connor, assessing. From the subtle straightening of his back and the way he bunched his fists, Connor could tell he saw him as a threat.

'Thanks,' Connor said. 'Gets me where I need to go.' He paused.

Considered. Thought again of Jennifer's smile. 'But I've got things to do today, so why don't you tell me why you're here, Paulie?'

Paulie gave a start, lips pulling back into a snarl as his eyes hardened. 'How the fuck did you . . .' he whispered.

Connor waved the question aside. It didn't take a genius to put it together. Whoever had followed them to the pub last night in a top-of-the-range Merc obviously loved expensive cars, and the look Paulie had given the Audi was almost pornographic. 'It doesn't matter. If you're looking for Jen, she's not here, so you can tell Daddy dearest that I acted like a gentleman. You'll understand if I don't invite you in to check for yourself.'

Paulie hunched his shoulders, marching forward, fists balled. 'Why, you cheeky little fuck, I ought to . . .'

Connor stepped forward, startling Paulie, who stuttered to a halt. This was a man used to people getting out of his way or running when he approached them. Having someone step towards him did not compute. Connor held up his hands. 'Sorry, didn't mean to antagonize,' he said. 'But, seriously, she's not here. And I'm not a threat. Promise. So why don't you tell your boss that and go have a nice day? Like I said, I've got things to do.'

Angry blotches of red peppered Paulie's forehead. His gaze darted across Connor's body, not assessing this time. Targeting. 'Now, listen, shithead,' he hissed, stabbing at the air in front of him with a chubby, misshapen forefinger. 'Mr MacKenzie has a message for you. Stay the fuck away from Jennifer. She doesn't need the likes of you sniffing around.'

Connor was unable to keep the smile off his face. He knew he shouldn't antagonize the man, found it impossible to resist. 'Ah, but you've got to admit, Paulie, she does wear some nice perfume.'

Paulie lunged forward, fist slashing through the air in a round-house blow that was aimed at Connor's jaw. He pivoted left, stepping into the swing of the punch, close enough now to smell the stale smoke that clung to Paulie like a shroud. He grabbed Paulie's wrist and kept moving, turning the bigger man's momentum against him. Paulie was dragged forward, unprepared for the sudden shifting of his weight and Connor adding to the speed of his follow-through.

Connor flashed his arm out, slamming Paulie in the chest with an open palm. He staggered back, careening off the bins that were neatly lined up against the wall, before stumbling and crashing to the ground, the impact of the landing forcing his breath, and a stream of expletives, from him.

Paulie beetled around on the ground, legs flailing as he rolled over and came up to a sitting position. His chest heaved, and Connor saw gravel stuck to his cheek. He swiped at it angrily, eyes burning with fury as he glared at Connor. 'You're a fucking dead man,' he whispered, his voice corpse-cold.

Connor placed two fingers to his neck, checking his pulse. 'Not yet, Paulie. Now how 'bout we leave this, eh? Who Jen sees is her call, not yours or her—'

Paulie exploded forward, showing a fluid grace that belied his bulky frame. His arms were stretched out, his hands grasping for Connor, his entire being consumed by the simple desire to sink his fingers into the man who had humiliated him.

Mistake.

Connor whipped his elbow up, the bone crashing into Paulie's outstretched hand like a wrecking ball. He felt the crunch of fingers as a cry of pain filled his ears, then dropped low and stabbed a left jab into Paulie's side, driving the last of the air from his lungs. Paulie collapsed to his knees and slid forward, Connor catching him by the collar before his face slammed into the ground.

Paulie reared to his knees, cradling his ruined left hand close to his chest. He looked up at Connor, tears of pain and outrage shimmering in his eyes. 'You fucking—'

'Paulie,' Connor cut him off, 'I didn't ask for this. Now, you can threaten me, come back with some pals and we can do this dance again. Or . . .' he paused, let everything human drain from his voice '. . . you can leave it. Tell Mr MacKenzie I'm no danger. Jen asked me to check the security at her place, and that's what I'm going to do. Have him look up Sentinel Securities. So leave it, Paulie. Go get in your nice Merc, get yourself fixed up and pretend this didn't happen.'

Paulie glared up at him, the need to lash out arguing with the pain in his hand. 'This isn't the end of it,' he said finally.

'Maybe not,' Connor said, 'but if I see you again, it will be. I'm sorry I hurt your hand, but you're a big boy, you know how these things go. So call it a draw, and be on your way.'

Paulie rose slowly to his feet, looked down at his once-immaculate suit. It seemed to fit him better now, as though rumpled after a tussle was more his style. He backed away slowly, keeping eye contact with Connor. Then he turned and stalked off, muttering under his breath.

Connor watched him go, the cloying, copper aftertaste of adrenalin congealing at the back of his throat. He spat once and shook his head, angry with himself. He shouldn't have antagonized Paulie, should have found a way to defuse the situation, avoid a confrontation. No doubt Jen's father would hear about what had happened. Would he send others to avenge Paulie's injuries? Or take the message and leave him alone?

Connor sighed and headed back to the flat. So much for the quiet life.

CHAPTER 15

The coffee was cold and bitter, but it was doing its job and holding the exhaustion that was settling into his muscles at bay. Ford drained the mug, then reached up and rubbed his eyes, as though he could massage some energy into himself.

No such luck.

He stood, his left knee making its all-too-familiar protest, then walked across the room to the incident board and the pictures that were pinned there.

The SOCOs' picture of the decapitated head had been joined by another, this time of the victim's mugshot when he was last arrested, four years ago. They were lucky, Ford thought, that Billy Griffin had been stupid enough to get lifted. Looking at the pictures side by side, the knot of sallow, bloodied flesh, its features frozen in a rictus of agony, bore little resemblance to the man in the mugshot. In life, Billy Griffin had been almost handsome, with high cheekbones, fashionably tousled dark hair and thick, full lips that made it look as though he were pouting for the camera. But, as Ford now knew, Billy Griffin's character did not match his appearance.

At least, not in life.

His record read like a CV for a petty thug. Born and bred in Bridgeton, east Glasgow, Billy had started his career early, with convictions for robbery, possession of class-A substances and assault. He was a known troublemaker on the terraces, banned from the grounds of both Celtic and Rangers, the city's two big teams.

He'd bounced along like that for years, supporting himself with semi-regular work as a painter and decorator for one of the big housing firms that seemed intent on buying up every open plot of land in Scotland and throwing up increasingly small properties. So far, so average. Just another young man with too short a fuse and too quick a fist.

But then came September 2014, and Billy had graduated to the big league.

It was the Friday after the independence referendum. With feelings still running high, Yes voters had descended on Glasgow's George Square, which had become something of a focal point for pro-independence rallies in the build-up to the vote on 18 September. That night, they'd come to commiserate with each other and vent their wounded defiance. But things had turned ugly when a group of pro-Union supporters charged at the crowd, chanting Nazi slogans, taunting with 'Rule Britannia' and firing off a flare that acted as a starting gun for a night of violence. In the end, eleven people were arrested for various offences, ranging from assault and breach of the peace to vandalism. Billy Griffin was one of them.

When the trouble had started, police officers at the scene had quickly formed a human barrier to keep the two factions separate and the chance of violence to a minimum. The problem was, Billy was already in the square when the pro-Union protesters arrived. When the situation descended into chaos, he kept his head down, waiting for his moment.

It came when Billy managed to grab a pro-independence banner and a flag bearing the Yes logo. Clambering onto a statue of Queen Victoria on horseback, which stood at the corner of the square, facing the pro-Union crowd, he had held both flag and banner aloft and set them alight, to roaring approval of the No crowd. Thinking back, Ford remembered the image of Billy that had been splashed across the papers and TV. In that moment, Billy Griffin had graduated from part-time thug to heroic totem of those who thought political debate started with questioning your opponents' parentage and ended with a hard boot to their ribs.

Luckily for Billy, a police officer got to him before the pro-independence supporters, who would have ripped him limb from limb. He went quietly, almost eagerly, his work done, his legacy secure.

Billy was sent to Barlinnie Prison and given a four-figure fine, both of which triggered intense debate in the media and gave them another chance to use the footage of Billy setting the flag alight. But then, as always happens, the story moved on, the commentators and the media looking for other topics and fresher meat. According to the reports, Billy had served his time quietly, been released and then gone back to his life.

Ford looked at the board, careful to keep his eyes on the picture of Billy when he was still alive. Something was missing. While Billy's pro-Union tendencies might explain the tattoo on his chest, why had he been murdered so savagely? And if it was some kind of revenge for what he had done at George Square, why dump his body in Stirling, more than twenty-five miles away? Why not leave it in Glasgow?

Ford looked down at Billy's file, suddenly aware of how thin it was. He needed more. Background. Detail. Who Billy was, what—

His thoughts were interrupted by the sudden shrill ring of his phone. He gave the inquiry board one last look, as though it might reveal its secrets to him, then headed for his desk, a growing unease roiling queasily in his throat. This must be the call he was dreading from the chief, telling him the case was being reassigned to Special Investigations or something else.

'Ford,' he said.

'Sir? Sir, it's DS Troughton,' the young detective blurted down the phone, his voice quickened by excitement, made tremulous by fear.

Ford sighed, suddenly irritated. 'Yes, Troughton, what is it? I'm in the middle of—'

Troughton cut him off, his words turning Ford's blood to ice, his lungs to stone. The world seemed to crowd in on him, taunt him. Torture him.

'Sir,' Troughton said. 'First, your wife is okay. She's been evacuated with everyone else and she's absolutely fine, okay?'

'Troughton, what the fuck do you mean? What's going on? What's—'

'Sir, there's been another one,' Troughton said. 'And this time it's at the uni.'

CHAPTER 16

Donna watched as Ford's car swept through the university entrance, the officers standing guard parting the throng of students and staff milling around.

'Fuck,' she muttered, driving straight on through the mini roundabout, then pulling in. She flicked her hazard lights on, ignored the impatient blare of the horn of the car following her.

Thinking back to the press conference, she had known Ford was the key to getting a line on the story. Despite his professional façade, Donna could see from the tics and twitches that drew his face into a tight grimace – hear from the tremor he worked a little too hard to keep out of his voice – that something about the case had got to him. And with Danny confirming that the victim had been tortured, Donna had decided she wanted a conversation with DCI Malcolm Ford.

She knew that going through the press office would be a waste of time – there was no way they were going to let the senior investigating officer on a splashy murder case sit down with a freelance reporter from the local radio station. So she had decided to go back to basics. She would doorstep him. Wait outside the concrete monstrosity that sat like a sixties gargoyle on St Ninians Road. So, after leaving her parents with Andrew, she had driven across town, parked on Clifford Road, which faced the station, as close to the entrance as she dared, and got comfortable.

She had just lulled herself into a state of boredom, her mind a jumble of thoughts about Fiona Clarke, Andrew and the possibility of getting the job she wanted, when she heard the harsh bleat of a siren from the police station. She looked up, training her camera on the building and trying to focus. A moment later a marked Fiesta bulleted out of the station, its engine giving a high-pitched howl of disapproval as whoever was driving floored the accelerator and took the gear as high into the red as the car would allow. She only glimpsed the man in the passenger seat, long, thin face, greying hair and hawkish nose, but she knew it was Ford. She started her car and took off after them, her fear at driving too fast competing with the thrill of the chase.

She had missed this. Been away from it too long. No matter what her mother said, *this* was what she needed. Not condescending pity, not a steady job or a settled life. No. This.

The police car was three vehicles ahead by the time Donna caught it on Polmaise Road, picking up speed. She followed as closely as she dared, praying that another wasn't setting off from the station and about to appear in her rear-view mirror. The car flashed past the golf course then hung a left, Donna keeping it in view and trying to figure out where it was heading. It was hopeless: on the road it was travelling along it could hit the centre of town in less than fifteen minutes, or be heading for Raploch or even Bridge of Allan. Forget trying to anticipate, she thought, just keep it in sight.

Ten minutes later she watched the marked car drive into the grounds of the uni, watched it speed up to take the hill past Airthrey Loch as it made for the heart of the campus. She parked, willing herself to release her grip on the steering wheel, thoughts racing.

Why was Ford here? What had happened? Did they have a suspect, a weapon?

Her mind was a riot of thoughts and theories. She needed to get in there, needed to know, but there was no way she'd get through that police cordon. If only . . .

Her head whipped up, phone in her hand before the thought was fully formed. She pushed aside the nagging feeling that she was crossing an invisible line even as she called the number.

63

She pressed the phone to her ear, willing it to be answered, willing it to—

'Hello?'

'Gav? Gav, it's Donna Blake, how you doing today?'

'Eh, it's all going a bit nuts here just now, to be honest, Ms Blake, something going on with the polis.' His voice, normally so deep she could feel it reverberate in her chest, was high and wavering, pulled taut by adrenalin.

Donna stared out of the window, swallowing down the excitement that crawled up her throat. *All going a bit nuts here.*

Perfect.

When she wasn't freelancing, Donna tutored on the journalism-studies course run by the university. It was easy work and good money, and some of the students could be fun. Like Gavin Webster, a lithe, almost lanky twenty-year-old from Perth whose pale complexion went a shade darker every time Donna walked into the room. She had played up to his obvious attraction to her, even though she hated herself for doing it. She'd worked hard to regain her figure after having Andrew, but still the self-doubt lingered. And Gavin's attention helped dispel it. 'Eh, Ms Blake?' Gav asked, confusion bleeding the tension from his voice.

'Yeah, sorry, Gav, sorry. So you're on the campus now?'

'Yeah,' he said, his voice brightening. 'The cops are clearing everyone out, but I was on the grounds with the camera, trying out some shots, so I'm still here. Looks like whatever's going on, it's up at the hotel.'

Donna knew the place. The Stirling Court had been built at the top of a hill looking down on the rest of the uni campus. With its views of the Wallace Monument and the Ochil Hills, it did well as an events venue and a conference centre. But what did that mean for the story? Why had Ford been called there?

'Listen, Gav, you fancy doing me a wee favour?'

'Yeeaaah?' he replied, wary eagerness giving his voice a brittle edge. She knew he was blushing.

'Fancy testing that camera a bit? See if you can get any shots of what's going on and send them over to me. Nothing that's going to get you in any trouble, but anything that could help with the story. I'll owe you one.' She winced as she said it, her earlier unease blossoming into something uglier. But she needed this. For her. And Andrew.

'Well, I . . .' Gav said.

'Please, Gav, it would really help.' She let the statement hang, his indecision screaming in the sudden silence on the line. Then she heard him inhale.

'Aye. I'll see what I can get and ping them over to your email. Okay, Ms Blake?'

'Yes, please, and it's Donna.'

'Donna, aye,' he said, his voice a whisper. 'Leave it with me.'

The phone went dead as Gav ended the call. Donna looked at it for a moment, studied the shadow of her reflection in the little screen as revulsion rose. She should call the poor kid back, tell him it was a mistake, not to bother. She spent a lot of her classes talking about the morality of journalism, that it wasn't all phone hacking and breathless accounts of which D-list nobody was shagging whom, and yet now here she was, feeding a poor kid the same bullshit Mark had used on her. Her finger hovered over the phone. But she held back. She'd call him in a minute. Just one more minute . . .

Twenty minutes crawled by, the phone unused. Then it buzzed. Donna's heart leapt as she unlocked it, saw the emails sitting there. She scrolled through them, her mouth dropping open.

Gavin. Sweet, naïve Gavin Webster. She could have kissed him.

She called his number, wasn't surprised when he answered on the second ring.

'That's all I could get Ms B– Donna,' he said. 'Cops are all over the place. They do?'

'They're perfect, Gav, absolutely perfect. You're a genius. Now, listen, I need to ask you a couple of questions on the record, but don't worry, I'm only going to quote you as an eyewitness. Okay?'

'So you're not going to put me on the radio?'

Donna bit back a surge of impatience, forced her voice to be calm. 'No, Gavin, not just now. I don't want you to be linked to the pictures or the story, and someone would recognize your voice. I'm going to write it up as a news story, put it on the website and see if we can punt it nationally.'

'Aye.'

'Great,' Donna said. 'So, from the beginning, just tell me everything you saw.'

CHAPTER 17

Connor finished his press-ups, then tidied the flat, trying to ignore the nagging annoyance he felt for goading Paulie into a fight. It had been stupid, unprofessional and, no doubt, there would be consequences – from the look the man had given him when he was leaving, Connor put even money on Paulie coming back for a rematch to reclaim some of his wounded pride. He couldn't blame him.

He thought briefly of his father, Jack, what he would have said, and gave a bitter laugh. He'd blame it on his own father, Campbell Fraser. Connor had never met his paternal grandfather, who had walked out on his wife when his son was in his early teens, but he knew him. Sometimes, usually after one too many drams, Jack Fraser would whisper stories that made his grandfather into a bogeyman – a cautionary tale to be learnt and an example not to live by. He was, according to his dad, a Jekyll and Hyde character. In public he was a charming if unexceptional surveyor with an interest in motor racing and an obsession with football, but in private an ugly drunk who took out his frustration and bitterness about the shortcomings of his own life on his wife and son.

'You've got the Fraser temper, son,' his father would tell him. 'Keep it in check like I have.'

Connor assumed keeping it in check meant being an emotionally aloof hypocrite, who thought nothing of ranting at his wife about 'the useless fucks at the hospital' who refused to see his genius. With the warnings about his grandfather ringing in his ears, Connor had become a shy, even introverted boy who loved to read, hated PE classes and had an aversion to football that bordered on pathological. He had been an obvious target for the bigger kids, the bullies that circled the playground looking for easy prey. And Connor took it. The punches, the slaps and the insults, he took it all, some part of him knowing that the pain would pass and the other kids would get bored soon enough.

But then had come *that* day, and everything changed.

It was lunchtime, and Connor had retreated to his preferred spot at the back of the school playing fields behind a clot of bushes that shielded him from prying eyes. He was planning to read while he ate his packed lunch, a sandwich his mum had prepared for him with about as much enthusiasm as he now picked at it. Not that he blamed her; after last night, and the muffled, angry exchanges he had heard between his parents as he lay in his bed, enthusiasm had been in short supply in the Fraser household. His dad had been long gone by the time Connor trudged down the stairs, but the fragile smile his mum had given him as she'd passed him his lunchbox had combined with the stagnant pressure in the house to give Connor a grinding headache.

All he wanted was to be left alone, to lose himself with Sherlock Holmes as he unpicked the mystery of *The Hound of the Baskervilles*, let the story soothe his mind and drown the echoes of the sharp, angry shouts from the night before. But it was as if the story had locked its doors on him. Like a stripper suddenly turned coy, it refused to reveal itself, the words on the page just lines of text put together.

The voice was like steel wool being scraped across marble. 'Hey, Connor, how you doing? Good book?'

He looked up to see Gordon Jeffrey standing over him, his face pulled into the same smile Connor had seen on his mum's face that morning. Fragile, contrived and filled with just enough false hope to make you at once pity and hate the person wearing it.

Gordon was a small, scrawny kid whose body would have made a scarecrow look buff by comparison. He had been at the school for a couple of months, having just moved to the area from Newcastle – his dad had taken a job at an accountancy firm in town. While they weren't friends, Connor knew Gordon from English classes in which they sat side by side. They had exchanged typical adolescent chit-chat, girls, books, films, recognizing on some level that they were both outsiders.

'Hey, Gordon,' Connor said, squinting up. 'Yeah, it's okay, just not really getting it today, you know?'

If Gordon had picked up the hint, he didn't show it. He glanced once over his shoulder, a quick, birdlike motion, then focused back on Connor. 'Oh, ah, that's not good. Hate it when that happens. I . . .' He trailed off as another figure appeared from the school side of the bushes, Connor suddenly understanding Gordon's desperation to be sociable.

His name was Stephen Franklin. At fourteen years old, he was already head and shoulders above everyone in his year, his glands twisting the soft putty of his child's body into something rougher, crueller. He seemed to revel in the power his size gave him, and was known for beating up any smaller, weaker kid who was unfortunate enough to get in his way. Instinctively, Connor got up as Franklin approached.

'So what the fuck's this?' the bigger boy asked. 'What you two bummers doing all the way back here? You letting this English fuck suck you off, Connie?'

Connor felt irritation prickle down his back and across his scalp. Connie. He hated that nickname. Not that he would let any of them know it. He forced a mirthless laugh through his lips. Flat, atonal. 'Aye, right,' he said. 'Good joke. Fuck knows what the wee cunt is after. I just wanted to be left alone.'

Gordon was looking at Connor as though seeing him for the first time. His face became a thin sketch of betrayal, mouth wide, skin pale, tears welling in his eyes.

'Aye, fuckin' thought as much,' Franklin said, nodding. 'Someone should teach him some fuckin' manners.'

'Aye,' Connor agreed, closing in on both Gordon and Franklin. His head was pulsing now, a bright blade of pain stabbing into his mind with each breath. The day was over-bright, over-sharp, as though the world was nothing more than a collection of harsh angles and jutting edges to skewer him. In that instant, he was back in his house, his parents' angry voices rising up through the floorboards, bouncing off the walls, leaving the air in his room bruised as the pressure grew and grew and . . .

'Would you no' just fuck off!' Connor roared, lashing out at Gordon with a kick. He whimpered and spun away reflexively, Connor's foot glancing off his hip even as he broke into a run.

Franklin gave a laugh that sounded like shards of glass being rattled in a tin can. His face was red, tears streaming down his cheeks, as he struggled for breath. 'Ah, that was fuckin' priceless, man!' he gasped. 'Did ye see the wee—'

Connor exploded. He was moving before he even knew the decision had been made, Franklin totally unprepared for the assault. He lashed out frantically, driving his fists into Franklin's face. Franklin tried to fight back, but Connor ignored the blows, punching faster, harder. He cried out in a voice that was not his own, the pressure from the night before building behind his eyes as tears stung. In that moment, all he wanted was Franklin to feel his own pain, to use his rage to blot out the memory of his parents' argument and the look of betrayal on Gordon Jeffrey's face.

A teacher broke them up a few moments later, attracted by the screams of kids who had sprinted across the playground to see what was going on behind the bushes.

'Ye're a fuckin' psycho, Fraser!' Franklin yelled, his voice trembling with shock as they were pulled apart. Connor saw the blood pouring from his nose and the welts forming on his face, and felt an almost irresistible urge to laugh.

His father had been right. He did have a temper.

Thanks to some fast talking by his father, not to mention the exchange of a brotherly handshake with Franklin's father, no one was expelled from school. Arrangements were made to keep Franklin and Connor in separate classes, but it was a worthless move. A typical bully, Stephen Franklin stayed clear of the boy who had shattered his tough-guy image, made him mortal in front of his classmates. Connor, meanwhile, became something of a school legend – the boy who had faced the playground monster and defeated him.

He had found his new popularity disquieting and confusing, his young mind unable to process the contradiction of his classmates admiring him for actions that seemed to drive an even greater wedge between him and his father.

And despite it all, despite the attention, the nods and the claps on the back, Gordon Jeffrey never spoke to him again.

Now Connor took a shower, trying to scald away the memories that flooded his mind. They were the last thing he needed, especially this weekend. Towelling himself as he stepped into the living room, he flicked on the TV, channel-hopped until he hit Sky News, and was just turning away when he paused and looked back at the screen. It was a live shot from outside Stirling University, police tape draped across the entrance, cars parked at diagonals to deter vehicles from driving in, and officers patrolling the cordon. The caption at the bottom of the screen read: 'BODY FOUND AT UNIVERSITY CAMPUS', with a second line of text below: 'Second violent death in Stirling in two days'.

He turned the sound up, perched on the edge of the sofa. A grim-faced newsreader with hair two shades too dark and teeth three shades too white stared sternly into the camera. 'The discovery was made at the Stirling Court Hotel in the university's grounds at approximately six a.m. On the line we have Donna Blake, a local reporter in Stirling. Donna?'

There was a moment's pause, then the same picture of Donna Blake that Connor had seen the day before filled the screen, accompanied by a redundant caption verifying that the newsreader had been right and Donna Blake was indeed a freelance journalist.

'Yes, Douglas,' she said, the tiredness of the day before replaced by an almost breathless excitement that Connor knew all too well. 'It's my understanding that a guest at the Stirling Court Hotel discovered the body at the foot of a fire escape at the rear of the hotel this morning.'

The picture of Donna disappeared, replaced by a still shot of SOCOs milling around on a section of manicured grass, the naked metal of a fire escape glinting in the background, white screens in the foreground to prevent anyone seeing what they were working on. Looking at the shot, Connor guessed it was taken with a powerful zoom lens, probably free-standing rather than fixed on a tripod, given the slight blurriness.

A series of images, mostly variations on the same scene, scrolled across the screen as Donna kept talking: 'While police have yet to make an official statement, sources have told me that DCI Malcolm Ford, who is leading the investigation into the discovery of a body at Cowane's Hospital in the centre of Stirling, is due to give a full statement within the hour. I also understand that . . .'

Connor stiffened, Donna's voice fading as though the TV had been muted. His jaw dropped open, tendrils of panic snaking around his heart and squeezing. *No* . . . He fumbled for the remote, hit rewind, then froze the shot. He approached the TV warily, as though it might suddenly explode.

No, it can't be.

He reached his hand out, tracing the shape of the object on the screen.

You could be wrong, a small voice whispered urgently in his mind. *You could be wrong.*

But he wasn't. He knew it.

At first glance, it was an innocuous shot. While the area at the foot of the stairs had been cordoned off behind white barriers, the stairwell remained exposed, merely cordoned off with police tape. Whoever had taken the photographs had managed to get a close-up of the stairs. On the second step from the bottom a shoe lay on its side, forgotten. Beside it there was a bag, a notepad and pens spilling from it in a frozen cascade. And on the step below, at the bottom of the shot, there was a book.

A book that told Connor he was connected to this murder in ways he didn't want to think about, and to a killer who was intimately connected to him.

CHAPTER 18

Ford slammed the phone down and glared at it. In the incident room outside his office, he heard a momentary silence, keyboards and conversations interrupted by the abrupt end to a conversation with an unknown caller.

Not that it took a room full of detectives to figure out who was on the call, and why. Chief Superintendent Doyle had seen the Sky report, the 'eye-witness' pictures from the scene and, after a bollocking from the chief constable himself, had phoned Ford to pass on the pain. Even in the new streamlined Police Scotland, shite still rolled downhill.

'You'd better get us a quick result on this one now, Malcolm,' Doyle had said, after he had exhausted his entire, admittedly impressive, repertoire of expletives. 'And, Christ, there's the press conference as well. How the hell did she find out we were planning that? Decision was only made on the ground.'

'I'm honestly not sure, sir,' Ford had replied. And he wasn't. He had his suspicions, though.

Doyle had finished the call with dark promises to complain to the head of news at Sky, throwing around the well-used and ultimately useless phrases 'jeopardizing an ongoing investigation', 'irresponsible journalism' and, Ford's favourite, 'interfering with an active crime scene'. He had swallowed a laugh at that one – the pictures, while ethically on dodgy ground, had clearly been taken with a telephoto lens, from outside the crime scene, beyond the screens that the SOCOs had hurriedly erected around the body.

Luckily for the photographer.

He sighed, closed his eyes and rubbed them, as though he could reach through the sockets and get to the headache nestled there. He considered calling Mary again, but she had already assured him she was fine – she had gone to one of the uni muster points and was now safely at home. Her only condition was that he didn't make today another late one. He agreed, both of them knowing it was a lie.

He straightened, smoothed his tie and headed into the main incident room. It was quieter than he'd expected, partly because officers had been assigned leads to track down, partly because staff shortages meant there weren't enough left to fill an incident room. He felt eyes fall on him as he headed straight for DS Troughton, who was perched at a desk just in front of the incident board, poring over reports.

The detective looked up as Ford approached, apprehension pulling his doughy features into a saggy grimace.

'Troughton,' Ford said, watching the DS flinch at the mention of his name. Christ, was this what passed for a police detective these days?

'Sir?' Troughton asked, his voice as soft as his gut.

'Troughton, I've got an update meeting with Specialist Division in less than half an hour. After which,' he sighed, the thought like toothache, 'I have to appear before the press and give the vague impression that we know what the fuck is going on. Anything you can tell me to help with that?'

Troughton's cheeks coloured, his eyes darting from Ford to the reports strewn in front of them, as though they were some sort of security blanket. 'Well, sir, I, ah . . .' He sat up straighter. Put some steel into his voice. It wasn't much, but it helped. 'SOCOs are still processing the scene, but you saw most of it yourself. The victim was severely beaten and dumped at the foot of a fire escape leading from the, ah . . .' Troughton consulted his notes '. . . the Wallace conference room.'

Ford knew the room in question, had attended dinners and functions there over the years. It was large, open-plan, only made exceptional by its commanding view of the Wallace Monument, which loomed down on the uni from its perch, like the hilt of some giant Gothic dagger that had been stabbed into the summit of Abbey Craig.

'While the post-mortem examination has yet to be completed, there are similarities to the injuries found on the body at Cowane's Hospital yesterday – severe trauma, signs of a sustained beating with a blunt instrument, especially around the joints.'

'One big difference, though,' Ford said, his gaze creeping irresistibly up to the picture of Billy Griffin. *Look at me.* 'This one wasn't decapitated.'

Troughton cleared his throat. 'Ah, no, sir, but there was a deep laceration to the victim's neck – might even have been the cause of death.'

Ford grunted, thinking back to the body he had seen less than an hour before. Limbs splayed at odd angles like a child's carelessly discarded toy, lying in a blast crater of violence and pain, blood spattering the grass, black against the lush, vibrant green. If it was the cause of death, at least it would have been quicker than what Billy Griffin endured. 'Any luck on identification?' he asked.

'No, sir,' Troughton said, flicking through the reports. 'The hotel doesn't report having any guests matching the description we managed to compile, and there was no definitive identification or even a mobile phone on the body or in the victim's belongings.'

Ford's headache was aggravated by the maddening itch that such details always gave him. Robbery obviously wasn't the motive, so why try to hide the victim's ID by taking their wallet and phone, especially when the bag and notepad had been left behind? Forensics had the bag, a book found nearby and the notepad for examination, but a cursory examination appeared to indicate it was a journal or a collection of notes.

'Okay,' he said, reaching down and sliding one of the reports across the table, away from Troughton. 'We've got nothing that conclusively links this to the Griffin murder, but there are enough similarities to suggest that's the case. Christ, the press are going to fucking love that.'

Troughton cleared his throat a second time, as though being deprived of his files had also robbed him of his voice.

Ford ignored him, found what he wanted. It was a picture of the victim. Thankfully, the face was masked by a thick mop of shoulder-length dark hair that had been thrown over the back of the head, presumably by the force of the impact with the ground.

One question clamoured for an answer in his mind, blotting out the fatigue and the headache.

Who was she?

CHAPTER 19

He looked at the phone cradled in his hands, the cold, calculating words he had just heard echoing in his mind like a fading gunshot.

'It's done. I'll expect payment in the next twenty-four hours.'

He seized on the harshness of the words, wrapped them around himself like a perverse blanket. Murder reduced to a financial transaction. Forget the throwing up, forget the guilt, the shock and the revulsion. It was a business transaction. Nothing more. A necessary evil to protect him and everything he had built over years.

Perched on a filing cabinet in the corner of the room, a muted TV told him the story. For the second time in two days, a body had been found in Stirling, this time at the university campus near Bridge of Allan. He knew it well, had spent many hours there, staring out across Airthrey Loch between lectures, the Wallace Monument looming on the horizon like a harbinger of things to come.

Which, he supposed, in a way it had been.

He was about to turn off the TV when he saw a line of text crawl across the bottom of the screen. Nine words. Nine simple words that plunged a shard of ice into his chest, sucked the air from the room and made time stop dead.

'Officers are investigating a possible link between the murders.'

He felt his calm begin to splinter, the terror bubbling beneath threatening to burst through the all-too-flimsy surface. No. It wasn't possible, was it? Could they make a connection? *Would* they?

And, if they did, would that connection be enough to lead them to him?

He closed his eyes, forced himself to think. The soft chatter in the waiting room outside his office became a cacophony of noise, deafening, accusatory, infuriating. He shut it out, remembering the call a moment ago. The cold, businesslike tone. The utter confidence in the voice.

I'll expect payment in the next twenty-four hours.

Payment. He seized on the word, clung to it. Payment. He had paid a heavy price for this particular service, on the understanding that discretion would be assured. Of course, a certain level of attention was understandable, but even if the killings were linked, there was no way to trace it back to him. And even if someone did manage to make a link, they would connect the murders with a ghost.

The man he had been twenty-five years ago was not the man now sitting at an office desk, with a roomful of people waiting for his advice and counsel. He had aged, matured, changed – metaphorically and literally. His old self had been brash, impulsive, even idealistic. The man he was now was governed by reason, intellect and a survival instinct so honed by twenty-five years of lies that it bordered on predatory.

He would survive. He always had. He always would.

He looked up at the TV, felt the panic recede as he slipped back into the role he had played for the last three decades. He considered for moment, then smiled. The thought that had made him smile surprised him. The fact that the smile was genuine surprised him even more.

Decision made, he stood, back straight, shoulders square. He flicked on the intercom, felt a slight tightening in his throat as he modulated his voice to mute the harsh consonants and extended vowels that would give away his true heritage.

'Margaret, send Mr Pritchard in, would you? And, when you have a moment, get the chief constable on the line, will you? I think it's about time he and I had a little chat about what's going on up the road.'

CHAPTER 20

'So, do you mind telling me what the fuck that was all about?' Gina had leapt on Donna the moment she had walked through Valley's doors, as though she had been lying in wait. Her face was pale, hectic blotches of colour clawing up her neck and across her chest like angry footprints. Her lips were drawn into a thin, bloodless line, and there was a chill in her eyes Donna had never seen before.

She had always wondered what it would take to get under Gina's skin. She had seen her take on-air meltdowns, equipment failures and the near-constant stream of trouble Matt Evans served up with a cool acceptance that bordered on the mechanical. But this was different. Was it, Donna wondered, that she'd scooped them? Or was it more personal than that? Gina was head producer and director of programming. The station was her baby. Did she feel betrayed by what Donna had done?

She reached her desk, stripping off her jacket and hanging it over the back of her chair, acutely aware of Gina standing just a little too closely behind her.

'Well?' she asked again. 'What the hell is going on, Donna?'

Donna turned, angry words leaping into her throat. 'I was doing my job,' she said. 'In case you'd forgotten, I'm only on a freelance contract here, as the bastards at MediaSound are too cheap to make me a staffer and pay for my holidays. My contract stipulates I can undertake work that doesn't "clash with or undercut" what I do here.

And, in case you hadn't noticed, that was a TV broadcast I did earlier, not radio. So there was no conflict. Okay?'

There was a moment of stunned silence, everyone in the office trying to look as if they weren't interested and failing miserably. Donna felt her cheeks burn, saw something flit across Gina's gaze.

'Even so, that was a pretty shitty thing to do, Donna,' she said. 'You could at least have called me, let me know what was happening. Christ's sake, the bollocking I got from Marcus . . .'

Marcus Hamilton. A career cockroach who had risen to be regional director of MediaSound, thanks to his unerring ability to know which arse to lick at just the right moment. Shit. 'He didn't say anything about . . .'

A small smile flashed across Gina's face, a fast-moving front of cruel humour, and then it was gone. 'No, you're safe. He didn't like your work for Sky but, as he says, you've attached yourself to the story now. And it looks good for him if he can say one of his freelancers is working a national story for TV broadcast as well.'

Donna let out the breath she had been holding, a strange mixture of relief and disappointment flooding through her. She needed the shifts here, especially at the moment. But still . . . 'Look, Gina, I'm sorry,' she said. 'Really, I am. It just all happened at once. I followed Ford to the university, a friend at Sky gave me a call asking if I could stand up a line for her, and the next thing, I'm being interviewed on the phone. Sorry, you know how these things go.'

If Gina saw through the lie, she gave no hint of it. And Donna had bent the truth only a little. The fact was that, after setting Gavin his mission to get photographs, Donna had phoned Fiona Clarke and told her she could give her an on-the-scene report about the breaking news from Stirling University. Maybe with pictures. Clarke had jumped at the chance and made the arrangements. She had been delighted with the results. So much so that she was sending a TV crew down to meet Donna at the press conference due to be held at Randolphfield in the next hour.

Gina adjusted her glasses, as though they were suddenly too heavy for her delicate nose. She took a deep breath, blew it out. 'Okay,' she said. 'But at least let me know next time. And get me something good from the press conference for the six o'clock bulletin. We could use something to brighten up a thoroughly crap day.'

'Why? What's up?'

'Guess,' Gina said, the weary resignation in her voice leaving only one possible answer.

Matt Evans. Why MediaSound had decided to give him a chance after the disaster he'd left behind in Edinburgh was beyond Donna, but then, as her dad would say, shit always floats to the top. 'What's he done this time?' she asked.

'Nothing. Literally nothing,' Donna said. 'He was meant to be at conference at three o'clock to go through the show and tonight's guests. Didn't turn up. And the smug git has his phone switched off, so there's no way of telling if he's even going to be in for the show tonight. Becky's agreed to cover if he doesn't appear, but still . . .'

Donna nodded. It was typical Matt Evans. Sloppy, unprofessional and totally selfish. Odds were he would arrive two minutes before the show was due to go on-air, give some crap about partying the night away with some idiot he'd convinced to spend the night with him, then breeze into the studio and nail a four-hour show. There was no doubt he was a wanker, but what really rubbed Donna up the wrong way was that he was a talented one.

And he knew it.

'I'll get you a good OB from the press conference, promise,' she said. 'Actually, I need to talk to you about that, but can you give me five minutes to catch up with my emails, make sure I'm not missing anything?'

'Okay,' Gina said. 'I'm going to get a coffee, then I'll see you in my office. Five minutes. No longer.'

Donna pushed down the impatience that frothed in her mouth like champagne. The story was live, she had an in with Sky and finally, *finally*, it looked like things were going her way. She didn't have time for this.

Gina stalked away and Donna logged in to her computer, watching as the screen went blue and her name appeared above a spinning circle as it booted up. She was willing it to go faster when her mobile rang. She fished it out of her pocket, saw a number she didn't recognize.

She hit answer and lifted it to her ear. Her world imploded as the voice at the other end said, 'Donna? Donna, don't hang up. It's Mark. We really need to talk.'

CHAPTER 21

It was like driving to a familiar destination and arriving with no memory of the journey. Connor couldn't recall heading for his bedroom, springing open the panel beneath his bed to reveal the safe that was set in concrete beneath the floorboards. He had no memory of opening it and reaching into the darkness for what was there, waiting for him.

Yet now he sat in front of the TV, watching the news reports from outside the uni, the Glock 17 he had not held in more than a year clenched in his hand. He looked down, at once horrified and comforted by the gun's presence, the solid, undeniable weight of it in his hand. He turned it slowly, letting the light play across the glossy black barrel. It was pristine, a year in the darkness doing nothing to dull its lustre.

He considered, his eyes darting between the gun and the television. Now that the initial shock had abated, doubt was creeping into his mind. Could it be a coincidence? After all, it was a popular book. Could he be wrong?

He snatched for the remote, rewinding the live stream of coverage to Donna's report. His hand tightened on the Glock as the still images of the crime scene flitted across the screen. He paused it when it came to the last image, felt the reptilian part of his mind hiss when he saw the book lying among the debris. He studied it, felt the first trickle of relief when he realized it wasn't the same edition as the one that had been delivered to their flat in Belfast.

The book that had ruined his life.

Connor had never meant to become a police officer, especially not in Northern Ireland. It had, he told himself, just been one of those things. He'd gone to Belfast to study at Queens University, partly because he wanted to be close to his grandfather, who ran a garage half an hour away in Newtownards, and partly because he wanted to get away from the constant low-level disapproval of his father.

From the moment Connor was born, Jack Fraser had never wavered in his conviction that his son would follow in his footsteps and become a doctor. But despite this conviction, and his constant attempts to mould Connor in his own image with tales of his life in medicine ('It even gave me a wife, son – that was how I met your mother') and even downright blackmail, it became apparent that he had failed.

Connor had thought his decision to study psychology would placate his father – he could still become a doctor. Instead, it widened the schism between them, Jack Fraser drunkenly dismissing his son's choice as 'the easy way out for a kid with a weak stomach and a weaker work ethic'.

A month after he left school, Connor moved to Belfast, setting himself up in a small flat a short walk from the main university campus, in an area of town called the Holylands. It had gained the name thanks to the divine intervention of a devout developer who had named the streets Damascus, Jerusalem, Cairo, Palestine and Carmel. He arrived in Belfast by ferry, taking his worn-down but much-loved Ford Focus with him so he could drive down to Newtownards and see his grandfather at the weekends.

Life fell into a soothing rhythm for Connor, studying during the week, nights out with other students at Lavery's, the Bot – or any other place that served cheap beer – then drive east at the weekend. Jimmy O'Brien was glad of the company. A stroke had taken his wife when Connor was only twelve. At the funeral, Connor remembered his mother beseeching Jimmy to come back to Scotland to live with them and 'see Connor grow up'. It was an offer she continued to make over the years, and Jimmy always declined. He had his garage, the pub and 'the lads'. What would he do if he moved away from the town where he had built his life with Grace McAteer? Who would tend her garden? Who would visit her grave?

It was on these weekend trips that Connor began the heavy lifting that would sculpt him into the image of his grandfather. Jimmy O'Brien had been an amateur bodybuilder in his time, channelling his fury at the Troubles into the iron instead of the pipe bomb. In an outhouse in the corner of the garage, past where the husks of scrapped cars sat piled like giant Jenga pieces, Jimmy had amassed a collection of weights and machines. When the garage was closed he would take Connor there and train him in the 'bang and clang', always with a Bushmills sloshing in an overfull glass. Over the course of his first year in Northern Ireland, Connor bucked the first-year student trend of losing weight and put on just over a stone and a half, most of it muscle.

And then, just at the point when women were starting to pay attention to the body he had built in his grandfather's garage and the university gym, he met Karen. It was her voice that first drew her to his attention: her clipped Edinburgh accent shrieked to him across the hushed calm of the McClay Library. He didn't feel homesick, but there was something about her tone that stirred a hollow wistfulness in him, as though she had reminded him of something he hadn't known he was missing.

He struck up a conversation with a corny joke: he'd come all the way to Belfast, he said, to meet the prettiest girl in Scotland. He had felt himself cringe even as he spoke, had known he'd blown his chance with her at that moment. But then she had smiled, and somehow he had known it would be okay.

And it was. For five years. He'd got to know Karen MacKay, who had come to Belfast to study English with the aim of being a teacher. They dated casually at first, then more seriously. By their final year, they were living together in Connor's flat, making the trip down to see Jimmy every weekend for Sunday lunch.

It was comfortable. Routine. Which was why they started planning to stay in Belfast. Karen would do her teaching diploma then find a position – as with everywhere else, Northern Ireland was desperate for teachers. Connor was considering getting a job with the NHS. But then, one night, the decision was made for him.

He was in the Apartment, a bar on Donegal Square that looked out onto the Baroque splendour of Belfast City Hall. The main bar was on the first floor, its floor-to-ceiling windows giving impressive views of the building, which was bathed with floodlights like a model on a catwalk. He was idly sipping on a pint and watching the square below, waiting for Karen to finish her shift at a restaurant nearby, when a sudden commotion drew his attention. Down on the street, a young, straggly-looking man sprinted diagonally across the road, narrowly missing a bus that was just pulling into the stop. He was running from two police officers who were sprinting after him, moving quickly despite the bulk of their stab vests and the weight of their belts. Connor heard them cry out for the man to stop, the shouts sending those on the streets below scattering and drawing other customers in the bar to the windows. The man – he was young, Connor saw, little more than a child – stopped, spun around with his hands on his head, a look of bewildered panic and utter hopelessness on his face. Even from thirty feet away, Connor could see the kid was seriously malnourished, with the pale, greying skin and nervous tics of an addict.

The officers were on him in a second, reaching out, grabbing, seizing. They spun him around roughly, crowding in on him. The panic gave way to terror on the kid's face and tears fell. Still the police shouted, intimidating and overpowering him. One raised his radio from his shoulder to his mouth, spoke into it. Cuffed now, the kid was frogmarched away to the half-hearted cheers of the crowd outside and murmurs of approval from those inside the bar. Connor watched him go, a police van pulling up at the other side of the square. The kid's head darted from officer to officer, and in his mind, Connor could hear his pleas.

He had heard them before, just as he had seen the look of pleading desperation, the day he had turned on Gordon Jeffrey.

Connor watched the police van pull away. He drained his pint, then went looking for Karen. At that moment he knew, on some level beyond reasoned thought, that he would join the Police Service of Northern Ireland. Not to arrest terrified kids in the way he had seen those officers operate, but to do it better.

For himself. And Gordon Jeffrey.

Despite her initial misgivings, Karen eventually agreed with his decision. With his natural physical presence and years of study he excelled at the training and became a probationary constable six months after he had graduated. Karen got a job teaching in Dunmurry and they moved into a flat in St George's Harbour, overlooking the Lagan.

And then came that night. And the book that had destroyed their life.

Connor sighed, pulled himself out of the memory. The news channel had moved on to another story, this time about the murder of a country rather than a single person. He weighed the gun in his hand. It *could* be a coincidence . . . But he had to know. For himself. And for Karen.

He placed the gun on the coffee-table and picked up his phone. Called the number from memory.

'Hello?'

Connor felt his breath catch in his chest as the voice from his past dragged him back to Belfast. His eyes settled on the gun.

'Hello, who is this?' Impatient now.

'Simon? Si, it's Connor Fraser . . . Yeah, I know, the ghost who walks. Listen, I'm after a favour. Need a wee check on Jonny Hughes. He on anyone's radar these days?'

There was a long exhalation of breath down the phone as DS Simon McCartney collected his thoughts. 'Christ, Connor, I would have thought you'd heard,' he said.

'Heard what?' Connor asked, his free hand reaching for the gun.

'Well, it's just that . . .' A sharp crack in the background drowned Simon's voice, followed by the sound of him swearing. 'Sorry, Connor, I'm down at Corporation Square. There's a power of building going on here.'

Connor knew the area. Not far from the Cathedral Quarter, heading down to the harbour and the Lagan. It was the latest part of Belfast to benefit from the investment that had come with the end of the Troubles; hotels, offices and apartment blocks springing up like blossoming flowers. But the development was looking increasingly fragile, the hard frost of Brexit threatening to kill it off as the EU pulled the plug on the money that was flowing into the town.

'No problem,' Connor said, dragging himself back to the present. 'What were you saying about Hughes?'

'Well, that's the thing, there's nothing to tell. He's gone. Three months ago. Got hit by a car on the Shankill, just outside the leisure centre. Whatever you wanted with the Librarian, it's a bit late now, Connor.'

CHAPTER 22

'Oh, come on, Donna, not again, for fuck's sake.'

Donna smiled at Danny's response to her call. He hadn't answered the first time she'd rung, probably enjoying the lie he had told himself that the last tip he'd given her had made them even.

She'd crushed that dream by texting him a picture of the cabinet secretary he'd blackmailed and a simple message: *No problem, Danny. If the story goes dry, I can always offer this one as a splash.* He had called less than two minutes later, his voice a whining blend of annoyance, desperation and anger.

'Come on, Danny,' she said, wincing as the line flared with static. He had obviously made the call outside to protect his privacy. 'The press conference is starting in less than an hour, and I need something to give me the edge. Anything.'

'Donna, I've given you everything I can. Ford may look like a creepy uncle, but he's no idiot. He's been watching me, I'm sure of it. If he links me to any of the stuff you've got . . . Christ, the chief constable's pissed off as it is with the stunt you pulled at the uni. If I give you any more . . .'

Donna's face tightened, her good humour at Danny's discomfort fading. She knew all about the chief constable's anger, and the complaint he had made to Sky. Fiona had called her less than twenty minutes ago, being very specific that their arrangement was freelance only: she could only take the heat from above if Donna kept

89

producing results. Translation: get me another scoop or we drop you.

'Danny, there's got to be something,' she said. 'It doesn't have to be big. Just something I can hook him with. Have they identified the victim yet? Has cause of death been established? Have they categorically linked this to the murder in town yesterday?'

Danny barked a humourless laugh. 'What do you think?' he said. Refocusing, the arrogance seeping back into his voice. 'Two violent murders in two days? Of course they're looking at possible connections. But there's been no formal connection made. As far as I'm aware they've yet to identify the victim, and cause of death has yet to be established. They might have more to say on that at the press conference – I've not seen the final release yet.'

Donna bit her lip. She needed more. 'Nothing else?' she asked. 'Nothing odd found at the scene? What about that bag I saw in one of the shots? Nothing there to identify the victim?'

A pause on the line, another wave of static as the wind picked up wherever Danny was. The silence told her two things. There was something, and Danny was weighing up how much trouble he would be in if he leaked it to her. She felt an electric rush of excitement, found herself holding her breath.

'Okay,' he said, after what felt like an eternity to Donna. 'There is one thing. But this is it, Donna. I'm no use to you if Ford catches on to me, right?'

'Of course,' Donna said, the lie coming with less effort than it took to keep the impatience out of her voice.

'Right,' Danny said, as though reaching some agreement with himself. 'There was one odd thing. There was no purse or other ID on the victim, yet the killer left behind a bag containing a journal and a paperback book. The journal looks like nothing more than random notes on local-government meetings and briefings, which supports the theory that the victim was a guest at the hotel. A council policy forum was held in one of the conference suites yesterday.'

'Hold on,' Donna said. '"Purse", not "wallet". So the victim is female.'

Danny cursed. 'Yes,' he said, voice brittle now. 'But that's the problem. None of the conference delegates has been reported missing, and the hotel doesn't have any guest unaccounted for that matches her description.'

Donna jotted notes, keeping her eyes off the Post-it note stuck to her monitor. 'Anything else? What about the book? Was that something to do with the conference as well?'

'Actually, no, it was just a paperback novel. Stephen King's *Misery*. Read it?'

'Yeah, long time ago,' Donna said, vaguely remembering the story of a writer held hostage by his number-one fan and forced to write a novel. Not her type of thing and, besides, she had enough real-life nightmares to deal with. The Post-it note was testament to that.

She forced herself to focus on the job in hand. 'Nothing more?'

'Nope,' Danny said, just a little too quickly. 'There was a handwritten dedication in the inside cover. Just looks like a note in a gift – doesn't give any definitive indication of who wrote it or who owned the book.'

'Oh?' Donna said. 'What did it say?'

Danny read out the dedication, Donna scribbling it down. She read it back. Considered it. Nothing important.

'. . . all I've got, Donna.'

'Sorry, what?'

'I said that's it, that's all I've got. I can't give you any more. If I do, Ford will be on to me in a second.'

So there was more, she thought. Interesting. 'Thanks for that, Danny,' she said. 'I'll maybe give you a buzz after the press conference, tidy up a few things, okay?'

'Do I have a choice?'

She laughed, then hung up, looking at the page of notes she had just scribbled down. Female victim. Probably at a conference being held at the hotel. Fan of horror novels. It wasn't much, but it was something.

She felt her eyes drawn back to the Post-it. 'Portcullis, after press conference,' it read.

She shook her head, anger gnawing at her like toothache. She should have hung up on Mark the moment she'd heard his voice.

Instead, she'd listened to his easy chat and, incredibly, found herself agreeing to meet him at the pub just down the road from the castle after the press conference was done.

Same old Mark. He'd lost none of his persuasive charm, the ability to make her say yes when she was determined to say no. But who was worse – him for calling after all this time or her for falling for it? She reached for the note, swiped it angrily from the screen and tossed it into the bin. She could deal with his crap later. For now, she had a press conference to prepare for, and a news editor to impress. She was close now, so close, to proving them all wrong. And no one, not Danny, Ford or even Mark, would stop her.

CHAPTER 23

After wrapping up his call to Simon with promises to keep in touch, and the assurance he would be welcome in Stirling at any time, Connor took the gun back to the bedroom. He was about to put it away when he paused. He reached into the safe, found the kit and set about stripping and cleaning the gun, the act second nature to him, the ordered routine soothing, the clicks as he dumped the magazine, cleared the chamber and pulled the gun apart like the ticks of a clock in the silence of the flat.

And as he worked, he remembered . . .

He was three years into the job, a newly minted constable. He had been teamed with Sergeant Simon McCartney, who was three years older than Connor and acting as his mentor. It hadn't taken long for a friendship to develop, Connor appreciating Simon's dark sense of humour, Simon picking Connor's brains on the best training programmes in the gym.

'Sure you're like the Hulk,' he had told Connor once. 'Just need to slap a bit of green paint on you and a pair of purple pants and you'd be all set. Not sure what your da' would think of that right enough, but fuck him.'

Connor had sneered. His father had been good enough to attend his graduation ceremony, had even been civil to Karen. He had smiled at all the right moments, posed for photographs, shaken hands. But

Connor saw the glances he'd sneaked at his son when he thought he wasn't looking. There was no pride, only a hollow disappointment that Connor felt echoed the loss he tried not to feel. That day he'd known he had lost any chance of reconciling with his father, that they would be strangers for the rest of their days. Time grew a callus of indifference over the wound but still, Connor would sometimes think of that day, of the look on his father's face, and wonder what it was he saw when he looked at his son.

The night had started simply enough, a standard cruise around the Greater Shankill area in North Belfast; a drive up the Shankill, then along Ballygomartin Road, past Woodvale Park, then a circuit of the Glencairn estate before looping back.

They'd stopped at the Tesco next to the park to grab a couple of cans of cola, Connor marvelling at the parents and children who wandered the aisles in pyjamas and dressing-gowns. Had they got ready for bed, then suddenly remembered they needed milk? Or had they been in their nightwear all day? He was paying when the call came in: reports of a domestic disturbance on Glencairn Street, a row of close-clustered terraced houses just across from Tesco. Connor exchanged a glance with Simon as they headed to the car, their shared concern passing between them unsaid. This was a tight-knit community and it was practically unheard of for someone to call the police to something that was happening behind closed doors.

Minutes later, they pulled up outside the house. It was just like any of the others on the street, if more run down – fading white paint peeling from pebbledashed walls, a low wall and rusting gate barricading it from the street. Simon paused as they approached the house, eyes lingering on the immaculate Subaru Impreza that was sitting half on the pavement.

'Ah, shite, I know that car,' he said, jutting his jaw towards the front door. 'I know who lives here. Fuck.'

'Who?' Connor asked, the first sparks of adrenalin making his skin itch. He was suddenly very aware of the weight of his stab vest, and the equipment belt that hung around his waist. He had yet to draw his gun from its holster on the job, but would tonight be the night?

'Jonny Hughes,' Simon said, nodding. He saw Connor's confused look and sighed. 'Low-level drug-dealer. Got some pull with the UDA as his uncle was a commander during the Troubles. Thinks of himself as a bit of a—'

He was cut off by a deep voice barking from the house. 'Catch yerself on, woman!' a man roared. 'Away and fuck I wasnae doin' anything, just helping with—'

Something heavy crashed to the floor in the house, followed by raised voices. Simon and Connor exchanged glances and rushed up the path. Connor stood to the side as Simon took point, hammering on the front door.

'Police!' he shouted. Connor darted a glance up the street, his eye caught by the ripple of blinds and curtains being pulled aside. He felt a flutter of unease in his gut. Glencairn was a known Loyalist area of town, proud of patrolling and policing its own. The official police wouldn't be welcome. And they knew how to deal with unwelcome guests.

'We've received reports of a disturbance here. Open the door, please.'

A moment of unnatural silence, punctuated by curses and the sound of fast footfalls. Simon raised his hand to hammer at the door again, but before he could there was the jingling clunk of a lock being released and a chain being slid aside. The door swung open to reveal an unremarkable-looking man in a Rangers T-shirt, his chest rising and falling rapidly, sweat beading across his forehead. An expensive pair of glasses perched on a nose that had clearly been broken at least once. He adjusted them with large, blunt fingers and peered out of the house.

'Evening, officers,' he said, his voice casual, his eyes not. 'How can I help?'

Simon took the lead. 'We've received reports of a disturbance at this address, sir, and we just heard raised voices, then what sounded like something falling over. Everything all right here?'

'Ah, yeah, sorry about that,' Hughes said, eyes dark and hard as eight balls behind his glasses. 'The wife and I were movin' me bookshelf, managed to drop the bloody thing. I may have lost the rag a bit, shouted and the like. Sorry.'

Simon returned Hughes's cold gaze. 'You mind if we come in and take a look, sir?' He moved forward a half-step, forcing Hughes back into the house.

'Well, actually, boys, it's not a—'

'It'll only take a minute, sir,' Connor said, as he stepped onto the centre of the path. He saw Hughes's gaze dance across him, evaluating. Something told him that, if it was to get physical, Hughes would be a problem. 'Really, sir, we'll be in and out,' he added, trying to focus past the dark excitement that was fizzing through his veins. 'Best to sort this out now, eh?'

Hughes hesitated, then dropped his chin to his chest, accepting the inevitable. 'Come on away in, then,' he said. 'But watch out, the place is a fuckin' mess.'

They navigated their way along a small hallway, with a steep flight of stairs at the end, and into a cramped living room. As Hughes had said, an upturned bookcase lay on the floor, books spilt around it.

Connor took a slow look around the room, nodding to the wall opposite where the bookcase had been and a fist-shaped dent in the plasterboard that spread splintering cracks of white across the dark purple paint. 'What happened there, sir?' he asked. 'Surely a book didn't do that Mr, ah . . .'

'Hughes,' he said, confirming his identity. 'Jonny Hughes. It wasn't a book. Like I said, I lost my rag a bit and I, ah . . .'

Simon made a point of looking around the room. 'You mentioned your wife, sir. Where is she?'

Hughes's expression darkened. 'Think she went to make a cup of tea, like,' he said. 'Amy! You through there?'

A door at the far end of the living room opened, and a tall, slender woman in jogging bottoms and a sports top was framed in front of a small, well-lit kitchen. Her eyes darted between the three men, a cold calculation taking place, and she stepped into the room.

'Aw, we didn't make enough noise to get the police involved, did we? Sorry, boys, my stupid fault, just let the thing slip out of my hand.'

Connor nodded, studying her. Like Hughes's, her forehead was beaded with sweat, her breath short and shallow as though she was recovering from heavy exertion. No signs of the two of them having been in a fight but, still, something niggled at Connor, something he had seen but not . . .

'So, you boys need anything else? All just like we said, right?'

Simon and Connor exchanged a look. The story checked out. Neither of them seemed to be in physical distress, and it was clear no one was going to be making accusations or pressing charges. Nothing more to be done.

And yet . . .

'There's no one else here, is there, Mr Hughes?' Simon asked. 'Not got a friend in to help you with the redecorating?'

Hughes twisted his lips into an approximation of a smile. 'Naw, no one daft enough to help out. But feel free to have a look. Got nothing to hide, me.'

'That won't be necessary, Mr Hughes,' Simon said. 'Just keep it down, okay? And next time you want to move a bookcase, get some help.'

'Sure, lads, no problem,' he said as they turned and headed for the door. Connor lingered for a second, his eyes catching on the fist-shaped dent in the wall. Then he left.

They walked out of the front door, watched as Hughes swung it shut. Got back into the car and studied the house for a moment, the Hugheses' silhouettes playing against the blinds of the front window.

'So, what do you think?' Connor asked.

'Domestic, most like,' Simon replied. 'You heard what he shouted as we arrived, "I wasnae doin' anything." Ten to one she's caught him at it and hit him where it hurts, in the books.'

Connor thought back to the books lying piled on the floor. 'Aye, what's that all about?' he asked.

'Jonny thinks of himself as a bit of an intellectual,' Simon replied, voice heavy with sarcasm. 'He did a stretch for aggravated assault a while back, caught the reading bug in the prison library. Collects them, for the titles rather than the content, I think. Always carries a book with him, picked up the nickname the Librarian on the way.'

Connor grunted a laugh. 'So what do we do now?' he asked.

'Nothing,' Simon said. 'Looks like just what they said, a domestic that got of hand. No signs of violence between them. Seems like the wall got it worse from Jonny than she did so we can . . .'

The wall. The image of the dent flashing across his mind. The size of it. The shape. The way Amy Hughes was standing, left hand clasped across right. 'He didn't hit the wall,' he said, more to himself than Simon. 'She did. That's why she was in the kitchen when we arrived. She was sorting her hand out.'

Simon smiled. 'Hell hath no fury, eh? Ah, well, we'll write it up, keep an eye on the place when we're around. Nothing more we can do for now.'

They didn't have to wait long. An hour later, they were heading back down Ballygomartin Road towards the Shankill, Woodvale Park a pool of darkness on their right, when the call came in. Glencairn Street again.

'Ah, for fuck's sake,' Simon hissed, as he hauled the car around and Connor hit the blues and twos. It was nearing the end of their shift, and this meant overtime neither of them would be paid for.

They pulled up to the house. Amy Hughes was stalking around the Impreza parked outside, keeping it between her and Jonny, who was brandishing a baseball bat. The windscreen had been shattered, the remnants of it twinkling like shards of amber in the sepia of the streetlights.

Connor was out of the car first, heading for Jonny, ignoring the jeering and whoops of the assembled crowd. This had gone beyond a domestic and curtain-twitching. It had moved outside, making it a spectator sport, and the neighbours had front-row seats. He tried not to think of who might be in that crowd, what they might be carrying. The Troubles were officially over, but animosity towards the police hadn't dissipated. It was in the blood, no matter which side of the divide you were on. And, right now, he and Simon were the perfect target for a half-brick, a petrol bomb or whatever else could be pulled from a backstreet arsenal.

Back-up was on the way, but Connor knew he needed to end this. Quickly.

'Mr Hughes? Put it down, sir, now,' he said, reaching for his CS spray as he spoke.

Hughes looked at him, wild-eyed, nostrils flaring. A crack had spidered its way across the right lens of his glasses, the flesh behind the frame puffy and already turning an ugly purple. Hell hath no fury, right enough.

Simon looped around to the left, trying to outflank Hughes and keep the crowd back at the same time. More jeers and hoots, a kid trying to spark up a chorus of 'Fuck the pigs'.

'Mr Hughes,' Connor said again, raising his voice. Not that it mattered. One look in Hughes's eyes told him the man wasn't listening. He wanted blood. And he didn't look like he much cared whose it was.

'Fuckin' bitch!' he spat across the car. 'Look what ye did to ma fuckin' motor. I'm gonnae—'

'Oh, aye? Gonnae what, Jonny?' Amy hissed back, cords in her neck straining, fists clenched. 'Hit me again? That what you do with her? She like that? A bit of slapping around? The rough stuff? Must be something like that, as you're shite at anything else, ya limp-dick fuck.'

Laughter exploded from the crowd, petrol to the rage burning in Hughes's eyes. He surged forward, slipping around the right of the car on the side closest to the wall, too fast for Simon to catch. A roar of approval from the crowd as Amy danced backwards from the bonnet, ready to face him.

Connor stepped forwards, grabbing her arm. He threw her behind him, fresh laughter and whoops erupting from the crowd as she lost her balance and ended up on her backside. She cried out, more in shock than pain, and Hughes's eyes darted between her and Connor. For a sliver of a second, Connor felt a surge of vertigo and sickness, the air now heavy with the promise of violence. Then, like a light being snapped off, the feeling was gone, replaced with something far darker and more dangerous.

Excitement.

Hughes raised the baseball bat above his head, ready to open Connor's head with it. But Connor was ready, the situation unfolding in his mind in a giddying kaleidoscope of snapshot images. He took a step left, away from the swing, then jabbed his fist into Hughes's exposed ribs. Not much, just a tap. It was enough to tip his balance and he staggered, bouncing off the low boundary wall of the front garden, skidding across its surface, then hitting the ground. He was on his knees in an instant, teeth bared.

'Fucker,' he said, his voice as hard as the pavement he crouched on. 'I am going to end you.'

Connor took a half-step back, giving Hughes all the space he needed. He rushed forward, the baseball bat forgotten, nothing in him but rage now. Connor heard Simon cry out, ignored it. Stepped forward into Hughes's path then went low, sweeping his legs out from under him. He landed roughly, chin cracking off the ground as his glasses skittered across the pavement. The crowd roared again: the neighbourhood big man with his UDA connections finally brought low. Connor sprang on him, got a knee on his back and hauled his arms roughly behind him. 'Jonny Hughes, I am arresting you for—'

His world exploded into a cacophony of screams that stabbed into his ear. Hot breath on his neck as Amy leapt on him, hissing, clawing, biting. She reached round, her hands curled into claws, scrabbling for Connor's eyes. 'Leave him the fuck alone!' she screamed. 'If you've hurt him—'

Instinctively, Connor snatched for the hand clawing at his face. Grabbed it and twisted. Heard something pop, then Amy's scream climbing from fury to agony.

He shrugged her off and turned his attention back to Jonny, who was thrashing beneath him but unable to move against Connor's bulk. He finished cuffing him and hauled him to his feet. With his glasses gone, Hughes glared at Connor with a naked, feral hatred. 'I'm gonnae make your life a fuckin' horror show, son,' he whispered. Then he spat into Connor's face.

The report was routine, the problem of Connor almost breaking Amy's wrist countered by the fact that she was assaulting him at the time. Jonny and Amy Hughes were charged with assaulting a police officer and breach of the peace. And that was the end of the matter.

Or so Connor thought.

Three weeks later, he came home after a shift, Karen already there, curled up on the couch with a glass of wine, the smell of her lasagne drifting from the kitchen, a package on the coffee-table in front of her.

He set down his kitbag. 'What's that?'

'That?' she said, a puzzled look on her face. 'I don't know. It was delivered to the school today for me, must be a mistake.' She handed it to him. 'Not something I ordered, strange they'd send it to the school though.'

It was a typical Amazon delivery package, a plain cardboard sleeve around the item inside. He opened it and slid out the book. With it was a printed card, Amazon's version of a dedication. As he read it, Connor felt the world tip and lurch: 'I promised you a horror show. Here it is. Hope you like it. L.'

He swallowed his fury and looked at Karen, who was studying him closely. 'You okay, Connor?' she asked. 'You've gone pale.'

He forced a smile, felt numb lips stretch away from his teeth. Hughes. And the obvious message? I know who you are. I know where your girlfriend works. I can get either of you at any time.

Connor snapped the slide back onto the barrel of the gun, pulled the trigger, then slid it back, resetting the mechanism with a satisfying clunk. He looked at the gun for a moment, memories he didn't want to face churning to the surface. Of what he had done. What it had cost him. What he had become.

He packed up his cleaning kit and put it back into the safe, then locked the gun into the darkness with all his other memories of Belfast. It was over. Jonny Hughes, the Librarian, was dead. The book found at the murder scene was a coincidence, nothing more.

Let the past lie.

He stood up, tired, the weight of the past draining him. Looked out of the window and decided he was in no mood to tackle his gran's house today. Headed for the living room to find his phone and call Jen. A day with her would help. He would check her flat as agreed, then suggest a drink. He was still musing on how he would tell her about Paulie as he scrolled to her number, not knowing the point was already moot.

CHAPTER 24

They held the press conference at Randolphfield, in a grim basement room that had the reporters complaining about poor lighting, lack of power points and crap sound. Sitting in an anteroom, Ford heard the griping, cut through with Danny's increasingly strident responses. Served the little shit right. Ford could have had another press officer run the show, but he wanted to make Danny suffer. From the sound of it, he was.

Ford returned to the notes in front of him, felt the prickle of annoyance again, adding to the headache that was pressing at the back of his eyes. It was a waste of time. He was being wheeled out in front of the press as cannon fodder, nothing more.

He had already received the call telling him that Special Investigations were taking over the case, and he was to offer his 'full and total co-operation'. That they were assuming command immediately after the press conference – leaving him to face the journalists with only a chief constable who thought every run-in with the media was an exercise in self-promotion – was a total coincidence.

Yeah, right.

He was the sacrificial lamb, the DCI who would stand up and tell the gathering how little progress they had made, which would give the chief the perfect opening to tell reporters he was taking a closer operational role and had called in Special Investigations to drive the case forward. It made Ford seem inept, the chief in control.

When, he wondered, had policing stopped being about catching criminals and become an exercise in political manoeuvring?

He thought again of retiring, jacking it in and walking away. Mary would approve. She had made no secret of her concerns about the toll the job was taking on him, the dark moods, the drinking, the sullen periods of silence when he would bottle up everything he had seen, unwilling and unable to burden her with it. He was close to his thirty years anyway, and he was still young enough to do something else.

But then he thought of Billy Griffin's head swaying in the breeze. The hellish squeal calling to him, beckoning him to look . . .

He had to face whoever had done that, look into their eyes, see what resided there, what made such violence and fury possible. He wouldn't be able to rest until he did.

The door to the room swung open, Danny stepping inside. 'Chief is ten minutes away,' he said, brandishing his mobile. 'You all set, sir?'

'I'm fine,' Ford replied. 'Tell me, has that reporter arrived? You know, the one who was on Sky, got those pictures from the university?'

Danny's Adam's apple bobbed as he swallowed, eyes narrowing. Ford smiled at his discomfort. So he was right: the little shite was talking to her. It was obvious, really – a quick look at Danny's CV, a Google search of Donna Blake's name showed they'd both worked in Glasgow, on the same paper, at the same time. The calls to a couple of contacts in what had been Pitt Street CID had hardly been necessary, but Ford liked to be thorough.

If only everything was so obvious.

Danny paled, fidgeted with his phone. 'Ah, I've not seen her, but I'm sure she'll be here. Why, sir? Is there something particular you want to discuss with her? Of course I can set up a sit-down with her but . . .'

Ford raised a hand, silencing him. 'Nothing like that, Danny,' he said. 'After the crap she pulled at the campus, I just want to know she's there so I can avoid calling her for questions.'

Danny's mouth opened, as though he was about to say something. Clearly he thought better of it. 'I'll make sure you know where she is, sir,' he said, his tone resigned.

'Good.' Ford nodded. 'Now make sure there's water on the conference table. The chief is always thirsty at these things and, who knows, I might need a jug to empty over one of the hacks.'

CHAPTER 25

The chief constable arrived twenty minutes later, killing any lingering goodwill the press might have had. Ford did his best but he could hear the irritation creep into his voice as he had to find different ways to say the same thing over and over again. Yes, another body had been found. No, we have yet to identify the victim. We have nothing to implicitly connect this murder to the body found at Cowane's Hospital yesterday, but we are pursuing every avenue of inquiry. Yes, we will keep you regularly updated.

Beside him, Chief Constable Peter Guthrie sat impassively, a serene Buddha who had been squeezed into a pressed police uniform that, instead of giving him an air of authority, made him look like a wee boy playing dress-up. Guthrie was a new breed of police officer, the type that believe in marketing plans, stakeholder engagement, community feedback and 'positive reinforcement of our core ideals'. He was a graduate who had been put on the promotion fast-track, skipping ranks and the experience a real police officer needed. With the advent of Police Scotland, he had thrived in the bureaucratic churn that trying to bring eight police forces together under one roof had created, and found himself elevated to the top job after the previous chief had racked up too many controversies, both internal and external, to stay in post. He had become, in the post-reorganization age, that most forbidden entity – a political liability.

At several points during the press conference, Ford saw Donna

Blake straining forward, trying to get in a question. Every time she raised her hand or tried to butt into the conversation, he ignored her. The chief did the same – given that he was using this whole debacle to gain a few Brownie points with his bosses at Holyrood, it was the least he could do. When Guthrie was summing up, looking into the camera with a voice as precise as his uniform creases and a delivery as polished as his epilates, Ford caught Blake's eye. Her gaze was cold. She looked as if she was biting back a mouthful of expletives.

When Guthrie had finished speaking, Danny stepped in to usher the press out as Ford made for the door to the anteroom. He opened it for the chief, was just about to follow him through, when his phone buzzed. He cursed himself as he pulled it out of his pocket. He had meant to switch the damned thing off before the press conference, but at least he'd remembered to put it on silent this time.

He glanced at the screen, an unfamiliar number displayed. Hit answer, raised it to his ear.

'DCI Ford,' he said, closing the door to the anteroom.

'Nice work just now,' a familiar voice said. 'What was that? Freeze me out for being a bad girl at the uni?'

'Ms Blake,' Ford said, pushing down the surge of fury he felt towards Danny. 'I'm curious as to how you got this number. I'm afraid I've no idea what you're talking about. I was merely—'

'Forget it,' Donna Blake hissed. 'I know exactly what you were doing, I heard about your boss's little call to Sky. But it doesn't matter. You can make it up to me right now.'

'And how can I do that?' Ford said, feeling a grudging amusement. He had to give it to her, Donna Blake was persistent. 'And, more importantly, why?'

Donna barked a laugh. 'I need a bit of background on the victim,' she said. 'See, I know you've had no luck tracking her down at the hotel, and her notebook makes it seem likely she was attending a conference there. But mostly I'm interested in the book you found with her, and the dedication.'

Ford's headache snarled back into life, anger pulsing through him. How the hell did she know this? The answer was obvious. Danny. He gritted his teeth and bit back what he wanted to say. When he spoke, his voice was atonal. 'Any details fit for public consumption were made available at the conference, Ms Blake. Anything else you may have is hearsay and I will not comment further. Are we clear?'

'Oh, that's fine,' Donna said. 'But the dedication in the book is confusing me a little.' There was a pause, the rustle of notes, and then she was back, quoting the words to him. Words he had puzzled over. '"Not the same edition, but the same horror story. Hope you like it. See you soon, L."'

She paused just long enough to enjoy his discomfort as it screamed across the silent phone line between them. The dedication meant nothing as far as she knew. But it was a way to show she was informed about the case and someone to take seriously.

'Any comment?' she asked.

'None at the moment,' Ford replied, fighting to keep the relief out of his voice. 'You should check with your sources, Ms Blake. They're not as good as you think they are.'

He killed the call, looked back at the now-deserted conference room. Considered. What the hell did Blake have over Danny to get him to tell her that? At least Danny had been smart and not told her everything. That one decision might just have saved his job.

Maybe.

She had been right on the dedication, with one glaring omission. It told them more than she thought, gave them their first and only real clue in the case. It was why they had decided not to release it to the public. Yes, it might have helped speed the identification, but it was also a good way of screening out the cranks who would undoubtedly come crawling out of the woodwork.

He thought again of the words, written in black pen in small, neat capitals on the inside front cover of the book.

'Not the same edition, but the same horror story. Hope you like it, Connie. See you soon – L.'

They didn't know who she was, what she was doing at the hotel or why she had been singled out to die so horribly. But they knew one thing about the woman dumped in the shadow of the Wallace Monument.

They knew her first name was Connie.

CHAPTER 26

The Portcullis was a hotel and bar at the top of the town, next to the castle esplanade. With its stained granite walls, traditional white windows and proximity to the castle and the Old Town Cemetery, which sprawled across the valley that connected the castle to the Holy Rude Church and Cowane's Hospital, it was always busy with tourists thirsty for a pint and a taste of local history.

Donna stood outside, heart hammering. She had told herself she wasn't coming here, had done everything in her power to drag out her post-press-conference work for as long as possible. She had taken extra time over the audio for Gina, and the video package for Sky. Luckily, it wasn't a live OB, and she was able to fluff lines and miss takes just enough to drag things out.

When she had finished, warning both Fiona and Gina that the story was likely to draw more ire from the police, she looked at her watch. She had been more than an hour. There was no way he would be waiting. It would be a pointless trip. And, besides, she had no intention of seeing him anyway.

But somehow, she found herself in front of the pub, watching tourists come and go. The sight of Mark's car was like a gut punch, robbing her of the ability to breathe.

They had met when she was working on the *Westie*, which had a reputation for breaking big stories and getting beyond the headlines. That was how Mark Sneddon had come to work there: a former political reporter based at Holyrood with one of the nationals, he had been courted by the editor of the *Westie* to head up their political coverage. He had a reputation as a good reporter, had broken a few big stories at Holyrood and had claimed the scalp of a backbencher who had been forced to resign from the committee hearing evidence on taxation: Mark had dug up his link to an Edinburgh hedge fund with a vested interest in protecting its clients' tax anonymity. Made political editor, he had quickly moved on to the newsdesk, allowed to draw from the general reporting pool to cover the stories he thought needed extra manpower.

They'd met when he was being given the tour of the office. And while he wasn't what Donna normally thought of as her type, there was something about him that caught her attention. The easy smile maybe, or the relaxed manner and self-deprecating humour. He was a welcome change from news editor Charlie Banks and his opinion that all his reporters were shite: the best way to motivate them, he reckoned, was to berate their copy and pile on the work.

She found herself confiding in Mark, telling him about her problems with getting stories placed in the paper, the feeling that Charlie Banks didn't rate her or her work. She was flattered when he took the time to listen to her, worked with her on her stories, stood up for her with Charlie and encouraged her to push herself more.

So obvious, she thought now, gazing at his car. Build up her confidence, be her confidant, her friend. The bigshot reporter who could see the talent in her that her bosses couldn't.

Things had started to change a couple of months later. They were both working a late shift, filing for the early edition the next day, and ended up having a quick drink at Sloans in the Argyle Arcade while he waited for his train to Edinburgh, where he lived with his wife. He had never made any secret of the fact he was married, always wore the wedding ring, spoke about his wife openly with Donna or other colleagues. On the outside, it seemed he had the perfect marriage, another reason Donna didn't see him as anything other than a friend.

But that night, as time wore on and the conversation thawed from the professional to the personal, he confided in her that all was not well at home, that his wife, who worked in HR and to strict hours, didn't understand that his days were unpredictable, the hours unsociable. 'You know,' he said, staring into his Guinness, 'she says I use the job as an excuse not to see her. And, Donna, I'm starting to think she's right.'

It was the moment the alarms should have rung for Donna. After all, it wasn't like she was looking for a serious relationship, or short of offers of company. But she liked Mark. And, besides, they were just friends, weren't they?

That changed on a leaving night for a colleague, who was following the increasingly well-worn path from the newsroom to a PR agency. The night started with drinks in Sloans, then moved to the Merchant City. There was food and more drink. And then more.

Sitting in a cocktail bar in Merchant Square, the crowd thinning out, Donna suddenly realized the time. 'Haven't you missed your train?' she asked Mark.

He gave her the slow, lazy smile of someone who was just pissed enough to be mellow, and leant in close. 'Doesn't matter,' he said. 'I've got a room at the Radisson across from Central. Told Emma I had an early job in town, so they were putting me up for the night. She wasn't happy about it, but . . .' He shrugged, raising his glass in a toast.

Nothing happened that night – Mark didn't push it and Donna didn't want to be the clichéd co-worker who ended up having a drunken fumble with a colleague in a hotel room. But it opened the door to the possibility in her mind, made it slowly solidify into an inevitability.

Six months later, they were sleeping together, and Mark was a semi-regular guest at her flat in Hillhead, on the west of the city. She should have known better – she *did* know better – but something about the illicit thrill of it was addictive: seeing him at work, acting as though nothing was going on, then her leaving and him following her home hours later. His nights in Edinburgh became fewer, until one night, while he was off and she was in the newsroom, she got a text: *I'm in Edinburgh. Miserable. This isn't home any more. I'm going to leave Emma. Want to be with you. xx*

The joy that text unleashed surprised her, as if it destroyed the dam holding back everything she didn't want to think or feel about what she was doing to another woman's life. They talked about it for weeks, planned his move, the perfect time, how they would tell everyone in the office. It was perfect, and Donna saw a new life start to unfold in front of her.

Until the pregnancy test.

She shook her head, the familiar anger glowing like a hot coal in her stomach. Blinked back tears as she looked at his car, then started to walk away. She'd only gone about a hundred yards when her phone beeped. She snatched it out of her bag, expecting it to be Gina or Fiona. The pieces should have aired on Valley and Sky by now, so the bollocking from the police was probably already well under way.

She stopped dead when she saw it was a message from Mark.

Saw you standing outside, understand if you don't want to talk. But this isn't about us, it's about the story. Think I can help you, Donna. I've got an in. I owe you that much at least. Will wait another five minutes then leave. Mx

She stared at the screen, felt a maelstrom of emotions churn within her. Bastard. He always knew the right buttons to push with her. She should walk away, leave him waiting, just like he had done to her and Andrew.

Andrew. She remembered Mark's promises of a new life together, felt the bitterness flare again.

But . . .

She looked down at the screen again. *I've got an in. I owe you that much.*

She chewed her lip, thinking fast. After Ford's little act at the press conference, she wasn't going to get anything else from him, and it was unlikely she could push Danny much further.

I've got an in.

Donna looked up at the afternoon sky and cursed. Then she took a deep breath and felt her face arrange itself into the cold, detached look she normally reserved for her mum. She would see what he had for her. But she would be damned if he'd get even a glimpse of what he had taken from her.

CHAPTER 27

Jennifer MacKenzie lived in a flat in the Woodlands, a development that had been carved out of a patch of ground just off Livilands Lane, a popular suburban area of the city known for its wide streets, large stone-fronted homes and access to good schools. It was a place for families – which might have been why it made Connor uneasy.

She lived on the top floor of a three-storey block tucked away at the rear of the development. The door was a standard intercom and deadlock routine: a visitor would buzz the appropriate flat, speak into the mic and the owner could buzz them in. Connor made a mental note as he pushed Jen's buzzer. She had asked him to give his professional opinion on security at her flat to placate her father. But how much should he tell her? The entry system was fine for day-to-day use, but anyone who really wanted to get inside could circumvent it easily enough. Copy the service key, tailgate a delivery driver inside, wait for the postman, override the system – but there was a fine line between security awareness and paranoia. He thought again of the gun he had held earlier, wondered if he knew where that line was.

The door buzzed and popped open, and he stepped inside to a narrow, well-lit hallway. He looked around, found no lift, which was good. Confined spaces for a target were always a problem, and lifts, especially in residential blocks like this, magnified it. It was all too easy to get into a lift, hit the emergency stop and stick a knife between your victim's ribs.

Connor shook his head, admonishing himself. There it was again. His gran called it his Doomsday gift – the ability to see the worst in any situation. And he couldn't argue. He had a tendency to fatalism, an ability to seek out the worst in every situation and dwell on it. It was like a dark cloud that shaded his thinking, filled every shadow with menace – it sparked his paranoia and the ludicrous thought that Jonny Hughes was somehow involved in the murders across the city. It was a characteristic he didn't like about himself but, he was forced to admit, it was useful in his line of work, where planning for the worst could keep his clients safe, secure, and breathing.

He took the steps to Jen's flat two at a time, gripped by a sudden urge to move, and found her door at the end of a short corridor it shared with one other. He expected the door to open as he approached, her waiting to let him in after buzzing the entry door, but it remained closed. Connor approved. It was an all-too-common mistake. Buzz the main door open, then swing open your own front door without thinking. It took away another possible line of defence, left you open and vulnerable.

He knocked on the door, the sound echoing along the corridor. A heavy lock disengaged, then it swung open.

Connor took a half-step backwards, cursing himself even as he stretched his face into a smile. He was so focused on thinking about Jen's potential vulnerability, he'd forgotten to think about his own.

Stupid. And careless.

A large, heavy-set man was wedged into the doorway, like an adult standing at the entrance to a Wendy house. What he lacked in height – Connor guessed he wasn't much more than five foot four – he more than made up for in width. A dark shirt was stretched tight across a barrel chest and strained at the waistband, the shirt-sleeves rolled up to reveal thick forearms stained with dark tattoos. Wisps of white-blond hair clung defiantly to his head, which gleamed in the light from the hall. He looked Connor up and down, his jaw working soundlessly, a darker, crueller version of his daughter's eyes boring into him.

'Mr MacKenzie,' Connor said, offering his hand. 'Pleased to meet you, sir. I'm Connor Fraser.'

If Jen's father was surprised that Connor knew who he was, he showed no sign of it. He grunted, took a slow step forward, easing the door shut behind him. 'Ah ken who you are, son,' he said, his accent putting him somewhere between Edinburgh and Broxburn to Connor's ear. 'Paulie told me all about you.'

Connor felt tension crawl into his shoulders, the first shot of adrenalin chilling the back of his neck. Shit. 'Just an unfortunate mis-understanding,' he said, keeping his voice as level as his gaze.

'Unfortunate, my arse. You broke three of his fuckin' fingers.'

'Purely in self-defence. I could have done a lot worse.'

Something sparked in MacKenzie's eyes, a flare scudding across a dark sky, and his jaw started to work faster. In the sudden charged silence of the hallway, Connor could have sworn he heard teeth grinding.

After a moment, MacKenzie seemed to deflate, as though whatever had been capering behind his eyes had fled. 'Aye, well, just don't try to be a smart cunt again, okay?'

Connor swallowed down a flash of anger at being told what to do. 'Never my intention, sir, I was just—'

He was cut short by the door swinging open, Jen standing there, giving her father a hard stare. 'Dad,' she said, her voice lyrical with the singsong admonishment only a daughter can give a father, 'I told you to leave it. If Connor said it was self-defence, it was. You know what Paulie's like. He probably asked for it.'

'Aye, he probably did at that,' MacKenzie said, his own voice heavy with the knowledge that he was never going to win this argument. He stretched out a hand to Connor, who returned the hard shake with a smile as empty as MacKenzie's.

'Duncan MacKenzie, pleased to meet you, son,' he said, although he and Connor knew the opposite was true. 'Was just popping in on Jen, see how she was.'

'What he's trying to say is he's just leaving,' Jen said, her eyes taking on some of her father's harsh focus. 'Weren't you, Dad?'

MacKenzie's eyes flitted between Connor and his daughter, torn. Then he took a breath and straightened himself to his full height, such as it was. 'Aye,' he said. 'I guess I am.' He turned back to Jen, kissed her cheek and gave her a clumsy squeeze of a hug. Connor watched as his posture shifted and relaxed, trying to contort his rough exterior into some approximation of tenderness for his little girl.

'See you later, Dad,' Jen whispered into his neck.

MacKenzie took a step back. 'Will do, sweetheart.' He was halfway along the hall when he stopped and turned, as though remembering something he had forgotten. 'I took your advice, by the way,' he said.

'Excuse me?' Connor asked.

'You told Paulie I should look you up. So I did. Sentinel Securities, protection for VIPs, politicians and the like?'

Connor nodded, the joints in his neck feeling as though they were filled with sand. 'Yeah, that's right.'

'Good,' MacKenzie said. 'Because Jen is a VIP. Understood, Fraser?'

Connor let the silence fall between them, his eyes locking with MacKenzie's. There was nothing he liked in that gaze, and everything he recognized. Fury. The overwhelming desire to protect. A pleading not to hurt the person he loved. He'd seen that look before: it had stared back at him from the mirror in Belfast as he tried to wash blood off his shaking hands. 'Understood,' he said, suddenly aware of Jen standing beside him.

'Enough, Dad,' she said. 'Connor's going to give the flat the once-over. And now you know he's a professional. I'll call you later, okay?'

'Okay,' MacKenzie said, his eyes not leaving Connor's.

The flat was bigger than Connor expected, one wall dominated by floor-to-ceiling sliding doors that led to a small balcony and views across Stirling to the Ochil Hills. The place was clean and tidy, almost Spartan in its appearance, giving the impression that Jen had just moved in. That might explain the reason for his visit.

'Sorry about Dad,' she said, as she ushered him to a large leather couch that sat against the wall opposite the sliding doors. 'He's always been over-protective. And after what you did to Paulie . . .' She let the sentence trail off, giving him a look that was half scolding and half encouraging.

'I'm sorry about that, Jen. He turned up at my place, must have followed me home last night. Guess I rubbed him up the wrong way. But he threw the first punch.'

She dipped her chin to her chest, as though making a decision. 'Yeah, Paulie always was a bit of a hothead,' she said. 'Not surprising that he got into trouble. And, to be honest, it might have done me a favour.'

'Oh?' Connor asked. In the pub the night before, she had admitted having her dad's employee watching her was a pain but, ultimately, she'd learnt to live with it. Was this what she'd wanted? To have Paulie taken out of action?

'Yeah,' she said. 'Dad didn't like what you did, but coming from his background, he respects it. Which means he respects you – and your word. So if you have a look around the flat and say it's okay, he's likely to believe you and back off a bit.'

She had asked him the night before if he would take a look at the place. At first, Connor had thought it was a pick-up line, a clumsy way to get him into her flat. But he had quickly realized she'd meant it. Which left only one question. No point in being coy about it. 'And why does your dad want someone to check out your flat?' he asked.

She fidgeted in the seat, the leather squeaking softly as she moved. She dropped her eyes, embarrassment diverting her gaze. 'Well,' she said, hesitant, 'it's just that he does a bit of business across the Central Belt, and sometimes he has to work with people who, ah, play a little rough. I only moved into this place three months ago, and Dad's a bit nervous.'

'Does he need to be?' Connor asked. He had checked up on the MacKenzie name when he'd got in last night. Didn't take long to link it to Duncan MacKenzie of MacKenzie Haulage, a freight company that operated across the Central Belt. A couple of calls to a contact at the Police Scotland call centre at Bilston Glen painted the rest of the picture. With his haulage firm criss-crossing the country, and reaching into Europe, there were rumours that not all of Duncan MacKenzie's cargo was strictly legal. Nothing had ever been proven, despite the police checking, but the off-the-record consensus was that, if it needed moving, MacKenzie would shift it. For a fee. Drugs, porn, booze, fuel, firearms, food, medical supplies, he didn't care. The only thing he wouldn't move, the reports said, was people. But even with that caveat, he would be dealing with those who wouldn't think twice about using his daughter to settle a grievance. Which raised another question Connor had yet to answer for himself.

What was he doing here?

Jen gave a sudden smile. 'Not really,' she said. 'I mean, yeah, okay, once, but I doubt anything will now. Dad's always been overprotective, so I thought you looking at the place might set his mind at ease.'

Connor studied her. He should leave. Stay the hell away from her and Duncan MacKenzie. He'd had one near-miss today and the last thing he needed was more trouble. But then he thought of the alternative, of facing his gran again and wondering if she would recognize him, of clearing her house, the memories and doubts crowding in on him as he packed up a life.

'Okay,' he said, standing. 'Give me the tour. But on one condition.'

Jen gave him a quizzical look.

'When we're done I get to cook you dinner.'

'Depends,' she said.

'On what?'

'Whether the offer comes with the takeaway guarantee. If you're a crap cook I want a pizza. No arguments. And you pay for the stuffed crust as an apology.'

Connor laughed. 'Deal,' he said.

CHAPTER 28

Donna stood outside the Portcullis, watching Mark's car pull away, a strange hollowness in her chest.

It was odd, she thought. She had walked into the pub, anger and defiance churning in her gut, but when she'd seen him sitting at a table near the bar, she had felt it drain away, replaced by something she couldn't quite name. He still looked the same, tall, lithe, with sharp features and a swarthy complexion, but there was a . . . vacancy about him. As though something vital had been stolen. She felt a stab of savage glee, then a flash of self-loathing as she found herself hoping it was losing her that had done this to him.

He gave a faltering smile as she approached, pushed a drink across the table towards her. They exchanged pleasantries, Donna keeping it brusque, businesslike. There was a conversation they weren't having, both of them dancing around it, like fighters trying to get the measure of an opponent, neither willing to make the opening gambit. But it was a conversation they had to have. About Andrew. About whether Mark would have any role in his son's life.

When Mark saw that Donna's attitude wasn't going to thaw, he abandoned the affable pretence and got down to business. He told her a story. One she barely believed. One that made her want to kiss and slap him at the same time.

'I'm telling you this as I owe you,' he had told her at the end.

Standing in the car park now, she knew that for the bullshit it was. He had told her because he needed her to break the story so he and everyone else could follow. Let the freelancer take the heat – didn't matter, the story would be in the public domain and every news organization in the country could follow up on it. He dressed it up as her continuing to lead on it, showing she could break exclusive lines for the nationals, but he was using her. She hated him for it, hated herself more for admiring the way he was manipulating the news cycle, moving her like a chess piece to get to the story he wanted to write.

She looked down at the pad she still held and scanned the notes she had made, focusing on the name she had written in the centre of the page and circled. Beside it, there was one word, underlined three times, surrounded by question marks. She read it again, felt the magnitude press down on her.

She took her phone from her bag and called the number, a shudder twisting down her spine as she gazed along the cobbled street, past the entrance to the cemetery and towards Cowane's Hospital.

The call was answered. 'Donna, I really can't—'

'Danny,' she said, cutting him off. 'I'm calling you as a favour, giving you ten minutes' head start on this, okay?'

'Wh-what do you mean?' he asked, his tone telling her he didn't want to know.

She felt excitement crackle through her veins. 'As soon as I hang up on you, I'm going to call Ford,' she said, unable to keep the smile off her face, even as her stomach churned with revulsion. 'And I'm going to ask him two questions. On the record. And believe me, Danny, he's going to come to you asking how to answer them. I'm going to ask him to confirm that the first victim was found to have a well-known Loyalist tattoo on his body, and that reports he was found decapitated in the grounds of Cowane's Hospital yesterday morning are true.'

Danny's voice was a strangled yelp of panic. 'Fuck's sake! Donna, how did you— You can't! The chief, he'll, well—'

'Danny, calm down. You're missing the point. This is good news for you.'

'Oh? And how the fuck do you get that?'

'Because, Danny, if he pushes me, I'll confirm that my source for this is not within Randolphfield or anyone else in Police Scotland's Forth Valley Division. Which puts you in the clear with Ford and the chief. And better than that, Danny, we're even. So do what you need to do. Get your lines ready, because I'll be calling Ford in ten minutes.'

CHAPTER 29

Connor enjoyed the heft of the knife in his hand as he chopped vegetables, the sound of the blade on the wooden board as he sliced the onions and diced the garlic oddly satisfying. From the living room, he heard the faint pop of a cork followed by the soft glug of wine into glasses, smiled to himself as he worked.

The check of Jen's flat hadn't taken long – the truth was, there wasn't much to see. Two bedrooms, two bathrooms, the open-plan kitchen/living room. Security-wise, it was a straightforward story: the entry door was adequate, as long as no one decided to leave it on the latch for friends or deliverymen. She knew not to open her front door without checking who was there. The balcony was a slight concern but, at three floors up and with a high guard rail, it was an unlikely point of entry.

Connor banished the thought, focused on his cooking. He had done as asked, and hoped his word would be enough to ease the paranoid fears of Duncan MacKenzie. Despite his reputation, surely he wasn't associated with anything serious enough to endanger his daughter. His employees, maybe – the way he had accepted what had happened to Paulie told Connor he was ready for such losses – but Jen? No. Connor didn't think so.

She came into the kitchen carrying a glass of red. After finishing his sweep of the flat, they had ventured out to the nearby Morrison's, Connor driving. He was surprised how much he enjoyed the simple act of wandering the aisles with her, picking up food. It was a chore he normally hated, putting it off until there was nothing left in the flat, but there was something about the prosaic nature of the errand that soothed him, reinforced his sense that the nightmare was over.

'Thanks,' he said, taking the glass and raising it in a toast. Sipped. Not bad, but he'd have to watch what he was doing if he was going to drive home later.

If.

'You sure I can't do anything to help?' she asked, peering over his shoulder at the array of chopped vegetables and meat. He was making a Thai green curry, one of the few dishes he knew how to make from memory. He enjoyed cooking, but the pleasure for him was in following the recipes as closely as possible, letting the cookbook make the decisions for him.

'Nope, just relax. It'll take me about half an hour.'

'Perfect,' she said, smiling over her wine glass. 'I'll put some music on.'

Connor went back to his work. Heard music drift into the kitchen from the living area a moment later.

'This okay?' Jen called.

'It's fine,' Connor replied. He didn't really care. Music for him was mainly for distraction, something to take his mind off the pain in his body as he trained or drown out the silence in the car as he drove.

He lost himself in cooking. After a few minutes, the jingle for the local station played, followed by the announcer saying it was time for the news.

'Investigations are continuing into two deaths in and around Stirling in two days, with further details emerging on both cases. This from our reporter Donna Blake.'

The station cut to Donna, her voice warped by the static of blowing wind. Connor wondered if that was intentional, to give the impression that she was on the scene as she spoke.

'The discovery of a body in the grounds of Stirling University was the second in two days, coming after police were called to Cowane's Hospital at the top of the town in the early hours of yesterday morning. While they have yet to comment on the bodies, or formally identify either of the victims, I understand that the first body was found to be severely mutilated and police are working on a solid line of enquiry regarding the victim's identity.

'Less is known about the body found this morning at the Stirling Court Hotel on the university campus, but sources have stated that police are pursuing a firm line of enquiry relating to a dedication found in a book nearby.'

Connor froze, the knife hanging in mid-air, the spitting of the wok forgotten. *Don't say it*, a voice whispered in his mind. *Christ, please, don't say it.*

'The dedication, written in a copy of *Misery*, by Stephen King, alludes to the book being a different edition of the same story, and is signed as "from L". Any listeners who are familiar with this, or think they may know who owned such a book, are encouraged to call . . .'

Connor didn't hear the rest of the report. It was as if God had wrapped His hands around his head and was squeezing. He felt an enormous pressure behind his eyes, heard a rising whine in his ears. The world seemed to lurch and spin, and he reached out to lean on the kitchen work surface, the knife clattering to the floor.

Jen came in, concern sketched across her too-pale face. Her voice seemed to come from a thousand miles away. 'Connor? You okay? God, you didn't cut yourself, did you? You look like you've just seen a ghost.' She bustled past him and moved the wok, which was starting to smoke, from the ring. 'Come on,' she said, touching his arm. 'Let's go and sit down.'

He let her lead him to the living room, sat heavily on the couch. He felt as though his lungs were filling with gravel, found it hard to breathe. Looked at her. 'What did that reporter say just now?' he asked, mouth as dry as sandpaper.

'I wasn't really listening,' she said. 'Look, Connor, what's going on? Do you need a doctor?'

He felt laughter rise in his throat. Swallowed it. A doctor? No, that was the last thing he needed. What he needed was lying in the dark in a safe under his bed. Somehow Simon had been wrong and Connor had been right, just as he had known from the moment he saw that fucking book on the TV.

Not the same edition, but the same horror story . . . L.

He pushed aside the desperate thought that this could all be a coincidence, knowing it for the hysterical lie that it was. Whatever was going on, it was all connected to Jonny Hughes. The book was a message for Connor, just as it had been in Belfast.

Connor seized on the thought, hugged it close. Felt his confusion and panic dissolve, replaced by a fury that seeped through him, darkening the shadows of his thoughts, shrinking his vision to a sharp focal point.

No. He had been down this road once before. In Belfast, he had let that message ruin his life. It had cost him his fiancée, his home. His future.

Not this time. Not again. Message received. And this time, whoever had sent it, even if it was Jonny Hughes somehow reaching out from beyond the grave, would pay.

CHAPTER 30

Ford stood in a hastily requisitioned office at Randolphfield, staring at the wall-mounted TV. The chief was in front of it, arms crossed, glaring. Danny was close to the door, watching Guthrie intently, as though he were some wild animal that was about to leap at him and tear his throat out at any moment. Given what they had just seen, Ford guessed the odds of that actually happening were fairly even.

At least, he thought, Danny had warned him the call from Blake was coming, which had given him time to get his anger out of the way, allowed him to handle it professionally. He had stonewalled her questions on Billy Griffin and the extent of his injuries, managed to persuade her to be vague in her report with the promise of further insights as the case progressed. It was an expedient lie that got him – and the investigation – out of an immediate and very dark hole.

But the question remained: who had told her? He had pressed her on where she'd got the information on Griffin and what had been found at the Stirling Court, threatened her with every charge he could think of, to no avail. All she would say was that none of the information she had was provided by anyone in Forth Valley or directly linked to the investigation.

Looking at Danny now, and the wary anxiety with which he was watching Guthrie, Ford almost believed her.

'So, gentlemen,' Guthrie said, eyes not moving from the television, 'what do you suggest we do next?'

Danny surprised Ford by speaking first. 'Well, sir,' he said, his voice as anxious as his gaze, 'it's not as bad as it might have been. I understand Blake did a report for the local radio station as well as the TV piece we've just seen, and if she kept the details we asked her to withhold out of that as well, I think this is a result. The story is out, we're seen to be working on the investigation, and this could jog memories and help us identify the second victim.'

'That's hardly the fucking point, is it, Brooks?' Guthrie said. 'The fact that this information got out at all is an absolute disgrace.' His eyes slid from Danny to Ford. 'Tell me, DCI Ford, just what type of investigation are you running here?'

Ford bit back the answer he wanted to give. So it was *his* investigation again, was it? At the press conference, Guthrie had all but said it would be handed over to Special Investigations, with him pulling the strings. Now that the shit was hitting the fan again, it was Ford's problem to deal with.

'Sir,' he said, keeping his tone neutral, looking at a point just over Guthrie's shoulder to ensure he stayed calm, 'with all due respect, my officers and I are doing the best we can. We're running the ID checks on the second victim as fast as resources allow, and we're double-checking with Glasgow about Griffin's last known whereabouts. We're also pulling all available CCTV footage to try to . . .'

Guthrie waved him into silence. 'Yes, yes,' he said. 'That's all well and good, but we need some bloody results. I've already had Ken Ferguson breathing down my neck, and at this rate I'll have the First Minister knocking at my door by the end of the day. This is not good, DCI Ford, not good at all.'

Despite himself, Ford felt a sliver of sympathy for Guthrie. The justice secretary, Ken Ferguson, had not had an easy time since he'd been given the job three months ago. With the government being constantly beaten over the head by political opponents and the press about the well-publicized problems at Police Scotland – and the matter of how a previous chief constable had left due to some of his more hands-on working practices – the service was a constant headache for Ferguson. He was known for his temper, enjoyed shouting down senior officers, who were stripped of their own authority the moment they walked into his office. It had gained him a nickname among the ranks: Fuck You Ferguson. And he would be looking for someone to blame for this mess, especially with that bitch Blake putting it all on show.

'Sir, you know what these cases are like – long hours and legwork. We're increasing foot patrols in the centre of town and around the castle area to reassure residents and tourists, and we're using every channel we have to get information. With Special Investigations taking a role, that should give us more manpower to help speed things up.'

Guthrie nodded, then turned his attention to Danny. 'Get this managed, son,' he said. 'I don't care what it takes, but no more fucking leaks, understood? Bad enough this got out, even if we managed to exert a modicum of control, but no more. Clear?'

'Totally, sir,' Danny said.

'Right. Get on it,' Guthrie said, as he pulled his hat so tightly onto his head that it forced his ears down. 'And, Ford, the moment you have anything . . .'

'I'll let you know, sir, though I take it you'll be at the update briefing later?'

'Actually, no. I have to update Fu– Ferguson, so I won't attend.'

Bastard, Ford thought. Trying to put some space between himself and the case while it was toxic. Typical politician.

'Very good, sir. Can I see you out?'

'No need. Brooks here can do that,' Guthrie replied. Ford was sure he saw Danny flinch.

'Uh . . . Of course, sir,' Danny said, swinging the door open.

When they had left, Ford closed his eyes and took a moment to soak in the silence. He wanted to go home. Wanted bed. Sleep. To see Mary. Instead, he had this, and no end in sight. 'Miles to go,' he muttered.

His mobile chirped in his pocket, forcing him from his thoughts.

'Troughton?' He listened, felt tension bunch his shoulders as the detective sergeant spoke.

'We've got an ID on the second victim. It's Helen Russell.'

'Who? I know that name, why would I . . .'

'She's a councillor, sir, Tory, Stirling North. Reported missing by her husband an hour ago. He thought she was away at a party event at the Parliament in Edinburgh, got worried when she didn't come home and she didn't answer her mobile.'

Ford felt his mouth go dry. Fuck. A councillor. A public figure. More headlines. That was the last thing he needed.

'Okay,' he said, the information hitting him like a shot of caffeine. 'Get everyone assembled. Case conference in one hour. Run her name with Griffin's, see if there are any connections. I doubt there will be, but the chief will ask.'

'Yes, sir. Anything else?'

'Not for now. I'll be back down shortly,' Ford said, and killed the call.

He stood for a moment, considering his phone, trying to order his thoughts. One came to him, randomly, and he spoke in the silence: 'Helen Russell. So who the hell is Connie?'

CHAPTER 31

Connor sat in his flat, mind racing with possibilities, each less attractive than the last. He knew the call would cause him trouble, but he didn't care. He needed information. Badly. And Lachlan Jameson could get it for him. He'd proven that the day they'd first met.

It was a month after everything had gone wrong in Belfast. Connor was back home, opting to rent a crappy flat just off Leith Walk in Edinburgh rather than living in Stirling, which, after the death of his mother, felt like a ghost-ridden no man's land in the ongoing war of silence between him and his father. He was mostly living off his savings, but the money was fast running out, and the side income he was making from giving personal training sessions at a high-class hotel on the Bridges wasn't cutting it.

He was on his way to one of those classes, resigned to spending an hour with a bored housewife – too much money, too little class and too much oestrogen – as he put her through her paces in the gym. He had already decided he would up the weights, intensify the cardio. It wasn't going to be the type of sweat she was hoping to work up with him, but it was the best she was going to get.

He was just walking up the Bridges admiring, as he always did, the view across the roof of Waverley station to the Scott Monument and the castle when his phone rang, an unrecognized number on the screen.

'Hello.' No names. Not for an unknown caller. Let them make the first move.

'Hello,' a voice boomed, the bass accentuating the clipped elocution. 'Connor Fraser?'

'Who is this?'

'Mr Fraser, I'm Lachlan Jameson, and I'd like to discuss an opportunity with you.'

He'd met him a day later, at the office of Sentinel Securities in a nondescript industrial park tucked behind the Gyle shopping centre. Against his better judgement, Connor found he liked the man straight away. He was tall and thin, given extra height and presence by the way he constantly seemed to be standing to attention, shoulders thrust back, spine ramrod straight, chest out. With his tweed suit, impeccable grooming and angular, almost hawkish features, he might as well have had 'ex-army' tattooed across his forehead.

The meeting was like Jameson's haircut: short, efficient, straight to the point. Connor was ushered into a corner office with windows for walls, the view of the industrial estate drab, the perfunctory greenery that had been dotted around to make it look less brutal only enhancing its functional appearance.

'Please,' he said, gesturing Connor to take a seat.

Connor took the chair directly opposite Jameson, who had barricaded himself behind a huge oak desk that was out of place with the cool, modern elegance of the rest of the offices but seemed to fit the room, and its occupant, perfectly.

'So,' he said, lacing his fingers together. 'I take it you've done a little background on us by now, Mr Fraser. What do you think?'

Connor smiled slightly. First test. Did you do your homework? 'Impressive,' he said. 'You've been running Sentinel for the last ten years, since you retired from the army and took a stint in private contracting, mostly in the Middle East, protecting oil execs from jihadis and kidnap threats. Since then, you've "built Sentinel into one of the most prestigious private and close security firms in the country".'

Jameson dipped his head, acknowledging the quote Connor had lifted from the company website, and the background detail on his military career he definitely had not. From what his contacts and background research told him, Lachlan Jameson was an enthusiastic private-sector operative. Connor had been coy in his description, but he'd been given enough hints that the man in front of him wasn't purely a protector. If the money was right, he could turn his hand to hunting too.

'We work with politicians, high-net-worth individuals, VIPs, diplomats. We offer a range of personal-security solutions, from escorting to reconnaissance and close protection. And I think this is where you come in, Mr Fraser.'

'How so?' Connor said, asking the question that had been plaguing him since the call the previous day. He had others too: how had Jameson got his number? How had he even known he was back in Scotland? But those would come later.

Jameson leant back in his chair. 'A large part of this business is intelligence, Mr Fraser,' he said, with a precision that told Connor he had given this speech before. 'Knowing which assets are on the board at any time. I have contacts. One of them reached out to me, told me that a talented officer with a bright future had abruptly abandoned a career with the Police Service of Northern Ireland to return home. He tells me the official reason was family bereavement, but I think we can dispense with that formality, can't we?'

Connor felt as though he had just been stabbed with a shard of ice. He blinked away the memory of Belfast, of air scalding his lungs as he fought for breath, his fists numb and blood-soaked, a crumpled body gurgling and moaning at his feet. 'I, ah . . .'

Jameson raised a hand. 'As I said, unimportant. You did what you thought was right. Took direct action. I appreciate that. But the fact remains, here you are, squandering your training and talent. My question is, would you be willing to use them for me?'

He had made the job offer on the spot, and Connor had taken a day to accept it. In that time he called every contact he still trusted in Belfast to see who had spoken about him – every one of them had come back with the same answer: Not us, but this guy must be connected.

Connor hoped that was the case now. He needed it to be.

He called the number. Waited.

'Connor. Nice to hear from you. Where's that report you owe me?'

He screwed his eyes shut, ground the cool of the gun butt against his temple. 'Lachlan, sorry about that. I'll get to it, I promise. But right now, I need a favour.'

'Oh, really?' Jameson said, irritation creeping into his tone. Connor could understand it. As a former lieutenant colonel, Lachlan Jamieson was used to having orders followed promptly. For an employee to ask a favour without completing an assignment was anathema to him.

'Yes, Lachlan. Please. I wouldn't ask if it wasn't urgent.'

A soft grunt at the other end of the line as Jameson sat in his office chair. 'Urgency is relative, Connor,' he said. 'Tell me what this is about, and I'll see what I can do.'

Connor paused for a second. How much could he tell him? How much *would* he tell him? He took a deep breath. 'I take it you've been keeping up with the news, the murders here?'

'Yes, indeed I have.' A pause, then humour lightened his tone. 'Don't tell me you're taking it personally and have decided to go vigilante on home ground?'

Connor grated out a laugh. 'Nothing like that, but there's something about the university murder that got me thinking. And I was wondering if you had anyone in the local police force I could talk to. With all your contacts, I thought you must know someone.'

He waited, hoping his pandering to Jameson's ego hadn't been too obvious.

'Hmm . . . There may be someone I could put you in touch with, but my question, again, is why? This doesn't concern you, Connor, and the last thing I need is an employee of Sentinel Securities making a mess in two murder investigations. Our clients demand discretion, remember?'

'Of course,' Connor said. 'Call it professional curiosity, but there's something I want to verify. I'll keep it quiet, Lachlan, I promise.'

'Very well.' Jameson sighed. 'I'll indulge you this once. I have someone in mind and I'll get them to call you shortly. This number okay?'

'Fine,' Connor agreed, trying to keep the edge of impatience out of his tone. How long was 'shortly'? The longer he waited, the closer

Hughes, or whoever it was, could be getting. He needed answers. Now.

'Very well. But, Connor, you realize there's a price to be paid for this?'

Connor tightened his grip on the gun. 'No problem, Lachlan. I'll have that report to you within the hour. And thanks, I owe you.'

'Yes,' Jameson said bluntly. 'You do. Just remember that, Connor.'

CHAPTER 32

Matt Evans languished in a place beyond terror, his thoughts shattered into a thousand jagged shards, each one slashing at his sanity as it formed then dissolved.

He was dead. He'd known that much from the moment his captor had loomed over him, those dead eyes boring into him as he held an iPad up to eye level and scrolled through the coverage of the Cowane's Hospital murder. He said nothing, the only sound his breathing, the silence of the room stretched taut by his presence. It had taken only moments for Evans to break the silence, his desperate, incoherent pleas echoing off the walls of his prison, accompanied by the clang of the chain around his foot as he bucked and thrashed, begging to be freed. He'd felt no shame as he babbled hysterically, his nostrils filling with the hot, rancid smell of his own piss. Shame was infinitely preferable to the agonies that could be visited on him at any moment.

Dead, empty eyes that seemed somehow to draw in the darkness of the room watched him. Then, with a smile that was little more than a baring of teeth, the monster knelt before him, drawing an object from a pocket.

When Evans saw what it was, understanding flooded his mind in a caustic torrent. It was as though he had been possessed by terror and the object had triggered an exorcism. He writhed and bucked and screamed, oblivious to the shackle around his ankle biting into his flesh and becoming slick with his own blood.

When the hand touched his forehead, he froze. His eyes bulged, his mouth worked soundlessly, trying to articulate a scream too big to be released. Warm fingers traced a path across his forehead in an obscenely intimate caress. He almost didn't hear the gentle 'Ssh,' his ears ringing from his own scream. But he heard what was said next, a question he had known was coming.

'You know what I want?'

He had nodded, eager to please, the thought of the object he had been shown flashing in his mind. He could imagine it biting into him, tearing, gouging, rending. He would do anything, *tell everything*, to avoid that.

He had been left then, alone with his thoughts and the memory of those headlines. 'Murder in Stirling'. 'Victims suffered prolonged, savage attack'. He pleaded to a God he didn't believe in, wept for his own wasted life and the days the headlines had told him would now never be.

Time lost all meaning to him. How long had he been left alone in the dark, with only his nightmares for company? Hours? Minutes? Days? A sudden thought seized him, hope swelling in his chest. Perhaps the police had caught him. Perhaps he wasn't coming back. A giddying wave of claustrophobia crashed through him, the thought of dying in the dark from hunger or dehydration seizing him. But even in this, there was relief. It would be a better end than the one he had been promised.

The fragile hope he nurtured was crushed by the sound of footsteps. Evans listened to them, the floorboards above creaking with his captor's weight. Then they stopped, and the silence rushed in on him again.

And in that silence, he heard one word. It tormented and terrified him, filled him with ever-escalating nightmares.

'Soon.'

CHAPTER 33

The call was an unwelcome surprise, triggering a frantic panic that made him feel as though the walls were closing in on him. The phone buzzed against his chest, insistent, and he pawed for it as though it was a burning coal.

He hit the answer button, clamped it to his ear, a thousand thoughts tumbling through his mind. 'H-hello?'

'Good afternoon.' The same voice, formal, businesslike, as though the devil himself had started making insurance calls. 'I take it you've seen the latest news.'

'Ah, yes. I have. But why are you calling? Is there a problem with the payment or—'

'No, the payment was fine. But I wanted to tell you there's been a slight change of plan.'

Another stab of panic, the phone growing heavy in his hand. 'What? What change of plan? I thought we agreed.'

'We did. But then I started thinking. While there's no risk of exposure, it couldn't hurt to muddy the waters a little.'

He felt as though the world was tilting, the floor threatening to fall away beneath him. 'W-what do you mean?'

A glint of humour, jagged and cruel, coloured the normally businesslike tone. 'You'll see soon enough. Just keep watching the news. Stick to your routine, keep your head down. And, trust me, you'll like this. It'll really give you something to talk about.'

The line went dead and he stared at the phone. His gorge rose, his stomach giving a watery lurch. He swallowed, forced himself to breathe, then smoothed down his tie with a hand that was almost steady. He reached for the door to ask Margaret to arrange his next appointment.

The caller was right. He had no option but to go on as normal, keep up the lie he had been living for so long. He would see what was planned soon enough. And when it happened, when he had 'something to talk about', he would do what he always did.

He would adapt. And survive.

CHAPTER 34

The discovery of Helen Russell's identity was like stabbing a syringe of adrenalin into the heart of the investigation. It galvanized resources and drew the attention of those who were content to keep the whole mess at arm's length when it was only an unidentified woman and a low-level thug who had been brutally beaten and slain. But when it was discovered that the second victim was a long-standing member of the Scottish Tories, everything was cast into a new light. Griffin's cheap tattoo and political background suddenly became a major line of enquiry, the manner of both deaths a cause for concern in the corridors of power.

Ford felt a strange mix of fury and weary acceptance when he and Chief Superintendent Doyle were summoned by the chief constable. He'd known what was coming the moment the case conference was cancelled. He told himself it was nothing personal.

Everything was political, these days.

'Given the profile of Mrs Russell, and the possible Loyalist link to the Griffin murder, it has been decided that Special Investigations will liaise with Special Branch, which will now be leading on both investigations,' Guthrie told Ford and Doyle, in the same cramped room where he had been briefed by Danny less than two hours before. He seemed smaller to Ford, diminished somehow, the only part of him showing any lustre was the epaulettes on his uniform, which winked in the glare of the strip lighting overhead.

'DCI Ford, if you could prepare your casework for transfer. You may need, of course, to second some of your officers depending on workloads, but your primary responsibility will be to ensure a smooth and efficient handover, and facilitate any request Special Branch may have.'

Ford kept his breathing steady as he murmured agreement, an image of Billy Griffin's mutilated head flashing across his mind. He knew all too well what Guthrie's order meant. Give up your office, get out of the way. Prepare to have your staff assigned every shit detail and piece of legwork going. The big boys are coming to town to show the local yokels how it's done. 'Of course, sir,' he managed, ignoring the sharp look from Doyle beside him.

Guthrie held his gaze for a moment, as though confirming something for himself. Then he straightened his back, as though the action would inject some authority into his voice. It didn't.

'You will, of course, keep yourself available at all times tomorrow in case Mr Ferguson wishes to speak to you and discuss your work on the case up to this point.'

Ford winced, hoped it didn't show on his face. Ferguson. It explained why Guthrie looked and sounded like a child who had just had his favourite toy taken away. Two murders in two days was a bad headline at any time, but given the negative press the police service had been experiencing recently, it had been seized on not only by the press but the politicians too.

Danny, who was doing his best to prove himself invaluable after the whole Donna Blake cluster-fuck, was providing Ford with regular updates on how the story was playing out. The short answer was badly, which made sense of Ferguson's imminent visit. He wanted – needed – to be seen to be taking charge of the situation, show that he could rise above politics to find a merciless killer and keep all the precious voters of Stirling safe. More importantly, Ferguson's visit would give him the perfect opportunity to find a scapegoat for this mess, deflect it away from the government's management of Police Scotland, the lack of resources and the overstretched staff, back onto the shoulders of the officers who were on the ground.

Ford was going to make sure it wouldn't be him.

Message delivered, Guthrie dismissed them. They were walking along a narrow corridor when Doyle's pocket buzzed. He pulled out his phone without breaking stride, clamped it to his ear and snapped a greeting in a tone that said he almost hoped it was bad news, something or someone to focus his frustration on.

It wasn't. He stopped dead, surprising Ford, who continued down the hall for a couple of steps before he registered what had happened. He turned, closed the gap between them, a silent question pulling his eyebrows high on his forehead. Doyle held up a silencing hand.

'Yes . . . No. Of course. I understand. But you have to realize . . . No. Not at all. How could I? . . . No problem. Text me the details.' He ended the call, gazed at the phone. It buzzed a moment later, the text he had mentioned being delivered.

'Sir?'

Doyle looked up, as though startled from a daydream.

'Sir, are you all right? Was that—'

Doyle held up his hand again. His eyes darted around Ford's face as he stared at him, a nerve pulsing in his jaw. Then his gaze hardened into a decision. 'I've got a favour to ask, Ford,' he said, his voice as still as his stare. 'There's someone I need you to talk to.'

CHAPTER 35

Donna was back at her desk at Valley FM, trying to ignore the flashing lights that danced across her phone, showing the calls waiting. Across the newsroom, she could see Gina pacing around her office, gesticulating wildly as she spoke into a mobile.

She'd managed to co-ordinate her reports, giving the exclusive to Valley first over the phone, then meeting the Sky cameraman at Cowane's Hospital and doing the piece to camera. She couldn't have asked for a better backdrop – the police still standing sentry, passers-by and tourists milling around, curiosity outweighing their fear. After the live feed, she had grabbed a couple for vox pops, asking what they thought of the murders, did they feel safe? It was predictable human-interest crap and she hated it, but she knew that it was just the type of meaningless filler Sky would need while they waited for the next big headline.

And there would be one. Donna was sure of it.

Her phone had started ringing almost as soon as the story broke. Old colleagues from the *Westie*, the BBC, even CNN and the Press Association all asking if she had any leads, if she was still stringing and able to provide content. She stood, letting the moment wash over her. So what if Mark had used her to get what he wanted? She had what she wanted as well. She was back, breaking a story, leading the pack.

The euphoria lasted until she was halfway back to the Valley office

– Gina insisting she come in so they could co-ordinate her workload. 'I've got no problem with you punting the story around other outlets,' she told Donna, 'but I need to know I can count on you, especially since that stupid fucker Matt is still AWOL.'

She'd made the mistake of not screening her calls on the mobile, caught up in the moment of being in demand again. Thumbed the answer key on the steering wheel, heard a wash of static fill the car, followed by the soft gurgling of a baby.

Andrew.

'Hello? Mum? Is everything all right? Is Andrew okay?'

'Yes, dear,' her mum replied. 'He's fine. We saw you on the TV and you looked great.'

Donna frowned at the steering wheel, off balance. Disapproval, passive aggression, these she could take from her mother, had learnt to expect. But praise? It sent a tremor of alarm through her gut. 'Eh, thanks. Could do better, but I'll get there.'

'Yes, dear, I'm sure you will. But from the sound of it you're in the car. Is that you heading home now?'

Donna ground her teeth, bit back a curse. Of course. She should have known. 'I'm heading back to the office just now, Mum, got a couple of things to wrap up. But I shouldn't be too much longer. Is that okay?'

A grumble down the phone. 'It'll have to be, won't it? Donna, it's not that we mind having Andrew, but he's hardly seen you today, and the boy needs his mum.'

Donna tightened her grip on the steering wheel, trying to drown out the part of her deep inside that was murmuring agreement with her mother, the part of her that would look down on her child as he slept in stunned wonder and wanted nothing more than to hold him close to her breast, get lost in his warmth and smell. But what would she be if she did that? Just another stay-at-home mum, her dreams and ambitions sidelined, replaced by an endless routine of nappy changes, nursery collections and visits to the soft play.

No. Not for her. She was doing this for them both. Rebuilding her career and her life, showing her son that, no matter what happened, you did not give up on what you really wanted.

If she concentrated, she could almost make herself believe it.

She took a deep, steadying breath. 'Mum, I'm sorry,' she said. 'But this story is big. You saw me today, Sky News. And they want more. I just need to straighten a couple of things out at the station, then I'll be home. Promise. It's not like I don't miss Andrew too.'

Her mother murmured something that could almost have been genuine agreement. 'Well, all right.' She sighed, her tone heavy with the weary disappointment she had perfected over the last thirty-four years. 'I'll have something in the oven for you.'

'Thanks,' Donna said, killing the call.

She arrived at Valley to find the newsroom in chaos. Every phone line was clogged with callers desperate to identify the second victim or claim responsibility for one or both murders. And, to top it all, Gina told her that Matt Evans was still AWOL, and they had no idea if he was going to make the evening phone-in.

Donna watched as Gina finished whatever call she was making, then stalked out of her office. She felt a shiver of unease as she realized she was heading straight for her.

'Days like this, I really fucking wish I hadn't given up drinking,' Gina said, her face pulled into a tight smile.

Donna smiled back at her. 'Tough call?' she asked, nodding towards Gina's office.

Gina barked a laugh that drew a few glances from around the room. 'You could say that. High heidyins from MediaSound's board-room. They wanted to make sure we were watertight on your story – seems the police have been on at them again, accusing you of jeop-ardizing the investigation.'

Donna had been expecting this. She knew that was why Mark had given her the tip – to let her be the one to break it and take the heat. Luckily, Ford had been smart enough not to deny anything and, in return, Donna had agreed to water down the content of her report. It made for an uneasy truce, but with the added attention, the police had to be seen to be going through the moves, which was why their lawyers had been so quick off the mark.

'It's solid,' she said, her cheeks starting to burn. 'The contact I got the information from is reliable. Besides, everyone will be all over it now – the moment they identify the second body, we'll move on to that and this will be a gruesome footnote.'

'About that,' Gina said, 'you got anything you can give me?'

'Not yet, but as soon as I have, I will. Sky still want me to do the follows for them as well.'

Gins pushed her glasses up her face, massaged her eyes. 'Look, Donna, I understand. You're freelance, you have to go where the money and the exposure are. But just remember who put you on air when you needed it, okay? Especially at the moment . . .'

Donna brushed off the slight. It was true. When Mark had sloped back to his wife, Gina had stepped forward and offered her the freelance contract. It had been enough to build up some savings, and give her a job to come back to when Andrew was born. 'So, Matt?' she said, trying to divert the conversation to safer ground.

Gina sneered. 'Useless bastard,' she hissed. 'I don't care that he was a big shot in Edinburgh, he's been a fucking liability here.'

Donna had heard the stories about Matt Evans. A shock jock talkshow specialist, who peppered his shows with profanity, humour and just the right amount of wolf-whistle controversy to win him regular tabloid coverage and an army of unnervingly loyal fans. But then came the 2014 independence referendum, and his on-air rant about which Unionists he was sure would be 'better together' with a baseball bat, a rabid dog or 'a woman who really hates a big Johnson'.

The firestorm of protest following the broadcast, which named as many high-profile politicians as it hinted at, had got him fired from his radio show on Edinburgh's EBA FM, and the late-night TV show at the local STV offshoot that he fronted. But in another fine example of shit floating, he had survived and, somehow, got a job at Valley FM. Donna hated knowing that they had that in common – both refugees from a mistake, finding sanctuary in Valley FM when no one else would take them. 'Anything I can help with?' she asked, blinking away the thought.

'Fancy doing his show tonight?' Gina asked, a half-smile twitching her lips. 'You're topic of the day anyway, and it's good exposure.'

Donna paused, thinking hard. The evening talk-show ran from

ten p.m. to two a.m., covering the stories of the day, a phone-in and topical guests. Okay, it was only local, but imagine what it could do for her show reel! She could see the line now – Donna Blake, reporter and presenter. And where would that lead?

Her mother's voice echoed in her mind, derailing the fantasy. *Andrew needs his mum.*

'Nah, I'd better not,' she said reluctantly. 'I need to get home.'

Gina murmured resigned agreement. 'Worth a shot,' she said.

She was about ten feet away when Donna called to her, 'If you get really stuck, let me know, okay? I'll see what I can do.'

Gina waved in acknowledgement, then walked away. Donna watched her go, a bilious mix of excitement and rage roiling in her gut. She snatched at her mobile when it rang, frustration curdling at the back of her throat when she saw the number calling. She hit answer and clamped it to her ear as she headed for the door. 'Wait,' she said.

She banged through the double doors of the station, took a left and followed a path to the back of the building, where cigarette butts lay puddled around a bin, denoting the unofficial smokers' area. She could almost taste the acrid tang of smoke on her tongue, feel the desiccated burn in her lungs. She hadn't smoked for ten years but in that moment she wanted a cigarette.

'OK. What?'

'Story seemed to go well,' Mark said, his tone somewhere between hesitant and triumphant. 'Just wanted to check in.'

She breathed hard, closed her eyes. What the fuck did he want? Another thank-you? 'Got another tip for me?' she asked. 'Or have I taken enough heat for you and the rest of the press for one day?'

'Donna, I . . .'

She sighed, felt weariness press down on her shoulders. 'Look, Mark, I'm grateful for the lead. It's helped. But if you've nothing else for me—'

His words came out in a rush: 'Well, it's just that I'm going to be covering this now. With the way you blew the lid off it, everyone wants a piece of the story. So I'm going to be in Stirling for the next few days, staying in town.'

Donna felt a twist of heat, her heart beating faster. She knew where this was going. She should hang up now.

'. . . was wondering if I could see you and Andrew at some point.'

She stared hard at the overflowing bin, felt an urge to charge forward and kick it over. She spoke as if on auto-pilot. 'Why? Why do you want to see him now, Mark?'

'Well, he is my son.'

Despite herself, she laughed. Hated the hard, bitter edge she heard in her voice. 'Your son? He was your son up until the moment you shit yourself when you found out I was pregnant, Mark. He was your son right up until the moment you scurried back to Emma rather than having the balls to be a father. Christ, was that what today was about? Throw me a bone and somehow all would be forgiven?'

'Donna, I didn't think – didn't mean—'

'Forget it,' she said, weariness replacing the burst of anger. 'You did me a favour today. I did you one in return. Call it old times' sake. But stay away from us, Mark. For Andrew if not for me. You made your choice. Live with it.'

She killed the call before he could answer, dropped the phone to her side as though it was made of lead. The rubbish bin doubled, then trebled, as tears stung her eyes. She wiped them away angrily, sniffed back the sob that ached in her throat.

Who the fuck did he think he was? He'd chosen his wife over her and Andrew, and now it was convenient, he thought he could just walk back into their lives.

No. No way.

Resolved, she went to find Gina. By the time she was back in the newsroom, she had convinced herself that the pang of regret she felt was nothing more than a figment of her imagination.

CHAPTER 36

He told himself he wasn't going to make the call.

When Chief Superintendent Doyle had broached the subject with him, Ford's first thought was that he was going mad. Here was a senior officer, a career policeman of almost thirty years' experience, asking one of his senior detectives to discuss confidential details of an ongoing inquiry with a civilian.

Ford was too stunned to speak, turning to walk away from his boss in a show of disrespect that would have been unthinkable only an hour ago. He got about ten feet away when he felt Doyle's fingers bite into his arm and spin him round. Doyle's face was a mask of tension, his lips thin and bloodless beneath the pencil moustache flecked with grey, his brown eyes darting over Ford's face, as though he was trying to read what he was about to say next on his detective's features. He found it, his gaze hardening, his voice a harsh whisper. 'Malcolm, please. Just hear me out. You don't like it, then report me, but at least hear me out first.'

And that was when Ford saw something he had never seen before in his boss. Something he had assumed was for lesser mortals like himself and Troughton.

Doubt.

He followed Doyle to his office, and took a seat when told to do so. Doyle sat heavily behind his desk then leant to the side, his balding head glinting in the overhead strip lights. There was the sound of a drawer opening, soft clinking, then Doyle reappeared, the effort of bending over putting some colour back into his pallid complexion.

He didn't ask, just poured two fingers of whisky into each glass and slid one to Ford. Almost on instinct, Ford lifted it to his nose, felt the peaty tang of Laphroaig bite at his nostrils. 'Very nice, sir,' he lied. He had no tolerance for the acrid burn of peaty whiskies, preferring instead the warming smoothness of a Speyside malt. But today was not the day to be discussing whisky with his boss. Better to keep things calm. Bide his time. Try to find out what the hell was going on.

Doyle raised his glass in silent toast, took a deep sip. He held it in front of him, swirling the amber liquid, staring into it as though it was a crystal ball. The silence dragged out, just long enough for Ford to start to feel uncomfortable. Eventually Doyle spoke. 'They're going to take it away from us, Malcolm,' he said finally, his voice as acidic and bitter as the whisky he had just poured.

'Excuse me, sir?'

Doyle looked at him, sorrow and anger in his eyes. 'The case,' he said. 'You heard the chief. Special Branch are going to take over due to the political links. So they're going to blunder around, focus on Helen Russell's past, do everything they can to make Ferguson feel reassured and keep the press happy. And in the meantime, other lines of enquiry are going to be left to die.'

Ford squirmed in his seat, felt a sudden urge to sip the whisky. 'Yes, sir, but—'

'But what?' Doyle spat, his voice low with anger. 'This is our fucking case. There are two victims here, and I'll be damned if the last major inquiry I work on is a fuck-up that is handed over to the big boys because us local yokels are too thick to work it.'

Ford said nothing, trying to process this new information. He hadn't known Doyle was retiring. As far as he knew, no one did. He was a lifer, a policeman who'd joined at eighteen and clawed his way up the ranks. The thought of him not being on the job raised fresh doubt in Ford's mind. Was it time to take the hint? To get out while he could?

But then he saw it in his mind, heard the low squeal of steel in the wind, Billy Griffin's head mounted on a spike like an excised tumour,

148

blood and gore dripping from it, the rat hanging from the mouth. Doyle was right. It was their case, their responsibility. But . . . 'Sorry, sir, I don't follow. What does the case being reassigned have to do with you asking me to talk to a civilian?'

Doyle drained the last of his glass, then reached for a refill. He left the bottle uncorked, a silent invitation to Ford. 'Let's just say I owe an old friend a favour,' he said, eyes focusing on something only he could see just over Ford's shoulder. He shook himself, brought his attention back to the present. 'I trust the man who called me, Malcolm,' he said. 'Like you and I, he took an oath to serve, just in slightly more exotic locations and with stricter discipline. And the man he asked me to put you in touch with is hardly a civilian either. He's a former PSNI officer.'

Ford took a sip of the whisky, let it soothe the jumble of half-formed questions and theories clanging around in the fog of his brain. The Police Service of Northern Ireland. An obvious link to Billy Griffin's Red Hand of Ulster tattoo. He had another sip as he felt his resolve waver, the thought of speaking to the man taking on an appeal that overrode common sense and the knowledge that he would be breaking every rule in the book by doing so. 'What else can you tell me about him?' he asked, playing for time, willing Doyle to say something that would slam the door shut on this insanity.

'Not much,' Doyle admitted. 'Look, Malcolm, I know this is highly unorthodox. But nothing in this case makes any fucking sense and, whoever this guy is, he might be able to help. My, ah, contact wouldn't ask if he didn't know we could trust this man's discretion, and if there's any blowback from this, I'll take it.'

'Sir, I . . .'

Doyle drained his second glass. 'Bottom line, Malcolm? I'm tired. I've seen this force bent and twisted into something I don't recognize merely on a political whim. Officers, Christ, friends I've known for almost thirty years are bailing out because they can't take it. And neither can I. Used to be that being a police officer was what counted. These days, all that matters is making the accounts balance. Whoever did this, if it is one killer and the cases are connected, is bad news, Malcolm. And he's on our patch. I'm out. But I want to be a copper one last time, follow the evidence, build a case. And if I have to step outside the bounds of the mighty Police Scotland to do so, then so be it. If you can't help me, fine. But you know the case, Malcolm, and I know you want this bastard as much as I do. So, please.'

Ford looked at his boss, seeing not the officer but the ground-down old man who sat before him. He felt as though he was teetering on a cliff edge, at once terrified and exhilarated at the prospect of leaping into the unknown. 'What's his name?'

Hope flashed in Doyle's eyes, bright and fleeting. 'Fraser. Connor Fraser. Lives in town apparently.'

The name was like a gut punch. Ford rocked back in his chair, felt whisky slosh over his hand, thoughts crackling through his mind.

Connor? What was it the dedication in the book said? *Not the same edition, but the same horror story. Hope you like it, Connie. See you soon. L.*

Connor. Connie.

The words spun through his mind, rattling around like a ball in a roulette wheel. It was a coincidence. Surely.

Connor. Connie. That tattoo. The injuries to the corpse around the joints. He'd looked it up. It was a paramilitary punishment method where the joints of the knee, elbows and ankles were targeted with a gun or blunt object, the brutality masked by its colloquial name 'the Belfast six-pack'.

Connie. Connor.

The squeal of the steel in the wind, the frozen scream on Griffin's face, the rat tail dangling from the mouth.

He downed the whisky, let it burn away his indecision. 'How do I find him?'

CHAPTER 37

After calling Lachlan Jameson, Connor found himself paralysed by indecision. It was a new and unpleasant sensation for him. He had always preferred quick, decisive action, an attitude instilled in him by his grandfather: 'Face a problem head on, and kill the monster when it's small.'

But the problem he now faced was what action to take? He knew the monster was out there, waiting. The message in the book was proof of that. But which monster? If what Simon had said was true, Jonny Hughes was dead, killed by a car on the Shankill Road. So who was sending him the message?

And, more importantly, why?

He forced himself to be calm, to resist the adrenalin that was urging him to get up and move. Told himself he had nowhere to go, no real leads to follow. No. Better to wait, see if Jameson came through with someone he could talk to.

For now.

He filled the time making phone calls from his land line, making sure he kept the mobile clear for Jameson's contact. First to the nursing-home to check on his gran ('She's having a fine day, Connor, bright and aware, working on her crossword') and then to Jen to apologize for his behaviour. He made light of it, brushing it aside as too heavy a weights session the night before, followed by too little sleep and too little food after. She agreed with him warily, her tone conveying nothing but indulgent scepticism, letting him end the call only after eliciting a promise that they would meet up later in the weekend. He agreed, motivated more by the need to get her off the phone than a desire to see her, the events of the last few hours making him crave solitude rather than companionship.

Calls made, he went back to watching Sky News, the volume turned low. It had moved on to other stories, but there was a constant reminder of Stirling in the ticker. 'Stirling murders: first victim mutilated, known to police,' it read. Connor mused on that. Who could it be? And what connection could they possibly have with Jonny Hughes?

Frustrated, he called Simon and went through the conversation again, his old partner reassuring him that Jonny Hughes was indeed dead. 'Look, Connor, there's no big conspiracy here. It's not like someone swapped the body or falsified the death certificate. He was run over trying to cross from the leisure centre, left him not much more than a smear of blood and shite across the Shankill. What's this all about?'

Connor considered the question. He knew that if he told Simon what he was thinking, what he had discovered, he would be dragging him into whatever was going on. But it was only a matter of time before he heard about the book, either on the news or from a contact, so perhaps he was only delaying the inevitable.

He sighed, felt the ache from last night's weights session settle like an old friend in his shoulders. Then he told Simon what he knew, about the book that was found on the second body, the dedication inside. Saying it aloud, dragging all his fears into the harsh light of day, he had a dizzying rush of hope as he realized how ridiculous it sounded.

Simon shattered that illusion with ten simple words. 'I'll check the death report. Get the next flight over.'

'Simon, you don't need to. I can handle whatever—'

'Really, Connor?' Simon said, anger in his voice. 'Just like you handled it the last time?' Connor felt a rush of shame scald his cheeks and neck. 'If this is connected to Hughes, I'm involved so I'm coming. I'll check flights. Can you pick me up at Edinburgh?'

Connor agreed, knowing further argument was useless. He

finished the call, telling Simon he would wait for his text, then see him at Edinburgh airport.

With the call over, the silence of the flat pushed in on him. He looked at the mobile, willing a missed-call message onto the screen. Saw nothing but the time and an unread text from Jen. He cursed, his eyes straying to the coffee-table and the gun that lay there. It was like a black hole, somehow sucking everything in the room towards it, making it the centre of the universe.

Connor reached for it, the cool of the surface welcome in his hand. It was strange how quickly it became familiar to him again, the weight, the feel of the barrel as he pressed his index finger tight against it, the snug fit of the grip in the web of flesh below his thumb. He raised it, looking down the barrel, confirming what he already knew. The sights were aligned straight and true, the events of that night in Belfast having had no effect on them.

After their arrest, the Hugheses had been processed quickly, charged with criminal damage, assaulting a police officer and possession of a weapon with intent to wound. Showing the sort of fidelity that had got him into the shit in the first place, Jonny had left Amy to languish in custody as he made bail, giving the address of a cousin on Shore Avenue just off Whitewell Road as an alternative home.

The house was a small, pebbledashed semi, Union flag proudly on display. It sat in the shadow of the Whitewell Tabernacle, a huge, strangely angular building that seemed to be fashioned mostly from red brick. Connor knew the place by reputation, a pastor there having been taken to court and ultimately cleared after giving a sermon in which he described Islam as a 'doctrine spawned in Hell' and 'satanic'. For Belfast, which was no stranger to bloody, often lethal disagreements over religion and the proper way to worship, it was an echo of the bad old times. For Connor, it was just another reason to be grateful that, despite his mother having been Catholic, he had been raised largely agnostic. 'I've seen God-fearing cause too many deaths in my time,' she'd told him. 'I'll be damned if that poison is going to warp my son's thinking.'

After the delivery of the book to his flat, Connor's first call had been to Simon. He should have called it in, registered it as a breach to the personal safety of an officer and his dependants, but he knew what that would mean – endless questions, change of duty, potential relocation until the threat was evaluated as low-level, no matter how hard he protested: the link between a book delivered anonymously and Jonny Hughes was thin.

But Connor knew. What was it Hughes had said the night of his arrest? 'I'm going to make your life a horror story, pal.'

He had met Simon in a pub around the corner from the flat, playing it casual with Karen but making sure she locked the door when he left. That flat had had a similar set-up to Jen's, with a main-door buzzer system and a substantial fireproof door on each unit in the block. But, still, he made sure his mobile was on and Karen's was in arm's reach when he left.

They found a snug at the back of the bar, Connor talking in a low whisper. Simon said nothing, merely sat and listened, but Connor could see the flashes of rage spark in his eyes as he spoke. It was the unwritten rule. You accepted the risk of being attacked on the street the moment you put on the uniform, especially in Belfast. It was why he and Connor still checked under their cars for tilt bombs and other devices before getting in, why they held their breath when firing the ignition. The Troubles may have been officially over, but the threat, and the lessons they had taught, remained.

The key lesson for Simon McCartney was a simple one. Fuck with me, fine. Crack on and take your chances. Fuck with my nearest and dearest? All bets are off.

When Connor had finished speaking, he paused, letting what he had just been told sink in. Then he grabbed his shot of Bushmills, swilled it around the glass and downed it in one. Connor saw his eyes redden, tears forming, and bit back a smile. Simon put on a good front, but he was no drinker – confiding in Connor once that whiskey to him was like turps. But it was part of the role he was playing.

Sitting in that bar, Connor couldn't help wondering which role it was that night.

'How do you want to do this?' Simon asked.

'Hard,' Connor said, Karen's confusion as she held up the book flashing across his mind. 'It's not on, Simon.'

154

Simon nodded in agreement. 'Fine. So this is what we do. . .'

It didn't take much to locate Jonny. After all, he had a business to run and Friday night in Belfast was peak trade.

Connor picked up his trail in the centre of town, Hughes following a pattern officers had tracked him on for months. He was targeting the bright young things who were out to impress: men with their achingly sculpted hair and precision-pressed shirts, women in dresses that sacrificed function to form. They were so eager to stand out, so intent to live on the edge, they had no idea that the coke they were buying from Jonny Hughes was so watered down and cut with shite that they'd have been better drinking an espresso.

Connor was at the bar in a Cuban place on Arthur Street, up behind City Hall. He watched as Jonny circulated like some kind of pasty, tattooed shark, his designer clothes ill-fitting, his glasses glinting in the strobe lights, fleeting pools of quicksilver. Soon Jonny caught the eye of a young man who was all false tan and designer labels, the pair heading for the back of the club and the toilets.

Perfect.

Connor let them get just far enough in front, watching them in the mirror behind the bar. Adjusted his jacket, felt the package in his breast pocket, then followed, no one paying them any attention. Blow or blow-job, they were just two guys out for some fun on a Friday.

But for one of them the night was about to become very serious.

The light stabbed dull pain into Connor's eyes as he stepped from the gloom of the bar into a well-lit corridor. At the end there was a set of double doors. Fast strides took him to the men's, women's and disabled toilets. He walked past, to another door, which he inspected. Smiled. Standard issue. It led to a small fenced-off area on the side of the building, which allowed easier access to the bottle bins, gas canisters and other supplies that were stored outside. Converted city-centre pubs lacked the basement capacity for full cellars. He retreated to the toilet for the disabled and waited. He swallowed a flash of panic that he'd missed them, then heard muffled voices and the rattle of the lock. The door swung out towards him, a barrier between him and the occupants. He pushed the door closed, saw two figures, the back of Jonny Hughes's head.

He stepped forward, snaked an arm around his shoulders. Pulled him in tight. 'Jonny!' he said, baring his teeth in a smile that made his jaw ache. 'I thought that was you! 'Bout ye?'

He saw panic flit across the man's face, a tremor tugging at the vein in his neck before his features arranged themselves into something like smug arrogance. His pupils were dark pits and, from the crust around his left nostril, Connor knew he'd been sampling the merchandise with his customer. Stupid. ''S all right,' he said to the man standing with them, his eyes darting between Connor and Jonny. 'Jonny and I know each other from way back, don't we, Jonny?'

Jonny gave a jerk of the head in agreement, a smile Connor didn't like slowly dawning on his face, like sunrise on the eve of battle.

'Actually,' Connor said, dropping his voice, 'I'm after a bit of the same stuff you were. Give's a minute with the lad, will you?'

The young man nodded, tapped his nose. 'Sure, boys, crack on,' he said, then scuttled back to the bar.

As soon as he'd turned the corner, Connor tightened his grip on Jonny, choking him in the muscled vice between biceps and chest. He wheeled around, marching Jonny towards the fire exit. ''Mon, Jonny,' he said. 'We need to have a wee word.'

Jonny bounced off the chain-link fence that made up the far end of the outdoor cellar, a grating, metallic shimmer filling the cool night. Connor eased the door shut, making sure the lock didn't catch. Cast an eye around for security cameras. None.

Perfect again.

He reached into his jacket, pulled out the package and brandished it at Jonny. 'This your work?' he asked, not trusting himself to move. Not yet.

Jonny pulled himself upright, smoothed down his suit jacket. And then he did something Connor had not been expecting. He smiled. 'So you got it. Ah, grand,' he said. 'Glad you did, Connor. It's a gift from the heart, so it is.'

'So you admit you sent this to Ka– a female I know?' he asked, his voice as hard as chips of flint.

'Course I did,' Jonny replied, his glasses flaring in the sepia streetlights as he nodded. 'You made a cunt of me in front of my woman,

Connie, only right I return the favour. Question you've got to ask yourself is how I found that little bitch.'

Connor was on him before he knew he was moving, hand clamped around Jonny's throat. He hauled him up, driving him back into the chain-link fence, which bowed and squealed under his weight. 'How did you find out about her?' he hissed. 'Who told you?'

'Let's just say,' Jonny coughed, hands clawing uselessly at Connor's arm, 'I know people who tell me things. So when I asked about you, well, they told me all sorts of interesting stories.'

Connor let him go, forced himself to take a half-step back. The thought had been there since the book had been delivered to Karen, hiding like a cancer in the shadows. 'Who's your contact?' he asked. 'Someone in the service?'

Jonny smiled. 'Tut-tut, Connie. You think I'd tell you that? Doesn't matter anyway. What matters is I know about dear old Karen. Made it my business when you fucked me over. Told you, Connor, I'm going to make your life a fucking horror story.'

Connor felt bone stab into his knuckles as his fist connected with Jonny's nose. Jonny staggered backwards, blood exploding from his face, glasses skittering across the cold concrete.

'Fucking bastard!' he spat as he clamped his hands over his face, blood seeping through the fingers. 'You broke ma fuckin' nose. I'm gonnae—'

Connor swung a roundhouse into Jonny's ribs, driving the air from his lungs and forcing him to his knees. He dropped beside him, grabbing handfuls of shirt, pulling him to his feet again, close enough to feel the heat of the blood, taste its iron tang at the back of his throat. 'Who fucking told you about her?' he snarled, glaring into Jonny's eyes, seeing his own rage reflected back in them.

'Away an' fuck, ya pig shite, ye,' Jonny spat.

Connor lashed out, catching Jonny with an uppercut that rattled his jaw and sent a snap echoing through the night. Jonny rocked back, dazed, then reached into his pocket, producing a lock-knife, the blade snicking into being like a magic trick.

Connor watched it, then let his eyes drift to Jonny's, trying to read his next move.

157

Jonny danced forward, like a boxer in the ring, shaking his head. Connor feigned left, avoiding a clumsy stab, then ducked down and pivoted right, bringing the spine of the book down on Jonny's wrist like a cosh. The knife clattered to the ground, an oddly musical sound, and Connor was on him.

The gun was in his hand before he knew it, robbing Jonny of his bravado, stripping him down to the coward he was. Connor blinked back a sudden memory of a playground years ago, and whipped the barrel across Jonny's cheek, making sure the sights cut into his flesh, then jammed the muzzle into his face. 'I swear to fuck, you don't tell me what I want to know, I'll end you here and now,' he said, his voice as cold and final as the bullet in the chamber.

Jonny's eyes widened, terror pulling his face into a waxy, blood-streaked grimace. His voice was a high, fast tremor, hysteria lurking in the sharp crash of consonants and vowels. 'Look, it's nothing. I was only playing, honest, man. I followed you, saw you pick up that bint in town, followed her to school the next day. Piece of pish to look at the website, find her on the teaching staff, wasn't it?' He held up shaking hands, eyes straining to see the barrel of the gun. Connor studied him. His fear was genuine, and he knew what lying would lead to. But still . . .

Still . . .

He smashed the gun across Jonny's face, rocking it to the side. Three blows in quick succession, blood slicking the grip of the gun. Then he ground the barrel deep into Jonny's cheek. 'How can I trust what you're saying, Jonny? Lying wee shite like you? How do I know you're not just saying that to get yourself off the hook?'

His voice was a begging whine that hurt Connor's ears. 'Please, man, please. I mean it. Honest. Look. I'm sorry. But you embarrassed me in front of Amy and the boys and, oh, God, I—'

Connor slashed the gun into his face again, his hand moving as if it was divorced from his mind. The wet, crunching thud of bone was sweet music, reverberating in his heart. The smell of blood burnt his nostrils and he lashed out again. And again.

The fury faded gradually, washed away by the exhaustion in his arms. He pulled back, looked at the diseased lump of flesh in front of him, sickened by what he had created, his father whispering in his ear: *You've got the Fraser temper, son. Keep it in check, like I have.*

Connor rocked back. 'If you ever go near me or mine again, we won't have this chat beforehand. I'll pull the trigger before you even know I'm there. Understood?'

Jonny mewled agreement. The sound was barely human.

'Oh, and, Jonny, one last thing. You tell anyone about this, anyone, I'll paint you as a tout and let your pals in the UDA deal with you. Clear?'

Jonny nodded enthusiastically, rodent eyes following the gun. Connor saw the hatred try to take hold again, make him a man, but it was swamped by the fear and the pain.

He had seen that look before. In the eyes of Stephen Franklin.

He got up slowly, looked around, found the gate set into the wire fence, took a second to burst the lock and swung it open. 'Fuck away off then,' he said, as Jonny got to his feet shakily. 'And remember, Jonny. One word, and I will fucking end you.'

Jonny edged past him into the alley, then ran. Connor thought he was going to stumble, but he found his stride and bolted. Connor watched him go. It was only when he was sure that he was alone that he doubled over and retched, the fear and revulsion churning inside him, clamouring to be free.

The mobile rang suddenly, startling him out of the past. He fumbled for it. Almost dropped it. Saw a number he didn't recognize. Hit answer. Waited.

'Hello?' the caller said, something familiar about the hesitant voice.

'Who is this?'

'Is that Connor Fraser?'

'Who is this?'

An impatient sigh. Someone obviously not used to being messed around. 'Mr Fraser, I believe you were told to expect my call by a . . .' a soft rustle of paper down the phone, the voice becoming stiff as a note was read '. . . ah, Lachlan Jameson. My name is Malcolm Ford, and I think you and I should talk.'

CHAPTER 38

After the unwelcome call from Mark, Donna had found Gina, then headed home. She presented her plan as an ultimatum, hating herself for her selfishness even as she told her parents she was only back for a couple of hours, and would need them to stay with Andrew while she covered the late show at the station. Didn't matter if Matt Evans turned up or not. Tonight, the show was hers.

Her mother had been ashen, the anger and disbelief etching itself across her face, making her look somehow younger, as though constant disappointment in her daughter was a source of nourishment to her. It was only when Donna mentioned that she would be paid double time for the shift, and get the following day off, that Irene relented, and agreed to stay at the flat with Andrew until Donna got home.

Sitting in the near-silence of his room, Andrew sleeping in her arms, Donna felt doubts and fears creep in on her from the shadows. The glass eyes of the bear her dad had insisted on buying Andrew – 'I bought the biggest one I could find for you the day you were born, only fair I should do the same for him' – turned dark and accusatory in the gloom. She was being utterly selfish, asking her parents to shoulder the burden of looking after Andrew, putting the job before her son. Her mother was right: she was a failure as a mother and a daughter.

But she wouldn't be a failure as a journalist. She would build something that would support her and Andrew. No matter what.

She looked down at him, felt a tug of something purer and deeper than any word as feeble as love could describe, even as the shame rose in her.

When she had found out she was pregnant, and Mark had scurried back to his wife, like the frightened child he was, she had considered an abortion, had gone as far as making an appointment. But the night before, alone in her flat, the tears long since exhausted, she felt a giddying, terrifying resolve. It would derail her career. End her life as she knew it. But she would have the child growing inside her.

Seven months later, Andrew was born at the Forth Valley Royal Hospital in Larbert by emergency C-section, Donna having moved back to Stirling a couple of months earlier. She hated to admit it but, with Mark out of the picture, she would need the help of her parents who, despite her mother's disapproval at Donna's single-mother status, made no secret of their excitement at becoming grandparents.

And now here she was, preparing to abandon them all again for the job that had led her there in the first place.

She left it as long as she could, reluctantly slipping Andrew into his cot when she couldn't delay it any more, the ghost of his warmth clinging to her arms and chest even as she pulled on her jacket and headed for the car.

The show ran five days a week, and was a popular addition to MediaSound's broadcasting arm. Matt Evans was on a short leash following his meltdown in Edinburgh, but he could still be relied on to throw in some calculated controversy now and then to keep the tabloids interested and him in the headlines, so the listening figures were good.

For Donna, the content of the show wasn't a problem – everyone wanted to talk about the murders and, as she had led the story on both TV and radio, there wasn't a shortage of callers. Still, she found it exhausting – the constant juggling of calls, the timing of segments to hit ad breaks, news updates or traffic reports, the need to keep the conversation casual but informative, entertaining but relevant. She tried a few diversions into other topics – the latest sex-abuse revelations in Parliament, the tweet storm whipped up by a man with all the integrity of a comb-over in a hurricane, the news that, yes, Brexit would be even more of a catastrophe than previously advertised. But no matter what she did, call after call dragged the debate back to the murders. Was a psycho on the loose? A serial killer? Was there a pattern? Would there be more killings? How badly mutilated was the body at Cowane's Hospital? As it was so close to the graveyard, was there an occult link?

Donna tried to snag some of the more rational thoughts to follow up later, but it was like trying to grab a twig from a raging river. The calls were moving too fast for her to do more than dive in and hang on.

She signed off at just after two, mentally and physically exhausted. Gina gave her a thumbs-up from the production office and Donna twitched her a smile. As she hung up the earphones, an autoplay of songs taking over until the station started broadcasting again properly at six a.m., she felt a grudging respect for Matt Evans. Yes, he was a self-serving wanker who traded on clichés, bigotry and populism, but he did it five days a week without breaking a sweat.

Mostly.

She went back to the main newsroom, cradling a cup of tea she didn't want but needed to revive her for the drive home. Gina followed a moment later, having checked all was well with the autoplay system. 'That was great,' she said, perching on the corner of Donna's desk. 'You're a natural. Thanks, Donna, you really helped me out tonight.'

'No problem,' Donna said, eyes drifting to the main door and the sound of squealing tyres beyond. It was a routine occurrence: with the station being in an industrial estate heading out of town, it was the perfect venue for the local boy racers to congregate in their souped-up bangers and hot hatches to practise their skills. The roads outside the office were constantly tattooed with tyre rubber from the night before, while a couple of the lampposts and street signs had been left at odd angles. They'd complained to the police, and Donna had run a story, but the truth was it suited the coppers for the kids to be racing around there rather than on the roads where they could hurt someone other than themselves.

She dragged her eyes, now gritty with exhaustion, back to Gina. 'I take it you've still not heard from Captain Fantastic?'

Gina gave a smile as tepid and grey as Donna's tea. 'No. The great Matt Evans has yet to check in. Fuck knows what's happened to him. Nothing minor, I hope.'

Donna gave a small laugh that made something hurt in the small of her back. Too long sitting hunched over the production desk: time to go home. 'Any chance you can use this to get shot of him?'

'I wish,' Gina replied. 'He's a useless bastard, but he's a popular useless bastard. And the bosses seem to have plans for him. I hear they're thinking about a TV slot on one of the late-night regionals.'

Donna hissed breath out between her teeth. Typical, she thought. Shit always floats.

She lingered for another ten minutes, flicking through her notes from the show, highlighting possible angles to explore on the story tomorrow. Then she sighed, rubbed her eyes and headed for the door, her mind filled with thoughts of Andrew asleep in his cot.

She pushed through the double doors, turned left past the bin where she had taken the call from Mark earlier that day, heading for the car park beyond. She was checking her phone for emails from Fiona or Danny, only looked up when the path gave way to the car park.

She stopped dead, her brain fleetingly unwilling and unable to process what her eyes were telling it. A mannequin had been propped up beside her car, its back against the driver's door, the legs spread wide, turning at impossible right angles at the knees. It was topless, the pale, mottled skin peppered with splashes of something that glistened like burnished oil in the orange glow of the streetlights overhead. But there was something wrong with the figure, something missing that . . .

The revelation hit her like a physical blow, grabbing her lungs and squeezing. She felt the phone slip from her hand as she lurched back on legs that suddenly felt boneless, disconnected. The sound of the phone shattering was like a gunshot. Her hands flew to her temples as though her head was about to explode, a growing scream clamouring in her mind, like an old kettle coming to the boil. Her eyes, unblinking, seemed to bulge at the horror of what was in front of her. She remembered Mark's words from earlier in the day.

Her gaze was dragged up, something wrenching free of its moorings, like the popping of a tendon or the tearing of a muscle.

She understood what was wrong with the figure in front of her. Why the shape refused to make sense. It was obvious, really. She should have seen it sooner.

See, Donna, the police found the body had been mutilated. Badly. It had been . . .

She gave a sudden, hysterical cackle, felt the growing scream scrabble up her throat on icy, spidery legs.

. . . decapitated . . .

She looked up to the roof of the car. Matt Evans stared back at her, eyes empty marbles shining in the streetlights, blood dripping from his neck, snaking down the driver's window, as though reaching out to reconnect with what was left of his violated and discarded body.

The dam broke. Donna fell to her knees and screamed. But she couldn't take her eyes from Matt's head, and its silent, accusatory glare.

CHAPTER 39

The picture seemed to scream at him from the phone's screen. He stood open-mouthed, shock and revulsion squeezing his vocal cords shut and denying the scream that ached in his chest.

He blinked, his eyelids feeling alien and foreign, which did nothing to blot out the vision of Matt Evans's ruined body. Forced himself to look again: Evans's body was propped against a car, the gloom of the night doing nothing to hide the blood that covered, like a shroud, the wounds that had been inflicted, the legs bent at sickening angles, knees obviously shattered. He focused on that, seized on the lesser horror as he swallowed burning bile, not wanting to see what was perched on the car's roof.

The phone buzzed in his hand, a text popping up below the picture: *Thought you would appreciate this. Will give you something special to talk about today. Enjoy Stirling.*

He stared at the message dumbly, its casual tone almost as shocking as the picture above it. Did he answer? *Should* he? And if he did, what would he say? 'Thanks for beheading the loud-mouthed little prick and slaughtering two other people, just what I wanted'?

No. No. He put the phone down on the coffee-table in front of him, pushed it across the table, out of his reach. Then he sat back, looked up at the ceiling. It was done. With Griffin and Russell dead, he was safe, his legacy assured. He could retreat into the life he had created for himself, go back to his – no, their work – make the difference he had always dreamt of.

There were always casualties in war, always collateral damage as innocents got caught in the crossfire. And Evans was hardly innocent. After all, it had been his greed and avarice that had started all this.

No. Better he was out of the picture. And the caller was right: it would divert the focus of today's meeting from other matters. He sighed, dropped his eyes back to the table and the phone that lay there, like an unexploded grenade. He reached for it, unlocked it, then forced himself to look at the picture one last time. Stared at it until the horror abated, replaced by the cool indifference he had honed over the decades.

He thumbed in a text, then considered. Glanced at the clock on the wall, seeing it was almost two-thirty a.m. He needed to sleep. Rest. Be ready for the meeting with the chief constable at Randolphfield in a few short hours.

He stood, and the phone buzzed again. He read the message – *A pleasure doing business with you.*

He felt a chill finger trace a path across his calm. He had done what was necessary to protect everything he had worked for, ensure his secrets stayed buried in the past. To do so, he had contacted a professional whose discretion was assured, whose credentials he knew were impeccable. It was a business arrangement, nothing more, and he had paid handsomely for the service.

He had met the caller in person only twice, the first time years ago, the second less than a fortnight back to agree terms and be given the phone they now used for contact, a phone he was assured was untraceable. He had seen in that meeting someone who reflected himself, a man living behind a façade.

But he had known. It was in his eyes. While he was hiding from his past, the caller was hiding something uglier, darker.

The contract was complete, but would the caller be satisfied? Or would he come looking for more blood, having decided there was one more loose end to be dealt with in Stirling?

And if that happened, would he be ready?

CHAPTER 40

The station was a riot of activity when Ford arrived just before six a.m., the air electric with the nervous energy, trepidation and excitement that a major case always brought with it. The paper-pushing and bureaucratic bullshit were swept aside by the brutal, visceral reminder of what they were facing, what they were trying to protect people from.

Chaos. Utter chaos.

He was halfway to the incident room when Doyle caught up with him, his skin pale and waxy, eyes sharp and glittering in dark sockets that spoke of a long, broken night.

'DCI Ford,' he said. 'Let's take a walk.'

Ford glanced up the corridor, felt the tug of the incident room.

'Now, Malcolm,' Doyle repeated, heading off down the corridor.

A minute later they were in Doyle's office, the smell of stale cigarettes doing nothing to mask the sour tang of whisky that hung in the air. Looking again at Doyle, Ford wondered how much of his appearance was down to exhaustion and how much to a hangover.

'Have you managed to speak to our contact yet?' Doyle asked as he settled behind his desk, the chair seeming to engulf him.

'Ah, not yet, sir. I mean, I spoke to him, and we arranged to meet later today, but now, with what happened at Valley FM . . .' He gestured to the window and the bustle of activity outside.

Doyle nodded slowly, his eyes not leaving Ford. 'Keep that

appointment, Malcolm,' he said. 'And do us both a favour, lie low today.'

Ford felt as though he had been slapped. 'Sorry, sir, but I don't understand. If there's been another murder, and by the sounds of it, it followed the same MO of the previous two, then surely it's my responsibility to . . .'

Doyle held up a hand. 'Malcolm, the best thing you can do is get out of here and lie low. This was turning into a nasty little political game before this DJ, Evans, was butchered, but now . . .' He trailed off, distaste twisting his face into something hard and unreadable.

'Sorry, sir, I'm still not sure I follow,' Ford said. He knew the words for the lie they were, knew what was coming. It was, after all, politics.

Doyle straightened in his chair, interlaced his fingers on the desk in front of him. 'I told you yesterday, Malcolm. Helen Russell's position as a councillor cast this whole case in a new light. It's why Special Branch have been dragged in, especially with the possible paramilitary link to Billy Griffin. It's all a bit . . . sectarian, for their taste. But last night's murder really kicked up a shit-storm. The justice secretary is due to visit today, a private meeting that, surprise, surprise, has been leaked to the press. And, just to really roll out the welcome mat for him, we've had another murder. That's three murders in two days, Malcolm. Makes us look inept, stupid. And it blows a fucking bastard of a hole in the government's claim that crime is at its lowest level in ten years. So, what do you think they want to do about it?'

It was obvious, really. 'They want a scapegoat,' Ford said, more to himself than to Doyle. 'And as I was the lead officer on Griffin and Russell, I'm in the frame. Right, sir?'

Doyle looked down at his hands, then back up at Ford. 'It won't be anything official,' he said, exhaustion making his voice a low growl. 'I've looked through your case files and you followed every procedure to the letter. Did some good work in pulling the background on Griffin, too. But you know they'll spin this, Malcolm. With the shit the force is in at the moment, they need to wash their hands of this one, show it was the fault of one officer, not a breakdown of the service or the work of an uncatchable psycho. They're keeping you off the case pending a review by Special Branch, and the Evans murder has been assigned to other officers who are being brought in from Edinburgh.'

Ford nodded. With the amalgamation of the eight police forces, it wasn't uncommon for officers to be moved around the country to plug the ever-increasing number of staffing gaps. He felt a surge of anger to have this placed on his shoulders. 'So, what am I meant to do, sir?'

'Officially you're to collate your paperwork for a handover with Special Branch and the Major Investigations team taking over. You're also to make sure you're at the disposal of the chief and Ferguson, should they wish to talk to you.'

'Bollock me, more like,' Ford said, the words out of his mouth before he could stop them.

'Quite right,' Doyle said. 'So make yourself scarce. Get the fuck out of here and let me try to work something out.'

'All right,' Ford said. 'But what about this Fraser guy? Surely with all this going on, the last thing I should do is talk to him.'

Doyle's face tightened, and Ford again found himself wondering who had called his boss for a favour yesterday. And what Doyle owed that person that had made him agree so easily.

'Meet him,' he said. 'Everything I said yesterday still applies. I want a result on this one, Malcolm, one last win before I go. Officially you're not actively part of the investigation. But you're still one of my best detectives. So meet him, see what he has to say and, if it's useful, you can show these pencil-pushing fucks what real police work looks like.'

CHAPTER 41

Donna sat on her couch, skin tingling from the scalding shower she had just stepped out of, hair damp, Andrew cradled in her arms. Since getting home, it had seemed important, no, vital, to hold him close, feel his warmth. Keep him safe. And looking at him, studying his face and his tiny, perfect hands, almost kept the memories of what she had seen at bay.

Almost.

She remembered what had happened after she'd found the body in a series of snapshots, random moments flashing before her mind's eye. Perfectly natural, a police support officer had told her. At times of trauma the memory could be affected.

Her screams had quickly attracted Gina and Mike, the technician who had helped produce the show. They had grabbed her, dragged her from the ground and back into the office. Donna remembered the harshness of the lights, the unyielding glare that seemed to give everything hard, jagged corners and lurid colours that made her head ache.

While Gina called the police, Donna had fired up her computer and, on instinct, started writing up the story. She stared at the screen without seeing it, trying to articulate the horror, the plan forming in her mind. Website copy first, then a news piece, then call Sky. She knew that if she stopped, tried to process what she had seen, rather than treat it as a story, she would grind to a halt, the terror and shock sucking her in like quicksand. And if she let that happen, she would never escape.

She was halfway to the door, camera in hand, when Gina grabbed her.

'Donna, where the hell are you going? Stay in here until the police arrive. Jesus, whoever did that could still be out there!'

Donna blinked, eyes drifting to the locked door. What did Gina mean, where was she going? She was going to get a picture to go with the story, of course. She was going outside, into the car park and . . .

. . . and . . .

The sobs ripped through her, sudden and overpowering, driving her to her knees again as the memory of Matt Evans's pulverized corpse crashed into her mind.

By the time the police had arrived and sealed the area, Donna was almost back in control. As the station was an active crime scene they were taken to Randolphfield, then led into a small room where the threadbare soft furnishings, lamps and cheerful watercolours on the walls did nothing to distract from the industrial grey paint and the feeling that this was an office going through the motions of being welcoming.

She answered the barrage of questions as fully as her shock-addled mind would allow, a police support officer giving her an encouraging smile every time she spoke. Yes, she had known Matt had been missing the whole day, but it wasn't unusual for him to drop off the radar. No, she didn't know if he'd received any threats or had any enemies. No, she had no idea why his body had been dumped at her car in particular. Yes, she got on fine with him. No, she never saw him socially.

The interview lasted about forty minutes, the constant repetition of the questions giving Donna the chance to process what had happened. There were memories and images her mind would not let her see, and she could feel herself flinch away from them any time they threatened to surface, but she was able to detach that from what had happened and see it as the story it was.

Matt Evans had been killed in the same manner as the first victim, Billy Griffin. Whether the dumping of his body on her car was incidental or intentional was irrelevant: Donna had received the message loud and clear.

These murders were linked. And she was going to report them.

When the interviews were over, she met Gina and Mike at the main doors of the station, huddled together in the pre-dawn chill as they waited for a taxi. The police had offered to drive them home but they had all refused for their own reasons, Gina and Mike not wanting Donna to know they were going home together, Donna not wanting to get out of a police car and face her mum.

Unwilling to talk about what they had seen, the conversation fell to practicalities. With the station deemed a crime scene and off limits, Gina would call MediaSound, make alternative arrangements, then let the staff know what was going on.

Donna offered to help, ignoring the guilty flash of glee that pulsed through her even as Gina spoke. With Valley FM out of bounds, she was free to offer the story, and anything else she found, to Sky first.

She called the night desk at Sky while she was in the taxi on the way home, gave an account on the spot to allow them to get the story on the air, then emailed Gina the copy she had written. It would be uploaded remotely to the Valley website. She felt a momentary pang of panic over the morality of reporting a story to which she was a key witness, but let it fade when the desk editor, Jack Mathis, said he'd interview her as a bystander and not the reporting journalist, with the promise of sending a camera crew to her for follows in the morning.

By the time she arrived home twenty minutes later, Donna had broken the story on TV and online. She couldn't remember anything she had said to the night desk at Sky or a word she had written for the online story. She wanted to run away and hide, hold Andrew and keep him safe. Knew that if she did that, she would never emerge from the flat again.

It didn't take the calls long to start flooding in, contacts and fellow journalists literally waking up to the story and keen to talk to her. She switched off her phone as she reached her front door. Time enough for that later.

She'd called her parents from the police station, telling them what

172

had happened. Tears threatened to overwhelm her again when her mother bustled her into the flat, arm around her shoulders, talking to her in a low, soothing tone that Donna hadn't heard since she was a child.

She showered as her mother made tea, Andrew stirring for a feed by the time she had towelled herself dry. She went to him, sending her parents to the spare room to sleep, then took him to the living room and held him in her arms.

She flicked the TV on, keeping it silent, watching the news ticker on Sky announce, 'Third murder in Stirling'. A twinge of excitement cut through the exhaustion, shock and horror. Three murders in two days. And she had scooped them all to get the story out. National news. And she was leading on it. A picture of Matt Evans flashed up on the screen, a cheesy publicity shot that had been harshly Photoshopped to make his hair fuller, his skin healthier, his eyes brighter.

A shudder twisted through her, the sudden image of the last time she had seen those eyes barging its way into her mind. She took a deep, steadying breath, forced away the tickle of panic in her chest. She looked down at her son: he was squirming in her arms, repositioning himself on her chest. He was so small, so defenceless. And she had effectively abandoned him tonight to cover this story.

The panic faded, replaced by a resolve that at once calmed and terrified her. The story had come to her now, literally dumped in her lap by whoever had killed Matt Evans. It was hers. She would work the story, get the job she wanted, keep Andrew safe and build a future for both of them.

And if a killer got in the way of that future, she would sweep them aside as she had every other obstacle and setback.

For herself. And for Andrew.

CHAPTER 42

Ford had no idea what Connor Fraser looked like, but he knew him the moment he laid eyes on him.

They had arranged to meet in a small café on Bow Street, less than a two-minute walk from where Billy Griffin's body had been found. Ford had felt a vague unease when Fraser had suggested the place, given its proximity to the crime scene. The last thing he needed was to be seen talking to a civilian. His anxieties began to ease as he approached the café – it was only a short walk away, but in the narrow cobbled streets around the castle, where tourists thronged even at this time of the morning, it might as well have been on another planet. And then there was Fraser. Whatever else he was, the last thing he looked like was a civilian.

He was sitting in the café, back to the exposed stone wall, as he watched the front door with an attentiveness only police officers had, the outward appearance of relaxation doing nothing to detract from the searchlight intensity of his gaze as he scanned for possible threats. He gave only the slightest nod when Ford entered, eyes never leaving him.

Ford returned the almost-greeting, ordered a coffee at the till, then wove his way through the tables to Fraser, who rose as he approached, uncurling and expanding, like a widening shadow. He was just shy of six feet tall, the broad shoulders, heavy jaw and wide chest offset by striking green eyes that spoke of quick thinking and calculation as they darted across Ford. The DCI took the outstretched hand, surprised by how gentle the handshake was.

'Thanks for agreeing to this,' Fraser said, as they sat down.

Ford chided himself for the surprise he felt when Fraser spoke. His accent was typical Central Scotland, halfway between the lyricism of Glasgow and the cooler precision of Edinburgh. What had he been expecting? 'Not my idea,' he said, leaning back to allow the waitress to set his coffee in front of him. She smiled at him, then was gone. 'My boss owes yours a favour. Let's leave it at that.'

Fraser knitted his hands together on the table in front of him, forming a shield around his coffee. 'Fair enough. Nonetheless, I'm grateful. Maybe you can help me straighten a few things out.'

Ford bristled, but swallowed the irritation with a gulp of coffee so hot it brought tears to his eyes. Who did this guy think he was? Bad enough he had pulled strings to talk to a DCI on an active case, but to think Ford was just going to sit there and help him solve his own little problems . . . Fuck that.

Fraser raised a hand, obviously reading Ford's thoughts. 'Didn't mean it like that,' he said. 'It's just there's something about the Helen Russell case that's bothering me. I was hoping you could help. Who knows? Maybe I can help you too.'

Ford put down his cup, took a second to consider its contents. Old trick. Dictate the pace of the conversation. Show who was in control. But looking into Connor Fraser's unflinching gaze, he wasn't honestly sure who was. 'What is it you think you know?' he asked.

Fraser rolled his shoulders, eyes darting around the room before settling on Ford again. 'When I watched the news report on Helen Russell's murder, something struck me. There were, ah, similarities to the MO of a shitebag I had dealings with back in Belfast. The book you found on the body, well, it was a – a calling card of his. Jonny Hughes. Nasty wee prick, called himself the Librarian. Had family links to the Loyalists, used them as a shield for drug-dealing. I . . . What?'

Ford cursed internally. He'd thought he had a better poker face than that, but obviously not with this guy. He had felt a sting of excitement the moment Fraser had said 'Loyalist'. It must have shown on his face. Stupid. He pushed it aside. 'We'll get to that in a minute. I'm glad you mentioned the book. I wanted to talk to you about that. There was an inscription in it, mentioning a Connie. And now, here you are, telling me you think there's a link to someone you collared while you were in Belfast. Something you want to tell me, Connie?'

Fraser's jaw twitched, his eyes narrowing slightly. Not the greatest poker player either. 'That's part of the reason I reached out to you,' he said, his voice slow and measured. 'It mirrors his actions in Belfast when trying to intimidate a . . . ah . . . witness in a case I worked on. But you looked like you were on to something a moment ago. What?'

Ford ground his teeth. Answer then redirect. Keep the conversation on track, going where he wanted it to. No, this guy was no civilian. He glanced around his surroundings, again wishing for the soothing familiarity of an interview room. But, with what Doyle had said, that wasn't going to happen, not when the top brass were looking to paint a bullseye on his back. 'Just something you said there,' he said, trying to sound casual, ignoring the whispering voice in his head telling him to be careful. He needed to know. Took another gulp of coffee, cooler now, decided.

'You said Loyalist,' he said, dropping his voice. 'That might tie in to something we found at the first murder.'

A glitter of interest in Fraser's eyes, keen and hungry. 'What?' he said, his tone telling Ford all he needed to know about the man. Doyle had told him he was a security consultant now, a former copper, someone they could trust. But in that moment Ford knew that Connor Fraser was none of those things. Fraser was a detective, driven by the desire – no, the need – to find the answer. It was the same compulsion that had driven Ford throughout his career.

'The first victim had a tattoo,' he said. 'Red Hand of Ulster. If you're saying you think there's a link between the perp you knew in Belfast and the Russell murder, it links her to the first victim.'

Fraser nodded. 'Who was he?' he asked.

'Just a small-time ned. Got into a bit of trouble during the independence referendum a few years ago.' Ford stopped, let that sink in, the incident taking on new context and significance given what Fraser had just said about Loyalists. The image of Billy Griffin holding a flaming Yes banner aloft flitted through his mind. What the hell was going on here?

Fraser seemed to consider the words, then tilted his head. 'Any links to Helen Russell?' he asked. Obvious question. It was the same one Ford had asked.

'Not that we've found yet,' he replied, his frustration giving his voice a hard edge.

'And you won't find it now,' Fraser said, leaning back. 'Given that Special Branch have effectively frozen you out of the case.'

Ford started, his coffee cup jangling against the saucer as it jerked in his hand. 'How the fuck did you find out about that?' he hissed.

Fraser shrugged. 'I got a call from our, ah, mutual friend about half an hour ago,' he said. 'Your boss called him with an update, apologized that you might not be able to tell me much.'

Ford forced himself to let go of the breath he had been holding. When Doyle had broached this madness, Ford had insisted on knowing where the request had come from – and why his boss would even consider it. Doyle had gone very quiet for a moment, then given him an answer that resolved every question.

'We served together in the first Gulf War, were part of Desert Storm. He saved my life. But that's my debt, not yours, Malcolm. So if you don't feel you can help, don't.'

Ford wasn't a military man, but his father was, so he knew what this meant to Doyle. He had agreed to speak to a man he absolutely shouldn't about a case he was being frozen out of.

Fraser nodded, an expression that might almost have been mistaken for sympathy stretching across his face. 'You totally out of the picture?'

'Mostly,' Ford said. 'Got to be on hand to take my telling-off if needed, though.'

'Arse-covering bastards,' Fraser said, draining his coffee. He straightened up, the first subtle indicator that he was winding the conversation up. He reached into his pocket, produced a business card, wrote on the back of it, then slid it towards Ford. 'You've got my work number already,' he said, 'but this is my personal number. If you need anything, call me. I'll be in touch later today with an update.'

Oily unease curled its way down Ford's spine. 'Update on what? What do you think you're going to do? Look, I agreed to meet you because Doyle asked me to. But if you think I'm going to let you just charge into this and . . .'

Fraser raised his hand, and Ford spotted the calluses that ran along the base of his fingers like an uneven wall. Weightlifter. 'Easy, DCI Ford,' he said, with a brief smile. 'I don't intend to make waves, but I do have a stake in this. I'm just going to talk to a few people. You said yourself you won't know if there are any links between the two victims because Special Branch won't let you near it. I'll ask around, see what I can find, let you know what I come up with.'

'Why?' Ford asked. 'Why are you doing this? And why didn't you report your concerns officially as a former officer? What went down with you and this Hughes character?'

Something flitted across Fraser's eyes, dark and predatory. It made Ford suddenly conscious of what an imposing figure he was.

'Let's just say I've got my reasons, not all of them professional,' Fraser said. 'Good to meet you, DCI Ford. I'll be in touch.'

'I could make this official myself,' Ford said, freezing Fraser as he rose. 'Hell, after what you've just said, I should make it official. Take you in, get a statement on the record.'

Fraser stood to his full height. 'You could,' he agreed. 'But you won't. You did this as a favour to your boss, I appreciate that. But if you report this, you'll have to explain how you found me, because the last thing I'm going to do is come forward voluntarily, which means exposing your boss. And yourself.' He looked up briefly, out into the street beyond. He placed his hands on the table. 'Look, chase up what I've told you, if you can. If it looks like it's leading somewhere solid, you have my word I'll give you a statement on the record. Believe it or not, I want whoever did this caught as much as you do.'

Ford stood slowly, felt a twinge of pain in his knee. 'Okay,' he said, the word tasting bitter in his mouth. 'This is between us and Doyle. For now. But no fucking around, Fraser. You're not a police officer any more. That's my job.'

Fraser gave a wistful smile, extended his hand. They shook, then Fraser left without saying another word, picking his way through the tables with an agility that belied his size.

Ford watched him go, wondering what he was about to do, not sure he wanted to know the answer.

CHAPTER 43

The ministerial car swept into Randolphfield just after ten a.m., Doyle standing beside Chief Constable Guthrie, who was doing his best impression of a waxwork dummy dressed as a policeman – back ramrod straight, eyes fixed ahead.

He was moving before the car even stopped, stepping forward and waiting as the back door swung open. A tall, lithe man with ash-blond hair unfolded himself from the back of the car, smoothing his tie into place as he straightened, fixing his gaze on the chief. He strode forward, hand out, even as the other two occupants of the car got out.

'Chief Constable,' the man said, the faintest echo of the west coast in his tone. 'Maxwell Higgins. I'm Mr Ferguson's senior special adviser.' He stepped to the side, clearing a path for the other members of the party. 'Of course you know Mr Ferguson, and this is Lucy Mitchell, who is chief of staff to the First Minister, and also leads our communications department.'

Panic flashed across Guthrie's face at the mention of the First Minister, the severity of the situation suddenly underlined. To his credit, he recovered quickly and offered enthusiastic handshakes, welcoming Ferguson and Mitchell with all the warmth he could muster. Doyle flinched at the scene. The chief had been hired because he was a grey man, good with numbers and unlikely to rock the boat, characteristics that shone in the lack of social ease he displayed.

Guthrie introduced the three to Doyle, who received the

perfunctory handshakes and murmured greetings before they turned their attention back to the chief. Message received: he was only a lackey, not important to them. Doyle didn't mind. He was in no rush to be useful, especially as, when he was, it would be as a scapegoat.

He thought briefly of Ford, of the wisdom of sending him to meet Fraser. The chief would explode if he found out. It ran contrary to every procedure in the book and every instinct Ford had developed over his long career. But what could he do when Lachlan Jameson asked for a favour? And, besides, if they were going to use him and his DCI to take the blame for the failings in the case, why not see if they could get a result through other means?

Guthrie bustled them into the building, leading them to a conference room that had been set up for the justice secretary's visit with refreshments and a laptop hooked up to a projector, a lectern at the head of the table. Doyle didn't think they were going to like the presentation Guthrie had made him prepare, and found he didn't care. They were here to get the facts of the case, make it look like Ferguson was fully up to speed and in control. And while it was unusual for a special adviser, who was effectively a member of the minister's political party and made suggestions accordingly, and the First Minister's right-hand woman to be privy to such a confidential briefing, Guthrie had insisted they be vetted and approved to hear the facts.

Fine. Doyle would get him up to speed. And fact one was that murder wasn't pretty.

He waited until they were settled, tuned out Guthrie as he made his opening comments – all the usual clichés about the team working well together, following firm lines of enquiry, solid police work and good progress. His ears pricked up when he heard the mention of Special Branch now being involved due to Helen Russell's political links and the tattoo on Billy Griffin's chest.

'. . . and I think that's a good point to hand you over to Superintendent Doyle,' Guthrie said, with a smile, to the minister. Ferguson, a small squat man with wiry hair slicked tight to his skull and a double chin that rubbed on his shirt collar, gave a nod, jowls quivering. 'Please, Superintendent Doyle,' he said, his accent clipped and Highland. Inverness, maybe.

Doyle stood up, walked to the lectern at the far end of the table, opposite Ferguson. He flicked a button on the small panel that lay there, the soft whine of a motor filling the room as the blinds swivelled shut and the projector flared into life.

'As of this morning, we have had three murders within five miles of each other.' He tapped a key on the laptop, a slide showing an aerial view of Stirling and the surrounding area with three large Xs marking the crime scenes dotted across it. He looked at it for a moment, pondered. Christ, but they were close. 'The first body was discovered at approximately six twenty-two a.m. by a dog-walker in the grounds of Cowane's Hospital. The victim was found to have been severely beaten before death, and badly mutilated.' He paused, looked at his visitors. Of the three, Mitchell was the only one who looked like she was taking anything in. The other two were braced in their chairs, unease tightening their faces. He felt a twinge of admiration for Mitchell, then wondered if her attitude was based on the fact that she didn't know what was coming next.

Too bad. Just the facts.

He hit the keyboard again, the next slide jumping onto the screen. Heard sharp intakes of breath from around the room. 'As you know, the victim, William Griffin, was also decapitated.' He had spared them the worst of it, left out the pictures of the body. But this was bad enough. There was something about the image of the metal spike, the head removed, a streak of gore running down it, that haunted Doyle. He was glad the others felt it too.

'The victim's head was mounted on this spike, and left at the door of the Holy Rude. He was also found to have had a rat stuffed into his mouth. From the damage to his tongue, cheeks and interior of his mouth, the pathologist has suggested the animal may have been alive when it was inserted.'

Doyle heard a groan, looked up to see Higgins cough into a handkerchief, his face drawn. Ferguson looked at him with bored disgust, while Mitchell kept her eyes trained straight ahead, her hands clasped around a pen.

Doyle flicked to the next slide, took them through the discovery of Helen Russell at the hotel on the grounds of the uni.

He hurried through the facts, not wanting to give Ferguson the chance to start asking about the news report that had been sent from the scene.

'Finally,' he said, flicking to the last slide, a nondescript shot of a small tent erected in the car park of Valley FM, a white-suited SOCO wraith-like in the foreground, 'we received a call at two eleven this morning, reporting the discovery of a body at the premises of Valley FM, a local radio station. As with the first victim, this body had been severely mutilated and, again, decapitated. We've identified the victim as a Matthew Evans, an employee of the station.'

Higgins's wavering voice floated from the gloom. 'And the, ah, the head. Was it, eh, mounted as the first victim's was?'

Good question. 'Not specifically, no,' Doyle said. 'But it was left on the roof of a car, which could be deemed to be displaying it in another fashion.' He went on, detailing the steps taken, the officers canvassing the areas, checking for links between the three victims, and finished with an update on the handover to Special Branch.

Ferguson spoke first, shifting his bulk in his chair and wrapping blunt, chubby fingers around a glass of water in front of him. 'The investigating officer who was initially involved in these enquiries, DCI Ford. How would you rate his performance in this matter, Superintendent?'

Doyle's gaze hardened on Ferguson. Prick. Forget the fact that three people had been murdered, probably by one nut job, who was still out there. Let's play the blame game. Thank Christ he was retiring. 'DCI Ford is an exemplary officer, sir,' he said, his gaze fixed on the soft pink flesh that spilt over Ferguson's collar. 'He has worked these cases to the best of his ability, in the face of extreme resource pressure and the demands of the press.'

Mitchell stirred in her seat, scrawled a note even as Guthrie fired Doyle a look filled with warning. Rein it in, that look said.

Doyle didn't care. Just the facts, after all.

'Hm, well, thank you, Superintendent. I'd like to speak to DCI Ford if possible. Where is he at the moment?'

Doyle felt heat in his cheeks, hoped it didn't show. 'DCI Ford is preparing the last of the case notes for Special Branch and assigning officers to support them,' he said, ignoring the cold glare from Guthrie.

'Quite so,' Ferguson said. 'Well, thank you, Superintendent. I wonder if you could show Maxwell and Lucy where they might find the canteen and get a little fresh air. I daresay they need it after that, and I want a word with your chief in private.'

Higgins and Guthrie exchanged worried glances, Higgins speaking first. 'Ah, Mr Ferguson, I'm sure it would be more beneficial if I—'

'Nonsense, Maxwell,' Ferguson snapped, with the impatience of a man not used to being questioned. 'I just need a quick word with Peter, that's all. Nothing for you to worry about.'

Higgins opened his mouth, closed it. Checked a watch that seemed too large for his wrist. 'As you wish,' he said. 'We have the press conference at noon. Shall we meet you back here at a quarter to for a briefing?'

'Ideal,' Ferguson said. 'Now go on. Peter and I need to have a chat.'

Doyle led them out of the room, turned back to see Ferguson leaning close to Guthrie, who looked more like a waxwork than ever, especially with the grey pallor of his skin. He caught his boss's gaze for just a second, saw the desperation of a man who knew he was about to get a world-class bollocking.

He closed the door and left them to it. Decided today wasn't such a bad day after all.

CHAPTER 44

It hadn't taken long for Connor to find the Russells' home address, taken even less time to bluff his way into the house with some vague talk of follow-up queries and questions to ask. He had his Sentinel ID tucked in his back pocket in case Mr Russell asked for some form of formal-looking identification, but found he didn't need it. The man just blinked at him for a moment then retreated back into the house, leaving Connor to follow. Down a narrow, dim hallway to the back of the house and a kitchen that looked out onto a garden every bit as neat and ordered as the one Connor had seen at the front. A decent plot of land, Connor thought, which fit with the seventies vibe he got from the row of bungalows on Munro Avenue. Nowadays, the gardens would be the size of postage stamps.

Russell beckoned him to sit, then busied himself making coffee. He hadn't asked what Connor took, just put a mug in front of him and retreated to his own chair at the opposite end of the table to watch him patiently. Waiting.

Christopher Russell was clearly in shock. His eyes fell to the mug he cradled between his shovel-like hands. His expression was blank, apart from a small frown that creased the skin beneath the stubble on his head as he gently spun the mug in circles, the coffee sloshing against the sides. Occasionally, it would spill over and splash onto his hands. If it burnt him, he showed no sign of it.

Connor considered. He didn't want to go over the same ground as the police, thereby raising this man's suspicions. But at the same time, he had to warm him up, not go straight to the question he wanted to ask. 'Mr Russell, can you think of any reason why your wife would have been at or near the uni campus yesterday? Did she have any meetings there?'

Russell looked up, as though he had forgotten Connor was there. The frown crinkled his brow now, as though Connor had spoken in a different language. Then he spoke, his voice soft and strangely high for such a big man. 'No, I can't think of any reason,' he said. 'Helen was meant to be in Edinburgh yesterday, at the Parliament. She had a reception with one of the MSPs, spokesman on culture, I think. Something to do with the plan to renovate the hospital at the top of the town.'

'Cowane's Hospital?' Connor said, gripping his mug. There had been plans to renovate the building and its gardens, make it more of a tourist attraction than it currently was. But an issue with the funding had thrown the project into doubt. Not that any of that mattered to Connor. No, what mattered to him was the link to the first murder. 'Was she due home last night, sir? Was that when you called to report her missing?'

'Ah, no, no.' Russell coughed. A kind of melancholy twisted his face, tears threatening. 'She was due to stay over. I knew she wasn't coming back.' Something in his voice told Connor that he also knew what his wife would have been doing that night. Question was, did he know with whom?

He shook himself. Forced himself not to get sidetracked. She was meant to be staying in Edinburgh. So how the hell had she ended up in Stirling? And then there was the question he really wanted to ask.

'Mr Russell, when your wife was found, she had several items on her person, including a paperback novel. Was she a fan of Stephen King?'

Russell blinked away whatever memory was gnawing at him, focused on Connor for what seemed like the first time. 'What? No. Helen hated that sort of gory stuff. Hell, she almost puked up her dinner the first time I flicked on an episode of *Game of Thrones* in front of her. What book was it? Why did she have it?'

'It was *Misery*, sir. It wasn't yours?'

Anger sharpened Russell's gaze. Finally, amid the chaos of his wife's death, there was something he could channel his fury at. 'Of course it wasn't mine, I've never read the damn book. Look, what is all this about, Detective . . .?'

'Anderson,' Connor said, the name plucked from the air, the lie coming out smooth and easy. 'I'm sorry, I know it sounds odd, but sometimes it's the small details that yield results. And I'm trying to establish a picture of your wife's movements and her life before her, ah—'

'She was a whore,' Russell said suddenly, the words as dark and bitter as the coffee he had served. 'I shouldn't speak ill of the dead, but she was, Mr Anderson. I knew she was in Edinburgh overnight for a reason other than party business. That book was probably a gift from whoever she was shagging.'

'And you have no idea who she might have been with?' He could see his time with Russell was coming to an end, the window closing. Might as well push it. 'Sir, does the name Jonny Hughes mean anything to you? Did your wife ever mention that name or Belfast at all?'

'No, but if he's who she was fucking, why would she tell me?' Russell said, looking down at the kitchen table. 'I don't know who it was, and I don't even know if she was in Edinburgh that night. She told me she was, but she could have been anywhere. Hell, they might have been at that hotel at the uni, right under my nose. And Belfast, fuck knows.'

He shook his head slowly, the pale sunlight bouncing off his scalp. Connor watched him, not sure what else to say, his mind racing with questions. Did the police know any of this? He'd assumed they'd checked the CCTV at the hotel for signs of Helen Russell: had they found any? And then there was the book. His last doubts were gone. Whatever was going on, that book was a message to him.

But from whom?

'Mr Russell, thank you for your time. I should be going.' Connor rose from the table, his chair squealing across the cold ceramic tiles in protest. Russell looked up at him, the anger gone, replaced by shocked bewilderment. He might have thought his wife was a whore, but she was still his wife. And someone had killed her, then dumped her like a piece of meat.

But who, and why?

He rose, mirroring Connor, then gestured to the hallway. Connor took the lead, aware of Russell's bulk behind him. He was halfway to the door when a figure appeared in the frosted glass and the bell rang.

Connor's pulse quickened. If that was the police, how could he explain this? Russell stepped past him, walking to the door. Connor moved to his right, trying to maximize the amount of clear space he would have when the door swung open. If it was the police, he would make his excuses and get out as quickly as he could, walk down the street and loop back for the car later, when he was sure no one was around to see him and note down the number plate.

The adrenalin left him as the door opened. A dark-haired woman, with thin lips and keen blue eyes that darted between the two men, stood in the doorway. There was no trace of the glowing smile, camera-ready make-up and calm authority Connor had seen in her pictures, but he knew her all the same.

'Yes?' Russell said.

She focused on him, gave a perfunctory smile that died when it got to her eyes, extended a hand. 'Ah, Mr Russell. Firstly, can I just express my sympathy for your loss. My name is Donna Blake. I'm a reporter with Sky News. I know this is a bad time, but I'd really appreciate a quick word with you. Of course,' her eyes moved to Connor, 'your friend is welcome to stay if that would make you feel more comfortable.'

Russell looked between them both, weary resignation causing his shoulders to slump. 'Detective Anderson was just leaving,' he said, his voice as collapsed as his posture, 'and I have nothing to say to the press, thank you very much.'

The door was closed almost before Connor was over the threshold, putting him face to face with Donna Blake. He was taller than her, but she did nothing to give ground, just looked up at him.

'Anderson, huh?' she said, a smile dancing in her eyes. 'Funny, I think Danny would have mentioned someone like you. So, Mr Anderson, shall we have a chat? Off the record or on, all works for me.'

Jameson's warning about discretion echoed in Connor's mind. The last thing he needed was to speak to a reporter. But still . . .

He moved past her, heading back up the driveway. 'I'm sorry, Ms Blake, but I have an appointment.'

She followed him, walking quickly to keep up. 'If you're a cop, I'm Doctor Who,' she said. 'Who are you? And what did you want with Christopher Russell?'

Connor stopped dead, turned to her. Again, she refused to back off, almost nose to chest with him, her jaw set, lips thin.

'That really is none of your business, Ms Blake. Now if you'll excuse me . . .'

'No, I don't think I will,' she said. 'You were wrong, Mr Anderson, if that's your name. This is my business. It became that when I found Matt Evans's head on my car roof last night.' He heard a tremor in her voice, her skin paling as she spoke.

Connor watched the memories battle the anger behind her eyes. He'd heard the news reports, knew about Evans. But why leave his body dumped by her car? A message from the killer? 'You want a coffee?' he asked.

CHAPTER 45

'So, how is sunny Stirling?'

He had been expecting the call. There had been something in the caller's voice when he'd told him about Matt Evans that had intimated this was not over. The contract might have been fulfilled, but the caller was obviously a man who enjoyed his work.

'How do you think it is?' he replied, surprised by the anger that rose in him. He had set this in motion, but to have the caller play with him, treat him like an amusement, phone whenever the whim took him? It was outrageous.

'I think it's giving you the perfect opportunity to polish your credentials and show yourself to be the man to take charge at a time of crisis,' the reply came, the voice dry with threat. 'I also believe it was a chance to reassure yourself that the investigation has no way to lead back to you.'

He tightened his grip on the phone. 'I've still to speak to Ford, the first detective to handle the case, but they know there's a probable link between the murders. Your little flourish with Evans tipped them to that, so, no, I'm not reassured. Why the fuck did you have to make the murders so public in the first place? Would quiet little accidents not have done?'

'I have my reasons. They don't concern you. You need to relax. Three people are dead in two days. Of course the police are going to look for a connection between the victims. And I've given them

189

one. The manner of death means they're looking for one killer, one deranged lunatic, behind all this. And I assure you that the last thing I am is deranged. I took every precaution. There is no evidence linking me to the murders, or you for that matter. Unless, of course, there is some detail you failed to tell me when you first came to me.'

Sudden panic turned his guts watery. The caller had been meticulous in his questioning on his possible links to the victims. He had told him everything, ensuring that all possible links to him or, more accurately, the man he had once been, were severed. The caller had checked, made arrangements, assured him there was nothing left to link him to this. But, still, the thought tormented him. Had he missed something? Some small trace of the past that could lead back to him?

'No,' he said finally, his voice more convincing this time. 'There is nothing to lead back to me. Not now.'

'Well, then, you have nothing to worry about. You've shown you're in charge of the situation, found the investigation is going nowhere anywhere close to you. I understand you've got a press conference shortly. I suggest you enjoy your moment in the sun. And don't worry, I'll be watching you.'

The phone died before he could reply. He stared dumbly at it for a moment, resisted the urge to reach out and support himself against the wall of the building. He looked out across the manicured expanse of lawn that surrounded the station like a green ocean. Felt panic claw in his throat. What had he done? He'd had no choice but to silence those who would do him harm. But at what cost? He'd invited a madman into his life. A madman who knew who he really was, what he had truly done. A killer who could expose him at any time, who could enforce his will over him with a single call.

He smiled, little more than a baring of his teeth. He had swapped one blackmail for another, inviting in a monster at the same time. What could he do? No, what *would* he do?

He stood, forced himself to become the man he was. Straightened his tie, took long, steadying breaths.

The answer was simple. The caller had said it himself. He would shine in front of the press. He would show them he was in control.

He just hoped he could believe the lie.

CHAPTER 46

With her car still impounded by the police as evidence, Donna was using taxis to get about, putting them on her credit card and hoping she could blag either Gina or Sky to foot the expenses bill. It was a risk, she thought, especially with money being so tight, but one worth taking.

It paid off when Anderson led her to his car, which was parked just around the corner from Christopher Russell's house. Donna was no car expert, but she knew an expensive motor when she saw it. It was a coupé, slung low to the ground. The man didn't say a word, just plipped off the alarm and swung the passenger door open.

'If you don't want to accept a ride from a stranger you just met who, incidentally, you suspect of masquerading as someone he's not, you're welcome to walk,' he said. 'But I'm heading back into town. Offer of the lift is there.'

She studied him for a moment, calculating. He was a big guy, heavy-featured but not in a thuggish way, bright green eyes that flitted around, taking everything in, only coming to rest on her face when he spoke to her. Smart-casual in a suit that was two pay grades above any CID officer she had ever met, expensive car – no way he was the copper he was pretending to be. So who was he, and was he a threat?

Anderson shrugged. 'Suit yourself,' he said, reaching into his pocket and producing a business card. 'Look, Ms Blake, you've obviously figured out I'm not with the police. Fine. After your ordeal last night, I can't blame you for being wary of strangers. So here's my card. Give me a call if you want to talk, okay?'

He passed it to her, then tracked round to the driver's side of the car and folded himself in. Donna glanced at the card. Connor Fraser, Close Protection Consultant, Sentinel Securities.

Interesting.

She let the engine start, a low, throaty burbling that promised speed, before she made her decision. She looked at the card again, then stepped forward even as she rooted around in her bag, swung the passenger door open and got in. 'All right,' she said, dropping into a leather seat more comfortable than her sofa. 'Drive, Mr Fraser. But if you try any crap, I'll use this.'

She brandished a small cylinder at him, about half the size of a can of deodorant, white body with a black lid. Pepper spray. She'd bought it online after seeing a reporter get harassed when he was trying for an interview with a suspected child-porn dealer at a court hearing. Best to be prepared.

Fraser looked at the can, and Donna felt a moment of absurd humour as she saw a smile crinkle the lines around his eyes. 'Fair enough,' he said, putting the car in gear. He hit the accelerator, pinning her back in her seat, the pepper spray rising up to point at the roof as she fought for balance. Her Caesarean scar gave a dull howl of protest. 'Sorry,' he said.

He didn't say much else as he drove, just concentrated on guiding the car back into town. Donna felt her patience fray, then snap. Fine. She would play along. For now.

'So, who exactly are you, Mr Fraser? And why is a "close protection consultant" poking around a murder case?'

His eyes darted from the road to her, then back. 'Let's just say I've got a professional interest in the case,' he said. 'And since you seem to have the inside track on what's happening, maybe we can help each other.'

She wondered about that. No way this man would go on the record, let alone on camera. So how could he help her? And why should she help him? 'What is it you think I can do for you?' she said, the CS spray feeling cold and somehow fragile in her hands.

'You said you found Matt Evans's body this morning, that it was left at your car. I know that the first body was also beheaded, so I think there's a link. Question is, what is it – and were you deliberately targeted?'

A shudder forced her to move in her seat, the leather creaking under her. Memories of Matt Evans rose in her mind, threatening to overtake her. 'How did you know the first body had been decapitated?' she said. 'The police convinced me not to reveal that in my report.'

'I guessed they'd do that,' Connor replied. 'They would have wanted to keep that back to weed out any crank calls or false confessions. But you knew it, just like my contact did. Tells me two things.'

'Oh, what's that?'

'First, you're not just a hack. You play by the rules, even if you push them a bit. Second, you've got good sources. And that might come in handy.'

Frustration burnt Donna's cheeks. Was that it? Was he just another Mark, ready to use her for what he needed? No way. 'Look, Mr Fraser, if you think I'm just going to tell you what I know and then—'

'I don't think anything of the kind,' he said, as he eased the car to a halt at a set of traffic lights. 'You obviously have sources. I'm saying I can be one for you too, maybe give you something to keep you ahead of the press on this. But in return, I need you to help me answer a few questions.'

She studied him for a moment, his patient eyes on her. They didn't waver, didn't roam to her chest or down to her legs, just stayed locked on her face. No aggression, no demands. He'd stated his terms. The decision on what happened next was hers.

'Right,' she said. 'But forget the coffee. Can you get me to the police station on St Ninians? They're giving a press conference there shortly. We can talk as you drive.'

'Fair enough,' Fraser replied, slipped the car into first and drove away.

CHAPTER 47

Connor dropped Donna just up the road from Randolphfield, not wanting to get too close to the station for reasons she didn't quite understand. Since he'd quit the PSNI, he hadn't set foot in a police station and had no intention of breaking the habit now.

His talk with Donna had proved informative, if not revelatory. He told her what Helen Russell's husband had said about his wife, hoped that her source had given her something Ford hadn't shared. That wasn't the case, but the fact she knew about the beheading, Billy Griffin's tattoo and the scale of the trauma that had been inflicted on him told Connor she had worthwhile contacts, who might come in handy.

He watched her walk up the street, heading for the station. She was a strong woman – she'd have to be to shrug off finding a decapitated body beside her car. There was something else too: a defiant hardness that Connor could sense rather than see. It was as though she was trying to prove something, but what?

Her clothes told him she wasn't affluent, her shoes that she was doing okay. There were signs of recent weight loss in the slightly sagging folds of skin around her neck, and the dark patches around her eyes spoke of a night's lost sleep. Understandable given what she had just seen but still there was something . . .

He considered his next move. No word from Simon yet about his arrival, so he had some time to play with. He wanted to speak to

Ford, see if they knew anything about Russell's mysterious lover, or whether she'd had any links to Belfast.

But even if she did, what would that prove? Hughes was dead, so whoever had left that book with Helen Russell's body had known him, and the trick he had pulled on Connor. He had never reported the incident, and Simon had offered to alibi him, if necessary, so who did that leave? The answer was obvious. Hughes had obviously told someone about the beating, and what he had done to trigger it.

But who had he told? And why were they sending him this message now? Was it to settle a debt to Hughes, to get retribution for the little shit now that he was dead? And how did it link with the other two murders? The tattoo on Billy Griffin's body seemed to indicate a link to Loyalists, but with Jonny's tribe or another branch?

Connor sighed, leant back in his seat, thoughts swirling. Too many questions. Not enough answers.

He was startled from his thoughts by the buzzing of his phone. He thumbed a button on the steering wheel. 'Hello?'

'Fraser, it's Ford,' the policeman said, his voice slightly distorted by the car's speakers. 'There's a press conference just starting here, and I don't want to be anywhere near it. Can you meet up? I've found something and I need to talk to you.'

Connor leant forward, interested. 'I'm nearby,' he said, looking up at the police station. 'Where do you want to meet?'

The answer surprised him. 'Can you get to the uni? I have business there, and the main SOCOs have cleared the site now so it should be quiet enough.'

Connor mapped out the route in his mind. Not a problem. 'Okay,' he said. 'Any chance you can give me a clue what this is about?'

Silence filled the car, heavy, expectant. Then Ford grumbled a curse. 'Seems Billy Griffin wasn't the only one who liked body art,' he said, his voice low. 'Pathologist found a site on Helen Russell's body that shows recent burning, the type you get from laser tattoo removal.'

'Take it you managed to get a partial look at the tattoo. But what's that got to do with me?'

'Depends,' Ford replied. 'When you were in Belfast, did you have any run-ins with the Red Hand Defenders?'

CHAPTER 48

Driving through the wide gates to the Stirling University campus, Connor felt as though he was passing through a portal into a world of what-ifs. The uni had been on his shortlist of places to study when he was leaving school, and he knew it was his mother's preferred option. A way to give him freedom but keep him close, with home in striking distance if he ever wanted or needed it.

Not that the prospect was a remote possibility. He'd wanted to get away from Stirling, the weight of his dad's expectation, but driving past the wide, glittering expanse of Airthrey Loch, the university buildings looking like a child's block toys beneath the granite monolith of the Wallace Monument, he found himself wondering: what if he had chosen to study here? What if he'd never moved to Belfast and seen the arrest that had caused him to join the police? What if he'd never met Karen, or Jonny Hughes? He would have been happy here, he knew. The campus appealed to him, and the international make-up of the student body would have made it easy for him to blend in, be another face in the crowd. He could even have pushed himself, used the facilities here to build his body. As the official 'university of sporting excellence', the approach would have been more scientific than throwing weights around at his granddad's garage.

What if, Connor, what if?

He found a space in the small car park on the hill just before the hotel, separated from the entrance by a neatly trimmed hedge. A couple of uniforms drifted by, heading back down the hill to the campus. Made sense. The police would want to reassure the students, and the tutors, that they were on hand, and that what had happened was an aberration, rather than the new normal. He grunted a laugh at the thought. As if anything about this was normal.

He locked the car, took a slow look around, then made for the hotel.

The entrance was standard – automatic glass double doors parted with an airy rattle, revealing a tiled reception area with a couple of couches and coffee-tables. The far wall was dominated by a dark-wood reception desk, behind which a woman stood, phone held in the crook of her neck as she pecked away at the keyboard in front of her. She looked up when the doors opened, gave Connor a nervous smile of welcome, then focused back on the task at hand. The tinny Muzak was doing nothing to improve the oppressive atmosphere. He'd felt it before, at crime scenes and at venues when someone had tried to get too close to a client he was escorting. The dissipated energy of fatal violence clung to a place, making everyone wary that it could be reignited with the wrong word or thought.

He spotted Ford in the bar area to the right of the desk, talking to a tall, dark-haired woman who had her back turned to him. He saw the policeman stiffen when he caught sight of him, take a step around the woman, blocking her from his view. Ford leant in close, kissed her cheek, then stepped forward, putting himself directly in Connor's path and walking straight for him.

So, Connor thought, he was avoiding the cop cliché of being unhappily married. He'd spotted the wedding ring on Ford's finger when they had first met but made no judgement – many widowers and reluctant divorcés found it difficult to part with their ring, as though taking it off would confirm the truth, make it real. But this was proof. He was married – or having an affair.

Connor pushed the thought aside as Ford stopped in front of him, taking the hand the policeman extended and shaking. 'Fraser, thanks for coming,' Ford said, his gaze set, as though he was willing Connor to focus on him and not the woman over his shoulder.

'Not a problem. Though I must admit your call has me curious. You mentioned the Red Hand Defenders . . .'

Ford glanced over his shoulder. Whoever that had been, he didn't want her touched by any of this. Connor couldn't argue with that. He wished none of it had touched him either.

'Let's go for a walk,' Ford said.

Connor followed him out, nodding to the receptionist, getting another smile in return. They took a right, skirted the front of the building, following the path until they were faced with a road that led to a large car park.

Ford turned, looking back at the hotel. On the side of it, clamped to the wall, was a fire-escape staircase. At the bottom, police tape fluttered in the breeze, a uniformed officer trying not to look bored.

'That's where they found Helen Russell,' Ford said.

Connor felt cold sweat prickle on his back as he remembered the pictures he had seen, the book lying among the debris. 'What's this got to do with the Red Hand, Detective Ford?'

Ford shook his head, a look Connor recognized all too well on his face. *Later*, it said. *We'll get to that later.* 'You have any dealings with them in Belfast?' he asked.

'Not really.' He looked past Ford, back to the staircase, his mind flipping over the name as though it was an interesting shell he had found on the beach. The Defenders was a Loyalist group that had sprung out of discontent with moves towards peace after decades of bombing, shooting and other violence in Northern Ireland. They claimed responsibility for pipe bombings of Catholic families, and in 1999, they had killed Rosemary Nelson, a lawyer who represented Republican paramilitaries. There were rumours the Defenders were merely a cover for the UDA and other Loyalist groups, allowing them to keep up the violence and intimidation while claiming to honour the ceasefire, but Connor had never been involved in those cases. Or had he? Jonny Hughes dealt for the UDA. Was that a link? Anyway, why was Ford asking?

Ford seemed to read the question on Connor's face. 'What I'm about to tell you is confidential. Only reason I'm telling you is that the moment Special Branch found out, the shutters came crashing down. I'm officially off the case, but you might be a way back in.'

Connor straightened. 'I'll talk to you off the record, that was made clear to your boss, but, as I told you, I don't want to make a formal statement unless I absolutely have to. I'm done with Belfast and all that shite. Last thing I want is to drag it all up here.'

'Okay. For now,' Ford said. 'But we both agree that if we find something that could affect the case, you go on the record and I take it in. I want this bastard, Fraser, so does my boss, but I can't let you go cowboying around and jeopardizing any leads we're working on.'

Connor pushed down the memory of Jonny Hughes lunging at him, baseball bat held aloft like a club. He wanted answers, needed them, but at what cost? That a killer might walk free on a technicality because he was too afraid or ashamed of what he had done?

No. Fuck that. 'Deal,' he said. 'So tell me what you know. And what did you mean about Helen Russell trying to get rid of a tattoo?'

CHAPTER 49

Ford was noticeable by his absence from the press conference, having fielded questions at the previous one. From the look of it, Donna wasn't the only one who noticed he wasn't there: the chief constable, Guthrie, was sitting on the small stage, casting withering glances between Danny and the door to the briefing room.

As with the day before, a table stood on the stage, a Police Scotland lectern set up at the middle seat where Guthrie sat. To his immediate left there was a cadaver in an ill-fitting suit, whom Donna recognized as Detective Chief Superintendent Martin Doyle. She'd heard stories about him, a former soldier turned copper who had worked his way up the ranks. Rumour was he was getting ready to jack it in. From the look of him on the stage, his body was ahead of his thinking.

Next to him, just far enough away to be an observer rather than a participant, was the star attraction, Ken Ferguson. The justice secretary glared out at the assembled press, arms folded over a massive chest. Beads of sweat clung to his hairline, glistening in the lights, his double chin cascading over his collar. Donna had watched as he entered the room from a side door behind the stage: he had the walk of the cataclysmically overweight. Arms thrust out to the sides, head and shoulders thrown back as though to counterbalance the pendulous gut that hung over his waistband. He was a political heavyweight all right, just maybe not in the way he wanted to be perceived.

A man who was the polar opposite of Ferguson loitered at the side of the stage. Donna studied him, a vague sense of familiarity at the back of her mind. Tall, wiry, with a suit that looked as though he had been stitched into it that morning, small, elegant glasses perched on a long, blade-like nose. While Ferguson sweated, this guy exuded a clinical manner. Beside him stood a woman in a sharp business suit, a folder barricading her chest, like a shield, her gaze fixed on Ferguson. Donna made a mental note to ask Danny who they were, made a bet with herself that they were officials from the party, here to make sure everyone got the message.

And it was crystal clear. This was a police operation. The government was merely there to observe. Closely.

She watched as Guthrie droned on, stuttering and muttering his way through an update on the investigation, which ultimately amounted to a lot of reassurance and very few new facts. She kept her head down when the briefing turned to the discovery of Matt Evans's body, glad to have bagged a seat near the back of the room. She knew she was on thin ice reporting on a murder she had discovered and, technically, could be a suspect in. Fiona Clarke had made the point in no uncertain terms when they had spoken earlier on the phone. Given the work she had done so far, they were going to cut her a little slack, but if she got into anything sticky, or the police uttered the magic words 'We are looking for one suspect in relation to these murders,' it was game over for her.

She jotted notes, pinged a text to Danny, watched as his phone lit up, drawing a frown from the wiry man standing next to him. Danny looked up, and the wiry man followed his gaze, eyes landing on Donna. It was the briefest glance, but it intensified her feeling that she knew him from somewhere else.

Just who the hell was he?

Her phone vibrated in her hand – a reply from Danny to her request for an on-camera with Ferguson when this was over: *He's doing a huddle out front, doesn't want to get in the way of the main presser. Get out early and get a spot. Front steps.*

She sent a thank-you, focused back on Guthrie, who was now talking about tracing the victims' movements and trying to establish any connections that would link them together and provide a motive.

Donna wondered about that. Three victims – a small-time ned, a local councillor and a loudmouth talk-show host with a penchant for insulting politicians and anyone else he could think of. There must be a link other than the way they had died. But, then, was that even a link? Of the three, only two, the men, had been decapitated. From what little Danny had been willing to tell her, Helen Russell had been beaten as badly as the others, but her head had been, mostly, left on her shoulders. Why?

She stirred from her thoughts, nodded to Gary, the lank-haired cameraman Fiona had sent from Edinburgh to put the report together with her. Excused herself, keeping low as though she was leaving a showing of the world's worst movie, then headed for the door. She could feel eyes on her as she moved, sensed other reporters getting nervous. Where was she going? What did she know?

She turned back into the room, saw a ripple of fidgeting and watch-checking sweep through the press pack, but the sudden happiness she felt at being back on the job died when she saw Mark looking at her with his easy smile.

CHAPTER 50

Simon was booked on the 14.45 flight from Belfast City, which would get him into Edinburgh at just after four o'clock. Connor left Stirling after his meeting with Ford, toyed with the idea of stopping in to see his gran on the way past Bannockburn, decided against it.

He needed to drive. And think.

Connor had always found there was something calming about driving. Being behind the wheel was like entering a Zen state, the focus needed to steer the car, accelerate, brake, change gear and check mirrors freeing another part of his mind – the place where his sub-conscious pondered the problems he was facing, stripped them down to find an answer. And that was what he desperately needed: answers.

According to Ford, the post-mortem examination of Helen Russell had shown injuries consistent with those of the other two victims – severe trauma, especially pronounced around the joints. Connor remembered his time in Belfast, seeing men walking down the street, their stiff-legged hobble or palsied arms at odd angles marking them out. They had been knee-capped or fried. In the bad old days, para-militaries on both sides had used those punishments as a way of exerting control through fear and intimidation. Since the end of the Troubles, the methods remained but the motivations changed as the paramilitaries turned their tactics to waging war on rival gangs. And the threat of having a kneecap or an elbow shattered with a bullet or a crowbar was a language everyone understood, which was probably why the volume of such attacks had risen instead of falling since the bombs and balaclavas had been put in storage.

The post-mortem had also thrown up another commonality: the presence of a tattoo or, at least, its ghostly after-image on Helen Russell's body. It had been found just above her left hip, a small, angry cluster of healing blisters, the shape of the tattoo a tracing below the wounded skin.

Connor remembered the image Ford had shown him – what looked like a letter G surrounded by four As, their apexes pointing outward, like the points on a compass. 'Took a little while to track it down,' Ford told him, 'but we found it eventually. It's the mark of something called Alba Gheal Ann An Aonadh, 4AG as they liked to be called. Sprang up in 1978 or '79, around the time of the first devolution referendum. Literally means "White Scotland in the Union", and was mostly made up of bored skinheads looking for an excuse to cause trouble. But guess who they got some help from?'

Connor didn't have to guess. The answer was obvious. Back then, it was common for paramilitary groups to look for allies and enemies across the water. And somehow, 4AG had forged links with the Red Hand Defenders.

So, Helen Russell had been a member of 4AG. But the work to remove the tattoo was recent, according to the pathologist, state-of-the-art laser work rather than the old techniques, which more or less boiled down to acid burns or sanding the tattooed area down to the muscle. Why had she waited until now to have it removed? What had triggered the decision? And how did it link her to Billy Griffin? The age difference precluded them knowing each other in the seventies: Billy would have been little more than a toddler in 1979, with Russell already into her mid-twenties. So how were they linked?

And why had they both had to die?

Whatever was going on, Billy Griffin was the key. According to what Ford had told Connor, he had disappeared without a trace following his release from Barlinnie after his little stunt in George Square. His last known address was a flat in the Govan area of Glasgow, but officers who had checked the place after his body had been identified had found only an empty strip of rubble-strewn land where the flats had been, another demolition of the past to make way for the regeneration of the area.

So where had Billy gone after he had been released from prison? What had he done to survive – and how had he ended up decapitated and dumped in Stirling? Whatever he had been doing was almost certainly illegal – there were no records of any National Insurance payments or even of benefits being claimed since his release. He was a ghost, working in the shadow industries where tax was a myth and employment rights meant the right to keep quiet about what you were doing.

The thought came to Connor as he was passing Grangemouth, the industrial heart of the town dominated by the apocalyptic sprawl of an old oil refinery, spewing white-grey smoke into the pale blue of the afternoon sky. He smiled, then tapped a button on the steering wheel, accessing the hands-free phone option. Told his phone to do a Google search, found the website, told it to dial the number.

The ring of a phone filled the car, followed by a dull clunk as it was answered.

'MacKenzie Haulage,' a voice that was no stranger to cigarettes said.

'Hi, could I speak to Mr MacKenzie, please?'

Boredom slowed the voice at the end of the phone to a drawl. 'Who's calling?'

'It's Connor Fraser. He'll remember me – we met at his daughter's place yesterday. I think he'll want to speak to me. I have a favour to ask.'

CHAPTER 51

The huddle arranged for Ferguson after the press conference was, in truth, little more than a scrum. The ministerial car had been brought round to the front of the building and conveniently parked in one of the bays opposite the main door. The only place for Ferguson to stop was just in front of the Police Scotland sign that hung over the front of the station. It made a strong image for the cameras, and Donna was forced to admire the political staging. No wonder they had won three elections.

Guthrie emerged from the station first, flanked by Doyle and Danny. They were followed by Ferguson, then the woman and the man Donna had seen at the press conference. Again, there was a momentary twinge of recognition, something about the way he moved, the small, birdlike dart of the head to whisper in Ferguson's ear. But then the cameras started popping and flashing, the questions were lobbed at them, and Donna was swept along with the story.

The woman stepped forward, placing herself between the press and Ferguson, who surveyed them with a smile that was as expansive as his waistline. The press conference was over, and he had moved from stern overseer to a more comfortable role: playing justice secretary, defender of police and public, friend to the press.

The woman held up her hand, calling for calm. 'As you'll appreciate, Mr Ferguson is on a tight schedule, but he has a few minutes to take your questions. So, please, wait until you're called, identify your-self and state your question.' She surveyed the crowd, the assembled reporters straining like children in a classroom to be picked first. Her eyes roved across the pack, looking for . . . 'Ah, yes, you, sir.'

'Thank you. I'm Mark Sneddon, *Chronicle*. Mr Ferguson, there have been claims that the investigations into these murders have been hampered by lack of resources in Police Scotland. Do you believe this is the case and, if so, what steps are you taking to address this, not just here but across Scotland?'

Ferguson's smile faded to the expression of a man disappointed to be asked a question by someone who clearly didn't understand what was going on. 'As you know, the Scottish government has made resourcing of the police across the country a priority. And while operational matters are for the officers in charge to comment on, I can assure you that we are doing everything we can to ensure that . . .'

Donna tuned him out – if she wanted that line she could pick it up from any of the dozen press releases it had already appeared in. The question was a no-brainer: it sounded tough but meant nothing, gave the minister the chance to reinforce the government line and keep away from the story.

She studied the woman smiling and nodding along with Ferguson as he spoke. She had found Mark Sneddon, a print reporter without a cameraman, in a sea of TV cameras and big-name news presenters? Nah, the question had been a plant: the woman had worked it out with Mark beforehand, known she would go to him first.

Question was, who was using whom?

Another surge forward as Ferguson stopped speaking. The wom-an's eyes roved across the press pack again, landing on Donna for a second, then moving on. Donna forced herself to think. Two more questions, max. She needed to stay low-key, keep away from Matt's murder but get a shot in, keep her name linked to the story.

The thought came to her suddenly. Connor Fraser's words: *You play by the rules, but you're not afraid to push them a bit.*

She smiled, the idea taking root. Something that kept them away from Matt Evans's murder but moved the story on. Something it was unlikely the rest of the press knew. Unless, of course, they had, like

Connor Fraser, paid a visit to Christopher Russell before the press conference.

'Just one more question,' the woman called, her eyes skimming across the crowd. Donna raised her mic, didn't wait to be picked, just started talking, her voice rising to cut across the throng. Directed the question straight at the main event, Ferguson, felt an electric thrill as the woman who had been controlling proceedings until that point glared at her.

'Mr Ferguson, Donna Blake, Sky News. I understand that Councillor Helen Russell, who was found at the Stirling Court Hotel, was at a cross-party reception at the Scottish Parliament sponsored by the Tories, the night before she was discovered. Were you at the event and, if so, did you see Mrs Russell?'

Ferguson smiled, coughed, played for time, glanced around, looking for an answer from the woman or the maddeningly familiar man who was with him. Found none, started talking. He quickly regained his composure, falling back on well-practised sound bites about 'attending a wide range of parliamentary events and, yes, I seem to remember being there, but I can't recall seeing Mrs Russell'.

'So you knew her prior to this, sir?' Donna asked, again ignoring those around her. 'You don't recall seeing her, so you would have recognized her if you had?'

Ferguson's jowls quivered, his small, pudgy hands knitting in front of his crotch as though he were trying to protect himself from a kick.

Too late, Donna thought, too late.

'Why, yes. I, ah, knew Mrs Russell. She was a vocal representative of her constituents in Stirling North, and I believe she was part of the delegation that made representation to me regarding policing in the area.'

The press erupted, questions lobbed like grenades at Ferguson. Donna looked over her shoulder, making sure Gary, the cameraman, had got it all. He gave her a brief thumbs-up, his eye not leaving the viewfinder of his camera. Kid must be psychic.

Donna looked back to Ferguson, and the woman who was trying to regain control of the event, saying they would have to wrap up as the minister had to leave. But it was the man who drew Donna's attention. He looked at her coolly, a still point amid the chaos that raged around him. Recognition pulled at Donna's mind, an echo of something almost remembered, like a song where the tune was clear but the lyrics were lost.

Something . . .

And then it came to her. She knew where she had seen him before. Years ago. Before Andrew. Before Stirling. When the fiction that she and Mark had some kind of future was being taken as fact. When Glasgow voted yes and Scotland voted no. When . . .

You have good contacts, she heard Connor Fraser whisper.

She cursed herself. Blind. And stupid. She hadn't asked Mark if he knew the name of the first victim, been so fucking grateful at what he'd given her that she hadn't thought to query it.

But she knew now. Billy Griffin. Had to be. The presence of the man in front of her guaranteed it.

A man who, four years ago, had tried to strong-arm the press into banning the infamous image of Billy Griffin torching flags. Flags he cared about very deeply.

Maxwell Higgins was a party man, through and through.

CHAPTER 52

Simon was waiting in Starbucks across from the arrivals gate at Edinburgh airport when Connor arrived. He sat in a corner booth, a coffee in front of him, leaning back in his chair, at ease with the world. Connor had always envied that about Simon, the casual demeanour that spoke of a man comfortable in his own skin.

It was something Connor had yet to master.

He looked up when Connor was halfway towards the table, a broad grin splitting his face as he stood. He was taller than Connor, thinner too, the lack of muscle bulk something he always complained about in the gym. Yet Connor had seen Simon McCartney sprint down Castle Lane in the centre of Belfast in pursuit of a shoplifter at a speed that would have put Usain Bolt to shame. And he could fight. As well as weightlifting, Connor and Simon had sparred together from time to time, mostly to blow off steam, sometimes to establish the pecking order without getting seriously hurt. And those bouts had taught Connor one simple lesson: Simon was a dangerous mix of speed and intelligence in a fight.

'Well, fuck me if it isn't the jolly green giant,' Simon said, grabbing Connor in an embrace and thumping him on the back.

'Ho, ho, fucking ho,' he said, feeling the knot of tension that had crawled into his shoulders when he saw that book begin to ease. His friend was here. Whatever was going on, they would figure it out and deal with it together.

Simon broke the hug, taking a half-step back. 'You look well, big lad,' he said. 'This private-sector lark obviously suits you.'

'It pays the bills,' Connor said. 'You weren't waiting long, were you?'

Simon ran a hand through his hair. 'Nah, not really. Gave me a chance to get a coffee and see the sights anyway.' He nodded to his left, where a lithe blonde girl was sitting, long tanned legs showing she was just back from somewhere sunny.

Connor shook his head. 'You never change,' he said. 'C'mon, let's get you out of here.'

'Grand,' Simon said, dipping down beneath the table and pulling up a large kitbag. He dangled it in front of Connor. 'Don't worry, I made a wee stop before the flight – got a decent bottle in here for later.'

Connor gave him a quizzical look. 'Don't tell me you've finally learnt an appreciation of the finer things in life?'

'Whisky? Nah, catch yerself on. Red wine, my friend. Got a bottle of Châteauneuf-du-Pape in here. You want to kill your tastebuds with paint-stripper, crack on. I'll enjoy the good stuff.'

Connor chuckled. Same old Simon.

They walked in silence back to the car, Connor having parked in the multi-storey attached to the main terminal by a covered walkway. Simon pulled up short when he saw the car Connor was heading for, whistling between his teeth. '"Pays the bills",' he said, eyes roaming across the Audi.

Connor popped the boot, Simon stepping to the back of the car and putting the bag in carefully. Then they hopped in and Connor fired the engine, Simon nodding approval as the V8 burbled into life. 'Very nice,' he said.

Connor smiled. 'It does the job.'

He got out of the airport, used the roundabout at the exit as a slingshot and powered up the ramp to Glasgow Road, Simon easing back in his seat.

Connor waited until they got onto the bypass and had settled into the outside lane before he spoke. He had been mulling over how to start this conversation ever since he'd left Stirling. There was no easy way to say it so direct was the only way to go.

'You manage to find anything on the Librarian?'

Simon sighed. When he had met Connor, he had been relaxed, at ease, a civilian. But now they were talking business. And that meant he was on duty. The earlier humour in his voice was gone. 'Not really,' he said. 'I checked the death report and it's sound – got hit by a car on the Shankill, just at the pedestrian crossing at the leisure centre. Some no-mark kid with too much acceleration and not enough brains. No link to his dealing from the UDA that the investigating officers could find.'

Connor glanced down at the speedo, eased off slightly from the 90 m.p.h. he was doing. 'Nothing else? No activity from known associates? No known leaks in the service that might have given me up to him? Nobody looking like they were wanting to settle scores on his behalf after his death?'

'Nothing like that. Seems he mostly fell out of favour with the UDA after your little, ah, encounter with him. He lost face with the leadership after the way you put him down in Glencairn, and then the way he got, ah, mugged in town. And besides, Connor, if there was someone looking to settle scores for Hughes, don't you think they'd come for me first?'

Connor nodded. They both knew it was true. After Connor had beaten the shit out of Hughes, they had known that, as officers who had last confronted him, they would be persons of interest, both to official investigations and those that were carried out in the backrooms of bars on the Shankill. So while Connor was tracking and confronting Hughes, Simon was making sure any video footage of him in town that night was conveniently lost. It didn't take much, just a few calls to the right people, a few favours called in. The Troubles may have been officially over, the weapons 'put beyond use', but there was still an unwritten war footing in Belfast. And the first rule of that was loyalty. A police officer needed a favour from a fellow law-enforcement professional? No problem. Ranks were still closed, reports still lost, shortcuts still taken.

All in the name of justice, of course.

Following the initial clean-up, the alibi Simon provided wasn't overly examined. They were at his place, having a beer and craic, then

212

decided to head into town, around the Cathedral Quarter. The latter lie was easy to prove: Simon was the first person Connor had contacted from the Harp bar after his gran had called and pulled the pin on the night that ended his life in Belfast.

Simon seemed to read Connor's thoughts. 'You seen Karen at all?' he asked.

Connor had known the question was coming, but still it stung like a hard jab to the kidneys. 'No,' he said. 'I know she's back here, teaching in Edinburgh. With the teacher shortage at the moment, it was easy for her. Seeing someone new, I think. But other than that . . .'

'Sounds to me like you've been keeping tabs,' Simon said, no judgement in his voice.

Connor sighed. It was true, he had been. He knew it was bordering on stalking, but he had to know she was okay. After what he had done in Belfast, he had shut down, folded himself in on the poisonous anger and pain he felt over what he had done to Hughes, then his mother's cancer diagnosis. Karen had tried to reach him, even as the distance grew, but it was useless. The relationship broke down, the stress and tension making Connor retreat even further for fear he would lose his temper again and lash out at her physically. He could not, *would* not, let that happen, let himself become that man.

His grandfather.

She had stuck by him, attended his mother's funeral with him, both of them knowing they were mourning more than a death that day. But still he checked. Facebook profile, employment records, electoral roll. All the usual stuff.

Day to day for him, really.

'Look, Connor, whatever the fuck is going on here, we'll figure it out. If someone is trying to leave you a message, we'll find out who it is. And why. And then we'll send our own message.'

'Okay,' Connor said, nudging the car up to 100 m.p.h., suddenly eager to get back to Stirling and find some answers.

CHAPTER 53

Donna wrapped up her to-camera piece as quickly as she could after the press conference, the terror of doing a live piece suppressed by the clamour of questions in her mind. That done, and Gary dispatched to the van to edit the footage into an extended package for the afternoon bulletin, she grabbed her phone and called.

'Hello, Donna, I—'

'What the fuck are you playing at, Mark?' she asked, feeling tension creep across her jaw. Seized by the urge to move, she walked down the sweeping hill that ran from St Ninians Road up to the front of the police station.

'Donna, what are you talking about?'

'Cut the shit, Mark. I'm talking about that little performance with your new best pal just now. Nice soft question by the way, just the thing to keep the story where they wanted it to go. That's what your wee tip to me the other day was as well – just another way to help your pals control the story.'

Silence, just long enough to make her think he had hung up. Then he spoke, his voice flattened by exhaustion. 'Look, if you're going to shout at me, can you at least do it face to face? I can see you now. Look left. I'm three cars down.'

She turned her head and spotted his car. Hung up without another word and stalked towards it. Considered a moment then got in. 'Well?'

He looked at her, a mixture of resignation and defiance flitting through his eyes. 'It's not what you think, really. But if we're going to talk, can we do it over a drink? I don't know about you, but I could fucking do with one.'

He drove to the Golden Lion, a hotel at the foot of John Street, where the redeveloped shopping area of Stirling gave way to the more historic section of the town. He buzzed at the gate and drove into a small car park, the surface of which seemed to consist of pitted tarmac and puddles. They got out and went inside through a small door that would have looked fresh in the seventies, up a twisting flight of stairs and into a reception area that led to a small bar. She got a table as he ordered, glared at his back as he hunched over the counter.

The place was quiet, a smattering of guests taking a break from sightseeing around the town, conversation soft and uneven, periods of silence broken by a burst of laughter or a cough.

'Come on, then,' she said, as he slid a vodka and tonic over the table to her. 'Let's hear it.'

He looked down at his pint, took a gulp, even though the Guinness was still settling. 'Okay,' he said, more to himself than to her. 'You're right. Yes, Lucy and I set that question up beforehand. And, yes, the tip I gave you the other day about the first victim was from her as well. But I didn't give you that to control the story, Donna, I swear.'

She snorted, tightened her grip on her glass. 'Aye, right. And I take it Lucy wasn't aware that Ferguson knew Helen Russell?'

Confusion clouded Mark's eyes. 'What? No, I . . .'

Impatience rose. Donna took a sip of her drink to dampen it down. 'So you're telling me that you weren't asking planted questions, that you weren't helping them keep the story pointed where they wanted it? Christ, Mark, has Emma got you so desperate for a shag that you'd drop your pants and your morals for a smile?'

Anger coloured Mark's cheeks. 'Now hold on a minute. Yes, I agreed to throw them an easy question but, no, I wasn't helping them control the story. Course I would have asked about Russell if I'd fucking known. And I was not using you.'

Donna laughed, a brittle sound that drew glances from the few customers dotted around the bar. 'If that's the case, then they're playing you as well. What did Lucy offer you, Mark? An out from Emma? An exclusive with the First Minister? A wee knee-trembler in Bute House? You used to like those.'

Mark opened his mouth. Closed it. Shame drained the anger from his voice as he said, 'A job. They offered me a job.'

'*What?*'

His head snapped up, and Donna was surprised to see tears welling in his eyes. 'The *Westie*'s cutting again, Donna, and this time I'm up for the jump. Compulsory redundo if I don't go – all the senior reporters above a certain pay band are in the firing line. So Lucy got in touch, said that if I helped her out at the press conference, they'd see about getting me a job with the party's comms team. They need experienced people, especially now with all this Brexit shite and another referendum on the cards any time.'

Donna raised her glass, held a chunk of ice next to her lips. Poor bastard. He really believed the line they had fed him. Christ, what had happened to him? This wasn't the Mark she knew. She put the glass down, hard, as though it would crush the momentary flare of compassion she'd felt. Not her problem. Not any more. 'So they gave you the tip-off about the first victim, asked you to get the word out? Did they tell you it was Billy Griffin who had been killed, or did they keep that from you as well?'

Momentary confusion flitted across Mark's face, before recognition forced his mouth into an almost comical O of surprise. 'Billy Griffin? Hold on, not Billy Griffin who torched the flags on George Square? How did you . . .?'

'Your new pals,' Donna said. 'I knew I recognized Maxwell Higgins from somewhere, couldn't pin it down. But then it hit me. It was the day after the referendum and the trouble in George Square, the Yes-campaign press call in Grand Central, remember?'

Mark shook his head slowly, which didn't totally surprise Donna: he had been running on adrenalin, coffee and post-sex endorphins back then. The press conference had been called by the Yes movement in the Grand Central Hotel in Glasgow's Central station, partly as a wash-up, partly as a wake. It had been a subdued affair: the First Minister had resigned hours earlier and everyone was still licking their wounds from the loss of the referendum and the trouble in George Square the night before.

There was, however, one moment that Donna remembered. As a backbench Nationalist took the podium and trotted out the standard lines about 'coming together for the country' and 'accepting the will of the people', Craig Mather, a reporter Donna recognized from the Press Association, stood up, holding aloft a copy of the *Westie* with Billy Griffin's infamous image splashed all over it. 'Does this look like uniting the country to you?' he asked.

The question was dealt with and the press conference wrapped up hastily. But afterwards Donna had spotted Craig huddled in a corner, a tall, wiry man leaning in, his lips close to his ear. She'd asked him about it later and was told that Higgins was warning him about such cheap stunts: his editor would be getting a call. Donna had later found out that every editor in Scotland had been contacted, Higgins trying to get the picture of Griffin banned on the grounds that it would aggravate social unrest and sectarian bigotry.

All of which had come to her in a flash as Ferguson flailed around at the press conference. Higgins was trying to control the story. Again. It was a leap to assume that it was Billy Griffin who had been killed, but she knew in her gut she was right.

'You know this for a fact? Got it stood up?' Mark asked.

'Not yet,' she admitted. 'That's my next stop: the DCI who was first on the scene. Get him to confirm what I know.'

'Think he will?'

'Someone will,' Donna said, her thoughts turning to Danny. 'You want to stand it up with your new pals, be my guest. But I want in on it, Mark. This is my story.'

'They're not my . . .' His words petered out as his gaze fell to his Guinness, as though speaking was too much effort. He took a drink, swilled it like mouthwash, then swallowed. Dared a brief glance at her. 'I wasn't using you, Donna, seriously,' he said. 'Lucy gave me the tip-off about the injuries on the first body. I let you know. Thought it might help you. Seems I was right. Sky TV, after all. Not bad.'

The coy smile he gave her, which she had once found so endearing, looked ugly. Yeah, it had helped all right. Helped her start to rebuild the career her willingness to believe his lies had destroyed. Helped her get a corpse dumped in front of her car.

Some help.

She drained her glass, stood up. 'Write your story, Mark. Your pals will need it for your CV. And don't bother giving me any more help. I'll work this story on my own from now on.'

She left him, taking the short flight of steps that led out of the front of the hotel. Stopped for a moment, looked around. To her left was the Thistles, the main shopping centre in the heart of the town. To her right was the long, cobbled finger of King Street, which led up to Cowane's Hospital and the castle beyond.

She took a deep breath, decided. Started walking up the hill to the site where Billy Griffin had been dumped.

She would call Ford on the way.

CHAPTER 54

After a warning call from Doyle about the press conference and Ferguson's eagerness to talk to him, Ford had decided to get lost for a while, try to clear his head.

He had driven back into town after dropping Mary at home with promises to get back as early as possible, no real destination set in his mind. Parked at the Albert Halls and taken a walk up the Back Path that led from the hall. The crooked path hugged the old town walls as it snaked up towards the castle, the Old Town Cemetery and the Holy Rude Church, where Billy Griffin's head had been found.

Ford knew it was a tourist attraction, found the notion of a place that commemorated death being of interest alien to him. But still the visitors came to wander through the sprawling site, marvelling at the ornate statues and headstones dotted around it. One of the most striking and, to Ford, disturbing, was a marble piece mounted on a granite plinth depicting an angel looking down on a woman reading to a child. The figures were sealed in a glass-fronted dome, its white-washed metal roof pitted and bleached grey with the passage of time. Ford stood in front of it, unease crawling through him. There was something about the frozen expression of the angel looking down at the pair, hand clutching its forehead, that awoke childhood memories of faceless ghosts and the terror he had felt at Sunday school when he had been told about the Angel of Death sweeping through Egypt, killing firstborn sons. As an only child with a vivid imagination, the story had horrified Ford, instilling in him a lifelong distaste of angels in particular and religion in general. It had driven him and Margaret to be married in a register office in Edinburgh, rather than the church her parents had tried to insist on.

His phone buzzed in his pocket, jerking him from his thoughts. He looked back at the monument, mouthed a silent admonishment as he pulled out his phone. It was a text from Doyle, as blunt and to the point as the man himself: *Reporter Blake stirring the shit again. Seems Ferguson knew Russell before her murder. Break for us – press harassing him instead. But stay lost for now. Any more word from Fraser?*

Ford pocketed the phone without sending a reply, uncertain of what he should say. He still didn't know what to make of Fraser. The man knew the right questions to ask, gave the impression of wanting to help, but still, ex-copper or not, he was a civilian and shouldn't be within a mile of the case. But, despite himself, Ford felt Connor Fraser could help, even if he had to be forced into doing so.

Ford walked deeper into the graveyard, heading towards the castle and an area known as Drummond's Pleasure Ground. A huge pyramid dominated the skyline atop a grassy mound, its sandstone sides dulled and blackened with age and damp. Ford struggled to remember its purpose, knew it was something to do with Presbyterians who had suffered during the Protestant Reformation back in the 1600s.

And there it was again. Religion. And what people would do in the name of their particular brand.

He stopped, Billy Griffin's mottled Red Hand tattoo flashing across his mind. And then there was Helen Russell's attempt to hide her own tattoo, the symbol for the Loyalist, mainly Protestant, Alba Gheal Ann An Aonadh. Whatever was going on, it was something to do with two Loyalist groups. But how the hell did Billy Griffin get mixed up with either of them? What was Helen Russell doing with the mark of a proscribed paramilitary group on her hip? And where did Matt Evans fit into all this? The murders were linked: the level of violence and similarity of the wounds on the bodies indicated as much. The fact that Special Branch had swept in and frozen the local cops out of the case practically screamed 'paramilitary links', which, in these days of cars being driven into crowds of pedestrians, and alienated youths killing those who didn't believe as they did, was a red flag that demanded the most serious response.

He knew it was one of the reasons they weren't formally connecting the cases yet. Let the public draw their own conclusions about a bloodthirsty serial killer stalking the streets. Once, the authorities would have done the same. But now, in a post-Manchester, post-Borough Market world, three ritualistic murders with some kind of sectarian link would instantly be ascribed to the twenty-first-century bogeyman: the radicalized terrorist acting for the honour of their God or country. And while the thought of a serial killer would cause parents to hug their children tighter and make sure their doors were locked at night, the prospect of a terrorist would ignite the flames of racial hatred being fanned so effectively by every nasty perma-tanned homophobe with a Twitter account and an axe to grind.

And if that happened, there was the very real prospect of blood on the streets.

But, still, Ford had to know. He had seen Griffin's body, knew it was no random act of terrorism designed to shock. No, it was murder as a message. But to whom? And what was the message? What linked the three victims? Why had someone decided they had to die?

Ford shuddered, glanced back to Cowane's Hospital as the squeal of the metal spike rocking in the wind echoed in his mind. Something caught in his thoughts, just for a second, a shape emerging from the fog of confusion. Something about the head. About the rat . . .

He sighed as the thought slipped away half formed, the need for a cigarette tugging at him. He had quit smoking about five years ago, had never got the hang of the modern trend of vaping. But there were days, when he needed to think, that he craved a cigarette. He considered buying a packet, along with a bottle of mouthwash, on the way home.

One couldn't hurt, could it?

He kept walking, heading for the exit to the cemetery that would lead him to the castle, decided he would walk back down past the front of Cowane's Hospital, check in with the officers who had been left on the scene, see if there was any update. He had been warned off the case, but there was nothing to prevent him checking in with his fellow officers. And if they happened to tell him the theory had been confirmed, that Griffin's body was driven up to the bowling green and dumped, then so much the better.

He had just turned out of the castle esplanade and back onto John Street when he saw a familiar shape marching up the hill, phone in hand, jaw set, dark hair whipping in front of her eyes in the wind. He felt no surprise when his phone vibrated in his pocket, just reached in to kill the call. He watched Donna Blake stop walking and pull her phone away from her ear, her face contorting in frustration.

Ford smiled despite himself. He was about to walk away when a thought occurred to him. Donna Blake had found Matt Evans's body. He had read the statement she had given, felt a certain grudging respect that she was still trying to work the story after what she had seen. But she had known Evans. And maybe she knew something that could help Ford link his death to Griffin and Russell.

Decision made, Ford started walking. Time for another interview with Donna Blake. But this time he would be asking the questions and, whether she liked it or not, it would most definitely be off the record.

CHAPTER 55

After Donna left, Mark Sneddon did the only thing that made sense to him: he ordered another drink. He took it back to his table, cracked open the laptop and filed his copy with the *Westie*. He wrote it quickly, clinically, the confrontation with Donna bleeding out the little enthusiasm he had left for the story. The job done, he placed a call to Lucy to see if there were any other lines she could give him, something he could use to help either her or himself. Felt nothing but resignation when the call went straight to her voicemail.

Of course he knew Donna was right – he was being used. And in his desperation to get a job and keep the money flowing he had allowed it to happen. But now he had played his role, done what was asked of him, and Donna had blown the story open anyway, torpedoing Mitchell's oh-so-clever plan to keep Ferguson talking about what she wanted him to talk about.

So where did that leave Mark?

Was this really it? A pitiful pay-off from the *Westie*, just enough to buy him a month or two before he plunged headlong into the abyss?

And after that, then what?

It was his own fault, of course. When Donna had told him she was pregnant, he had panicked. His marriage to Emma was dull, tedious, routine – routine lives, routine boredom, routine sex – but that was what he needed. Routine. He had never been good at organizing his own life, preferring to live as he worked: from deadline to deadline, crisis to crisis. And his marriage allowed him to do that. So when the moment came, and the choice of diving into the chaos of parenthood and creating a new life with Donna or staying with the safe, reliable, ultimately empty marriage he had that let him live his life, he did what he always did.

He chose himself.

Emma, of course, knew something was wrong. It was in the pointed questions, the lingering looks, the rolled eyes every time he picked up his phone. So Mark took the only option he had: he threw money at the problem. Holidays, presents, the new kitchen she had wanted, even a new car the moment her two-year-old BMW coughed the wrong way one cold morning. Anything to make her feel loved, special, the centre of his world.

He had bought his way back into the routine of his marriage. And as the credit card bills had mounted and the loan amounts had risen, he'd told himself it would all be okay. His marriage, his life, was worth it. And, besides, he was scraping by.

Just.

And then he had been told about the redundancies at the *Westie*, with the specialist reporters – who had laughingly been deemed to be on the highest wages – up for the chop.

Mark had panicked. One lost wage was all it would take for the house of cards he had built to come crashing down, for the lie of a life he had built around Emma to be exposed. He had looked for a job, any job, to jump to – a life raft to keep things moving. And, in his desperation, Lucy Mitchell had found him.

Looking back on it now, it was so obvious it was embarrassing. The offer of a job with the party, a job 'tailor-made to use his political expertise'. With a snap election a very real possibility, there was work to be done, the case for independence to be made.

Mark didn't need to be convinced. He'd written the stories, knew how much special advisers and high-ranking party officials could earn.

They had him at 'civil service pension'.

But then he had seen Donna again, the way she was throwing herself at the story, and the shame had boiled up in him. He had left her with a child on the way and nothing but a bagful of broken promises. And yet she was out there, chasing the story, being the reporter he had once thought he was, while he did . . .

What?

He put the pint down, slid it out of reach. Forced himself to focus through the beer buzz. Thought of Donna and the press conference, Ferguson's reaction to her question. Faced the question he should have asked the moment Lucy Mitchell had got in touch with him.

Why *was* Ferguson so scared about being linked to Helen Russell?

He thought about it for a moment, staring at the blank screen of the laptop as if he could see the answer there. They both moved in political circles and, the Scottish media village being what it was, it was almost inevitable they would know each other.

So what *was* Ferguson scared of? No. Wrong question. What was Mitchell so scared of?

He splayed his fingers across the keyboard, thought for a moment, then started typing, gingerly at first, pecking at the keys hesitantly. If Mitchell had no further use for him, fine. There was something she was trying to hide. And if she had something to hide, then maybe, just maybe, he had something to sell.

CHAPTER 56

'Fuck's sake, you're not pissing about, are ye?'

Connor glanced at the Glock-loaded pancake holster he had laid on the coffee-table. In truth, he had almost forgotten about the gun, its weight becoming familiar on his hip all too quickly. He looked up at Simon, who had paused in uncorking the bottle of wine he had produced from his bag. 'Can't take any chances,' he said. 'Even in peacetime, you always check under the car before you drive.'

Simon smiled. It was a phrase he had instilled in Connor early, a reminder of the Troubles, when paramilitaries would booby-trap police officers' cars with bombs strapped under the tyre sills or wedged further in the chassis. Even though a ceasefire had been called and such attacks were now less common, the message was simple: keep your guard up. Be prepared. Don't take chances.

Simon sat down, went back to the cork with his waiter's mate, his eyes not leaving the gun. Connor knew why it was bothering him. He had dropped everything, flown to Scotland, all on the hunch of his former partner who thought that, somehow, a dead man was stalking him. The gun was a sign that he was taking the threat seriously. And they both knew that Connor Fraser with a gun was not a happy mix for anyone who got too close.

The cork came out with a dull pop, and Simon poured the wine into the glasses Connor had brought from the kitchen when they had arrived at the flat – Simon again commenting on how well Connor was doing for himself. Looking back at the last twenty-four hours, Connor could have argued with him on that but decided to save himself the bother. There were bigger issues to discuss.

Simon took a glass, went through the pantomime of swilling the wine around, watching its legs as they crawled down the sides of the glass, taking a deep sniff. Connor smiled inwardly. Simon McCartney, the great wine snob. Not bad for a guy who used to think a pint of Guinness and a fish supper with a wooden fork was the height of sophistication.

Simon took a sip, gave an appreciative sigh. Then put the glass down and leant forward, elbows on his knees. Looked down again at the gun. 'Let's go through it from the top,' he said, the cold, on-duty edge returning to his voice.

'I've told you most of it already,' Connor said. 'There was a murder two days ago. A man called Billy Griffin was decapitated and left at a church at the top of the town. Didn't pay much attention when the first news reports came in, nothing really to do with me. But yesterday there was another report. A councillor had been killed. She'd had the shite beaten out of her like yer man Griffin, then was dumped at a hotel on the grounds of the uni. And . . .' he paused, catching Simon's gaze and holding it '. . . that was when I heard about the book. *Misery* by Stephen King. A reporter who's been ahead on all of this found out about the inscription in it: "Not the same edition but the same horror story. Hope you like it, Connie. See you soon – L."'

'And you think that's a message for you, from someone who was linked to Jonny Hughes? Someone who's looking to settle scores now that he's dead?'

Connor swallowed his frustration with another slug of wine. 'What else could it be, Si? The message is almost identical to the one that bastard left in the book he sent Karen – and "Connie"? Who else could it be? The question is why: why Helen Russell, and what does this have to do with the Red Hand and the UDA?'

Simon let the silence stretch out. It was a tactic Connor had known him use in countless interviews. Let the quiet gnaw at the interviewee, pressure them into filling it with something, anything. And all the while Simon would sit across from them, implacable, like he had all the time in the world.

'Okay,' he said, when Connor felt his patience was about to snap. 'I see what you mean. It's an intimate message, and one that only you or I would understand. But I told you, Jonny is dead and, from what I could find out, there's no one actively looking to settle any beefs for him. He was on the outs with the UDA, just another small-time pusher trying to use the paramilitaries to make a rep for himself and buy a bit of street protection. Way I heard it, his uncle was getting fucked off with the whole thing. Don't think there were too many tears when he died.'

Connor felt something catch in his mind, a train of thought that hid in the shadows every time he tried to look at it. Pushed it aside. He needed to stay focused. 'Any indication Jonny's death wasn't an accident?'

Simon gave him a withering look. 'Come on, Connor, this isn't the movies. There's no big conspiracy here. He got stupid, tried to cross the Shankill at the wrong time, ended up with half his dome caked on some boy racer's exhaust, nothing more.'

'Okay,' Connor said, that nagging discomfort needling him again. What was he missing? 'But that still leaves the fact that three people are dead, and if it is one killer we're looking for, they've got some link to Jonny Hughes and know about what went down between him and us.'

'Why use Helen Russell to send that message?' Simon asked. 'Makes more sense to dump the book with the first body. From what your copper pal said, he's the one with the Red Hand on his chest, links to the Loyalists. Right up your street.'

'Yeah, but the woman, Russell, had links too. The detective, Ford, asked me about the Red Handers, if I'd had any run-ins with them. Seems she had work done to try to erase an old tattoo from a Unionist group here, active in the seventies, which ran training camps with the Red Hand across in Northern Ireland. Rumour is they came across here too, had a few survival weekends in Perthshire.'

'You mentioned Russell's husband said she was shagging around. Any chance it was with Griffin?'

Connor wrinkled his nose in disgust. 'Unlikely,' he said. 'From what Ford said, Griffin was only in his late twenties, while Russell was closing in on her seventies.'

Simon smiled at some private joke. 'Even if they weren't shagging, there's something that links them together, and you to them. So what? Have you heard of either of them before today? Has Sentinel done any work for Russell or someone linked to her?'

It was a good question, one that had occurred to Connor after his conversation with Ford. 'Nothing. I checked earlier. We've done some private work for the Tories, shadow security for some cabinet ministers who get a nosebleed and a case of the shits any time they have to go further north than Clapham Junction. But nothing for Russell.'

Simon considered his wine glass, his pose just casual enough to tell Connor it was practised. I'm a big thinker with a taste for the finer things in life, it said. He had to swallow a bubble of laughter.

'Any word back from your contact about Griffin's movements?' Simon asked.

'Not yet,' Connor said, reaching for his phone on a reflex. Duncan MacKenzie hadn't been pleased with the call from Connor, but after some fatherly warnings about looking after his 'wee girl' he'd agreed to look into Billy Griffin for him. If he had been working something illegal anywhere in Central Scotland, MacKenzie would be the man to find it.

But, so far, nothing.

'In that case, I suggest we go to the pub,' Simon said, smiling.

Connor looked at his friend sitting there, waiting. Almost said something, then bit back the words. It was a test. Plain and simple. And he'd almost missed it.

Sloppy, Connor, he thought. Sloppy. And right now, sloppy is the last thing you need.

He reached for the gun, eyes falling on the waiter's mate on the table. Felt the tug of recognition, something he was almost seeing. 'Good plan,' he said, standing. 'Get out, see the sights. If someone's after me, they're less likely to make a move in a public area. Everything we've seen so far shows they like to work in private. And with you there, we're more likely to spot anyone watching us.'

Simon clapped his hand softly against the wine glass, smile widening, finally hitting his eyes. 'Very good,' he said, draining his glass. 'Just give me a minute to change my shirt and we'll get going.' He made his way to the hall, went into the spare bedroom.

Connor cleared the glasses, thoughts turning back to what was bothering him. Something about what Simon had said? Something about the waiter's mate he had used on the wine?

He was startled from his thoughts by his phone buzzing on the table. He reached for it, felt a twinge of guilt when he saw the caller ID. Thought about ignoring it, knew that was a bad idea. Hit answer. 'Hello, Jen,' he said, forcing an enthusiasm he didn't feel into his voice.

'Hi, Connor, how you doing? You recovered after yesterday?'

'Yeah,' he said, embarrassed. 'Sorry about that, stupid mistake not to eat after a weights session like that.'

'Aye, stupid,' she said, her tone telling him he was fooling no one. 'If you're feeling better, you up to anything tonight?'

He looked around at the sound of a floorboard creaking, saw Simon step back into the room, a fresh T-shirt hanging off his sinewy frame. 'Actually, I'm just heading out to the pub. Fancy joining us? I've got someone here who I think you'd like to meet.'

CHAPTER 57

The headline seemed to scream from the screen, a white-hot outrage that seared his eyes and made his nerves quiver and sing, like the over-tightened string of a guitar.

'Justice secretary linked to Stirling murder victim,' the caption read, below images of the press conference, reporters surging forward as Blake asked her question, the screen flaring bright as every flash popped, trying to catch the moment in all its failed glory.

He had known using Sneddon was a risk when he was approached with the idea. Anyone who met him could practically smell the desperation bleeding from his pores, the need to please, to ingratiate, to make himself indispensable. But he had allowed himself to be convinced, trusting those advising him that they knew what they were talking about.

And Sneddon had proved how wrong he was when he opened his mouth to parrot the lines he had been given like a good little puppet. He shuddered with embarrassment at the memory. A fucking baseball bat would have been more subtle.

And then, just to complete the cluster-fuck, Blake had pushed her way into the press conference with the one inference he had worked so hard to keep everyone from drawing.

So you knew her prior to this, sir? You don't recall seeing her, so you would have recognized her if you had?

He fought the almost irresistible urge to swipe the computer from his desk as the anger boiled up: a wave of acid at the back of his throat. He clamped his hands under the desk and pressed up, as though trying to lift it, feeling his muscles ache with the effort. All he had to do was stand up, extend his arms and flip the table. Grab his chair and throw it through the glass wall that faced into the rest of the office, sweep up a shard of broken glass as he stepped through and then . . .

He closed his eyes, the after-image of that fucking headline dancing across the darkness. Forced himself to breathe, relax.

Think.

He opened his eyes, looked again at the insult. His fury slowly abated, replaced by a cold hatred that he seized on and nurtured as he fed it the facts.

So they knew there was a link. So what? Politicians had meetings with each other all the time: it was the nature of the business. A Nationalist minister meeting a Unionist councillor was perfectly normal. Routine, even. It could be explained.

Evans, on the other hand, was a complication. He admitted to a dark elation when he learnt what the caller had done, hoped that the little prick had been made to suffer before the end, just as he had asked for Griffin to suffer. After all, betrayal deserved to be repaid with pain. But now, with this fucking bitch Blake setting the press pack salivating, it felt like an indulgence, an unnecessary risk that only increased the chance of exposure.

And yet . . .

If everyone was looking at Russell, no one was looking at Evans. At the moment, the official theory was that, as a local media personality with form on a bigger stage, he had attracted the attention of the killer. Which was true. What no one knew, what he could not afford anyone to know, was *why* he had attracted the killer's attention.

The sound of his intercom startled him from his thoughts. He reached for it, unnerved to see his hand was not steady. 'Yes, Margaret, what is it?'

'Ah, Ms Mitchell is calling for you, says you'll know what it's about.'

He shot a poisonous glance at the door. Stupid, senile old bitch. He should have got rid of her when her eyes started to fail. She was more

232

trouble than she was worth. But, no. She had been with him from the beginning. And her dedication deserved – no, demanded – his loyalty.

He closed his eyes, concentrated on keeping his voice even. No point in delaying the inevitable. 'Put her through, will you?'

The clunk of a call being connected, Mitchell's voice on the line. He listened, eyes still closed, as she unravelled his world around him. He thought of hanging up, just slamming the phone down and walking away from it all. But that would be the coward's way out. The way of Evans or Griffin. No. He had come too far, worked too hard, to fail now.

He turned his attention back to the call, listened to the forced calm of Mitchell's voice. And, as he did, he came to a decision. It was one he could live with. After all, what was one less journalist in the world?

CHAPTER 58

Connor and Simon arrived before Jen and headed to the bar to order a drink. They had decided to meet at the Settle Inn, a small pub about five minutes from the Castle, its whitewashed walls glowing softly in the dwindling light. A sign above the bar boasted that it was the 'auldest pub in Stirling', dating back to 1733. Connor wasn't sure about that, but the stonework looked like it could pass the test, one wall of the pub being a mosaic of time-stained sandstone and granite that dwarfed a small wood burner set into the fireplace. The furnishing reminded him of his grandfather's club, long, heavily varnished benches and small circular tables surrounded by high-backed wooden chairs.

They found a place at the bar and stood shoulder to shoulder, the sounds of a folk band tuning their instruments in the back room echoing off the vaulted stone ceiling and drifting back to them. Simon looked around with vague amusement.

'What?' Connor asked.

'Oh, nothing. Just that, for a man who drives a flash car and is obviously doing all right for himself, you've got a taste for the, ah, rustic.'

Connor laughed. It was true. Despite the flat and the car, neither of which he would have been able to afford without the money his mother had left him, he never felt comfortable with either those who were obviously wealthy or the world they lived in. He supposed it was why he was so good at his job: the hotels, offices and parliaments to which he escorted clients had a rarefied air of opulence that set him on edge. And because he was never totally at ease, he was always alert, watching. Waiting. Simon was right, he preferred places like this, places that reminded him of his grandfather and the world he had lived in. But that wasn't the reason he had chosen this place tonight.

Not that Simon needed to know.

They finally caught the eye of a barman who was definitely making a brave attempt at being the auldest barman in Stirling. He pulled their pints with hands that were warped and gnarled with arthritis, shirt-sleeves rolled up to expose twig-thin arms dotted with a patchwork of liver spots and cheap tattoos.

'Six pund aiktie,' he said, his voice as rough as his beard, as he placed the second pint of Guinness on the bar towel in front of Simon. Connor reached for his wallet, felt Simon jostle him with an elbow.

'Catch yersel' on,' he said. 'I'm getting this one, least I can do.' He pulled his wallet from his jacket pocket, opened it to reveal a thick wad of notes and pulled a tenner from the sheaf. Connor's eyes lingered on it, his thoughts lost, until Simon spoke, breaking the spell. 'Cheers,' he said, raising his glass and turning to lean on the bar.

'Aye, cheers,' Connor replied, lifting his own glass, his thoughts filled with waiter's mates and Simon's wallet.

He took a swig of his pint, the cool velvet of the Guinness sticking to the back of his throat. He looked across the pub, saw nothing that appeared to be a threat. Simon was right: in a cramped, public place like this, a professional wouldn't dream of taking a shot at him.

And Connor was convinced that whoever he was dealing with was a professional.

The pub door opened and Jen walked in, glancing around. He raised his pint to her in greeting, saw her smile even as her eyes jumped from him to Simon. 'Evening,' he said, as she approached. 'Thanks for coming. Jen, this is Simon McCartney, an old, ah, friend, from Northern Ireland. Simon, this is Jen. And before you say it, she's too good for you.'

Simon laughed, punched Connor in the shoulder, just hard enough to tell him it was a cheap shot.

'So, you going to tell me all about the mystery man here?' Jen asked.

'I can, but I may have to kill you after,' he said, widening his smile and squaring his shoulders. In that moment, he felt bad for his previous remark. He was only teasing, but he knew Simon liked the woman he had just met. 'If you two are going to talk about me, I don't want to hear it,' he said. 'Listen, go and get a table, talk behind my back, and I'll get you a drink, Jen. Same as the other night? Vodka tonic?'

She nodded, her hair playing in the light, turning gold. Connor knew it would feel like cool silk running through his fingers. 'Yeah, please,' she said. 'Come on, Simon.'

They moved off, dodging customers and finding a small table next to the fireplace. Connor turned back to the bar, caught the old man's rheumy gaze and ordered. Looked back at Simon and Jen as he waited, watching as they got to know each other, the stifled, defensive body language, Jen's arms crossed over her chest as she leant on the table slightly, Simon's legs crossed at the ankles as he leant away, giving her all the space she needed. But, still, they seemed to be getting on. They were holding eye contact and, occasionally, Connor saw a flash of Jen's white teeth.

'Three twenny, pal,' the old man said.

Connor fished into his back pocket for his wallet, drew it out. Opened it and reached his fingers in for a note . . .

A note.

Realization flooded through him, froze him to the spot as random thoughts collided and connected in his mind. He felt more than saw the old man shuffle on his feet, trying to attract his attention. 'Sorry, mate,' he said, fishing out a fiver. 'Keep the change.'

The barman cracked something that might once have been called a smile, then beetled back to the till. Connor watched him go, forced himself to follow the path his mind was trying to take him down, see if it was a dead end. It wasn't.

He pulled out his phone, took a long swig from his pint to kill some time. Opened the browser, found what he was looking for. Felt a punch swing into his guts and drive the air from his lungs as he saw what he didn't want to see, what he had desperately hoped wasn't there.

He clicked the phone off, pocketed it. Picked up Jen's drink, took another gulp of his own. Bitter.

He made his way back to the table, took a seat between Simon and Jen, who were sitting opposite each other. 'So,' he said, putting the glasses down gently, 'what nasty lies has he been telling you about me?'

Jen smiled, raised her glass in thanks. 'Nothing yet,' she said. 'Actually, he says you're the perfect gentleman, so I know he's talking shit.'

Connor pulled his lips back from his teeth in what he hoped was a vague approximation of a smile. 'Aye, that's our Simon, always with the bullshit.'

He saw confusion flash across Simon's face, replaced by a bashful smile. 'Only bullshit here is what line you used to get Jen to talk to you,' he said. 'How did you meet this lunk anyway?'

It was a pointless question: Connor had told Simon all about Jen and her background on the way to the pub.

They bandied small-talk for a few minutes, Simon and Connor falling into the old act of trading insults. Jen seemed to enjoy the routine, relaxing into the conversation as they spoke.

'Right,' Simon said, when they hit a lull. 'I'm for the toilet, then a top-up. You both want the same?'

Jen considered her glass. 'Please, but I'm only having one more after this, got an early shift tomorrow.'

Simon smiled. 'Never a good thing. Connor?'

Connor stared at him, let the mask slip for just a moment. Saw Simon flinch. 'Aye, a pint, please,' he said.

'Grand. I'll nip to the toilet and sort that out. Where would they . . .?'

Connor gave him directions, watch his friend stalk off. Counted to twenty in his head, slowly, nodding along to whatever Jen was saying. Then he stood up. 'You be okay for a minute?' he said. 'Sorry, Jen, but Simon's put the idea in my head now.'

She looked at him, cocking her head to the side and giving him a mischievous smile. 'And I thought it was only women who went to the toilets in pairs,' she said. 'Aye, on you go, but no measuring contests, okay?'

'No promises,' he said.

He got to the toilet a moment later, stood outside the door, breathing heavily. Steadied himself, then walked in. It was a basic toilet, one long trough running along its length, a row of sinks opposite. Simon was at the far end, his back to the cubicles, a young guy who didn't look old enough to shave washing his hands. Connor straightened to his full height as he passed, gave the kid the cold stare in the mirror. He got the message, shutting off the tap and grabbing a wad of green-paper towels to dry his hands.

Simon smiled at Connor. 'Nice girl,' he said, as he finished up. 'Don't know what she sees in you, like, but . . .'

Connor grabbed him by the shirt, swung him round and barrelled him into a cubicle, the slam of the door like a gunshot. He kept going, driving the back of Simon's legs into the toilet, forcing him into the cold porcelain of the wall.

'Connor, man, what the fuck?' Simon gasped.

Connor felt a bitter sorrow rippling through his head in cramping waves, Jonny Hughes's voice a taunting whisper in his mind: *I know people who tell me things. So when I asked about you, they told me all sorts of interesting stories.*

'How long have you been here, Simon?' Connor hissed. 'You said you got the fourteen forty-five flight from City, but that's bullshit, isn't it?'

Simon's eyes widened, the colour draining from his face. He dropped his head, took a deep breath, muttered something.

'What was that? I didn't—'

Connor almost didn't see it coming. Simon's arms flashed up, as though he was surrendering, then he brought his fists down on Connor's wrists. Bright pain exploded in Connor's arms, crawling all the way up to his shoulders. Involuntarily, he eased his grip and Simon lashed out, driving a hard right into Connor's exposed armpit. He grunted, twisting to the side, Simon writhing and trying to get free by using his momentum against Connor.

'Fucking quit it!' Connor roared. He straightened up, ignoring the pain in his arms, grabbed Simon by the shoulders and squeezed, forcing him down, buckling his knees with the sheer force of his mass. 'I just checked the flight times,' he panted, arms quivering. 'Nice try, but your fucking flight was delayed by ten minutes, so there's no fucking way you got off the plane, had enough time to buy a coffee and be lounging about waiting by the time I got there. So how long *have* you been here, Simon? Who sent you?'

'Fuck, man,' Simon replied, bucking up as hard as he could and pushing Connor back. He stared at him, cold defiance in his eyes. 'You no' think I was maybe at the front of the plane, managed to get away ahead of the crowd?'

Connor sneered. 'With that fucking waiter's mate you were carrying? In hand luggage only? No fucking way, pal. Even if you flashed your ID, no way they're letting you on board. And then there's your fucking wallet. Got a little look at the bar. Full of Scottish notes, not an Ulster Banker among them. So last time, Simon. How long have you been here? And who fucking sent you? Was it Hughes? His uncle? Were you working for them the whole time?'

Simon's eyes flashed with disgust. He took a half-step forward, fists bunching. 'Fuck you, Connor,' he said. 'After all the shit we pulled to cover up what you did, you think I was working with those wankers? Fine. So I've been here for a couple of days. Headed over the moment they found that wee scrote at the church. But it's not what you think, promise.'

Connor forced himself to lean back, give Simon space, his fury at the betrayal arguing with the vague hope Simon was actually on his side. But he had lied. And then there was the book, the message . . .

I know people who tell me things.

'Tell me,' he said, his voice as cold as the tiles on the wall, 'no bullshit, Simon, what the fuck is going on. If you're not working for Hughes, then why are you here? And why didn't you tell me? Did the PSNI send you over? To check on me?'

Simon shook his head, a crooked smile on his lips. 'Nothing like that,' he said. 'But you are being checked on.'

'What the fuck is that supposed to mean?'

Simon glanced to his right, as though he could see through the toilet wall. He straightened, tried to smooth the T-shirt crumpled by Connor's grip. 'Let's not leave the wee girl waiting,' he said. ''Mon, I'll buy you another pint. And I can put it on expenses. After all, Lachlan Jameson is paying. The least the old bastard can do is stand us a jar.'

CHAPTER 59

Parents dispatched after a raft of tentative questions about how her day was, and if she was coping after 'what happened', Donna stood at the front door of the flat, soaking in the silence.

The confrontation with Ford had been unexpected, and gruelling. She found his sudden appearance on the street put her off balance. He had pushed her hard on who had leaked to her the details on Billy Griffin's murder, how she had managed to get those pictures at the uni and what her relationship with Matt Evans had been like. 'You see, Ms Blake,' he told her, 'three murders and you're a common factor in all of them, popping up like an unwanted aunt at Christmas. So, I've got to ask, why are you so closely linked to all of this?'

It was a good question, which put her even further off balance. She had seen the first murder as a way to get her career back on track, escape from the backwater of Valley FM into the deeper waters of the national media. She'd been so focused on that, on getting her byline back into the story, that she had allowed herself to be sucked in by Mark, used in his pathetic little ploy to buy himself a job with the government. But now another two people were dead – one of them dumped, literally, in front of Donna's nose.

So what was she doing involved in this? Was it worth it?

She moved through the flat quietly, found her way to Andrew's room. He was huddled in his cot, the covers pulled up to his chin, his right arm defiantly on top as ever. She felt a stab of melancholy as she remembered it was the same pose Mark adopted when he slept.

Mark. She should have given him to Ford, let him deal with the awkward questions. So why hadn't she? She owed him nothing, no matter how he'd tried to spin his little 'favour' the previous day, and it would get Ford off her back if she just gave him Mark's name.

And yet . . .

She rubbed her eyes, felt the weariness settle on her like a weight. Saw a flash of Matt Evans's dead, leering grin in the darkness, snapped her eyes open and swallowed, throat clicking. She crossed the room quickly, peered into Andrew's cot and felt comforted by the regular rise and fall of his chest.

She cursed when she heard her phone ring in the living room. Reached out to smooth Andrew's hair, found herself not wanting to touch him, overtaken by the irrational thought that she would some-how infect his dreams with her nightmares. She swore silently, then hurried from the room to silence the phone. Fumbled through her bag as it rang, convinced it would switch to voicemail at any moment, half hoping it would.

No such luck.

She read the display, saw an unfamiliar number. Felt a sudden dread creep through her, the urge to click the phone off and ignore it flitting through her mind. 'Hello?'

Heavy breathing down the line. A soft sniff. Then a voice. Female. Low. The precision of a Morningside accent hardened into something brutal by hatred.

'Is that . . . is that Donna Blake?'

'It is. Who's calling?' Donna said, not wanting to know the answer.

'Is he there?'

Donna felt her guts chill even as heat flashed across her cheeks. 'Is who there? Who is this?'

'This is Emma. Emma Sneddon. And I'm asking if he's there. You know, my husband. Mark. Is he there, Ms Blake?'

Donna felt as though she had been plunged into an ice-cold pool. She tried to breathe, found her lungs were useless. Her heart hammered in her ears, even as something brittle clawed its way up her throat. 'I, ah, I'm not sure what you—'

'Please don't,' Emma said. 'I thought there was something wrong when he said he was going to be staying in Stirling to cover a story. Knew it wouldn't be long until he found his way back to your door. So I decided to pay him a visit. But he's not here, and the hotel staff say he's not been back since early this afternoon.'

Donna felt the room spin, a kaleidoscope of thoughts crashing through her mind. Closed her eyes. Forced herself to think. 'Hold on. You're in Stirling now. At the Golden Lion?'

A sneer down the line. 'So you know where he's staying. Why doesn't that surprise me? Is he with you now? Is he hiding from his phone or did you ask him to switch it off in case the wifey interrupted while you were fucking?'

Donna felt anger spark in her, seized it, used it to burn away the shock and confusion crashing through her mind. She spoke slowly, deliberately. 'Now listen, I don't know what you think you know, but you're wrong. Mark is not here, has never been here and never will be here. Yes, I saw him earlier – we were discussing the story we're both covering, if you must know, but I've not seen him since.'

'So you're saying he's not there?'

'Yes!' Donna barked, cringing as her voice rose, not wanting to wake Andrew. 'I saw him earlier this afternoon at the press conference and then at the Lion. I've not seen or heard from him since. If he's not answering your calls, that's your problem, not mine.'

'So where is he?' Emma asked, more to herself than Donna.

'I don't know, and I don't care.'

'Look, I'm sorry,' Emma said, 'but when he wasn't here, I just thought . . .'

You just thought he was fucking me again. A shard of ice roiled in the pit of Donna's stomach. She forced the chill into her voice. 'I don't care what you thought, Mrs Sneddon. He's not here. Check with his newsdesk – he's probably out chasing a lead. And don't call me again.'

She hung up before Emma could reply, then tossed the phone onto the couch as though it was diseased. She fought back the tears burning behind her eyes.

242

She knows. Fuck. She knows!

Reluctantly, she reached for the phone. Called Mark's number. Got his voicemail. Left a curt message, then hung up. Considered. Her phone told her it was a little after eight o'clock. She'd left Mark at just before three. Five hours to go quiet? That was nothing when he was working a story, except . . .

The image of Matt Evans's ruined corpse rose in her mind again. She thumbed through the phone, found the number she was looking for. Hit call.

'Newsdesk.'

'Brian? Brian, it's Donna Blake, how you doing? . . . Yeah, long time no speak. Look, after a wee favour. You heard from Mark at all? I know he was up here on a story, but I've not seen him.'

Brian sighed heavily, and Donna could picture him in her mind. Brian Donald. Boring Bri, they used to call him at the *Westie*, mostly down to his taste for wearing cords, dull ties, and his hair in a rigid side parting. But there was nothing boring about the way Brian Donald worked: he was, quite simply, the best night editor Donna had ever seen. Incisive, fair, balanced, and bereft of one single fuck as to what the advertising men thought was popular or would sell papers. He was a dying breed, a journalist committed to telling the story and nothing more. Which was why their boss, Charlie Banks, had banished him to the night job of watching the wires and reacting to any big stories. The last thing Banks needed was a popular, talented journalist on the desk, challenging his style of rule through fear and loathing.

'No, I've not seen that useless twat, or heard from him. He was meant to ping me a wrap after the press conference, got nothing from him. And I've been trying his fucking phone all afternoon without a reply. He on the pish up there?'

Unease unfurled. 'Not that I've seen. Thanks, Brian, I'll give him a nudge if I see him.'

'Make it a fucking left hook, would you?' Brian replied, then added: 'And don't be a stranger, Donna. I cannae pay much, but I'll take any copy you fancy sending over, especially with Mark MIA.'

She murmured her thanks, promised to stay in touch, then ended the call, the silence of the room crowding in on her as her mind raced. She could buy Mark avoiding his wife or her – that was to be expected. But not to file his take on the hottest story of the day, one that was guaranteed to get him the splash?

No. No way. Something was wrong.

Suddenly aware of the gloom in the room, she headed for the door and switched on all the lights, trying to dispel her dark thoughts with the shadows.

Ford's words now: *Three murders and you're a common factor in all of them, popping up like an unwanted aunt at Christmas. So, I've got to ask, why are you so closely linked to all of this?*

Three murders? Mark was missing. Had it just become four? No. That was paranoia, insanity. And yet . . . She shuddered, glanced around, the flat suddenly too big for just her and Andrew, transformed from a safe home to a cage. She headed for the hall, dug into her pocket for the card she had been given earlier that day. Studied it.

Whatever was going on, Ford was right. She was a common factor. And here she was, alone with her son, when a maniac who took people's heads was out there. She could tell herself it was a coincidence, just Mark being his usual selfish self, but deep down she knew that for the lie it was.

She had started out wanting to report this story. Now she was part of it. And in that instant, as she started to dial the number on the card she held, Donna knew two things.

She needed protection.

She needed Connor Fraser.

CHAPTER 60

Connor marvelled at the performance Simon put in as the night wore on. He was the life and soul, carrying the conversation, making all the right jokes, showing just enough interest and teasing Connor just enough to win Jen over. For his part, Connor felt like an actor thrown on stage without a script. He nodded at the right moments, laughed along when needed, kept his body language casual. But all the time he kept his focus on Simon. On the man he thought he had known.

The friend who had been lying to him.

Jen seemed to sense his distance, kept sending him curious glances. Not that he could blame her. With this and the way he had acted in her flat the day before, she must be having serious reservations about Connor Fraser.

She finished her drink, pushing the empty glass across the table to signal she was done. 'Right, well,' she said, making a show of adjusting her hoody and sitting up straighter. 'As I said, I've got an early shift tomorrow, so I'll leave you boys to it.'

'Sure I can't persuade you to have another?' Simon asked, giving her his best disarming smile. 'You leave, I'm going to have to deal with this one all night.'

Connor glanced up at him. *Deal with this one?*

'Nah, really, I can't,' Jen said, rising from her seat, Connor and Simon mirroring her. 'An early shift at the gym is grim enough, but with a hangover? No thanks.'

'Fair enough,' Connor said. 'C'mon, we'll walk you back.'

She looked at him, gaze cooling. 'Who do you think you are – Paulie? I'll be fine, Connor. Stay here and catch up with Simon. I'll see you soon.'

Before he could say anything else, she kissed his cheek, squeezing his arm as she did so. He felt the heat of her skin on his linger as she pulled away and looked into his eyes. 'Call me tomorrow, okay?'

'Okay,' he said. 'But at least text me when you get back. Been a few things going on in town recently, in case you hadn't noticed.'

She rolled her eyes and cocked her head, but Connor could see she was pleased at his response. Wasn't sure why he felt pleased as well.

'All right,' she said, turning away from him. 'Simon, nice to meet you. Hopefully see you again before you go.'

'Sure you will. I'm not letting him keep you to himself.'

Jen dipped her chin to her chest to hide her blush. Then she headed for the door. Connor watched her go, again felt the urge to go after her, make sure she got home safely. But then he saw another figure get up and follow her. A figure who had been hugging the bar, out of sight. A figure with a slight limp, one hand encased in a bandage that seemed to glow in the low light of the bar.

Paulie.

Connor smiled. One problem solved. Jen would be safe. He turned to Simon, the good-humoured mask he had been wearing for Jen slipping from his face.

'Talk,' he said. 'And don't lie to me, Simon. I'm not in the mood for any shit.'

Simon held up his hand, drained his pint. 'Whole truth. Honest, Connor. But let's get out of here. Suddenly I'm not that thirsty any more.'

They headed back up onto Bow Street, then followed the long downhill stretch that led away from the castle and back to the heart of the town. Connor tried not to think of Cowane's Hospital as they walked, the body that had been found there.

Simon was looking ahead, the muscle in his jaw pulsing, as though he was chewing on the words he was trying to say. Connor watched him, determined that, this time, Simon would be the one to speak first. As they walked, he felt the cold, hard weight of the gun pushing into the small of his back, like an invisible hand propelling him along the street.

'Jameson called me as soon as you asked him for a contact with the local police,' Simon said, not looking away from the street. 'He was worried that you were going to cause a scene for the firm and, from the way you were talking, that there might actually be a threat to you. Who better to call than your old partner? I arrived yesterday, flew into Edinburgh, hired a car and drove straight here. Checked the place out, made sure you were okay. Saw what you did to that twat who noised you up at the flat – nice work by the way. Stayed in town, back there.' He turned slightly, pointing vaguely in the direction of a high-end hotel further up the hill that was popular for conferences and weddings. 'Then I drove the car back this morning, dumped it at the airport, and was waiting to meet you.'

Connor nodded, anger and relief battling for supremacy in his mind. 'And that's it? No more? Lachlan called you because he was worried about me making a splash and dragging Sentinel's name through the mud?'

Simon stopped. 'Well, you can't really blame the man, Connor. You do have a tendency to make a mess when you lose your temper.' The smile on his face faded under Connor's stony gaze. 'But, no, it wasn't just that. He was worried about you, Connor. Said he wanted me to see if there was a credible threat to you. Look, if you don't believe me, call the man yourself.'

'Oh, don't worry, I will,' Connor said. But what would he say? Thanks for sending an old friend to look after me, boss, but fuck you for thinking I'd be dumb enough to make a mess on my own doorstep?

Questions. Too many questions.

He looked at Simon again, studying him. He wanted to believe him and, in truth, it was exactly the type of move Lachlan Jameson would pull. Control the situation from afar. It was no different from what he had done when he'd asked about Robbie's performance on the Benson job. Except this time he had been the one under observation. The thought didn't sit well with him.

He took a breath. Whether or not he believed Simon was almost irrelevant – either way, he was part of this, which meant Connor had to keep him close. 'So what did you find out on your snooping?' he asked.

'Well, I—'

Connor's phone rang, cutting Simon off. He pulled it out, ready to kill the call, when he saw the number. Gave Simon a hold-that-thought look and hit answer.

'Mr MacKenzie, thanks for getting back to me.'

'Aye, whatever. I'm doing this for Jennifer, Fraser, not you. Clear?'

'Totally,' Connor said. 'Did you manage to find anything out?'

'Aye, yer fuckin' right I did,' MacKenzie growled. 'Who was this kid, Fraser, and what was he to you? And how is my Jen involved in this?'

'He's just someone I need to track down for work, Mr MacKenzie. He's no threat to you or Jennifer, I swear it. Do you think I'd let anything happen to her?'

A pause, the heavy breathing of an old bull echoing down the line, a father considering his options. 'You best not, Fraser, believe me. But Jen seems to like you, so I'll give you the benefit of the doubt. Billy Griffin was—'

A beep on the line told Connor another call was coming in. Irritated, he swiped the phone from his ear, staring at the screen. Saw Donna Blake's number flash up, hit decline.

'Sorry, Mr MacKenzie, had another call coming in. What were you saying?'

CHAPTER 61

Home for Billy Griffin was a flat in a nondescript pebble-dashed estate in Castle Vale. The block stood opposite the high fences separating it from Cornton Vale Prison, for Scotland's female convicts. Connor vaguely remembered a story about refurbishment work taking place on the site.

The Audi stood out like a sore thumb among the scattered assortment of mid-range Vauxhalls, Renaults and Fords in what looked like a small car park serving the prison. Connor pushed down vague unease at leaving the car. The street was quiet and well lit, the cameras that loomed over the fence from the prison presumably deterring any problems with staff cars.

And, besides, he didn't intend to be there for long.

It hadn't taken Duncan MacKenzie long to establish Griffin's movements, given the notoriety he had gained from his little stunt in George Square. As Connor had expected, he had dropped out of the mainstream after leaving Barlinnie, opting for work that was cash in hand and no questions asked.

Just the sort of workforce MacKenzie preferred.

From what he had been able to piece together, Griffin had realized Glasgow was scorched earth for him and headed east, where he'd set himself up as a small-time drug-dealer. He had kept himself to himself, until a run-in with one of the bigger dealers in the city – an old-school gangster called Albert Swanson, who had built an empire for himself over the last thirty years – had seen him driven out of Edinburgh with his tail between his legs and a couple of teeth clutched in his hand.

For reasons no one understood, he had surfaced again in Stirling, getting back to his dealing. MacKenzie had reached out to a few contacts in the local pub trade, found that Griffin had a reputation as a quiet dealer who made no trouble and was happy to give landlords a cut of his take in return for an easy time from the doormen. And it was this arrangement that had led MacKenzie to the address that Connor and Simon now sat outside – one of the landlords of a city-centre nightclub Griffin dealt in was renting him the flat, which explained why Griffin didn't appear on any electoral roll or property register. He was living under the radar, effectively in the back garden of the prison service.

Connor had to admire the balls in that.

Simon looked up at the block of flats, the pebbledash jaundiced in the lights cast from the prison, the windows like dark, empty pits. 'You sure about this?' he asked. 'Yer man said the cops hadn't been able to find this place yet, so if we go in there, we're technically polluting a potential crime scene.'

Connor squinted up at the flats. Simon had a point. He'd promised Ford he wasn't going to make waves, yet here he was, about to trigger a tsunami. And then there was Simon to consider. He was still a serving officer of the PSNI: if any of this washed back on him, it could destroy his career.

If, of course, what he had told Connor was true.

'Fuck it,' Connor said. 'I'm done holding my dick, waiting for something to happen. We're here. Let's take a look. You can stay with the car if you want.'

Simon gave him a hard stare, cocked an eyebrow. 'Fuck ye,' he said. 'Look, I'm sorry I lied to you, Connor, really I am. But I'm here to help. That's the truth. If Jameson hadn't called me, I'd still be here. You know that.'

Connor nodded. It was true. The man he had known in Belfast, the man who had covered for him when he had beaten Hughes to a pulp, would have done anything for him, dropped everything to stand at his side at a moment's notice. But was the same man sitting beside him now? Or was he someone else, with motives Connor couldn't grasp?

He was out of the car before he knew he was going to move, driven to act by the desire to get away from his thoughts. He waited for Simon to slip around the front of the Audi to join him, then clicked on the car alarm and glanced around the street. Quiet, just as he wanted.

'Flat three, second floor,' he said, jutting his jaw towards a peeling white-painted door at the end of a small pathway that was more weeds and dying grass than concrete. Simon sighed, then started walking, the meaning in Connor's words clear – you want to come with me, fine, but I'm not turning my back on you.

On the wall to the left of the door a panel was filled with three rows of buttons, each a buzzer to one of the flats. Most of the names were faded, the tag for Griffin's flat missing. Connor tried the door. It rattled on an old lock. He gave it a sharp nudge and it opened. Exchanged a glance with Simon, who shrugged and slipped inside. Connor followed, keeping his back to the wall, minimizing his exposure to the stairwell. He reached back and touched the gun nestled into the small of his back, fought the urge to draw it.

They made their way up the staircase, navigating the obstacle course of kids' bikes, scooters and footballs that littered the landing. Got to the second floor, and found the flat they were looking for at the end of a corridor that glittered a sickly, industrial green from years of repeated repainting with a cheap paint that was meant to deter graffiti.

They took up positions at either side of the door, glancing over their shoulders to the other end of the corridor and the flat opposite. Last thing they needed was a nosy neighbour poking their head out.

Connor inspected the lock. It was a standard Yale below a cheap door handle, a simple, slender bar of steel that reminded Connor of his school days. He looked across at Simon, nodded. A Yale lock didn't present many problems, and he had a few options. Given the construction of the door, he could probably shoulder his way in, nothing dramatic, just a steady increase of pressure until it gave under his weight. But that would create noise. No, better to take the silent approach.

He knelt, Simon taking a half-step around him to shield him from view. He shrugged off the prickling of unease he felt at turning his back on his friend, and slid two long, slender rods of metal from his pocket. Lock-picking wasn't difficult, especially on something as cheap and generic as this. Just feel for the tumblers, align and turn. No problem at all.

Except . . .

Connor studied the lock for a second, its glossy sheen. He wiped a finger tentatively across it. It came away greasy.

He reached up, tried the door handle. It swung down easily and the door opened. He stood up, held out his finger to Simon, rubbed it with his thumb. 'WD40,' he said.

Simon nodded, message received. Lock-pickers sometimes used lubricants on old locks to make them easier to pick. The lock had been picked before, and whoever had done it had left it open.

Connor stepped into the gloom, hugging the wall, making sure he kept his back tight to it. Simon followed him, taking the other wall, easing the front door shut as he stepped inside.

The pencil light Connor carried stabbed into the gloom, revealing a small, neat hallway with exposed floorboards and a coat rack running up one side. To their left was an open door that hinted at a bedroom beyond, and to their right, another open door led to a bathroom.

They nodded to each other, took a room each. Swept them, then moved back into the hall.

'Clear,' Connor said of the bedroom, which was a stark room, with only a bed and a small bedside table.

'Clear,' Simon echoed.

They moved forward, down the hall to the room at the end. Connor felt a dull electrical throb in the back of his head as he looked at the door. Again, the weight of the gun pressed into his back. He looked at Simon, nodded, then swung the door open. Simon stepped in first, dropping to a low crouch in case someone was waiting for them. Connor mirrored him, stepping into a long living room-cum-kitchen that took up the entire width of the flat. He looked at the windows that made up the far wall, noted the curtains were drawn tight. Closed the door then felt along the wall for a light switch. Flicked it on to reveal an unremarkable living space – a tired beige couch and armchair faced a large television, with what looked like an old record player sitting beside it. In front of the couch was a coffee-table, a mug on top of it.

Connor looked around, a vague confusion tugging his thoughts. Had he been wrong about the door? Had it just been left open by mistake, the lock not picked? As with the bedroom he had checked, there was no sign that anything had been moved or disturbed, that someone had broken in to search for something.

'Well, this is disappointing,' Simon said, glancing around.

'Let's take a proper look,' Connor said, moving into the room.

They split it up, Connor taking the small bookshelf behind the TV unit, Simon retreating to the kitchen area behind a low breakfast bar. Connor scanned the collection of books, surprised by what he found: row upon row of volumes on Scotland's history, ranging from the commercial to the academic. He scanned the shelves again, confirming that what he was looking for wasn't there – no fiction and, specifically, no copy of *Misery*. There was also a smattering of DVDs and these were more of what Connor expected – action movies and sci-fi, along with a couple of martial-arts films.

He ran his finger along the spines of the books, then turned back into the room. What was he looking for anyway? Something that explained why Billy Griffin had been the first to die, and what his connection to Helen Russell was. But what would that be?

Frustrated, he stepped back and crouched to inspect the record player beside the television. Nothing remarkable, an old-style variable-speed turntable and a random collection of seventies rock and eighties power anthems, from AC/DC to Guns N' Roses. He flicked through the records, pushed them back into the rack until they sat flush.

It was, Connor thought, a strange collection, at odds with the books he had found. And something about the sleeves nagged at him. Each album had a small red tag on its top right corner, a six-digit number printed on it. Connor considered. Second-hand? Bought from an auction maybe? The tags holding lot numbers?

'Anything?' Simon called, as he emerged from the kitchen.

'Not that I can see,' Connor said, glancing to the couch as he considered pulling the cushions out and looking beneath it. But, again, what would be the point? If the place had been broken into and searched, it had been done by professionals who had left no trace of their work. They had either found what they were looking for or nothing at all.

He stood up, glanced around the room. At the bare walls behind the couch, the seats tucked neatly beneath the breakfast bar, the reclining chair moulded to a man's shape over time, the . . .

Connor darted his head back. He took a step forward, ran his hand up the wall. Yes. There. Sticking out of it, at eye level, a small nail, painted the same colour as the rest of the wall. He looked closely, noted the faintest discoloration around the area, signs of a picture that had been hung there, but only recently.

He looked around the room, thinking. Was that what was missing? What whoever had broken in was looking for? A picture on a wall? And, if so, what did that picture show, and how did it explain Billy Griffin's role in this?

'Looks like this is a busted flush, Connor,' Simon said.

'Maybe. Come on. Let's take a proper look at that bedroom.'

They moved back into the hall, Connor careful to switch off the living-room light before he opened the door. He stepped into the bedroom, saw the curtains there were closed too. Coincidence? Or had whoever had been there drawn the curtains to give them more privacy to search the place? Either way, it was a gift he wasn't going to ignore. He flicked on the light switch, a naked bulb flaring into life.

The room was bigger than Connor had thought on his first look, dwarfing the double bed and cabinet that were pushed up against the wall. The bed was made, smooth and creaseless in the way only someone who had served time in either the military or prison could achieve.

Simon stepped forward, around the bed, heading for the chest of drawers. He slid them open and peered in. 'Nothing,' he said. 'Cheap pants and socks and . . . oh, wait . . .' He straightened up, holding a plastic bag that contained a small amount of white powder. Connor guessed it wasn't icing sugar.

'Party favours,' Simon said. 'Makes sense if this guy was dealing, like you said. Brought some home for himself.'

Connor nodded. Not unusual for a dealer to test the product. And it didn't seem like there was much else to do in this place. He got the impression it was less a home, more a barracks – a place to sleep between shifts. He gestured to the double doors of a built-in wardrobe on the far wall of the room. 'Let's have a look in there, then call it,' he said.

The wardrobe was as Spartan as the rest of the flat: three pairs of jeans hung from cheap wire hangers, alongside four unironed shirts. Above them, an assortment of what looked like T-shirts and jumpers were neatly stacked. Again, no sign anyone had been here or looked through the clothes.

Connor stood back, a thought occurring to him. Why would they look here? If someone had broken in to get hold of a specific item – the missing picture in the living room – then would they bother searching the rest of the flat? Why risk it? No. They would come for what they wanted and leave.

Which raised the question: could they have missed something here?

He reached forward, pulled out the first pile of T-shirts and placed them on the bed.

'Have a look through them, will you?' he said to Simon, as he took out the second pile and placed it beside the first. The shelf empty, Connor ran his hand around it, probing the corners. He sighed with frustration as he found nothing.

He looked at the laundry basket in the bottom corner of the wardrobe, pulled it open. Nothing, just white underwear and a T-shirt at the bottom.

He turned back to the bed, where Simon had spread the first pile of T-shirts. Nothing remarkable – a few designer labels and some older ones with the logos of the same bands Connor had seen in the record collection.

'This is a waste of time,' Simon said, reaching for the second pile. Connor nodded, his eyes drawn to the scattered T-shirts, then back to the jeans in the cupboard. An itch in his mind, something . . .

'Here, hold on, what's this?' Simon said, pulling Connor from his thoughts. He was holding up a small piece of plastic, about the size of a credit card, a tatty red lanyard hanging from it.

Simon passed it to Connor. It was just a standard security pass, with a passport-style photograph, the type any number of office workers slipped around their necks every day and forgot. But Connor knew it wasn't just a security pass. It was a key. He looked back at the T-shirts on the bed, the scene making sense to him now, just like the tags on the records in the living room.

He stepped back to the wardrobe, checked the jeans hanging there. Like the T-shirts, they were in two sizes – 32-inch waist on two pairs, 38-inch on the other. He stepped past Simon to the chest of drawers, knowing what he would find. Pants in two drawers, not separated by colour or make, but by size.

Two people sharing one set of drawers.

The picture might have gone, but Connor had a good idea now of who it had featured. A glance at the headshot on the security pass confirmed it – in the image, he was wearing the AC/DC T-shirt that was now lying on the bed. 'Come on,' he said. 'Let's tidy up and get out of here.'

'Where we going?'

'To talk to Donna Blake,' Connor replied. 'She called me earlier on and I haven't got back to her yet, but we need to speak to her now.'

'Why?' Simon asked, roughly refolding the T-shirts and stuffing them back into the cupboard.

Connor held up the security pass. 'Because maybe she can tell us about this. About why Matt Evans was leaving his pass for the radio station and changes of clothes at Billy Griffin's flat.'

'Hold on,' Simon said, realization spreading across his face. 'You mean . . .'

'Exactly,' Connor said. 'Matt and Billy were connected. Maybe intimately. There's a picture missing from the living room. I'm betting that's what whoever broke in here was looking for. But why were they so determined to hide the link between Matt and Billy? And why did they have to die for it?'

CHAPTER 62

Ford was at home, stomach heavy with a dinner he had made for Mary. He was no chef, but he was competent, and the sight of him in the kitchen after the events of the last few days had seemed to put Mary at ease.

They chatted as he cooked, sharing a bottle of white wine he had picked up along with the ingredients for the meal. The closest they got to discussing the murders was when Mary had asked about 'the man at the uni'. 'I hope he's a new colleague, Malcolm,' she had said, smiling at him over the rim of the glass. 'He's big enough and ugly enough to look after you, especially at the moment.'

Now, sitting in his chair, Mary dozing on the sofa in front of a film she had insisted they watch together, Ford's mind turned back to Connor Fraser. Just what was Fraser to him? A witness? A suspect? Or, as Mary had said, a colleague of some kind?

From the hall, he heard his mobile buzz. He shot a glance at Mary, saw she was undisturbed by the sound. He grunted as he got to his feet, the weariness of the last three days making his legs alien and heavy. He got to the hall, fished in his coat pocket and found his phone. Smiled in spite of himself when he saw who was calling. Speak of the devil. 'Fraser, funny you should call.'

'DCI Ford, thanks for picking up,' Connor said. The echo on the line told Ford he was using a hands-free, the background noise that he was driving. 'I need to ask you a question.'

Again, Ford was irritated. Just who did this guy think he was, assuming he could ask questions of a serving detective? And on what? The strength of a favour to a friend? 'Go on,' he said, his tone conveying he reserved the right not to answer.

'Matt Evans's place. Have you taken an inventory at his flat yet?'

'What? Why would you ask if—'

'DCI Ford, please, this is important. No dicking around. I might be on to something here. The flat. Did you take an inventory?'

'Not personally,' Ford said, hearing the resentment in his tone, not caring. 'I'd been sidelined by that point, but I know it was on the actions list at the case conference. Why? What's this about? What have you found?'

'Can you access the inventory? Check it?'

'Why? What are you looking for? And why should I help you? You said you weren't going to go poking around, Fraser, and yet here you are . . .'

Fraser's voice rose, partly to compensate for the increase in engine noise, partly from anger. 'Look, I'll make you a bet. You check the log. You'll find something that doesn't fit. There's going to be two sizes of clothes in that flat, I'm guessing thirty-two- and thirty-eight-inch men's trousers. Looking at his pictures, my money's on Evans being the thirty-eight. If I'm right, call me back and tell me what I need to know.'

Ford felt his pulse rise, impatience and curiosity overwhelming him. What did it matter if he helped him? He was off the case and, from the sound of it, Fraser had made more progress than he or anyone else had been able to.

And then there was the head. The spike squealing in the breeze.

He had to know. 'What are you looking for?'

'A picture, something, anything that confirms a link between Billy Griffin and Matt Evans. I think they were connected, using each other's homes to store clothing and other items.'

Ford clamped the phone tighter to his ear, as if he could use it to calm the hurricane of thoughts whirling through his mind. 'How the hell did you come to that conclusion?'

A pause, the deep snarl of an engine as Fraser downshifted. The murmur of another voice, unintelligible. Then Fraser again: 'Because I just found Matt Evans's security pass for Valley FM at a flat being used by Billy Griffin. I also found clothes that looked like they'd fit both men, along with tagged albums that I'm assuming came from Valley FM's collection. There are signs that the door to the flat was tampered with, and there's an indication that a picture is missing from the wall of the living room. My guess is it's a picture of Evans and Griffin together, and whoever broke in was looking for it, to ensure we didn't make a connection between the two men.'

We? Ford pushed the thought aside. He had more immediate problems. 'You're telling me you found Billy Griffin's residence? Christ, Fraser! We've been looking for that place for three days! And now you're telling me you lifted evidence from the scene! Fuck's sake, do you realize what that means? Look, this has to end now. It was a mistake from the start. Meet me at Randolphfield. I'll take your statement there and we can figure this out. I can't promise you that I can—'

'I can't do that,' Connor said. 'I don't have time for pointless questions, and I don't think you do either. Please, I'm going to follow up another lead now. Just check the inventory for Evans's flat and get back to me.'

Ford heard his teeth grind, felt his jaw ache. He never should have let Doyle talk him into this. Having a civilian running around, poking his nose into an active investigation, an investigation government ministers were taking a close interest in, was wrong on every level.

But . . .

He looked at the door to the living room, where Mary slept on the couch. Remembered her words from earlier. *Who was that man? A colleague? I hope so.*

Fuck it.

'Fine,' he said. 'Give me an hour. But then you come in, Fraser, and give me a statement on this. My arse is far enough out on a limb with this as it is, I don't need you sawing the branch off under me.'

'One hour. Understood. And thank you.' Connor killed the call, leaving the line as empty as the promise he had just made.

CHAPTER 63

Connor had called Donna before Ford, was driving to her place while he spoke with the detective. He hadn't bothered to listen to the voice-mail he saw she had left him.

It turned out to be a mistake.

'You took your fucking time getting back to me,' she'd hissed. 'What part of the word urgent don't you understand?'

'Sorry, I've been busy,' Connor said, rolling his eyes at Simon, who was giving him a quizzical look. 'Listen, Ms Blake, I need to speak to you about Matt Evans, ask you a few questions. I was—'

She cut him off with a barked laugh. 'Funny, that's what I need to talk to you about. One of the things, anyway. Can you come here, to my place?'

Connor paused, the statement surprising him. Earlier in the day, she had kept a can of pepper spray trained on him as he gave her a lift across town. Now she was offering him her home address, no questions asked. What had changed?

'As long as you don't mind me bringing someone with me,' he said, trying to buy himself a moment to think.

'Fine.' She had given him the address, which the satnav showed to be on the road out to Cambusbarron.

'No problem,' he said, slipping the Audi into gear.

'This isn't exactly how I saw tonight panning out,' Simon said, eyes on the road.

And how did you plan on it going? Connor had wondered, with only the slightest pang of guilt.

Ten minutes later, after he'd spoken to Ford, Connor pulled up outside Donna Blake's place, a three-storey block of flats so new Connor could have sworn the smell of fresh paint still hung in the air. She hadn't been there long.

He peered over the steering wheel to the top floor, saw a soft light on in what he figured was the living room. Pulled out his phone and texted her that they had arrived. It had been a slightly odd request, which rang a vague alarm bell in the back of Connor's mind. Why didn't she want him buzzing the intercom? It wasn't to stop him waking a partner – that would happen the moment he stepped into the flat. Did she have a dog that would bark and disturb the neighbours? Or was she using the text to prepare someone else for their arrival?

Only one way to find out. And, besides, it wasn't like he had much of a choice.

The response was almost immediate: *Come on up, I've buzzed the door.*

'Well, then,' he said to Simon, 'let's not keep the lady waiting.'

The door was open, as promised, and they made their way up the stairs, Connor letting Simon go first, just in case. When they reached the top-floor landing, Donna was waiting for them, silhouetted in the crack of an open door.

Connor saw her tense when she spotted Simon and stepped forward with what he hoped was a disarming smile. 'Ms Blake, this is Simon McCartney, an old, ah, friend of mine,' he said. 'Simon, this is Donna Blake of Sky News and Valley FM.'

He saw Donna blush at that, pleasure sparking in her eyes.

'Good to meet ye,' Simon said. 'Sorry about the circumstances, but yer man here is the world's biggest shite magnet.'

Donna smiled, an expression that seemed unfamiliar to her, and again Connor wondered what drove her. She was determined, defiant, fearless. And now, here she was, ready to invite two men she barely knew into her home.

'Come in,' she said. 'But, please, keep quiet. My . . .' she looked up, her eyes filled with challenge as she found Connor's gaze and held it '. . . my son is asleep and I don't want to wake him.'

Things fell into place with an almost audible click. It explained a lot.

She led them down a short corridor into a small, neat living room. Connor noticed she had arranged a bottle of wine and three glasses on the table. Saw from the smear on one of the glasses and the slight blackening at the corners of her mouth that she had already had some, then wiped the glass clean in a hurry. 'Can I offer you a drink?' she asked, gesturing them to sit.

Simon eased himself into the couch. 'That would be grand,' he said.

'Not for me,' Connor said. 'Driving. But thank you.'

She poured a glass for Simon, then splashed a small amount of wine into her own. She almost succeeded in hiding the tremor in her hand, but Connor spotted it in the pitter-patter of the wine as the bottle danced gently in her grip.

'So, you wanted to ask me about Matt?' she said, sitting back.

'Yes, in a moment, but can I ask why you were so desperate to see me, Ms Blake? And what it is that's got you so rattled this evening.'

She looked up at him, something he couldn't place darting across her eyes. Then she looked into the wine glass. When she spoke, her voice was low, almost atonal. It reminded Connor of the tone Simon used with suspects. No emotion. All business.

'I got a call earlier, telling me that, ah . . .' she looked deeper into the wine glass '. . . a colleague has gone missing. He was at the press conference earlier, hasn't been seen since.'

'And why would that trouble you?' Connor said.

She looked at him as though he were a child who had just asked why water was wet and the sky was blue. 'With everything that's happened over the last few days, you don't think I should be worried when someone goes missing? Shit, where have you been?' She took a sip from the glass. 'Sorry, it's just the whole Matt thing. Mark, ah, my colleague, was at the police press conference earlier. I confronted him about feeding soft questions to the minister, to make sure the story stayed away from Ferguson's links to Helen Russell.'

'And what did Mark have to say for himself?' Simon asked, leaning forward, his elbows on his knees.

'Not a lot,' Donna said. 'Just a sob story about trying to get a job, the usual crap.'

'That can't be the only reason you wanted to see me, Ms Blake,' Connor said. 'You could have told me that over the phone. There's something else, isn't there?'

She chewed her lip, jaw setting as she made a decision. 'I know who the first victim was,' she said. 'And I told Mark. I worked a story back in Glasgow about him – you might know the name. Billy Griffin? The kid who was photographed burning a Yes flag in George Square after the referendum in 2014.'

Connor stiffened, exchanged a look with Simon.

'What?' Donna asked, eyes darting between the two men as the air in the room thickened.

'Billy Griffin,' Connor said. 'We've come across that name ourselves. Did Matt Evans ever mention him?'

Confusion dug furrows into Donna's brow. 'No. Why would he? What would Matt have to do with . . .'

Connor held up his hand. 'I'll get to that. But tell me more about your friend. You're worried because he's disappeared, so worried that you wanted to see me, here, tonight. Why? For reassurance? Protection?'

Donna's cheeks reddened, her face hardening with defiance. 'Yes,' she said. 'You said it yourself, Mr Fraser, you're in the protection game. I saw what happened to Matt Evans first-hand, then I told Mark about Billy Griffin and suddenly he's off the radar. So, yeah, I'm alone here with my son, and there's a nut job out there who thinks nothing of hacking people's heads off and leaving them lying around like trophies. I panicked, okay?'

Simon spoke before Connor could reply, his voice soft and soothing, honed from years of talking to victims of crime and their families. 'Ms Blake, no one is blaming you for wanting to protect yourself and your son, especially after what you've seen. But Connor is right. We believe there's a link between Billy Griffin and Matt Evans. You worked with Matt, so if there's anything you can tell us, anything at all . . .'

She shook her head. 'I didn't really know him,' she said. 'We worked together, but he kept himself to himself, was a bit of a dick, to be honest. And he never mentioned anyone he knew, let alone Billy Griffin. Why would he know him anyway?'

Connor was about to speak when his phone buzzed. He flashed an apologetic smile at her, then turned away and answered it. 'DCI Ford. Thanks for getting back to me so quickly.'

'You were right,' Ford said. 'Inventory shows two different sizes of clothes in Evans's flat. Officers also found two different brands of deodorant and two toothbrushes in the bathroom.'

'Anything that definitively links Evans to Griffin?'

'Not explicitly. We can use the toothbrush, see if we get a DNA match, and print the flat. But there's no picture, nothing that shows them together.'

Connor bared his teeth, worried at his thumbnail as he thought. Damn. He had hoped . . . The idea came to him suddenly, the thought of the ID flashing across his mind. 'And nothing in the inventory from his office either?'

Ford muttered something Connor thought questioned his parentage. 'Not been searched yet,' he said. 'Whole office was sealed as a crime scene, but the interior's not been looked at as the body was outside and we've only so many bodies on hand.'

Connor winced at the poor choice of words, decided not to needle Ford with it. 'Thank you, Detective. That's useful to know.'

'Your turn, Fraser,' Ford said. 'You found anything from that lead you were chasing?'

'Nothing yet,' Connor admitted. 'But I promise I'll call you the moment I have anything.'

'Good. You can come to the station, tell me all about it on the record.'

'Look forward to it,' Connor said, cutting the line.

'Ford?' Simon asked, as he turned back to them.

'Yeah,' Connor replied. 'Suggestive evidence at Evans's place linking him to Griffin, but nothing definitive yet. Which leaves only one option.'

Simon nodded, eyes sliding to Donna.

'What?' Donna asked, sensing the unspoken conversation between the two men.

Connor hunkered down beside her, making sure he was at eye level. 'Ms Blake, Donna. I need a favour. I promise I'll protect you and your son, but you have to do something for me in return.'

'And what's that?' she asked, tensing in her chair, voice frosted with suspicion.

'Can I borrow the keys to your office?'

CHAPTER 64

With her early shift in the morning, Jen hadn't been keen on helping Connor. But he had persisted, the vague guilt he felt at laying on the charm and promising her whatever she wanted in return for helping him only slightly ameliorated by the realization that he meant to honour his promise.

She arrived twenty minutes later, Simon letting her into the flat. She had changed out of the tight-fitting jeans and T-shirt she had been wearing in the pub earlier, opting for a pair of joggers and a sweat shirt. Connor couldn't help but notice she looked all the better for it.

'Jen, thanks for coming,' he said, as he led her into the living room of Donna's flat. 'This is Donna Blake, who I told you about on the phone.'

Jen extended a hand, Donna taking it. They were about the same height, but it was like looking at a flipped image. Where Jen was fair, Donna was dark. Jen's skin seemed to glow with health, her eyes bright and clear, while Donna's complexion was pale, her skin taut, eyes surrounded by dark shadows of exhaustion and glittering with a keen awareness fuelled by a mixture of adrenalin and fear.

'Pleased to meet you,' Donna said, cracking what was almost a genuine smile, warmth guttering through the façade. 'Thanks for this.'

'No problem,' Jen said. 'Just means this one will owe me. Again.'

Connor squirmed as both women turned to him. 'Right, as I said,

Jen's going to keep you and you son company while we're away. You'll be perfectly safe, but if there are any problems, just call my mobile.'

'Uh-huh,' Donna said, her eyes telling Connor she wasn't convinced.

'Right,' Connor said, nodding to Simon as he bounced the keys Donna had given him. 'Let's go. You remember that alarm code?'

Simon sighed. 'Seven four three five nine four,' he said. 'You happy now? C'mon, let's get going.'

Out in the cool night, the smell of rain in the air, Connor glanced around, saw what he was looking for and threw the car keys to Simon. 'Go on, I'll be there in a second.'

He watched as Simon walked to the car and plipped the alarm, then took a straight path to the Mercedes parked at the end of the street, doing nothing to mask his approach.

He wanted to be seen.

The driver's-side door opened as he closed in on the car, the interior light bouncing off Paulie's shaven head. Connor held up his hands as Paulie unfolded himself from the car, careful to keep his bandaged hand against his chest. Connor thought about that. Why would MacKenzie trust his daughter's safety to an injured man – a man who had failed once already? Smiled. Obvious, really.

'What the fuck you playing at, Fraser, dragging her all the way across town just to see you?'

'Not here to fight, Paulie,' Connor said. 'Look, I know I already owe you, but I need a favour. I have to run an errand, and I need you to keep an eye on that flat,' he turned and gestured to Donna Blake's window, 'while I'm gone. Jen's in there with someone, and I need you to make sure they're safe until I get back.'

Paulie pulled back his lips in a snarl, revealing teeth that weren't over-familiar with a brush. 'What the fuck? You think I'm babysitting for you? Fuck off. All I care about is Jennifer.'

'I know that,' Connor said, holding Paulie's gaze. 'And why shouldn't you? She told me you've been around since she was a kid. It's obvious you care about her – why else would you be here on your own time?'

'What the . . .?'

267

'Come on, Paulie, I don't have time for bullshit. You're hurt. You've let your boss down once already, yet here you are, driving around with a busted hand, still keeping an eye on Jen. Must hurt like a bastard, even with an automatic like that. You wouldn't be doing that unless you cared for her. So I'm asking you, please, do this for me. Keep her safe until I get back.'

Connor saw the hatred in Paulie's eyes flicker. It was only for a second but, in that moment, he knew the man would do what he asked. Not for him. For Jen.

'And why the fuck should I do anything for you?' he said.

Connor stepped closer, moving to Paulie's left, making sure he was out of Simon's eyeline as he reached behind his back.

'Because I'm trusting you,' he said. 'And because I'm giving you this to make sure you get the job done.'

Paulie looked down, eyes widening as he saw the holstered Glock Connor was holding tight to his chest. 'What the fuck are you . . .'

'Just take it. I don't think anything's going to kick off here, but if it does, this'll even the playing field with your hand being fucked. It's chambered. Just flick the safety, point and shoot. Okay?'

'Who the fuck are you, Fraser?' Paulie asked, even as he reached for the gun.

Connor kept his gaze level, hoping none of the panic he felt at handing over the weapon had bled into his eyes. 'Someone like you,' he said. 'Someone who wants to keep Jen safe.' He reached into his other pocket, produced a business card. 'If everything goes to plan, I'll be back in less than an hour. But if anything happens, or you see something you don't like, call me.'

Paulie took the card, his eyes moving between it, the gun and Connor, as though they were parts of an equation he couldn't figure out. 'Okay,' he said finally.

Connor nodded and turned away, keeping himself between Paulie and the Audi, not wanting Simon to know he had just given away his gun. He kept his pace slow and casual, fought the almost irresistible urge to run, duck, get out of the line of sight of Paulie and the gun. He thought he could feel it trained on him, the barrel poking into his back as he walked.

'The fuck was that all about?' Simon asked, as Connor slipped into the driver's seat of the Audi.

'Insurance policy,' Connor said as he fired the engine. Settling into the seat, he felt his T-shirt plaster itself to his back, the cold sweat that covered him acting like icy glue.

The studio was only a ten-minute drive from Donna Blake's flat, on streets that were quiet. Connor kept to the speed limit, not wanting to attract undue attention. He needn't have worried: turning off the main road into the industrial estate where the radio station was based was like falling off the world. He had expected a police car or an officer stationed at the entrance, but there was nothing. He remembered Ford's words – *We've only so many bodies on hand* – and realized that whoever had been stationed there had been reassigned. Made sense. The main crime scene was a car park, and that would have been picked clean by the forensics team by now, Donna Blake's car taken away for further testing. Which left the office. Not a primary crime scene, just adjacent to one, which meant that the police could seal it up and return to it when they had the time and the manpower.

Which gave Connor an opportunity.

He drove past it, a squat, ugly building with a gaudy Valley FM sign stuck in the grass and peeling red paint on the awning above shuttered glass double doors. He looked around for CCTV cameras or anything that would indicate a police presence, saw nothing but the yellow and black 'Police: Do Not Cross' tape that surrounded the building and fluttered listlessly in the breeze. He pulled around the corner, tucking the Audi into a pool of darkness under a tree. Killed the engine, looked at Simon.

'You sure about this? We're going to break a police cordon and search a potential crime scene. That's bad enough for me, but you've still got a career to think about, Simon.'

Simon grinned in the gloom, teeth glinting in the light from the Audi's dash. 'Catch yerself on, Connor. I'm not letting you go in there to have all the fun. Besides, we both know you want me right beside you so you can keep an eye on me.'

Connor shifted uncomfortably in the driver's seat. Simon was right, but the notion sounded absurd. He got out of the car without another word, Simon following him. They ducked under the cordon and walked quickly up the path to the double doors, Simon riffling through the keys as he moved, dropping to the ground for the shutter lock in one fluid movement.

Connor heard the lock click, winced as the shutters squealed and rattled up their tracks. Simon stopped them halfway, leaving just enough space for them to access the front door. He ducked under and saw the police tape pulled across the middle of the two doors. There was a soft snicking sound, and a blade suddenly winked in Simon's hand.

'Where the fuck did you get that?' Connor asked.

'Says the man carrying a cannon,' Simon said, as he sliced the police tape and unlocked the door. 'I'm going to slip in and disarm the alarm. You follow and pull the shutters down behind you.'

Connor watched as Simon stepped into the blackness. Heard the beep of an alarm as the motion sensor tripped, felt his pulse raise as he heard Simon punching keys. What if Donna had given them the wrong code? What if Simon had remembered it wrongly or keyed it in wrong? What if—

The beeping ended abruptly. 'Clear,' Simon called.

Connor took a deep, steadying breath, pulled the shutter down behind him and stepped inside, pulling out his pencil torch.

It was just as Donna had described it, a large, open-plan space, untidy desks dotted around it. The back of the room was taken up by a booth that was separated into two sections – a production unit and the main recording studio. Through the glass window, Connor could see a mic hanging on a boom arm. He wondered how many times Donna Blake had sat in front of it.

'Here,' Simon called, snapping Connor from his thoughts. Connor swung the torch in an arc, saw Simon standing next to a desk that was neater and less cluttered than the others. Just as Donna had said, a Saltire hung from an Anglepoise lamp at the corner of the desk, one end twisted into a loose knot and looped around the neck of a small teddy bear with a Union flag cape draped down its back. Donna had told him that no one in the office could decide if it was Evans's idea of

270

a joke or a deliberate attempt to bait people into confronting him. But, with what he now knew, Connor suspected it had another meaning. Something deeper. An in-joke between Evans and one other person.

Connor stepped forward, swung the torch over the desk. Nothing there of interest. A notepad sat beside a laptop, which was patched into a desktop monitor. Donna had told them all the laptops were password-protected but still, it was worth a look.

'You check that,' Connor said. 'I'll look in the drawers.'

Simon cracked the laptop and hit the power key, its tinny *bong* as it powered up loud in the gloomy silence. Connor watched him for a moment, then turned his attention to the three drawers on the right of the desk.

He opened the first, again the question of what he was looking for occurring to him. Something that provided the missing link between Evans and Griffin, something that made sense of all this.

He heard the soft chatter of keys. 'Password,' Simon muttered. 'What the fuck could that be?'

'Try Billy,' Connor said, speaking before he thought about it.

More chattering from the keyboard, followed by the chirp to tell them the password was wrong. 'No go,' he said, 'and if this is a normal log-in system, we've only got two more tries before it locks us out.'

Connor bit his lip. *Think. Think.* He kept his own passwords random, but knew other people were less contentious, opting for something simple and memorable, something with meaning to them. The name of a pet or a loved one. But how did he figure that out with a perfect stranger? 'Gimme a minute,' he said, turning his attention back to the drawers.

The first was a disappointment, holding only pens, a stapler and a stack of Post-it notes. The second and third were slightly more promising, with old notepads and a flash drive. Connor lifted them out, pocketed the flash drive, then riffled through the notepads. Nothing interesting, mostly notes on stories, ideas for interview subjects and topics, along with a few newspaper cuttings, headlines highlighted, notes scrawled in the margins.

'Any other ideas?' Simon asked, impatience edging his voice. 'Would he make it as easy as his own name? Fuck it, why not try?'

He typed. Got the *bing* of rejection. 'Ah, fuck it. Let's take it with us, man, work it out later.'

Connor nodded agreement, looked at the notepads in front of him. Couldn't see any reason to take them. Besides, leaving the drawers totally empty, along with the disappearance of the laptop and the slicing of the police tape, would be like leaving a huge 'We only searched this desk' sign for the police.

He dropped the notepads back into the drawers, pushed them shut. 'Aye. Come on, then. We've got those notepads and the laptop, maybe we can . . .'

The bottom drawer had stuck.

Connor looked down, thinking he had overfilled it, one of the notepads catching on the runner. But, no, it was only half full, the notepads sitting well below the lip of the drawer.

He tried it again. It refused to slide home.

He dropped to his knees, pulled the drawer all the way out. As he'd suspected, it had caught at the end of the runner, and he angled it up to pull it clear. Set the drawer aside, reached into void space and felt around.

A pulse of excitement as his hand touched something cool and smooth. He ran his fingers over it, finding its edges, then pulled it out and reached back in to make sure he hadn't missed anything else. He hadn't.

'What's that?' Simon said, leaning over.

'No idea,' Connor said, opening the laminated envelope file. It might be nothing, just a folder that had slipped down the back of the drawers and been forgotten. He slipped out a sheaf of papers and trained the torch on them. His breath caught as he processed what he was seeing, the pressure rising behind his eyes as though he was straining against a heavy weight in the gym rather than holding a few pieces of paper.

Simon's voice seemed to come from very far away. 'Connor? What is it? What?'

Connor stood up abruptly, felt the world sway. Looked across the desk, at the small display there. 'Try teddy bear,' he whispered, his tongue and lips numb.

272

'What? Oh . . .' Simon typed, the screen flaring to life as the laptop kept booting. 'How the fuck did you figure that out?' he asked. 'Connor, what?'

Connor bent down, slid the drawer back into place. It fitted perfectly now. A lot of things did. 'Later,' he said. 'Grab the laptop and let's get out of here.'

Simon wasted a second on a confused look, then got moving. They retraced their steps, both careful to touch only what they absolutely had to, even though they were wearing gloves. Connor stepped out into the night, grabbed the shutters as Simon reset the alarm, then pulled it down behind them. The police would find that the cordon tape was cut, but it was a neat slice, so at first glance it would look all right.

Not that it was a real concern. Not now.

They hurried back down the path and to the car, the file seeming to pulse with heat under Connor's arm. Back in the Audi, he had the engine fired and the car in gear before Simon had had a chance to speak. He was just clearing the industrial estate when a chirp from the stereo told him he had a call. He thumbed the answer button on the steering wheel. 'Connor Fraser.'

A low whisper down the line. 'Fraser, it's Paulie. You'd better get back here. Looks like we've got company.'

Connor floored the accelerator, the car roaring to life, the sound echoing in his chest, seeming to resonate somewhere deep within.

'Connor, what the fuck's going on, man?' Simon asked, raising his voice over the sound of the engine.

'I know why they died,' Connor said. 'Donna was right. She is in danger. And – fuck! – I put Jen right in harm's way too.'

Simon stared at him for a moment, then turned to face front. 'Drive,' he said. 'Forget the guilt. Just fucking get us there. You can fill me in on the way.'

CHAPTER 65

Paulie was leaning on his car when Connor pulled up, smoking a fat cigar and blowing the smoke lazily into the night. He seemed relaxed, satisfied, like a man enjoying a smoke after a fine meal. Connor got out of the car, the acrid tang of the cigar hitting his nose as he approached. He glanced around for the problem Paulie had called about but saw nothing except the darkened street and the light still burning in Donna Blake's flat.

'Well?' he asked.

Paulie smiled, showing off the yellowed stumps of his teeth. Rolled himself off the car and stood upright, the outline of Connor's gun obvious in the awkward way his rumpled jacket hung from him. Connor felt Simon's eyes on him. Ignored it.

'Had a wee, ah, incident,' Paulie said, as he walked round the car. 'Taxi pulls up about fifteen minutes ago, guy gets out. Twitchy little fucker, all jerky movements and big eyes, like he'd taken a few too many hits of speed.'

Connor looked around the emptiness of the street, felt a sour dread curdle in his gut. 'What made you think he was a threat?'

Paulie sneered, tension rippling through his shoulders. 'I knew,' he said, voice as dark as the shadows. 'He had the look, seen it enough times. And he headed straight for yer woman's block of flats.'

Connor snapped a look between the flats and Paulie. 'Hold on, you're not telling me that you let . . .'

'Fuck off.' Paulie laughed. 'You think I'd let anyone into that flat after what you said earlier? Course I fucking wouldn't.'

'So, what happened to him?' Connor asked, unease rising. He didn't like where this was going.

A smile blossomed on Paulie's face, warm, generous and utterly authentic. For an instant, it changed him from a brooding thug to a kindly uncle, full of good humour and content with the world. In that instant, Connor understood Paulie was the worst kind of predator: a monster without hesitation, who only felt pleasure in the pain of others. 'Decided to keep him for us to have a little chat with, didn't I?'

He walked to the rear of the car, fiddled for a moment and opened the boot.

'Squirrelly little shit, I'll give him that,' Paulie said, standing aside to let Simon and Connor look at the captive.

Wide, terrified eyes gazed up at them, framed in sockets that were already turning a dusty purple from the punches he had received. Blood was caked around his nose, dark and lurid against the waxy sheen of his pale, sweat-soaked skin.

'Puh-please!' the man said, his jaw chattering as though he were sitting in a bucket of ice. 'Please don't hurt me! I'll stay quiet, I promise! I was only joking around earlier on. I would never, could never . . .'

Connor reached into the boot, grabbed a handful of damp shirt and hauled. Weak fingers skittered across his wrists as he pulled the man out and dragged him to the kerb. 'Sit down,' he said.

He obeyed, feverish eyes darting between Connor, Simon and Paulie. Connor could understand his terror. He'd been put in an indefensible position, three men looming over him. Not good.

Connor hunkered down, getting face to face with the man. He felt the briefest moment of recognition, washed away by the reek of stale sweat and beer that seemed to roll off him in waves. 'Who are you? Why were you trying to get to Donna Blake?'

'Donna? Donna who? I don't know who you're—'

Connor leant forward, unblinking. 'Don't bullshit me. My friend here,' he nodded up at Paulie, 'said you were heading for her block of flats. If you weren't going to see her, who were you going to see?'

275

The man looked down, took a deep breath. When he looked back, Connor saw nothing but desperation in his eyes.

'Please, just don't hurt them, okay?' he said at last, his voice as pathetic as his eyes. 'I'll tell you anything you want but, please, just leave them alone. Please . . .'

Connor stood back as the man began to cry, soft sobs that racked his thin shoulders.

I'll stay quiet. I was only joking.

Don't hurt them.

'Who do you think sent us?' Connor asked, the pieces of the puzzle falling into place. 'And why do you think we're going to hurt Donna Blake and her son?'

The man's head whipped up, hope guttering in his eyes. 'He didn't send you?' he whispered. 'You're not here for me or Donna? Then who . . .?'

Connor sighed, frustrated. 'Let's start again,' he said. 'Who are you, and why were you trying to see Donna Blake?'

The man's eyes flicked between the three men, desperate calculations giving him a feral, feverish look. 'My name is Mark Sneddon,' he said at last. 'I work for the *Chronicle*. I need to see Donna because I'm in a world of shit and I don't know where else to turn.'

CHAPTER 66

Emma snapped awake, disoriented. Why was her bed in the wrong position? Why was the pillow too soft? Who had put that chair in the corner and where was . . .

Realization hit her as the fog in her mind gradually cleared. She remembered now. After her call with Donna Blake, she had demanded access to Mark's room at the Golden Lion. The concierge, a young, slope-shouldered kid who was all acne and wide eyes, had demurred at first, citing security for the hotel's guests. Emma admired the sentiment, but she didn't have time for his professionalism. A few withering glances, a description of Mark's luggage, then veiled threats about talking to the management, followed by a flash of her ID to prove her name, and she was following him up a small, narrow staircase.

The room was on the second floor, one up from a large ballroom that Emma guessed saw a lot of weddings. The concierge let her in, gave her a spare key, then retreated. It was a typical mid-range hotel room, compact, neat. Mark's suitcase, a battered old thing he had bought before their honeymoon, was tucked into the corner of the wardrobe, a shirt for the next day hanging freshly pressed above it. Typical Mark. Fuck around all you want at night, but always be ready for the next day.

Other than the shirt, there was little sign of his presence. The bed was made, sheets and pillows undisturbed. She had sat on it, suddenly tired, then lain back, staring up at the ceiling, hands steepled over her stomach, thinking. If Donna Blake was telling the truth, where had he gone? What was he doing?

And with whom?

The thoughts followed her into a fitful doze. Now, fully awake, she stood up and went to the bathroom. On the wall above the toilet there was a mirror, which flared into life as she stepped into the room. A stranger stared back at her, a flushed, haggard version of herself that she recognized from the eyes and the small mole just above the left eyebrow.

She used the toilet, then washed her hands, splashed cold water onto the face that had taunted her from the mirror.

Where the fuck was he? How could he do this to her? Especially now.

The thought snarled in the corners of her mind. Donna Blake had said Mark wasn't with her, but had she lied? Was he fucking her right at this moment even as Emma stood there, like the mother she had sworn never to emulate, anchored to a dead marriage, the invisible chains of an outwardly comfortable life and the crushing knowledge that it was too late to start again?

She felt tears bite at the back of her eyes and whirled into the room. No. That would not be her. They had never spoken about it, silenced by their own cowardice. Besides, when the moment of decision had come, when she had seen in his eyes that he wanted to tell her it was over, he had chosen her. Not the pathetic bitch he had met at the office.

Or so she had thought. But now?

She walked to the small dressing-table beside the wardrobe, looked down at the hotel-branded notepad that lay next to the phone. The top of the pad was ragged, showing a page had been torn from it, a pen discarded beside it. She ran her finger across the indentations she felt on the page. A phone number? An address?

Donna Blake's address?

She flicked on a lamp above the phone, angling the page, trying to see the impressions. It took a moment for her eyes to adjust, but when they did, she could see it wasn't a number Mark had written down, but a word.

Or a name.

She looked around for a pencil, something she could use to rub on the notepad and pick out the markings. She had no idea if it would work but had seen enough TV shows to hope it would. Glancing around, she spotted the small bin under the table and cursed herself.

She grunted as she bent down and saw a small piece of paper scrunched up into a tight ball clinging to the bin's plastic lining. She fished it out, put it on the dressing-table and smoothed it.

Yes. She couldn't be sure, but she was fairly certain it was the same words she had seen on the indented notepad. They made no immediate sense, but filled her with a strange relief. At least it wasn't *her* name – or an address.

She turned in the chair, grabbed her bag, which she had left beside her on the bed, took out her mobile and tried Mark's number again. Once more it rang through to his voicemail.

'Mark? It's me. I'm still in Stirling, still at your room. Call me back, will you?'

Call finished, she flipped over to the web app, deciding to try to make sense of what she had found written in Mark's heavy hand. She squinted again at the scrunched-up note, confirming she had read it correctly, then turned to the phone. Keyed in 'Skye, Dundee, Kenneth Ferguson' and hit search.

CHAPTER 67

Connor drove in silence, hands clenching and easing on the steering wheel in time with the tide of his thoughts. Simon sat silently in the passenger seat, chewing over what Sneddon had told them.

After ascertaining who he was, Connor and Simon had bundled Sneddon into Donna's flat, leaving Paulie on guard duty. When the door had swung open, Donna had stepped forward, eyes shimmering with tears, a smile of relief fighting with a grimace as she saw Sneddon. Then she'd caught herself, body stiffening and face hardening.

Connor understood. It would take an idiot to miss that Donna and Sneddon had a relationship that ran far deeper than merely former colleagues. Given the way she retreated to the living-room door as Connor sat Sneddon on the sofa, creating a barrier between him and the child, it didn't take much to fill in the gaps. Having him there was an intrusion, a violation of the life she had built since she was with him. If Connor had the time to care, he'd almost feel guilty about bringing Sneddon there.

Almost.

It had taken a few minutes to calm the man, convince him he wasn't in immediate danger. It was time Connor didn't think he had. But, slowly, the reporter had regained his composure, and then he had told them a story.

When Donna had left him at his hotel, he had gone back to what he knew, adding in what she had told him. Ferguson's team of handlers had tried to steer the coverage away from the politician's links with Helen Russell, so it seemed as good a place as any to start. Checking back in the cuttings from the *Westie*'s archive, he'd found what he was looking for in coverage from 2014 and the run-up to the independence referendum.

Connor wasn't surprised by that. It fitted with what he now knew – what had given him the password for Evans's laptop.

As part of the referendum campaign, a series of town-hall-style public meetings had been held around the country. At these events, members of the Yes and No camps faced questions from the public about the case for independence or remaining in the UK. Connor had been in Belfast at the time, but he had followed the coverage. He knew the events could get pretty heated, the debate turning sour and ill-tempered as logic and reason gave way to patriotic fervour, sloganeering and the knee-jerk desire to defend an entrenched position shaped more by the screaming headlines and wall-to-wall TV coverage than any real consideration of the issue.

While the SNP administration had walked a tightrope at the time, and faced some tough questions on the use of supposedly apolitical civil servants to push a pro-independence line, the party had dutifully wheeled out its big guns for these debates. And one of its biggest guns, literally and figuratively, was Ken Ferguson.

A bullish debater, Ferguson was seen by the party and the press as a journeyman Nationalist, who had made the transition from the firebrand wing of the party to the measured elder statesman who could make the dispassionate case for independence and a constructive relationship with England: 'our nearest neighbours and closest friends'. As such, he had been sent around the country, attending events in Dundee, Elgin, Portree and Stirling.

What Sneddon had found interesting was that, at each of these events, one of the panellists he was debating was Helen Russell. Sneddon had done his best to connect the dots, checking with hotels in the towns and cities, trying to track down footage from the debates to see how the two had interacted, and while what he had found was suggestive, there was nothing concrete.

That didn't pose much of an ethical dilemma for Sneddon, whose tabloid instincts were excited by the possibility of a political sex scandal to add spice to a juicy murder. Deciding to take a punt, he had called Ferguson directly, told him what he had found, and asked why he had been so coy about how well he had known Russell. He had recounted the conversation with a pride that swelled his chest and made his eyes glitter from their bruised sockets.

'I played it just right,' he had told them, pointing at the records he had pulled up on his laptop, 'asked how long he had known her, had they got close on the campaign trail, any expenses for late-night dinners, drinks, that sort of thing.'

'So why did you run?' Donna had asked, her voice low and tired. 'Sounds like a hell of a splash, especially since you tried to help Higgins and Mitchell steer the story away from Russell and Ferguson's past relationship in the first place. Or were you too scared to write the story that showed you were a sell-out?'

Anger had flashed in Sneddon's eyes for a moment, replaced by shame and fear. 'It wasn't that,' he said. 'Ferguson clammed up pretty quickly, couldn't get off the phone fast enough. But two minutes after I put the phone down on him, I got a call back. From Mitchell, the special adviser.'

'Ah,' Donna sneered. 'What did she say?'

Sneddon dropped his gaze, digging his thumbnail into the back of his hand. 'It was weird,' he said. 'She told me she'd heard about my call to Ferguson, told me how disappointed she was. Then she started telling me I was a level-headed reporter the party could use, and it would be a shame to lose my head and my prospects over an unsubstantiated story against the minister. After all, look what had happened to Matt Evans when he'd started throwing the insults about.'

He had looked at Connor then, a desperate pleading in his eyes. 'Don't you see? She was threatening me! They got rid of Evans – and all that talk about losing my head? Christ, she was telling me to drop it or I was next.'

Connor kept quiet. He knew Donna would dismiss it as a coward's paranoia but, as much as he was coming to despise Sneddon, he knew the other man was right.

He was being threatened. Just not for the reasons he thought.

After hearing Sneddon's story, he had called Ford, not wanting to leave Donna and her child alone while Paulie, still armed with Connor's gun just in case, made sure Jen got home safely. The detective had agreed to come and take the statement – it was nothing that would stand up, but it was another link in the chain, and Connor wanted it on the record.

They had left after Ford had arrived, heading back to Connor's flat. As they drove, Connor was trying to put it all together. It was like doing a jigsaw in the dark. He had all the pieces, could feel them fitting together, but he needed someone or something to flick the light on, let him see the full picture.

If, that was, he had the courage to look at it.

CHAPTER 68

'So, are you going to tell me what you found, and what the hell this all means?'

They were in Connor's living room, the folder from the radio station on the coffee table. Simon had made himself busy with the drinks, pouring himself another large glass of the wine he had bought. Connor had asked for a large whisky. He had no intention of drinking it, but he wanted the heavy-based short glass Simon would put it in.

Just in case.

He took a breath, collected his thoughts. 'Okay,' he said, reaching for the folder and opening it, splaying the papers inside across the table like a deck of cards. 'I think Sneddon was right. Someone doesn't want the link between Ferguson and Russell exposed. But not for the reason he thinks. See, I found this.'

He picked up a photograph from the table, studied it. It made sense, really. It was one of the first questions Ford had asked him: had he had any dealings with the Red Hand Defenders? Why? Because the Defenders had known links to Alba Gheal Ann An Aonadh, the ultra-Unionist group that was known to have run joint training camps with the Defenders.

Training camps just like the one in the picture Connor handed Simon. It was grainy, slightly out of focus, clearly taken on the spur of the moment, then uploaded to a propaganda-filled website in which any face that wasn't covered with the traditional balaclava or scarf pulled up to the nose had been digitally blurred. But this shot was raw, without any of the faces doctored. It showed a small, tight group of people, mostly young, shaven-headed, brandishing a variety of weapons ranging from pistols to baseball bats. They were standing in a scruffy version of a regimental pose, two flags in the centre – the Red Hand of Ulster and a white flag with the black compass points of the Alba Gheal Ann An Aonadh logo branded swastika-like in the middle. And grinning out of the image were two faces Connor knew.

Billy Griffin and Helen Russell.

'Fuck,' Simon whispered. 'So the first two victims knew each other. And Billy was linked to Evans. But how? And why did someone go so medieval on them?'

Connor stopped for a second, looking at the picture. That was bothering him too.

He brushed the thought aside. Focused on what he did know. 'Think about it. Sneddon said it himself. With all the shit going on with Brexit and talk of a second referendum at any moment, can you imagine what would happen if it came out that a leading government minister – the minister in charge of law and order – was revealed to be a marriage wrecker who was shagging a leading member of a proscribed Unionist terror group? The papers would have a fucking field day, and the pro-independence movement would have a total shit-storm on their hands.'

'I don't know,' Simon said. 'I can see it's embarrassing, but worth killing for? Especially like this? Nah, there's got to be more to it. Something we're not seeing.'

Connor riffled through the papers, mostly background on Russell and Ferguson, written in what he assumed was Evans's hand. And there was another question – the clothes: why did Evans and Griffin have each other's clothes in their homes?

He looked back at the picture. Clothes. That was what had given Connor the password to Evans's laptop. In the picture, Billy was wearing a Rangers FC top, for a club with a traditionally Unionist background. The club had a nickname, Teddy Bears, and, with the flag-draped toy on Evans's desk, it had been an obvious connection to make.

Obvious . . .

'Gimme the laptop,' Connor said, reaching across the folder for the flash drive he had found. Simon leant down, picked up the laptop from the floor and passed it to him. Connor powered it up and waited while it booted. After a few moments it revealed a standard desktop littered with an assortment of Word and Excel files that looked like broadcast scripts and timetables. He flicked into the web browser and its history, found nothing more than a collection of news websites, Amazon and searches on Russell and Ferguson stored there. But again he felt the pull of recognition, something about files he had seen earlier . . .

He slotted the flash drive in, waited for the icon to appear on the desktop, double-clicked on it and scanned the directory. They were .mov files, uploaded from a smartphone. Connor clicked on one and watched as the drab interior of Billy Griffin's flat filled the screen. He was sitting opposite the wall where the missing picture had hung. He smiled nervously at the phone, laughed, waved. Then a voice came from off-camera, a voice Connor recognized from Valley FM as Matt Evans's.

'Okay, Billy, no rush. Tell me again about the training camp.'

Billy fidgeted in his seat, rubbed his hands on his legs, glanced nervously at the camera. 'I'm no' sure I should . . .'

A blur as a figure passed in front of the camera, walking diagonally across the view, then dropping to his knees in front of Billy. Matt Evans ran his hand up Billy's legs in a slow, comforting caress. It made sense of the shared wardrobes, the teddy bear on his desk at work. 'Look, Billy, I'm not trying to force you into anything here,' he said, his voice radio-sonorous and soothing. 'If you don't want to do this, then I'm sorry, I shouldn't have asked. But if we do this, handle it right, we can get everything we wanted, everything we've spoken about. Away from here. Clean. Together.'

Billy nodded, the gesture so full of blind hope that the whisky soured in Connor's stomach. 'All right, Matt,' he whispered.

'Good,' Evans said, returning Billy's smile. He stood up, placed a hand on his shoulder, and leant in, a reassuring peck on the lips. Then he turned and walked behind the camera again.

'When you're ready,' he said, the voice colder now.

Billy knotted his hands in his lap, studied them for where to start. 'Aye, well, it was like I said before, like. I heard about it from the boys at the game, got into it that way. Signed up when I could, wasnae easy to get in, they're suspicious bastards, but with the way things were then, I wasnae surprised. Anyway, I went to a couple of meetings, then got asked away on one of these "outdoor retreats", you know, meant to be all camping and team building, but it's just a cover to get you trained up with the kit and the fightin'.'

He droned on about the details of the camp, weapons, crap food, too much booze, lots of propaganda about the 'indy scum who want to rip our country apart'. Connor skimmed through the files, noting that the location of filming occasionally changed, swapped for a brighter, more homely flat with other pictures on the wall. Evans's home, surely. It was mostly the same content, Billy bragging about his growing links with both 4AG and the Red Hand, how they had given him an important assignment: he was to make a real statement after the independence referendum. 'Aye,' he said, cheeks reddening with pride. 'They wanted me to make a real scene, show those Yes bastards who they were dealing with. Told me to get a flag, make sure everyone saw me light the fucker up.'

Again, Evans's voice from off-camera: 'Who told you, Billy?'

'That Russell bint,' Billy said, staring into the camera, his eyes growing dark and sly, a rat-like intelligence seeming to sharpen his features. 'But it wasnae just her. See, she told me we had friends in high places. And one of her pals, who everyone thought was a Yesser, was really a friend of ours, and would see me right.'

Connor paused the clip, took a swig of whisky before he had even thought about it. There it was. Billy Griffin claiming Helen Russell knew that a key Nationalist was actually a Unionist sympathizer. Ferguson? Given their links, probably. At any rate, it was explosive pillow talk, and information worth killing for.

On an impulse, Connor clicked back into the web history, ran through it until he saw what he was looking for, clicked on it and held his breath hoping, hoping . . .

Yes. One of the previously visited sites was for a gmail account.

But Evans had been sloppy, closing the window but not logging out of the account, meaning it opened automatically. A lot of it was crap, internet shopping, Nigerian millionaires and promises to 'extend his manhood'. Connor skimmed a page, then clicked on the sent items. Again, nothing of interest. But on the left, in the folders, there was one marked 'Handy'. Connor clicked on it, hit the jackpot.

It was a back-up of the recordings Evans had taken of Billy and sent to himself, no doubt as insurance. But there was also a message, simply entitled 'Proposal'. It had been sent a week ago to Lets4Kennynatsnper@gmail.com. Not difficult to decipher.

Connor clicked on it and read:

Sir,

I tried to call you earlier on but was rudely fobbed off. You may know, I presented *Nightline* on EBA and have recently moved to host a show in Stirling. I believe we have a mutual acquaintance, a charming young man who I met during my time in Edinburgh and who is now safely residing in my care. He told me quite an illuminating story about you and your links to a Unionist group that is best not mentioned in polite company. I must say, I was shocked to hear you would associate with such people, let alone agree to help them.

As you will appreciate, this is a story of significant public interest, and I am very keen to get your input. Depending on what you say, I may be persuaded that there is a greater story to pursue, but that will take *sum* talking on your behalf. However, if I do not hear from you within twenty-four hours, I will make this story public.

Connor sat back, Simon craning over him to read the file. So that was it. Blackmail.

What was it MacKenzie had said? Billy was drug-dealing in Edinburgh? No doubt he'd run into Evans as a client and the two had got talking. Something had happened between them, taking the relationship from merely user and dealer, though from the way he had handled Billy on the tape, Connor knew Evans was both. At some point, Billy had told Evans his story. And all Evans had seen was a payday – 'that will take *sum* talking'. So he had approached Ferguson, who had moved to shut him up and sever all links to him. Permanently.

Connor closed his eyes, saw the obese, sweating form of Ferguson standing in front of the cameras. He wasn't the killer – there was no way he was capable of it. The physical exertion of moving a body, let alone decapitating it, would give the fat fuck a heart attack, so who . . .

Connor froze, the glass halfway to his lips. He lunged forward, barging Simon out of the way, ignoring his curses as wine sloshed onto his T-shirt. Suddenly, he understood what was bothering him. What he had seen on Sneddon's screen but not recognized.

Until now.

He fished his phone out, opened his own email, found the message he had made Sneddon send him, the one that had all his research attached. Clicked on the records of the Electoral Commission from the time of the town-hall tour and scanned down until he found what he was looking for.

The world stopped. Simon called him from the end of a long corridor. Far away. Unimportant. All he could hear was the hammering of his heart in his ears, his pulse making his vision brighten and expand in time with his heartbeat.

He tore his eyes from the screen, looked at Simon, the questions and doubts tumbling through his mind as he felt his grip tighten on the glass.

'Jesus, Connor, you okay? You look like you've shit a brick, big lad . . .'

Connor ignored him, flicked through his contacts. Found the number he needed. The number he had made a point of finding the first day he had met Malcolm Ford.

'Superintendent Doyle? This is Connor Fraser. I'm sorry for contacting you like this. But I have a question, sir. You told DCI Ford that you served with my boss in the army. Could you tell me where that was, please? It's vital to the case and my employer.'

The answer Connor had feared slithered down the line, stabbing into his ear and ripping through his mind like a blade. He mumbled a thank-you, then ended the call, the phone skittering across the table as he tossed it with a numb hand.

'Connor, what the fuck . . .?'

He looked up at Simon, at the man he had thought was his friend. The man he had seen wield a wicked-looking knife earlier in the evening. The man who might have been lying to him all along.

He stood, his legs heavy, adrenalin beginning to spark and crackle through his veins. It was like a short-sighted man putting on glasses for the first time, the world jumping from soft focus to brutal, sharp-edged detail as he finally saw everything. He took in Simon's relaxed posture, saw his shoulders and jaw tighten with dawning unease, his pupils dilating and his breath deepening as he readied himself for what was coming next.

'Connor,' he said, rising now, holding an arm out. 'Big lad, what's going on? What was that all about just now?'

'The rat,' Connor said, feeling a smile draw his lips tight. 'Did you know they found a rat stuffed into Billy Griffin's mouth? I thought it was a message, that maybe he was traitor, a rat, who had been silenced. Is that what you are, Simon? A rat? A traitor?'

Simon's mouth fell open as though he had been slapped. 'Connor, what the fuck are you talking about? I thought we were past this. I'm sorry I lied to you, but God's truth, Lachlan called me over here to keep an eye on you when it all kicked off here. What the fuck are you . . .'

'The rat,' Connor said again, as though Simon hadn't spoken. He was focusing on the angle of Simon's lower jaw, just below the ear. It was where he would hit him first if he had to. He prayed he was wrong. Prayed he wouldn't need to.

'It was a message, just not the one everyone thought it was. See, it was a calling card. Which leaves me with only one question, Simon.'

'What? Connor, Jesus, what . . .'

'Are you really my friend? Or are you just another rat working for him?'

CHAPTER 69

He felt no surprise when the call came, had been expecting it since the moment his client had told him about the press conference and that little prick Sneddon insinuating a link between Ferguson and Russell.

The client had been panicked, on the verge of hysteria. What would they do? All Sneddon had was insinuation and conjecture at the moment, but that was more than enough for most members of the press. They would start digging into all of it. Find out about Russell, her past, her links with Billy Griffin. It would be a disaster, the apocalypse. Not just for them but for the movement as a whole. After all, how could any Nationalist be trusted ever again after it emerged that their own justice secretary had secretly been a Unionist sympathizer?

He made soothing noises into the phone, more to silence the pathetic mewling rather than to offer any real comfort. The truth was, he didn't really care what this meant for his client or their petty political aspirations. He had known this was a possibility since the moment he had agreed to this job. He had taken steps to avoid this outcome but, still, the thought of this conclusion, so tempting and alluring, had played on his thoughts, filled his imagination in quiet moments.

And now here it was.

He reached for the phone, let it ring for a moment. Then took a breath. Answered.

'Connor. I thought I might get a call from you. How are things in Stirling? You making the most of your time off?'

He smiled at the predictable response, the venom and fury injected into Fraser's voice, which was normally so quiet and even, like a slow-flowing stream. He felt a surge of satisfaction. If nothing else, he had got under Connor Fraser's cool façade, antagonized the man behind the veneer.

And, after all, wasn't that the point?

He waited until the fury had abated. 'You know, if you feel that way, perhaps we should meet, discuss all this. I hear there are some sights to see around the castle and the cemetery, so how about we meet there? . . . Yes, where the first body was found. Say an hour?'

He clicked off the phone, rocked back in his chair. He didn't need the hour, was a lot closer than Connor or Simon would have guessed.

But he needed the time.

He called the number from memory, didn't have to wait long for the reply. And why should he? After all, this call was going to make his client's day.

CHAPTER 70

Connor pulled into a parking space across the road from Allan's Primary School, a short walk down the hill from Cowane's Hospital and the Old Town Cemetery. He killed the engine and looked across at Simon, who was staring back at him.

The confrontation had been inevitable, as Simon had continued to insist that Lachlan Jameson had summoned him only to keep a surreptitious eye on Connor when the bodies had started to pile up in Stirling, and Connor had been looking for a favour. Connor had continued to dismiss that explanation as bullshit, both men's voices rising with their anger.

'Tell me the fucking truth, Simon,' Connor had hissed, 'or I swear to fuck I'll make you eat that fucking glass.'

'Away tae fuck,' Simon replied, his voice a harsh rasp. 'I am telling you the truth. I came because Lachlan asked me to keep an eye on you. Thought you needed back-up. I swear. So get it done, choke me out, 'cause my answer's not going to change.'

Connor gave a grunt of frustration and forced his shoulders to ease. Grabbed the laptop and spun it round. 'So if that's true, what the fuck does this mean?'

Simon's eyes darted between Connor and the screen, trying to make sense of what he was seeing.

It was the email Sneddon had sent, detailing the expenses and accounts of those involved in the independence roadshow debates. When he was checking the Electoral Commission's spending records of the parties for accommodation and looking for crossovers, he had stumbled over something else. A seemingly innocuous line in the accounts that referred to payments made for 'travel and transportation costs' for Ferguson as he travelled around the country. Deprived of his ministerial car and entourage, he'd been forced to rely on private means to get around.

Private means that were provided by Sentinel Securities.

On one level, it made sense to Connor. With the debate becoming increasingly polarized and toxic, those involved had been looking for a little extra security and reassurance when travelling to meet the great unwashed. And Connor knew it was happening again now: with Brexit on everyone's lips, there had been a surge in political clients looking for close protection experts to act as drivers and bodyguards when attending events.

But there was something else, something that echoed in Connor's mind the moment he had seen the company's name in the records. A memory of his call with Jameson after the Benson job in Edinburgh.

'Seems there's been a murder in Stirling, not far from where you stay. Not a lot of detail at this stage, but sounds fairly grim. Body badly mutilated. Maybe you should come in to work after all. Might be quieter than home tonight.'

Body badly mutilated. How had Lachlan known? He had called before Ford's first press conference, when all that had been available was the scant information Connor had seen in Donna Blake's initial story: it's a murder, and we don't have a fucking clue.

It was possible that Jameson had called his pal Doyle for an off-the-record update, but why? Concern for Connor? Unlikely and, besides, Doyle had told him that he hadn't asked for details of the case.

Then there was Jameson's military service with Doyle. They had served together in the first Gulf War, in the 7th Armoured Brigade, a tank division also known by a more colourful nickname: the Desert Rats.

Rats. Just like the one that had been stuffed into Billy Griffin's mouth.

Not a message. A calling card.

Simon had blinked up at Connor, nothing but confusion in his face. 'Connor, honestly, man, you've got to believe me. He called me, said you might be in a bit of bother, asked me to come and keep a quiet eye on you, watch your back. Said he didn't want to tell you as it would be like an insult – that you couldn't look after yourself. Look, you've got to believe me, man.'

Connor wanted to believe Simon, but it didn't make sense. The picture he had formed in his mind told him that Lachlan Jameson had a previous relationship with Ferguson, who had reached out to the 'security and protection expert' asking for help with his little blackmail problem. Killing wasn't an issue: before forming Sentinel, Jameson had taken on private contracts; a little digging had told Connor they had attracted high fees and bloodshed. Wet work, they called it. And the intelligence was that Lachlan Jameson loved to get wet.

But if that was right, if Jameson was the killer, why had he called Simon in to watch Connor's back? Why put him in touch with Doyle and, subsequently, Ford? And why, if he was trying to play this quietly, was he taunting Connor with a message from his past? A message he would have known demanded a response?

It was a question that had lingered unspoken between them on the drive back into town.

'You got any idea what the fuck is going on here, Connor?' Simon asked, as he stared up the hill. The night had made good on its threat, and rain tapped on the roof of the car, like the drumming of impatient fingers.

'Haven't a clue,' Connor said. 'But why don't we go and find out?'

CHAPTER 71

They split up at the Stirling Highland Hotel, Simon heading through the car park for the Back Walk so he could loop around the church and approach from the cemetery. It had been his idea, and Connor knew he was testing him – trust me to cover your rear. Connor had agreed: he wanted to believe in Simon and their friendship, but trust wasn't the issue. If he came in from the rear, it split up him and Jameson, meaning Connor could deal with them individually rather than together. He felt a momentary pang of regret at leaving his gun with Paulie, then pushed it aside. A gun was a coward's weapon, and this was better dealt with by hand.

He stopped at the gate to the Holy Rude, the rain-slicked cobbles gleaming in the streetlights. There was no sign of the police or the violence that had been committed there, which made sense – Stirling might have a history steeped in blood and violence, but tourists tended to prefer more romantic reminders than decapitated corpses and blood-stained grass.

He walked up to the gate slowly, felt no surprise that it was open. Stepped into the gloom, giving his eyes a moment to adjust to the light, then moved up the curved lane, aware of the hedges to his left that led to the bowling green, which dated all the way back to the sixteenth century. He kept walking, following the path as it swept gently left, past the Holy Rude and towards the hospital.

As he approached, a shadow peeled itself from the darkness

pooling around the building and stepped forward. Connor kept his eyes on Lachlan Jameson, stopping to force his boss to come to him and move away from the old stone steps that led up to the graveyard, buying Simon more time.

'Ah, Connor,' Jameson called, as though they had run into each other on a pleasant Sunday afternoon. 'I must say, you picked a hell of a night for it.'

'Why, Lachlan?' Connor felt as though the rain should evaporate into steam as it touched him, boiled away by the rage that coursed through him. 'Why kill those three people? And why drag me into it?'

Jameson smiled, a predatory leer Connor had never seen before. He shook his head as he stopped, Connor tensing as he reached into his pocket. 'Business, dear boy,' he said, as he held aloft another copy of the book he had used to torment him. 'Merely business. A client came to me asking for a job to be done, a message to be sent. The means of sending that message was left to me. Judging by the reaction, it was definitely effective.'

Connor felt frustration blend with his anger, turning it into something darker, more feral. He itched to lunge forward, grab Jameson and squeeze the answers he wanted out of him. 'But why the book? Why stir up all that shite with Jonny Hughes if you wanted to keep your part in it quiet? You should have known something like that would only make me look into all this. And you should also have known I'd work it out eventually.'

Jameson's smile intensified, and Connor felt a trickle of unease that was only fuelled when the other man nodded with a gleeful chuckle. 'Ah, Connor, you're good, very good. Always have been. But you're missing the big picture. After all, I never said how many clients I had, did I?'

Connor cursed his sloppiness even as he whirled to his left, a sudden blur of movement from the darkness snapping his focus away from Jameson's attempt at distraction. Cold agony, as bright as a star, exploded in his leg and he lurched backwards, clutching his thigh and feeling the world sway as blood coated his hand.

Shock shattered his thoughts as his past stepped into the light, the knife gleaming. And suddenly he understood. Simon had been wrong. Someone else would understand the message of the book, someone else who knew what Jonny Hughes had done and how Connor had reacted.

''Bout ye, Connor?' Amy Hughes asked, her smile mirroring Jameson's. 'Been a while. You're looking well on it, though. Well, apart from that.' She gestured towards him with the knife.

'Fuck! Connor!'

Connor whirled, the world heaving and swaying as his head snapped right, just in time to see Simon race down the steps from the graveyard. Connor tried to call out, warn him, but it was too late. Focused on getting to his injured friend, Simon gave Jameson all the time he needed. He stepped into Simon's path, driving a crashing fist into his cheek and sending him tumbling to the ground. Even over the static hiss of the rain, Connor heard the dry, twig-like snap of Simon's jaw, saw the knuckle-dusters glint on Jameson's hand like obscene jewels as he pulled back his fist and turned to face him.

'Connor, meet one of my other clients, Amy Hughes. I believe you knew her husband, Jonny, had some dealing with him. Amy was very keen that I talk to you and Simon about that, and what happened the night you visited their home. And now here we all are.'

Connor smiled. 'What happened? Marriage counselling not work out for you?'

'Fuck you!' Amy spat. 'You cost us everything! Jonny was a fuck-up, but he loved me, made sure we were provided for. Then you came along and beat the fuck out of him over a cheap hoor, and that's him. You fucking ruined him, made him look weak. No one wanted him to deal for them after that, said he was a fucking embarrassment. Weak. You fucking pig *cunt*!'

She lunged forward with the knife and Connor collapsed against the church wall, rain-slicked granite driving icy needles into his back and shoulders. He focused on the sudden chill, tried to use it to clear his thoughts, calm the white noise of pain, confusion and rage.

'You okay, Connor? Watch your step. Last thing we want is you slipping and breaking your neck. Been enough death here recently, hasn't there?'

The knife rose slowly, flaring orange as it caught the glow from a streetlight overhead.

Connor braced himself against the wall, tried to draw strength from the ancient stone. 'Come on, then,' he hissed, dragging his gaze from her eyes, trying to focus through the growing fog in his mind. 'I've not got all night, and this is getting fucking boring.'

'Mr Take Charge, huh, Connor? I always liked that about you.' A glance down at the knife. 'Well, if you insist.'

Connor pushed off the wall as hard as he could when Amy lunged, using inertia to make up for the weakness in his leg. They collided in a tangle of limbs and fell to the cobbled ground, writhing. Connor's leg was engulfed in agony as he jerked the wrong way, the sudden pain forcing another scream from him. He felt small, hard fingers scrabble across his face and twisted away, eyes searching desperately for the knife. He grabbed for it, felt Amy's crazed strength behind the blade, inching it closer, closer, to his face.

He took another breath, tasted blood at the back of his throat, and gripped the arms that were quivering with the effort of driving the knife towards his face. He thought about letting go for an instant, the knife digging into the soft flesh under his chin, the blade slicing sideways and down to tear open his windpipe, blood and gristle splattering onto the cobbles. He could let it end with him. Let his blood be the last.

But then he looked to his side, saw Simon sprawled on the ground, Jameson looming over him. Simon, who had been manipulated as Connor had been, all to fulfil a deranged woman's perverted lust for revenge.

No fucking way.

He snapped his head straight ahead, focusing on Amy Hughes's face. It was a mask of hatred, teeth bared, eyes dark pits as she used her weight to try to force the knife down.

Connor let it happen. He released his grip, darted his head to the right, dragging Amy forward with the sudden momentum, the knife biting into the cobbles. Drove his hips up, bucking her, adding to her speed. He whipped his head to the side, crashing his forehead into her temple with a sickening crunch that detonated a shrapnel grenade of agony in his mind. Amy screamed and slumped to the right, Connor following her. He grabbed for the knife, his fingers thick and clumsy, the world swaying and nausea squeezing his gut. With the blood loss and the blow to the head, he had to finish this. Fast.

Grabbing the knife, he reversed it, drove the butt into Amy's other temple. She gave a gargling grunt, blood exploding from her mouth in a fine, warm spray that peppered Connor's face. Then her head lolled forward, eyelids fluttering over glassy eyes that were filling with the rain.

Connor watched her breathe, blood bubbling on her lips. Then he got to his feet slowly, his good leg screaming at being forced to take his weight, his wounded leg strangely numb.

'Bravo, Connor,' Jameson called, stepping over Simon and approaching him. 'I was sure you'd get the best of Mrs Hughes, but it was entertaining to watch.'

'Fuck you,' Connor snarled, closing one eye to focus on him, thinking. He needed him angry if he had any chance of ending this. 'You're fucking diseased, Lachlan. You kill three people to save a minister's career, then drag me into it to get revenge for a clapped-out gangster's ex? Christ, how the hell did she make you agree to that? Or did she go the extra mile to seal the deal?'

'How fucking dare you?' Jameson spat, and lunged. He killed for money and pleasure, but by insulting his professionalism, Connor had made it personal.

Connor staggered back, feeling his leg threaten to give way as he dodged Jameson's blind swing. He took a firmer grip on the knife, held it butt forward, the blade tight against his forearm.

Jameson turned, took a moment to aim, swinging for the open target Connor had left him. Connor dropped low, letting his leg give way and drag him down, then whipped the knife out, drawing a long slash across Jameson's exposed midriff. Ignoring the pain, he drove up and forward, charging Jameson, pinning his arms to his sides in a bear hug and sending him stumbling backwards. He felt breath on the top of his head, hot as Jameson thrashed and writhed, trying to free himself.

No fucking chance.

Connor tightened his grip, put everything he had into it as he kept charging forward. Jameson, off balance, lost his footing and fell backwards, breath erupting from him as he hit the hard cobbles.

Connor reared up, a blood-streaked god in the rain-soaked shadows. He dropped the knife and drove his fist forward, splinters of teeth stabbing into his knuckles as he felt the back of Jameson's head bounce off the stone ground, the shock juddering up his arm, like a gun's recoil. 'Fucking bastard!' he roared, hitting him again. Jameson's nose exploded, the crack reverberating deep in Connor, a cry to action for the part of himself he hated. He threw punch after punch, selecting targets on instinct – cheekbones, jaw, eye sockets, temples. As he struck Jameson, his mind was a kaleidoscope of pain – his mother's funeral, his gran's pleading confusion, the loathing he felt when he thought about what Jonny Hughes had made him become, the loss of . . .

He whirled as a hand fell on his shoulder, lashing out with a wild left.

'Fuck, man, easy,' Simon said, his words mangled by his obliterated jaw, his eyes glittering and over-bright. Connor could see he was going into shock.

'That's enough, Connor,' Simon drawled. 'Leave him now. Not worth it.'

Connor looked down at Jameson. His face was a bloodied, pitted ruin, the scaffolding that had held his features in place shattered by Connor's blows. He tried to feel guilt, then looked back at Simon and knew he never would.

He staggered back, the act of getting to his feet robbing him of the last of his strength. Sat down, hard, the pain of the landing bringing his thoughts into focus. He fumbled for his belt and looped it round his leg, pulling it tight in a rough tourniquet. Grabbed his phone, squinted against the gathering dark as he looked for the number he needed. He hit call, then waited for an answer.

'Ford? It's Connor Fraser. You wanted that update? Cowane's Hospital. Now. And if you could bring an ambulance . . .'

He let the phone fall to the cobbles without waiting for an answer, then looked at Simon. Fingers of guilt prodded him, even through the shock and the pain. 'Sorry, man,' he whispered. 'I should have trusted you.'

Simon shook his head, eyes still over-bright. Concussion. Definitely. 'No,' he whispered, voice fading. 'You shouldn't. Rule one, Connor. Even though it's peace time, always check under the car.'

Connor leant forward to catch him as he toppled forward. He held him close, refusing to let his body touch the cold cobbles greased with Jameson's blood, and forced himself to ignore the warm blanket of unconsciousness that threatened to wrap itself around him.

Instead he listened to the sound of the rain.

And waited.

CHAPTER 72

In the week that followed, a feeding frenzy erupted over a story that was part murder, part political conspiracy and all embarrassment for the government.

Ferguson endured a trial by media, forced in front of the cameras to admit his affair with Helen Russell but deny any knowledge of her links to Alba Gael Ann An Aonadh or sympathy with their aims. Watching one interview, in which he was cornered by a crowd of reporters in the corridor leading to the Scottish Parliament's debating chamber, Connor almost believed him. The blend of stress-induced scruffiness, bewilderment and righteous fury was convincing. And, besides, it was all circumstantial. Yes, Ferguson knew Russell, but did that mean he was really a Unionist in disguise, willing to kill to bury the truth that he was working against a party he had been a member of for more than twenty-five years?

In the end, it didn't matter. As the embarrassing questions piled up, and the lurid speculation hit fever pitch in the media, Ferguson was suspended. In the minority administration, the loss of the justice secretary triggered a major cabinet reshuffle and growing calls for a snap election.

Connor didn't care if that happened, had no intention of heading for the ballot box if it did.

For his part, Lachlan Jameson kept quiet, confirming only that he had carried out work for Ferguson back in 2014, providing security services during the referendum. He even offered emails between himself and Ferguson's office to prove it, in which he stated Sentinel would be 'delighted to assist with any further issues he may have in the future'. He admitted assaulting Simon, claiming it was self-defence because Simon had turned on him 'for reasons unknown'. Reading that in the interview transcript Doyle had shared with him, Connor was forced to smile. If Jameson didn't know the reason for the attack and what had happened that night, Amy Hughes did. And, unlike Lachlan Jameson, she was more than willing to talk.

Displaying the kind of blind loyalty that always mystified Connor, Amy had gone back to Jonny as soon as she had been released from custody, forgetting his abandonment of her after their arrest when he had told her he loved her. But following his confrontation with Connor, Jonny Hughes had struggled, an embarrassment to his relatives as an unsafe pair of hands in their drugs business. That was why he had been on the Shankill Road the day he died: reduced to trying to sell steroids to gym users, he had been confronted by the staff at the leisure centre and forced to flee – straight into the path of the car that had killed him.

It had been too much for Amy who, as the grieving widow, had tearfully asked Jonny's uncle, a low-level UDA thug called Miles Hughes, to seek vengeance on the man who had brought 'our Jonny' low. Miles agreed, and put an open contract out on the peeler who had beaten the shit out of Jonny Hughes. Connor read this with no great surprise: ordering a hit on a copper who had left the island was little more than lip service to keep Amy happy and ensure family honour was maintained.

Until, that was, Lachlan Jameson had heard about it.

Connor could imagine how it had happened. Jameson had received a call about him from a contact in the PSNI – a contact Connor was determined to find one day in the near future. Deciding to check Connor out, he had found out about the open hit on him, either from his PSNI contact or his network of informants from his private contracting days. Connor knew how that world worked: contractors looked after each other, shared information and potential business. It was a dark, violent world, which bred a strange loyalty among those living in it. And in that world, information wasn't just power, it was a survival tool. So Jameson had approached Amy.

'I really thought the fucker was going to do something there and then,' she had told Doyle, when asked about her first meeting with Lachlan Jameson, eighteen months before. 'He asked all the right questions, even how I wanted that shite Connor Fraser done and if I'd like to see pictures as proof he had suffered. But then he went quiet and I didn't hear from him for months, until he called out of the blue two weeks ago.'

Connor paused when he read that. Jameson had known about Amy Hughes the day they'd first met, the day he'd offered him the job. What was it he had said about Robbie? *If he's not an asset, he's a liability. This is a business, after all.* Was that what he had been thinking when he had offered Connor the job? *If he works out, great, but if he doesn't I can always make a profit by executing him for that bitch back in Belfast?*

Sitting in his flat reading the report, his wounded leg bandaged and resting elevated on a pillow on the sofa, Connor pushed the thought aside. It didn't matter, not really. What did matter was Amy's confession that it was her, not Jameson, who had killed Russell. 'He asked me to do it, told me that, if I did, he'd do Fraser for free. Good deal for me. After all, what do I care about some dozy bint who's shagging around?'

But Connor didn't need to read the confession to know that Jameson hadn't killed Russell. It was something that had been niggling in him, an observation Simon had made about the murders: why go so medieval on two of them, beheading only Higgins and Evans? Now he had the answer: beheading was Jameson's calling card, a bloody little flourish he had learnt during the war.

Connor closed the file, laid it aside as he struggled up from the couch. Let Jameson keep his silence. Amy had said more than enough to make sure he would spend the rest of his days in prison. A prison Connor intended to visit from time to time.

He tested his leg, felt a flash of pain when he put his weight on it. He'd been lucky, the doctors had said. The blade – a wickedly sharp implement that matched the wounds on Griffin's and Evans's necks

– had just missed his femoral artery. If it had hit that, he would have bled out in minutes, improvised tourniquet or not.

Connor hobbled for the door, grabbing his keys as he glanced at his watch, calculating. Simon had been transferred to a specialist unit at St John's Hospital in West Lothian to treat his shattered jaw. The drive would take about forty-five minutes, and he had to factor in a stop on the way. He had no idea how he was going to smuggle a bottle of wine into Simon's room, but he would figure something out. He owed him that much.

The Audi's clutch was heavy and unyielding to the pressure Connor could exert with his wounded leg. He got out of Stirling, felt a pang of guilt as he passed the turn for Bannockburn, and resolved to see his gran on the way home. Maybe smuggle something in for her as well.

He joined the M9, the quiet of the car filled with thoughts of his gran and whether she would recognize him when he visited. Restless, he flicked on the radio, unsurprised to hear Donna Blake's voice. Connor had no idea what sort of deal she'd cut with Sneddon, but he'd let her break the story about the links between Russell, Ferguson and Sentinel Securities, the founding partner of which was now 'assisting the police with their enquiries'. She ran through the case again, cutting back to Ken Ferguson's latest stumbling attempt to defend himself.

'Yes, I had a relationship with Helen Russell, which, in hindsight, was inappropriate. And, yes, arrangements were made to engage the services of Sentinel Securities and Lachlan Jameson for the duration of the independence campaign in 2014. I stress, I am a proud Nationalist who would never . . .' He droned on for a few seconds longer, Donna mercifully cutting him off before the desperation in his voice could hit a crescendo. 'Mr Ferguson remains suspended pending a full investigation of his relationship with Mrs Russell, which party sources say is being expedited. One source, who asked not to be named, cited the rise of the "Me Too" movement, saying it gave "added impetus to get to the truth".'

Donna wrapped up the report, sounding confident and assured. She'd done Connor and Simon a favour by keeping them out of the coverage as far as she could, all on the condition that Connor gave her the exclusive when the time came. 'Won't mention your name, but I want that story,' she'd said.

Connor knew she needed it. With a new contract as a Scotland reporter with Sky, to go with her work at Valley, she had to hit the ground running. He found he was happy to help. There was something about her hard-headed defiance that he found appealing.

The Kelpies flashed past as Connor drove on, the two massive horse heads looming over the motorway. He found his gaze drawn to them, pulling his eyes off the road as they slid past.

He felt a twinge: something wanted to step out of the shadows in his mind as random thoughts tumbled and collided.

Two heads.

Ferguson's words now, from Donna's report: *Arrangements were made to engage the services of Sentinel Securities and Lachlan Jameson for the duration of the independence campaign in 2014.*

A nail driven into Billy Hughes's wall, the ghostly after-image of where a picture had hung almost visible in the fading on the paint.

Jameson: *If he's not an asset, he's a liability.*

Arrangements were made to engage . . .

He eased off the accelerator, took the first off ramp he saw and found a lay-by. He leant over to the glove compartment, his leg protesting as he shifted his weight, fishing out the iPad that was there. He'd given all the files on the case to Doyle and Ford, including the tapes of Evans's interviews with Billy, but he had kept copies of them. He wasn't sure why at the time, chalked it down to his own paranoia, but now . . .

He tapped into the files, found the one he was looking for. It was the same set-up as usual: Billy sitting in the chair, looking straight to camera. But this time, about halfway through, Billy got up, heading for the small bookshelf Connor had inspected. The camera tracked with him, Matt pivoting to keep him in shot as he walked around the room, past the picture . . .

The picture . . .

Connor spooled the recording back. Froze it. There it was. On the wall, just to the left of Billy's shoulder. He took a screenshot of the frozen image, enlarged it as much as he could, then fiddled with the contrast and tone, trying to clean it up. Squinted at it, then called up a web page on his phone, keyed in a name and compared the images even as he felt his breath quicken, the pain in his leg forgotten.

Not conclusive. Nothing that would stand up in court. But it was enough for him.

He tossed the iPad into the passenger seat, started the car again, fumbled for his phone and called Donna Blake, even as he punched Holyrood Road into the satnav.

CHAPTER 73

Maxwell Higgins, Ferguson's senior special adviser, was waiting when Connor arrived, pacing around one of the ponds set in the concrete at the front of the Scottish Parliament. He was taller than he appeared on TV, and bristled as Connor limped towards him, striding forward to cut the distance between them, as if he were impatient to get the conversation over with. Or, more likely, Connor thought, to make sure no one heard them speaking.

'Who the hell do you think you are, Fraser?' he spat, face pale, eyes glinting behind his glasses. 'Calling me out of the blue, making wild accusations. This whole business with Ken is distasteful enough. The last thing we need . . .'

Connor smiled, heard Lachlan Jameson's words again as he raised the iPad and unlocked it.

If he's not an asset, he's a liability . . . If he's not cutting it, we cut him.

'I'd be happy to discuss this in court, Mr Higgins. Perhaps when we do, you can explain what I have here.' He tapped the video still he had taken, the picture on the wall in Billy Griffin's flat. The image Jameson had broken in to steal. It was blurred by magnification, but it was still clear enough to drain the colour from Higgins's face, make him flinch from the iPad as though he had been slapped.

It was another semi-military pose, a group of ragtag youths clustered around the Nazi-like 4A flag, flanked by two figures standing to attention. Helen Russell. And Maxwell Higgins.

'Well, I just don't, I can't . . .' Higgins said, taking a half-step back as he glanced around, desperately checking who was in the vicinity.

Connor smiled, warm and genuine. 'So, about that date in court, when were you thinking?'

Higgins stared at him, hate and feral desperation stripping the mask from his face. 'What do you want?' he hissed. 'I'll buy that from you or . . .'

Connor locked the iPad and dropped it to his side, out of Higgins's reach. 'I'm sure you could too,' he said. 'After all, Mummy and Daddy have a few quid – I bet they'd be happy to shell out to help you.'

Higgins blinked rapidly, confusion diluting the hatred in his gaze. 'What do you . . .?'

'I did a little checking on my way here,' Connor said, shifting his stance as his leg began to ache. 'Quite the story back in the day, wasn't it? You, the son of a minor Tory peer, breaking generations of family party loyalty to side with the cause of independence? A coup for the party, and it seems you made yourself useful, working in just about every position you could until you found Ferguson and became a senior special adviser. And he was very, very useful, wasn't he?'

Higgins seemed to regain some measure of control. He slowed his breathing, smoothed his tie. But it was a façade: the quick, rat-like glances at everyone around him told Connor as much.

'I don't know what you mean. I worked for Ken for years and I—'

'You used him,' Connor said. 'Must have been handy having the ear of someone that high up in the party, someone you could mould into a success, use to gain their trust. And all the while you were still having your little weekends with Helen Russell and the boys at 4AG. My friend Donna told me all about you back in 2014, how desperate you were to have the picture of Billy Griffin pulled from the papers. Didn't make much sense at the time, but I get it now. You weren't worried about how it would affect the cause, you were worried it would make Billy too much of a star, get him to talk about his pals. But he kept quiet, didn't he? Until Matt Evans, of course.'

A dark flash in Higgins's eyes at the mention of Evans's name. It was all the confirmation Connor needed.

'That bastard,' Higgins whispered.

Connor nodded. 'Yeah, that bastard. See, I read it wrong. It was you he emailed, not Ferguson, wasn't it? Lets4kenny – that email account was set up on Kenny's behalf, but it wasn't used by him, was it? I bet if I looked on your computer I'd find the log-ins there. Evans knew what he had, and he was blackmailing you with it. And, as it was you who spoke to Lachlan Jameson back in 2014, you who "made the arrangements" to hire him for Ferguson, you had just the solution to your problem, didn't you?'

Defiance straightened Higgins's spine, forced him to lock eyes with Connor who, despite the pain, took a half-step forward into the gaze.

'You have nothing,' Higgins said, more to himself than to Connor, a sneer twisting his features. 'A blurry picture, a claim I had access to my boss's private email and records showing I arranged security for Ferguson a couple of years ago. Nothing.'

Connor shrugged. 'Maybe,' he said. 'But it's enough to start with, enough to get the questions going, isn't it? And how's it going to look when the man behind the minister is exposed as a regular at ultra-Unionist camps?'

Higgins's resolve seemed to crumple, fast calculations running across his eyes. He ran his tongue over his lips, swallowed once, throat clicking. 'What do you want?' he breathed, his voice taking on a pleading that hurt Connor almost as much as his leg. 'I wasn't joking before – I can get you . . .'

Connor felt the anger rise in him then, cold and black. When he spoke, he heard his father's voice. 'What I want is my friend to recover from the broken jaw you caused. What I want is Donna Blake not to be haunted by the image of what you had done to Matt Evans. What I want is for my leg to stop aching every time I fucking move. But what I'll take is watching the police and the press rip you apart. Don't worry, though. You won't have to wait too long. I've already sent them all the records of your contact with Jameson, the emails to Kenny's account and, of course, this picture.'

He lifted the iPad, waved it in Higgins's face. 'They should be here very, very soon.'

Higgins whipped his head around, like an animal suddenly

realizing it was in a cage. Connor turned and walked away, gritting his teeth and forcing himself to walk smoothly, not let Higgins see how badly he was hurt. As he walked, he heard the first wail of a siren in the distance and wondered if it was headed this way. Looked back over his shoulder to see Higgins rushing for the Parliament.

Not that there was a safe hiding place for him there – or anywhere else for that matter. If the police didn't get him, Connor would. For Billy Griffin, Matt Evans, Helen Russell – and Simon.

He got back to the car park where he had left the Audi, paused in front of it, wiping the cold sweat from his brow. Took deep breaths as he swallowed the pain shooting through his leg. The siren sounded closer now, more urgent. He hoped that, wherever Higgins was, he was hearing it too.

Connor circled the car slowly, bending at the wheel arches, intent on his task. Then, satisfied, he got in and fired the engine.

Even in peace time, you always checked under the car before you drove.

ACKNOWLEDGEMENTS

Writing can be a solitary business, so I owe a massive thank-you to everyone who regularly turns up at the scene of the crime with support, advice and bad jokes. You all know who you are, and you are the best.

To my publisher, Krystyna Green, who had the faith to sign me, thank you. The gin and dog pics are on me! I also owe a huge debt of gratitude to Craig Russell, whose support and advice have been invaluable, just as his work has helped me grow as a writer.

Thanks are also due to everyone in the wider crime-writing community: you help make sure this work never feels like a job. There are too many to mention, but special thanks to Vic Watson and Jacky Collins who do such great work with noir at the bar in Newcastle and Edinburgh and, of course, Lucy Cameron, who gave me the highlight of my career by getting me to play half a pantomime horse in Dumfries.

My life wouldn't be worth living if I didn't mention my fellow blokes in search of a plot, Gordon Brown and Mark Leggatt. Thanks for making sure I burst a gut laughing every time we step on stage. And, Mark, make sure that tea cosy is washed before the next time we need it. Thanks also to Alasdair Sim for the early red-folder read-through, and Elaine Cropley for letting me drone on about books over drinks.

The biggest thanks go to Fiona, who understands when I get lost (i.e. grumpy) in the work, and Alex and Madeleine, who are always there for a hug when I need it.

And, last, to my agent, Bob McDevitt, who got me into this, and my other fellow bloke Douglas Skelton (bet you thought I'd forgotten you) who got me through it, thank you. I honestly couldn't have done it without you.